C0068 88869

TELL
ME
YOUR
LIES

KT-382-036

Kate Ruby is a pseudonym for an award-winning TV drama producer and screenwriter. With several previously published novels and original TV projects developed at the BBC and Sky, she balances her writing career alongside her role as an executive producer.

TELL ME YOUR LIES

KATE RUBY

**SIMON &
SCHUSTER**

London · New York · Sydney · Toronto · New Delhi

First published in Great Britain by Simon & Schuster UK Ltd, 2021

Copyright © Kate Ruby 2021

The right of Kate Ruby to be identified as author
of this work has been asserted in accordance with the
Copyright, Designs and Patents Act, 1988.

1 3 5 7 9 10 8 6 4 2

Simon & Schuster UK Ltd
1st Floor
222 Gray's Inn Road
London WC1X 8HB

Simon & Schuster Australia, Sydney
Simon & Schuster India, New Delhi

www.simonandschuster.co.uk
www.simonandschuster.com.au
www.simonandschuster.co.in

A CIP catalogue record for this book
is available from the British Library

Paperback ISBN: 978-1-3985-0026-6
Export Trade Paperback ISBN: 978-1-3985-0126-3
eBook ISBN: 978-1-3985-0027-3
Audio ISBN: 978-1-3985-1323-5

This book is a work of fiction.
Names, characters, places and incidents are either a product of the author's
imagination or are used fictitiously. Any resemblance to actual people
living or dead, events or locales is entirely coincidental.

Typeset in the UK by M Rules
Printed and bound by CPI Group (UK) Ltd, Croydon, CR0 4YY

MIX
Paper from
responsible sources
FSC® C171272

For Anne, with love

TELL
ME
YOUR
LIES

LILY

I know what you're thinking. You've read about us in the papers, haven't you? Something scurrilous in the *Mail* with a picture of our perfect family, our perfect daughter, before she burnt it to the ground, or an 'opinion piece' in a broadsheet masquerading as a treatise on modern life. You've probably seen that terrible picture of Nick and I coming down the stone steps of our house – correction, *my* house – his arm lassoed around my shoulder, looking more like a harness than an expression of love. You thought how much older I looked than in the previous shots, how unkempt. It's ironic: I used to think nothing of a blow-dry or a manicure for some pointless drinks party in Shepherd's Bush on a Thursday night, and now I'm so far divorced from my old life that I'm prepared to be googled into perpetuity looking like some kind of crazed bag lady.

It pains me to admit it, but Nick was probably right to hold me back. He knew how much I wanted to scream at the huddle of journalists – bedraggled and desperate in the grey drizzle, like foxes skulking around the bins – to tell them that it was *her* who needed restraining, not me.

I won't say her name. Whatever she says, whatever Rachel's

behaviour implies, it's a lie. They've re-cut the truth, stitched a false flag from the scraps. I loved Rachel with all my heart – with a mother's heart – even when she was at her very worst. All I wanted to do was protect her, from herself most of all.

What I know now is this: you don't know what rock bottom feels like until you're face down on the ground.

ONE YEAR EARLIER

RACHEL

He was coming into focus for me now, as if my head was pushing up from underwater. My eyes were clearing, the sickness lessening. He was handsome.

'Can you follow my finger?'

His wedding ring hovered above my head – he was left-handed. Creative, thoughtful, but still clever enough to ace the sciences. The metal was battered and tarnished, but that was probably a sign of commitment, not carelessness. He looked like he was only a little bit older than me, thirty-five or so. He'd probably met her at medical school, nailed his colours to the mast early.

'That's good, Rachel. Do you know where you are?'

How had I done this? Sunk this low? I turned the shame inside out, smiled up at him.

'Judging by your nice white coat, I'm guessing a hospital.'

I looked down at myself. Some kind of weird cotton sack clung to me like a shroud. A monitor was emitting an insistent beep that acted like a screwdriver on my eardrum. I sat up abruptly, grabbing at the plastic beaker of water on the bedside table, dizzy suddenly. Thank God it was only the one bed in this room. But then – I knew what that meant. If I was in a private room, she must already know.

'That's right. You're in the Chelsea and Westminster Hospital. Do you remember why you're here?'

I lay back down, retreating from him. A starburst of memory, a hot flash of shame. A tight cubicle, smelling as rank as they always do when it's long past the witching hour. Mopping the cistern with a damp piece of loo paper, leaning low over it as Rob's hand covered my bum so tightly it felt like suction. And then?

'It was a bit of a late one, wasn't it?'

The doctor looked down at the manila cardboard folder he was holding. He took a theatrical pause to read the notes.

'You could say that, Rachel. Sounds like having a bit of a late one is something of a pattern. Am I right?'

'It was my best friend's birthday. It got out of hand. I mean . . . it's not a regular occurrence and I'm not going to get in this state again.' I sat up, pointed to my no-doubt ravaged face, regretting immediately making him study it. 'This kind of hangover is definitely not a lifestyle choice.'

His frustration was visible. 'This is more than a hangover, Rachel. We had to pump your stomach. You tested positively for cocaine. It's no exaggeration to say you could have died.'

You can make words into other words in the space between a person's lips and your own ears. They hang between you for a few precious milliseconds, open to reinterpretation. I vaporized these ones before they had any meaning.

'I'm sorry,' I said, deliberately plaintive. If I could make him feel sorry for me, or attracted to me – if I could make him feel anything – I'd know I was in charge. 'I just really wanted to honour my friend, and it went too far. She's like a sister to me.'

Let God forgive me: no one was like a sister to me, apart from my beloved Sophie.

'You were lying on the pavement. You were covered in vomit. You're lucky a cab driver stopped and called 999. If that's your idea of fun ...'

His words were getting harder to pulverize. So Rob hadn't even brought me here. Did we say goodbye in the club, or could he just not be bothered to make sure I got home in one piece? I groped for more facts, but none came.

'Okay, I get it. I'll do a detox. Dry October. It could catch on.' His gaze was cold. 'I'm sorry, I don't mean to be flippant. I'm just trying to process what happened.' I let my voice drop. 'It's a shock.'

I felt a tiny softening. I threw a smile at him, took another sip of my water.

'There's plenty of help available, Rachel. Twelve-step programmes, counselling ...'

Twelve steps? It took everything I had not to throw that back in his face, but before he could even finish his laundry list, Mum had appeared at the door. She was pale that day, the thinness she prized so much making her look unexpectedly fragile. It punctured me.

'Rachel.' I could hear it, that familiar cocktail. Anger and relief, each fighting for supremacy. She hurried across the room to my bed, touched my face. 'You're awake.'

'Hi, Mum,' I said. My voice had a crack in it. It was for real this time, and I wondered if the doctor could tell the difference. Men rarely could in my experience.

'Darling ...' she said, voice thick with worry. She found steel. 'You cannot keep doing this. You cannot.' The good looking doctor's eyes ping-ponged between us. 'Thank you so much,' she said with a hint of noblesse oblige. 'Let's talk outside in a few minutes.'

Once he'd gone, she sunk into the armchair underneath the window. I looked past her, my eyes fixing on the naked, wintry branches of a tall tree outside.

'It was Lou's thirtieth. You know what she's like.'

Mum held up a manicured hand, eyes closing in disgust.

'No. I know what *you're* like. I don't want to hear it. None of us do. You were meant to be a godmother next week. I'm not sure Josh will even allow it now. Aunt is quite enough for that little girl to handle.'

Some part of my brother would be loving this. I pushed the thought away. My thoughts still felt so muddled. But perhaps they always did back then, even without a gram of coke and a bottle of vodka to contend with. Clarity was dangerous.

'Mum, I'm sorry. I'm really sorry.' A sob choked its way out of me and I twisted up a corner of the sheet to dry my eyes, leaving a smudgy black mark on the pure white cotton.

'We can't carry on like this. I barely sleep. I'm just waiting for the call.' She paused for dramatic effect. '*That* call. What's wrong with you, Rachel? Why are you destroying yourself?'

'I . . .' My heart beat an insistent tattoo in my chest. I wanted to wrap words around it all – the creeping feeling of being not quite good enough that ran for cover when I drank myself happy. The other pieces, the shadows from long ago that kept me permanently wrapped in darkness. But we both knew she didn't want to hear too much truth, so I swallowed it down, bitter medicine. 'I'm sorry,' I said, pathetically.

Mum sank into the chair, let her head drop forward. Her

blonde shoulder-length hair, highlighted by a salon so expert
that their clients could go to the grave without ever experiencing
a whisper of grey, framed the smooth planes of her face. It was
hard to believe she was a grandmother. I don't remember a time
when people didn't tell me how beautiful my mother was. Even
at nursery school, I doubted I'd ever measure up. There's pretty
and there's beautiful – I'm still not sure which one serves us best.

'Sometimes when I'm lying there, waiting for the phone to
ring, I wonder if it's me. If it's something I did – it's always supposed to be the mother, isn't it? But then I look at your brother
and sister ...'

I heard my cue, clear as a bell.

'Of course it's not you,' I interrupted. 'You're an amazing
mum. I'm just ... you and Dad, you taught us to be the life and
soul.' She smiled: she couldn't help but be flattered by that. 'I
know I've been behaving like I'm still in my twenties, and I know
it's time to grow up.'

'When I was thirty-two, I'd had you and Josh, the business
was taking off—'

'I know,' I said, interrupting again. 'I know I haven't ticked
the boxes, okay? But I really want to change. I want to feel like
a grown-up.' It was true: every wedding invitation made me feel
like even more of a loser, even though the feminist in me knew
that was pathetic. 'And it's over now, I promise. This was the
wake-up call I had to get, Mum.'

The words felt dry, lines from a play that I'd performed a
hundred times, but they somehow had the desired effect. Mum
abruptly stood up and leant over me, enveloping me in a hug so
tight that I could only breathe in that familiar mix of Coco and
expensive shampoo. I let myself sink into her, melding my body

against hers. Perhaps some cellular part of us never forgets what it was like to be a single entity, nestled inside our mother's body, their gentle cage our only hope for survival.

'We're going to get you proper help,' she said, the words whispered into my smoke-stink hair. 'I've had her number in my phone for months now, but I was too frightened to call. To make all of this real.'

'What are you talking about?'

'Her name's Amber. She's got ... – well, apparently she's a miracle worker. She's an angel for addicts. All the people I've talked to can't stop raving about how she changed their children's lives.' She manoeuvred my tear-stained face upwards with a light touch of her hand, looking into my swollen eyes. 'What we need right now is some divine intervention.'

Addict.

I couldn't quite screen out those two harsh syllables, but nor was I ready to accept them. I knew better than to challenge her, however.

Divine intervention. That was one phrase for what was coming.

LILY

I thought it would be a comfort. Her childhood bedroom, freshly ironed sheets, home-cooked meals. But of course 'gratitude' has never been Rachel's middle name. She was surly and combative when she returned home. Nick was too infuriated to bother with her after a day of it, so I was left to take the flak. She holed up in her bedroom watching endless episodes of American dramas, tinny and nasal, through her battered laptop, ignoring the surround-sound TV in the living room. '*Binge* is such an unattractive word, isn't it?' I prompted her, but she kept her eyes trained on the screen as if my voice was the buzzing of a fly she was too lazy to swat.

The truth was that it hurt me. I would never have told her that – a fatal mistake perhaps – but every time I sent a spiky dart in her direction it was my heart that it pierced. I don't know what I'd expected – your daughter being scraped off the pavement, unconscious, drooling tequila, is hardly the perfect precursor to quality mother/daughter time – but clearly some part of me was as deluded as she was. By the time the doorbell rang out on day five I was desperate for someone to break the spell.

There was something about the way she stood there that

11

unsettled me – the sureness of her stance, as if the doorway was a gilt picture frame and she was a priceless piece of art. She didn't speak immediately, just smiled.

'Amber?'

She didn't look entirely like the picture on her website either, but nor was she brandishing a copy of *The Watchtower*, so it had to be her. Her dark hair was cut to just below her ears, where it kicked up in the kind of girlish curls that demanded product and a roller brush. She wore gold earrings, tiny, shiny tassels that brought out the brightness of her cornflower-blue eyes. There were gold studs, too, that ran up the ear lobes in a punky flourish. The eyes themselves were watchful, quickly scanning my face as if an internal computer was downloading the data faster than the speed of light.

'Yes,' she said, sticking out a gloved hand. 'And you're Lily?'

'I am,' I said, stepping aside.

I swallowed, suddenly unsteady. I clung to the door handle, fixing a smile on my face. Every step was like this. The phone call. The drive to the hospital. Each one was an incontrovertible admission that there was something deeply wrong with my child.

'I'm so glad to be here,' she said, her voice soft, and I felt something inside me unfurl.

'It was wonderful you could fit us in,' I said, opening the door fully and ushering her into our wide hallway. There's a large bamboo-framed mirror that hangs down the length of it, an inlayed lacquer table where post and keys get dumped. I automatically de-focused my eyes, not wanting any stray folds of jowly skin to make themselves known to me. 'Tea? Coffee?'

'Something herbal would be great,' she said, her gaze still

trained on me. I was glad. Everything looked so untidy: Nick's giant, muddy wellies discarded by the doormat, a pizza leaflet shouting loudly about extra mozzarella. I kept a brisk pace towards the kitchen.

'Rachel's resting upstairs. I'll put the kettle on and go and find her.'

'No rush,' she said, smiling at me.

I grabbed it, then filled it from the fiddly little filter jet. My hands were shaking, and a few drops of scalding water dripped onto my bare flesh. I winced, tried to hide the pain.

'No ...' I said. 'I'm just conscious we've only got an hour with you.'

She waved an airy hand.

'The first session has its own pace. I try not to get too hung up on time ...' She pantomimed hitting an imaginary watch on her wrist, which was ringed by a set of silver bangles. '*Heal faster!* Not really my approach. Kind of counter-productive, don't you think?'

And I realized with a jolt that I didn't know what I thought. I hadn't thought beyond ... her turning up, her making it better. I hadn't imagined how any of this would unfold. Looking back now, I want to slap myself for the lack of foresight, even if it was born out of desperation.

'Yes, no – absolutely,' I said.

Suddenly my feet felt rooted to the tiled floor.

'You've made a really brave decision,' she said softly. Her words hung in the ether; the silence broken by the ping of the kettle. 'If you tell me where the bags are, I can do it?'

'No, no,' I said, finding my mojo. I made her a lemon and ginger and shoved the strongest capsule in the Nespresso for my own delight. I kept my back turned as I did it. If she thought coffee was unspiritual, I didn't need to know about it.

*

Rachel's door was closed, no sound from within. I tapped gently.

'Is she here?' she eventually shouted.

I opened the door. She was wearing a pair of Nick's pyjamas, which she'd pretty much had on since she'd arrived. They must have been fetid by now, stiff with sweat. Looking at her there, hunched over her phone, you'd never know she was a thirty-something woman with a civil service job others would have killed for. I couldn't let the pain in. I snapped at her instead.

'Rachel . . . you knew she was coming at eleven. Get some clothes on. We're paying for this.'

Amber's words rung in my ears. *Heal faster.* I wondered if she had children. If she understood how hard it was to smile beatif-ically when they gave every indication that they simultaneously hated you and loved the soft cushion of your indulgence.

'I know,' she snapped back. Her eyes looked puffy. Had she been crying, or was it a byproduct of peering incessantly at all those screens? 'I'll be five minutes.'

I wanted to tell her that I was doing this because I cared. *We* cared. That we didn't want her to plunge even further down a rabbit hole that we'd soon have no hope of freeing her from. That I wished more than anything that she was still tiny and there was no peril big enough to defeat my maternal might. But I didn't. Perhaps I thought I'd outsourced human kindness to Amber. Perhaps I couldn't risk too much analysis of what it was that had sent her underground.

'Make it ten,' I snapped. 'Have a shower.'

*

She punished me for that. The minutes ticked past, Amber and I perched at opposite ends of the oatmeal linen sofa in the living room like it was a seesaw. Amber put her mug down on the occasional table, a Bridgewater one that Josh had given me when his twins were born. 'Most Marvellous Granny,' it said, in curly script, hearts painted all around it. I wished I hadn't used it today: it made me feel ancient at the best of times.

'So these are the grandchildren?' she said, pointing at the mug and examining the jumble of family pictures on the table. There were silver-framed portraits of the boys when they were newly born and a recent shot of a toothless, grinning Nancy, a bow on her bare head. 'She looks like a real live wire.'

It seemed like an odd description for an infant too young to even take a step unaided, but I seized the chance to distract from Rachel's mortifying refusal to emerge from her bedroom.

'She's adorable. First granddaughter, and my son Josh's pride and joy.'

Amber studied the photo for a beat longer than felt necessary, but didn't say anything more.

'And that's your wedding, is it?' Nick and I, in a dusty leather frame. There were plenty of other pictures she could have zeroed in on. School photos of all three of them, six-year-old Rachel wearing a stripy *Dennis the Menace*–style jumper she used to love. It was a hand-me-down from an older cousin which I hated back then, but now she looked nothing but adorable in it, all gap-toothed and innocent. 'You look fabulous!' said Amber, summoning me back. 'So retro.'

I laughed, not entirely naturally. My hair cascaded in

15

lacquered waves down my shoulders in that picture, my dress a creamy satin bell. Nick's hand clasped mine tightly, the ancient doors of the Ealing church framing us both, grinning as confetti came at us from all directions. We were only twenty-two, teenage sweethearts who kept a promise.

'Trust me, considering it was only two years after Diana and Charles's ridiculous affair, I was the picture of restraint.'

Now it was my turn to conduct an examination. Amber's skin was smooth, but there was no hiding the lines that fanned out from her eyes like sun rays. There were no greys peppering her dark hair, but that proved nothing, a fact I could attest to. Her hands were a giveaway – they had the kind of sun damage that could only have been caused by decades of beach holidays. She had to have been at least a teenager when our wedding photograph was taken, however much she was choosing to behave as if it was a fascinating artefact.

My sneaky studying was stopped by Rachel's appearance, her bare feet rendering her as quiet as a cat. Her wet hair was slicked back, her pale face left bare. Amber smoothly stood up, cocking her head to take her in. She smiled a smile that looked as if it contained the warmth and wisdom of the ages, and my spiky inner dialogue melted into ambient noise.

'Rachel,' she said, extending both hands just far enough that they welcomed my sullen child, without demanding a response. 'I've been so looking forward to meeting you.'

'Have you?' said Rachel, her voice like a knife. Normally she liked to drop the odd T and scuff her vowels, making sure the expensive education she'd endured would go unnoticed. It drove me mad, myself the product of a grammar school followed by an unfeasible amount of hard work.

16

'It was an instinct,' said Amber, unruffled. 'I like to help. If I can.'

'Right.'

I looked between them, my whole body thrumming with tension. I had too much riding on this. It was a dangerous place to be.

'Darling, why don't you sit down?' I said, both of us hearing the honey I'd injected into my tone. 'I can make some more coffee.'

She looked at me, unsmiling, but at least she backed into the armchair near the television. It seemed to swallow her up whole.

'Thanks. Can I have the strong one?'

'Of course. Anything more for you?' I asked Amber, but she demurred, still smiling her buddha smile in Rachel's direction. I took a last look between them before backing out of the room, relief engulfing me as soon as I hit the kitchen. Would it be so wrong to just stay here, flicking through *Vanity Fair* and imagining my life was entirely different?

*

I could hear both their voices as I walked slowly back down the hallway, each step an individual act. My pace became glacial. Rachel was – was she laughing? Amber was still on the sofa, but she'd scooted down to the other end, breaching the gap between the two of them. Rachel was sitting properly now, her back straight and her body angled forward, no longer using the leather armchair as her personal cave. I stood there a second, the silver tray in my hands. For a brief second I felt like a nervy waitress at a posh function, paid by the hour to shut up and smile.

'Coffee is served!' I trilled, and suddenly the air felt heavy again. I wished I'd stayed where I was, looking at pictures of a sad-eyed Angelina Jolie and speculating about how much her artfully photographed LA mansion was actually worth.

'Thanks, Mum, you're amazing!' said Rachel, with a brief smile that was pathetically gratifying.

'Are you sure I can't get you anything?' I asked Amber, lowering myself into the armchair opposite Rachel's.

With Amber holding court on the sofa, we already formed a perfect triangle: it would take time for the sacred geometry she'd created to cut me to the quick.

She slowly turned her head towards me, her large eyes like a sad lemur in a cage at the zoo. 'Just sit. Join us. Rachel's been giving me a little bit of background about the past few months.'

'Right!' I said. My heart was racing again, even though this was exactly what I'd asked for. I searched for a continuation of my sentence, but it felt as though my windpipe was knotted. Rachel leant forward, her hands gripping the arms of the chair.

'Mum, I'm so sorry I've been such a mess the past couple of years.' It was longer than that, but I kept my careful accounting to myself. 'It looks like I'm so much worse than I am, though. I don't want you to worry. There's still all the thirtieths going on, and now the weddings have started up. The fact is, most of the time during the week I'm just on my own at home after work watching Netflix in my tracksuit bottoms.'

I didn't know which half of that description was more sad. My eyes involuntarily flicked to the side table – the cluster of frames, the smiles of goals being achieved and love being cemented. I glanced back towards Amber, gratified to read in her face that she wasn't buying Rachel's PR spin on what normality looked like either.

'Landmark moments can be hard, can't they?' she said.

Rachel gave a half smile of assent, her bottom lip trapped between her teeth from the inside. I knew that expression of old. She'd have it when we stopped her pocket money or refused to let her go to a teenage party where there were no parents to supervise. Amber continued, her voice a soft caress.

'Life has seasons, even if we don't want to admit it. There's something they talk about in astrology, the Saturn return, which comes in when you're twenty-nine. It's a big time of transition, on every level. You'll still be living in the aftershock.'

I fought down a wave of irritation – if I'd wanted to hire a tinpot astrologer I'd have googled one – but then I looked at Rachel. Her shoulders had dropped, her eyes had softened.

'I know it's ridiculous, but being past thirty feels – when I was twenty-one, thirty-year-olds felt ancient,' she said. 'It felt like a lifetime away.'

'I understand that,' said Amber. 'It's the decade for babies and husbands and . . .' she wriggled her thin shoulders. 'But it's not as simple as that, is it?'

Isn't it? I thought meanly. I was barely an adult when I got married – it had been far from perfect, but it was a decision. Sometimes in life you just needed to make a decision.

Rachel was shaking her head as if she couldn't trust herself to speak.

'No,' she said eventually. 'Nothing makes much sense to me, really. I don't know why I feel like this all the time.' She looked down into her coffee like I might have piped the answer into the froth, her face desolate. I looked at her, willing her to look back at me, but she seemed to have forgotten that I was even there.

'It's okay not to know why you feel this way,' said Amber

after a pause. 'I think it's okay to just know that right now it's confusing. And that you're finding the confusion painful.'

And then Rachel began to sob – big, honking sobs that blind-sided me. It was so loud and messy – it was almost as if she was exploding. I stood, grabbing for a box of tissues, but she waved me away without even looking at me, a single hand emerging from the chaos of her tears. She wiped at her wet face with a sleeve, her sobs reaching a crescendo. I looked down at my child, her face still hidden in the bunched-up sweatshirt fabric, and felt a sense of utter uselessness. I thought about ignoring her or marching across the room and wrapping my arms around her shaking body, but I didn't know if she'd throw me off or shout at me. I couldn't risk the humiliation.

I sank backwards, reluctantly grateful for Amber's air of studied calm. She leaned across the sofa, took the tissues from me, touching my hand for a second as she did so, a tiny caress. My breathing slowed, my aloneness less total. Almost simulta-neously, Rachel's sobs started to lessen. Amber moved further down the sofa towards her.

'Would you like one of these?' she asked her gently.

Rachel gave a barely perceptible nod. Amber pulled out a handful from the box, putting them directly into her wet grasp, and laid a hand on her forearm.

'Is it okay that I'm touching you?' she said. 'I thought you might need a bit of contact to help bring you back into the room.'

Rachel nodded again, mopping at her raw face.

'Darling . . .' I said, but then I ran aground.

'I'm okay, Mum,' she muttered.

'Yes, you are!' said Amber. 'You're in touch with your

emotions. You're not numb, or dead inside. Your feelings are close to the surface, longing for permission to express themselves. And you just did that. You just gave them that permission. You should be really proud of yourself.'

I felt a flood of relief: was that what it was – not a breakdown, but a catharsis? Was that all she needed? Rachel looked up and gave her a shy, watery smile.

'Thanks, Amber,' she said.

'You're very welcome,' said Amber, beaming back at her. Relief and irritation duked it out again. *She's not a radiator*, I thought. *You can't just sit there congratulating yourself on how well you bled her.* It was jealousy too; my surly daughter already seemed like putty in her hands. 'You're starting the journey. You're saying yes.'

I cut in. My voice sounded nasal and harsh to my own ears. 'So, you're thinking a series of sessions?' I said. 'A few weeks?'

Amber slowly rotated her body away from Rachel's, turning that intense gaze of hers onto me. 'Good question,' she said.

I was caught in her headlights.

'What do you want, darling?' I asked Rachel, nervously.

'Not to feel so horrendously shit,' said Rachel, smiling an actual smile for what felt like the first time in living memory.

'Good answer!' said Amber, almost playful. She paused, and the room stilled with her. 'But maybe we should turn that question around. What would *you* like, Lily?'

I froze.

'The same thing, obviously,' I said. 'For my daughter to be happy and healthy.'

'But that wasn't the whole question. What would *you* like, for *you*? For Lily? It's important. You're not just Rachel's mum.'

Or Nick's wife, I thought. I tried to formulate a response, but Amber's soft voice had started up again. 'I can see how hard you're working too,' she started. 'Even if you can't answer it now, just stay with the question over the next few days. See what emerges for you.'

'Okay,' I said, as monosyllabic as Rachel had been for the past few days. The question vibrated inside of me, like a wasp trapped in a hot summer car.

'Shall we leave it there for today?' said Amber. We both nodded our assent. Rachel looked different, there was no denying it. Now her tears were dry, you could see the brightness in her hazel eyes, a new alertness in her expression. Still, I didn't want to get my hopes up. 'And can I just say, I think you've both been incredible. Strong and vulnerable all at once. Warriors for truth. I'm really looking forward to our work together.'

Rachel gave her a look of pure gratitude.

'Thanks for coming.'

'You're very welcome. What I would ask is, as we take the first few steps on the path, you try to make a commitment to yourself. Do you think you can agree to no alcohol or drugs until we see each other again?'

I cut in. 'That's a given. The doctor's been very clear that Rachel can't drink for at least three weeks. Her stomach was pumped, and as for drugs . . .'

They weren't even listening. They were looking at each other, the same half smile on each of their faces.

'It's hard though, isn't it?' said Amber. 'When alcohol's been keeping you feeling safe. Taking away your nerves, bonding you with your friends.'

Rachel's look to her was uncertain at first, but then it became determined.

'I won't go near it.' She screwed up her face and as I watched it contort, I thought about how incapable she'd always been of perceiving how pretty it was. How lovable she was when she wasn't being deliberately unbearable. 'To be honest, the thought of it makes me feel ill right now.'

'Great! And are there any trigger points you can think of now that we should talk about? More parties? Social events you might need to think about skipping?'

'Well there's the christening,' I said. 'Josh's new baby. Rachel's a godmother. But we'll all be there to keep an eye.' Rachel looked blank suddenly, that vacancy returning. 'Sorry, darling – I mean, we'll look after you.'

Amber's eyes flicked quickly between us, reading our silent exchange. I tried and failed not to mind. 'Do whatever you need to do to be prepared for it – that's inevitably going to be a big deal. And let's not leave too long a gap between appointments. Next week would be perfect timing.'

'Thank you,' said Rachel, her voice small. She didn't stand, just gave a half-smile from the safety of the chair.

'It's time to take yourself seriously,' said Amber, eyes lingering on her. 'You deserve your own compassion, Rachel.'

I stood myself, breaking the moment. My legs were shaking as I walked her to the door.

'We really appreciate you coming,' I said, aware I sounded a little like she'd cleaned the windows, not somehow exorcised my child.

'You're welcome,' she said, her eyes lingering on me now. 'You take care of yourself too, Lily. I'll be holding you both in my thoughts. Sending compassion to you.'

She sailed off down the path, without a backward glance. I know that for sure, because I left the door wide open, watching her progress until she disappeared from my eyeline.

RACHEL

I started with the best intentions. I knew a week out of the office would be pushing it, what with the months of imaginary tube delays and doctors' appointments that I subtly implied were too personal for my boss, Duncan, to question. As managers went, he was ridiculously tolerant, but exasperation had recently started to morph into anger, maybe even hurt. He was a civil servant to his bones, and I could tell that he took my lack of respect as a moral failing. The truth was that I felt that same disappointment in me that he did, but I was too distracted polishing my excuses until they gleamed to let myself own it.

That first morning, it was easier than I expected to get out of bed and push myself back out into the world. How hard could a single Friday be? And besides, Amber's visit had infused me with a weird kind of energy. It was a high, a natural high – the kind that people in kundalini yoga classes claim exist, their eyes all glassy, with a chaser of B.O. – that I'd always assumed was down to the fact they'd never had a real one.

Mum was on a client call in the living room when I came downstairs, and I half hoped I'd be able to slip out without seeing her, but as I slugged back a quick coffee, she came through to find me.

'Thanks for looking after me,' I said, giving her a quick hug. Was it guilt telling me that she felt bonier than ever? 'Say thanks to Dad too. I'm going to go back to mine after work. Please don't worry about me. You've done enough of that, I think we can agree!'

She didn't raise a smile. Instead she looked at me beseechingly.

'You will see her again, won't you?' she said, her thumb hard against my palm, blocking my way out of the kitchen.

We hadn't really talked about the session since the moment Amber left. She'd looked at my swollen, blotchy face with a slight disgust that I'm sure she thought I wouldn't notice.

'Well, that was certainly intense,' she'd said, efficiently scooping up the coffee cups, not quite making eye contact. 'But worth it, yes?' I couldn't form a coherent thought yet – that would take a few, dangerous weeks – so I'd simply muttered 'Think so' and dived for my phone.

'Definitely. Mum, I actually want to carry on,' I told her now, trying to work out how to dodge my way past her without any more reminders about what a disaster I was. I knew I'd been moody while I'd been here, but I'd been too ashamed to risk emerging – at least until Amber opened the door. It scared me. I wasn't sure yet what to do with it. 'This is a new start. I actually mean it this time.'

I felt her body relax, her grip loosen. Back then, I still wanted to make her happy, maybe even more than I wanted to make myself happy. Or was it that I still believed that only the first one mattered?

'I'll call you later.' She gave a tight nod. 'Stop worrying about me, okay?' I kissed her cheek again. 'That's your job for today,' I added, laughing, and slipped down the corridor away from her. I hoped my lightness would infect her.

By the time I approached Shepherd's Bush tube, that lightness had evaporated, anxiety rushing into the void. *Could I do this?* The tube heard my prayers, idling in a tunnel for a good five minutes, but soon it started up again, and I was standing in front of the slab of concrete in Westminster where I worked. I swiped my pass through the barriers, then watched my finger approach the button for the lift, seeing it light up. For a moment, it felt as if I was watching a reconstruction of my last day on earth.

I was edging my way across the floor when he spotted me.

'Rachel!'

I'd hoped to sneak to my desk and then hide behind my computer, staring so determinedly at the screen that my dili-gence would repel any conversation, but Duncan was heading straight for me.

'I didn't think you'd make it back this week.'

Flecks of white gunk – baby food, I guessed, unlikely to be cocaine – peppered his moss-green jumper, his shaggy brown hair sticking up in spikes like a drunken hedgehog. He and his wife – a policy adviser in the Treasury – had had expensive IVF twins a year ago, and since then he exuded 'harassed dad' as if it was a particularly overpowering aftershave. Duncan's wariness made his smile go crooked, but he couldn't quite stifle his natural warmth. 'Well done.'

'I didn't want to leave you all in the lurch. There's so much to do . . .'

He lowered his voice. 'So, it wasn't appendicitis in the end? From what your mum said, it was pretty dramatic.'

'They're still running tests,' I said, my voice staying impressively steady. If lying was something people actually looked for on a CV, I'd be headhunted daily. 'It's possible it was a virus. They'll monitor me for a few weeks, but hopefully it was a one off.'

'Well ...' His shoulders slumped downwards. Admitting to himself it was a blatant untruth would add an extra ton of stress to his already impossible load. Better to kick the problem down the field, deal with it later. 'Excellent. We should still be on track to get the proposal on teachers' housing done for the end of next week. If you can just plough on ...'

'Consider me your favourite lady farmer,' I said, then cringed in case he thought I was flirting. He had nothing to fear. Duncan – or at least single Duncan – was exactly the kind of man I should have fancied, but never did.

'Great,' he said, and we lingered awkwardly for a second too long before heading to our respective desks.

It was a graduate traineeship originally, hard won. Dad's a property lawyer with a big practice, and I'd worked for him in my year off, and then in all the university holidays, so I'd had the kind of practical experience that sparkled alongside my first-class degree. Mum and Dad were thrilled when I'd got it – I think they even had ludicrous fantasies of me being prime minister – and the first couple of years were great. I moved between departments, soaking up knowledge and smugly reflecting on how much more 'important' my work was than the friends who were selling their souls as city traders or fledgling PRs. While they were writing press releases about new waxing treatments or swotting up on the Yen, I was learning about urban regeneration and social care.

But then, somehow, I stalled. I stopped staying late: it was far more fun to stay out with those friends I'd sneered at, with their fat salaries and their glamorous party invites, and then sneak into the office stinking of the night before. I took my eye off the ball, missed the promotions and the pay rises that the eager beavers I came in with were all too happy to hoover up. Soon the friends with the glamorous invites started staying in with boyfriends or, with alarming speed, fiancés. Now I was a mid-level government drone in the housing department – it felt like a job for life in the worst possible sense.

'Are you really better?' said Julia as I slid into my chair. She was a couple of years younger than me but you'd never know it: she and Hillary Clinton must've signed a pact to take joint responsibility for keeping trouser suits relevant. She was wearing a navy one that day, a crisp silk shirt peeking out beneath it, her neat blonde bob jutting forward over her strong jawline as she swiveled towards me, eyes bright with concern. Julia was horribly good.

'Think so,' I said, ostentatiously powering up my ancient government issue computer as if I couldn't bear to waste another moment. 'Thanks for asking.'

'Of course.' She kept her swivel chair angled in my direction. 'Fred had appendicitis when we were at Oxford.' Julia never said university, like a normal person might. 'It was a complete miracle he didn't miss his finals.'

Her gaze didn't leave my face – a cold trickle of unease ran down my spine. Was she testing me? I should have forensically studied the symptoms, worked out how my mystery illness diverged from the real thing and confused the doctors. A wave of shame washed over me, but I refused to engage with it. I had work to do here.

'Poor him,' I said sympathetically. 'Typical Fred, though! He'd never miss an exam, would he?'

Julia beamed. Masterful swerve – she couldn't resist such a golden opening to talk about the world's most perfect husband. I'd only met him a couple of times, while chinking a glass of soupy white wine with his at some lame work function, but she bought the casual intimacy hook, line and sinker. I scanned my 216 emails as she described his emergency admission, turning and cocking my head enough times to convince her I was listening. It took a good three minutes before we reached his triumphant limp into the exam hall, ready to ace it. At least now I'd have a few bits of medical colour to add to my own story.

'Anyway, sorry, I'll let you get on,' she said, finally petering out.

'Don't apologize, I really appreciate that you give a shit,' I said, realizing as I said it that I actually did, and immediately hating myself for the lies I'd been scattering so easily since I entered the building. 'I loved that picture of Hobo at the dog park on Instagram by the way.'

Hobo was their Pit Bull, a rescue with a gruesome snarl and his own social media paw print, @homeofhobo. Judging by the number of photos they posted, any future human offspring would likely crash the internet.

'He's so adorable, isn't he?' she said, her face lighting back up. 'I never regret giving our little guy a home.'

I started to subtly swivel my chair – this line of conversation could run and run. 'Ugh, so many emails!'

Julia gave a sympathetic yelp and turned back to her monitor. Duncan's dishevelled head was bent over his desk too, the low hum of phones and earnest policy conversations a monotone lullaby. I felt deflated, the sugar high of surviving their questions crashing to nothing. Was this it? Was life back to normal? Was this actually what I was meant to want?

I started to plough through the emails – some of the research about the impact of rising suburban commuting costs had started to come in, ready to be woven into my report. It mattered – and yet . . . It was too soon for coffee, so instead I opened up a browser window, my eyes darting left to check that Julia's gaze was trained on her own machine. A couple of quick keystrokes later, and I had landed on Amber's homepage.

I wouldn't have admitted to anyone – least of all Mum – how many times I'd visited it since Wednesday. Amber's dark hair was longer in the picture, flowing down over the shoulders of a floral red boho dress. Her face was cocked towards the camera, an almost-smile playing around her lips. Her eyes drew you in, as if it was you specifically they gazed on, not some random internet stalker who'd chanced on her site. It was crazy, but it felt in that moment like she knew I was sitting here, on a government-issue swivel chair designed specifically to guard against costly lower back pain, wondering what the point of my existence really was. Maybe it wasn't crazy: she'd said she would be keeping me in her thoughts. No, she'd said she'd be keeping *both of us* in her thoughts. Mum, too.

I clicked on the 'About Me' section.

Amber Greville has a passion for helping her clients become their best selves. After a hugely successful career in the advertising industry, Amber was set to take over as creative director of a blue-chip agency. It was not to be – within days of starting the role, she was struck down by a crippling autoimmune disease, with no apparent medical cure. Looking back, Amber couldn't be more grateful – as for many of her clients, her breakdown proved to be the ultimate breakthrough!

I risked reading that sentence a couple of times, even though it made me emotional. I steadied myself and carried on.

While her doctors remained baffled, Amber took herself to an ashram in South East Asia, which began her journey on the spiritual path. Working with a range of healing modalities, she finally got to the root course of her disease and became determined to help other stressed-out Westerners recover from the spiritual burnout that blights our frenetic lives. Amber's sincere desire is to help you rediscover your innate goodness, your right to be here and the blissful tranquillity that is your true destiny.

My innate goodness. I rolled the phrase around my mind – it felt alien, a language I didn't even have a phrasebook for. I clicked back to her photo. She looked different this time. More enigmatic. Wiser.

I looked down at the pile of printouts on my desk, then over to the row of glass-fronted meeting rooms that ran down the length of the room. Duncan was in one of them with a whiteboard, a gaggle of graduate trainees hanging off his every word. One more section, then I'd carry on. The next tab across was *Testimonials*. I hadn't read these before. I felt a little thrill of anticipation.

'Thank you Amber. Thank you, thank you, thank you. Without your wisdom, your patience, your stubborn belief in me, I'm not sure I'd be here today.' (Freya, 35, London)

'You were right, it wasn't too late! A year after we finished our sessions, I was holding my beautiful baby girl in my arms. Thank you for teaching me that my dreams could come true – what we can believe, we can achieve. xxx.' (Maria, 43, Winchester)

'If you're wondering whether to take the plunge, just do it. Amber will challenge you, enlighten you and, best of all, make you laugh like you've never laughed before. Tomorrow really is another day!' (Chris, 44, Gloucestershire)

Was Chris a man or a woman? Were there even men like that, men who longed to be 'enlightened'? That guy Rob, the friend of Lou's who'd left me to swim in my own vomit on a cold London pavement, certainly didn't seem like a guy who had enlightenment on the top of his Christmas list. Shame twisted up inside me at the memory, followed by a further blast at the realization that I was currently drawing a government salary to dick around on the internet.

I swiftly shut down the website without gobbling up any more of the ecstatic quotes. Besides, even a skim told me all I needed to know – they were riddled with excited capital letters and exclamation marks and little paths of kisses like birds hopping through snow. Amber meant a lot to a lot of people, it seemed.

I pulled up my emails again, forcing myself to become immersed. This work was important. It mattered. So why couldn't I make it matter more to *me*?

*

I kept it up for the rest of the day. I powered through my report, refusing to let myself waste any time on pointless apps. I distractedly ate a soggy BLT at my desk, all my focus on how we were going to square the circle of flat teacher salaries and rising London rent with our ambitious building project in commutable towns. I emailed the draft of my document to Duncan around four, earning a double thumbs up from across the office. This surely earned me the right to a cup of coffee and a KitKat?

Each floor of our offices had a little kitchenette in the corner, known as tuck shops since before the war. Hot water whooshed into my cup, the tea bag floating up towards me. I squished it, comforted by the mundanity of the action, by the sense of simply performing a task and awarding myself a tiny, deserved reward. But then my phone began to ring: Josh. His name flashed up again and again, an accusation.

I knew I needed to speak to my brother. Mum had wasted no time telling me my refusal to pick up his calls was 'deeply hurtful'. I'd asked her to tell him that I needed time to get my head together, but if I ignored him all the way up to the chris-tening – even thinking the word *christening* made my stomach lurch – it would become an international incident. I reluctantly pressed my thumb down on the angry, flashing surface of my phone's screen.

'Josh, I'm sorry. I was going to call you tonight—'

My brother cut across me like I was a hapless witness in his courtroom. He was a human rights barrister, used to defending the downtrodden with ferocious, articulate indignation. It had provided him with an excellent skill set for this particular phone call. He was mid rant within seconds.

'It's bad enough that you put Mum and Dad through this – this *shit* – without ignoring me and Chloe too. Do you not want to be in this family, Rachel? Is that it?'

When he was behaving like some Victorian patriarch, it was hard to believe he was only two years older than me.

'Jesus, Josh, I was in hospital! It's fair enough if I needed some space.'

A couple of heads twitched in the old leather armchairs around the periphery of the tuck shop. I abandoned my tea, the bag drowning itself in the darkening water, and headed for the semi privacy of the corridor.

'We needed to talk to you.' I hated the way he always styled himself as a 'we', gave himself strength in numbers. My sister-in-law was aggressively, blandly pleasant, but always made it crystal clear where her loyalties lay. 'We asked you to be Nancy's godmother. You can't just ignore us.'

'That's why!' I said, my voice rising, my vulnerability catching me unawares. 'I felt shit enough, without you having to tell me I'm not good enough to be responsible for a baby's moral welfare.'

Air audibly swept up Josh's nostrils, the pause stretching out meaningfully. It had the desired effect: anxiety prickled my flesh as I waited for his next insight.

'Oh, Rachel, what are we going to do with you?'

'I'm sorry,' I said, my voice as high and reedy as a child. I dug my bitten nails into the soft flesh of my palm. He continued, conversational now.

'I was with this nineteen-year-old in court this week. Somali prostitute, oldest of six. Her brother's disabled, her parents are dead. It's no wonder she fell into the hands of a pimp. She had no options. Trafficked here and locked up in a brothel for nine months before they got raided. Now we're fighting to let her stay.' I looked out onto the oval, cobbled courtyard at the back of the building: its steely grandeur was the perfect backdrop to my brother's lecture. 'Mum and Dad gave us everything, Rachel. Why do you keep throwing it in their faces?'

Amber flitted across my mind, her calm gaze searching me out. The thought of her was weirdly comforting.

'I don't know,' I said. There was nothing else I could say. He didn't want to hear the truth, and I was still only groping for it. It would sound like a rambling excuse, pinned to teenage angst I should have long since left behind. Who knew if that really was why I was such a fuck up, anyway? 'Sometimes it all feels incredibly hard, finding the point of it all. I know you can't understand that.'

'Don't tell me what I do and don't understand,' he snapped, before his voice unexpectedly softened. 'We care about you, Rachel. We just want you to stop this – this craziness.' He paused again. 'I was going to say it wasn't appropriate for you to be Nancy's godmother. That's what we'd decided. But now I think it's exactly what you need. Surely there's a point to Nancy?'

He gave a dry little chuckle. I was dreading him telling me I was unfit, but the news that I *was* fit filled me with an equally violent tidal wave of dread. No skulking at the back of the church and quietly slipping away from the drinks.

'Thank you,' I said stiffly. Any exchange with my brother somehow seemed to involve a grovelling apology and a tugging of the sisterly forelock. 'It's a real honour.'

'Don't make me regret it,' he said. 'I've got to go back to court. See you next weekend.'

I stood there a few seconds longer, looking down at the ground. A gaggle of pigeons squabbled over a crust of bread, wind ruffling their feathers as their beaks pecked in a desperate frenzy at the ground. Then, before I went back to my desk, I made a call.

'Lou, it's me. What are you up to later?' The words escaped my lips before I could swallow them. 'I'm feeling Tigger-ish.'

LILY

I think I knew before I knew. I felt the soft whisper of my high-lighter brush smoothing my left cheek, my eyes gazing back at me in the dressing table mirror. It wasn't the usual dull mono-logue about crepey skin or dark circles. 'You can't control today,' said a small, definite voice. 'She's not a child anymore.'

Nick passed swiftly behind me, an apparition in a well-cut grey suit. I shivered. Then I picked up my mascara and contin-ued the well-worn internal argument about whether I looked like an ageing film star or a delusional bag lady when I dressed up.

By comparison, it felt as comforting as a nursery rhyme.

RACHEL

Of course Josh couldn't have his precious baby girl christened in the mean streets of Shepherd's Bush where we grew up. Instead I started Saturday morning gingerly picking my way through the cobbled back streets of Kensington, which were lined with white stucco houses as grand as fairy-tale castles and small, yappy dogs attached to careworn-looking women being paid minimum wage to pick up their poo. The idea of ever being able to afford to live in one of these houses was certainly a fairy tale for me. It would require Nancy's godfather to be an eligible bachelor in possession of a vast fortune who fell madly in love with me the second our eyes met over the font. A vicious gust of wind slipped its way up my green Zara dress, which immediately felt too short, too cheap, too bright. Too me. *Of course that won't happen*, spat the spiteful voice inside my head. *You're not the girl they marry. Look at the evidence.*

And there, indeed, was the evidence. I rounded the final corner, coming upon the ancient church Josh and Chloe had chosen for the momentous day. Its tawny stone glowed in the warm morning light, the outside thronged by well-heeled couples. How was it that Josh managed to profess his socialist principles while simultaneously living this life? The fact his wife had a trust fund certainly helped.

I slowed my pace to a snail's, grateful for the excuse granted by my precarious high street heels. I could taste a metallic tinge at the back of my throat, the legacy of last night's vodka tonics. I discreetly wrapped up the tab of gum that I'd been chewing en route: Mum's sixth sense for these things was strong, and I was too fragile for a fight. I'd deserved that night out, I reasoned; anyone would need a dose of Dutch courage when this event was coming up.

But the truth was that my night out with Lou the week before had broken the seal on my days-old sobriety. And the fact I hadn't been able to find a time to make a second meeting with Amber since was ... Right then, I couldn't bear to interrogate the reasons.

Josh spotted me the second I reached the churchyard. His smile was more appraising than warm as he strode over to kiss me hello. He's tall and fair, and his well-cut suit emphasized the whole impressive package. In principle at least: to me he just looked like some kind of brutal AI who could turn on the human race at any moment. He leant down to brush his lips against my cheeks.

'Well done. Twenty whole minutes to go.'

Tiny pinches, the kind that leave no bruises. My brother's speciality.

'What a beautiful church,' I said. 'Lucky Nancy.'

'They don't really notice though, do they?' he said, as if I'd meant it literally. His sharp grey eyes didn't leave my face. 'How are you?' he said. 'We've been fretting about you.'

'Yeah, no, I'm fine,' I said, looking away and waving at Chloe.

She was grappling with a squirming Nancy, their four-year-old twin sons squabbling around her feet in tiny, matching waistcoats which made them look like very expensive toys. 'Looks like Chloe could do with some help.'

Mum and Dad both emerged from one of the chattering groups, the four of us converging on Chloe like a SWAT team. As Mum hugged me, I smelt the familiar and complicated cocktail of love and anxiety that was seeping out of her pores. I held on to her a second longer than I normally would have, a wave of guilt sweeping through me at the thought of how late and how messy my Friday night had really been. Dad's greeting had less undercurrents to it: he didn't want to have to worry about me unless he was forced to. He was much more willing to believe my bullshit, and the current narrative – sober, apologetic – suited him just fine.

Nancy had calmed in Chloe's arms: there was something almost unbearably vulnerable about the pudgy outline of her upturned face.

'Can I hold my goddaughter?' I asked.

'Seventeen minutes to go,' said Josh, making a pantomime of looking at his large chrome watch. 'You're not there yet, Rach. Still time for us to reconsider.'

I ignored him, my arms outstretched, and soon felt the soft mush of Nancy's body meld with my own. The truth was, my emotions had felt dangerously close to the surface ever since I'd seen Amber. When the baby emitted a piercing cry, it was almost a relief to break the moment of connection with her. It felt too intimate somehow.

'Still in need of some practice!' said Dad, as I swung Nancy's wriggling body back to Chloe. 'You'll get the hang of it when you have to.'

His baggy grey suit was trying too hard to be casual, with its oversized buttons and patch pockets, and the white shirt underneath it was left open at the neck, exposing a V of suspiciously tanned skin. He was too used to being handsome, the extra power it brought to his already bulging portfolio. He wasn't going to give it up without a fight.

As my eyes flicked away then, I spotted her, a last-minute arrival slipping through the church gate. She was gripping the hand of a lanky man with greying curls, leading him towards the milling crowd. I froze with shock, then knew I had to get away from them.

'I'm just going to run to the loo,' I gabbled. 'I don't want to need to go when we're by the font,' I carried on, my legs carrying me towards the church before any of them had time to reply.

*

I sat on the closed wooden seat for far longer than I had time for, my heart thumping in my chest. She was here. She was actually here. How could she turn up like this? I could hear people streaming into the church now. They'd be looking for me soon.

The first thing I saw as I emerged was the smiling moon of my little sister Sophie's face. Normally I'd have been thrilled to lay eyes on her, but shock still gripped me like a vice. She grabbed my arm.

'There you are – I've been in here sorting out the orders of service. You're meant to be at the font!'

'Yeah, no. I know that,' I said.

Sophie would be the world's worst professional poker player. The light in her hazel eyes dimmed as soon as she heard my tone, her round body slumping with disappointment. She wanted so much for me to see the world through her rose-tinted glasses: she literally wore them – glasses at least – round ones, with wire frames, which added to her nerdy cuteness. Life had flowed for Sophie with an ease it never had for me. She was the adored late surprise baby, petted and fought over by all of us. She'd sailed through school, then met a boyfriend she adored at university, who'd put a ring on it by the time she was twenty-five. I could see him now, his head, with its thinning crown of ginger hair, swivelling around from his spot on the front row to seek her out. Toby wasn't the most exciting choice, but he made her happy.

'Are you okay, Rachel?'

My eyes roved around the church, my sister's words no more than background noise. Esther was sat halfway back on the end of a row, the curly-haired man's hand a long-legged spider that entrapped hers.

'Esther's here,' I said, my eyes still trained on the two of them. Esther was Sophie's au pair back in the day, at least in part. She didn't look back at me, but I sensed she was feeling the laser bounce between her shoulder blades.

'I know!' said Sophie, smiling as she twisted her head to look over to her. 'It's been ages since we saw her. Who do you think the hottie is?'

'He looks creepy to me.'

Disappointment swept across her face again. Why was her big sister such a shrew?

'Alright, he's not George Clooney,' conceded Sophie, 'but . . . it's nice if she's met someone. What is she, nearly forty? It's not easy at that age.'

Or thirty-one, as it turned out. My sister's well-intentioned pity added to my spikiness.

'She's thirty-five,' I snapped back. I could pretty much run through all of Esther's vital statistics if anyone ever needed them. A coroner perhaps. Or a judge.

'I think it's really nice that Josh and Chloe invited her.'

'Yeah, but do you think it *was* them that invited her?' I asked.

'Yeah, it's their baby's christening.'

Josh was glaring at me now, angrily tapping his watch. I felt a stab of loneliness, then steeled myself. I just had to get through the next few hours. In a way, it was a good thing no one was by my side. How would I make sense of any of this to them, when it made absolutely no sense to me?

'Come on, then,' I said, setting off down the aisle. 'Let's get this over with.'

'You'll be great,' said Sophie, squeezing my arm. 'Lucky old Nancy.'

I gave her a grateful smile. It turned out I wasn't alone: I had my sister.

*

The guests funnelled up the stairs of the predictably *chi chi* restaurant that Josh and Chloe had picked for the reception, their braying confidence amplified in the narrow space. The upstairs function room was festooned with pink balloons, smartly dressed waiting staff handing out flutes of champagne at the door. My primal monkey paw grabbed one before my brain had caught up. Mum's eyes burned with disappointment.

'Oh, come on, it's a celebration!' I said, the sweet-sour taste hitting the back of my throat in a welcome gush. 'I want to be able to toast Nancy. I'm her godmother.'

Her face flickered with uncertainty. I took a more measured

sip, smiled at her. She was seduced by the normality, I could tell. Her visible relief flooded me with shame. Made me dangerous.

'Can we have one for my mum, too?' I said, reaching out a hand towards the silver tray. The waiter holding it was dark-haired, with almond-shaped eyes. 'She's the grandmother after all!'

He gave me a languid smile. 'Sure thing,' he said, an Aussie uplift to his tone, and I felt a tiny charge. I could chase a high in a dustbin in those days.

'Cheers, Mum,' I said, chinking my glass against hers, my high feeling almost real.

'Cheers, darling,' she said, giving my glass a tentative tap. 'Just the one. You know what Amber said. I want you to make sure that you see her next week like you promised.'

The room was filling up rapidly, the hum of conversation almost drowning out her voice.

'I will, I swear.' My promises had scarred us both too many times by then: her smile was no more than a thin line drawn by her lips.

There was Dad, rounding the top of the stairs. Why had he arrived separately from us? My gaze swept the room. No sign of Esther. He crossed the space, slipped an arm around Mum's waspish waist and signalled effortlessly for a drink with his other hand.

'I thought we'd just paid through the nose to keep you sober?' he said at the exact same moment the good-looking waiter leaned in to hand him his glass. My cheeks flamed red with shame, but he was too professional to let his face register Dad's comment. Mum touched Dad's arm as the waiter melted back into the crowd.

'She's promised to just have the one. It *is* a celebration, Nick!'

'I'm fine, Dad, just leave it,' I said, feeling approximately thirteen years old. How was it possible I was into my fourth decade, with my parents paying for therapy and monitoring my booze stats? I might as well have had a maths tutor and a time limit on Facebook.

My brother, the golden child, was chinking a champagne flute with a fork now, clearing his throat.

'Thank you all for coming here to celebrate our beautiful daughter.'

Chloe raised the white-frocked baby a little higher to trigger the admiring coos of the crowd, the twins still glued to her ankles. As she did so, I saw Esther slip into the room and head for the back. Was it my imagination, or did Dad's eyes narrow, following her progress?

'She's truly a blessing. We couldn't be more proud of her, and she's only fifteen months old.'

There was a tremor in his voice, a trace of emotion that I rarely saw in my brother, who was so ruthlessly efficient at life that there was little room for glitches. I stood there, frozen between the frosty twin poles of our parents, my shame mounting. Nancy was already making her parents proud at fifteen months: I seemed to be doing the absolute opposite with my thirty-plus years.

'Thank you to Guy, my best mate since our first year at Trinity.' Josh had made sure he made it to Cambridge. His ruddy-faced rowing buddy, Guy, was one of his many souvenirs. 'Do you promise not to teach her how to down pints in a moving punt?'

There was predictable laughter as Guy took a self-deprecating bow. 'Thank you to Melissa, who shared a dormitory with Chloe and definitely knows her wickedest secrets!' I looked towards the humourless Amazonian who'd made little to no effort at all to be friendly when we'd crowded around the font. 'And finally, to my little sister.' Josh turned his body towards me and paused for dramatic effect. 'What is there to say about Rachel? Please don't teach my baby to sink pints on a punt or – more your style – get shit-faced on cocktails and go home with a lechy waiter.' The room erupted with guffaws. 'Only joking, sis, we love you. We know you're a reformed character.'

I gave a weak smile as Guy turned to give me an ironic grin. He had no idea.

'Nancy's lucky to have this motley crew to see her through what we hope will be a charmed life. Will you charge your glasses and drink to – the godparents!'

There was a raindrop of champagne left at the bottom of my glass. If I wanted more – and I did – this was my moment. I slipped away from my parents, holding my flute out to a waitress among a throng of guests, so they wouldn't be able to see the alcohol cascading into it.

'So, we look like a couple of prize plonkers.' It was Guy, pinker than ever, holding his glass aloft to chink against mine. He looked like he'd been cut out of the Millennium party pages at the back of *Tatler* and glued into a scrapbook, frozen in time by Pritt-Stick. I clinked my glass with his, grateful for an excuse to take a long gulp. 'I haven't seen you for donkey's years, Rachel.'

'I think the last time I saw you, you were wearing some particularly stylish red Speedos by the pool in Marbella,' I said, the champagne emboldening me.

'Budgie smugglers?' I took a quick look at his bare left hand. I'd been too distracted by Esther's presence in the crowd when we'd been stood at the font – besides, he was Josh's geeky housemate from freshers' week the last time I'd seen him. The truth was, Guy's puppyish freshness worked in his favour now. Josh's other friends seemed cynical and tired, whereas Guy bubbled with fun. Could my godfather fantasy be coming true? Had Josh engineered this – a rare good deed in our flammable relationship?

'Something like that,' I said.

Guy smiled, his eyes lingering on me with a certain intensity. I liked the way he towered over me, like that he could defeat any predator. 'Sorry, I'm being remiss,' he said. 'I'm leaving a damsel in desperate need of another drink.'

The irony. I froze a second, knowing this was a doorway. Knowing that, when Amber's gentle insistence had oiled the lock, my sobs had come from somewhere deep inside. Her face flickered in my mind's eye, the reams of testimonials – lives saved and transformed – spooling through my already champagne-fuddled mind.

I chose the other path.

'You're a crushing disappointment,' I said, handing Guy my flute, letting my gaze linger on him this time.

'Let's remedy that, sharpish,' he said, pushing his way through the crowd in search of help.

My heart lurched as he walked away. It felt cataclysmic, like he'd abandoned me in a sea of hostile bodies. It was extraordinary how quickly I'd start to think a man was my saviour. It was such a grim, inevitable reflex.

'Rachel!'

Her voice was like nails down a blackboard. I'd recognize it blindfolded. I spun around.

'Hi, Esther,' I said, monotone. She was wearing a white shift dress, the bare pink flesh of her arms covered in goosebumps. Her wide, nervy smile was painted pink, and a smudge of the lipstick decorated her slightly goofy front teeth. They'd made her look even younger than she was when she lived with us – and she was young then. I could remember her seventeenth birthday, the cake Mum bought, the handmade card from Sophie with the dried flowers painstakingly stuck down. And the flowers – the huge mixed, colourful bunch that Dad brought home 'from all of us'. I felt my body contract, my champagne glass slick in my clammy hand. Esther dived forward suddenly, planting a sticky kiss on my cheek.

'How are you, darling?' Her eyes flicked almost imperceptibly to my glass. Or maybe she wanted it to be noticeable. My mind went into overdrive – I hadn't seen her for years. How could she know my family thought I had a problem? Why exactly was she here, back in the heart of our fractured world?

'Really well,' I said airily. 'I've just heard I'm going to get a big promotion at work. And it's such an honour to be Nancy's godmother.' I hardened my expression. 'Mum and Dad are so happy to have their first granddaughter.'

Mum was standing near the bar, elegant as ever in her claret wrap dress. Had she seen us marooned here together? She certainly wasn't looking in our direction now.

'I know! Little Nancy. So adorable.' That goofy grin again, never quite reaching her clear blue eyes. 'Such an honour to be invited today.'

An internal shudder swept through my body. I wanted to ask her who had been the one to ask her, but I didn't want to hear the lie she'd concoct. 'Right,' I said lamely.

She gave a little giggle. 'It's so nice, still being treated as part of the Appleby clan.'

Dad had appeared alongside Mum now: their bodies looked as stiff as marionettes – I longed for them to put on a better show. I had to get away, but I didn't want Guy to lose track of me.

'And who's the new man?' I said. 'I saw how he was looking at you in the church. Is it serious?'

Esther gave another grating giggle.

'We met online. Time will tell, I suppose.' She gave a little shrug.

Just then, Guy reappeared at my elbow, two champagne glasses held firmly in his meaty paws.

'And who's this?' Esther asked.

I dumped my empty glass, grabbed the fresh one and, without taking the time to think through the wisdom of it, grabbed Guy's free hand with my own.

'This is Guy,' I said, letting his name linger significantly, stepping closer to him.

'Hi,' he said, awkwardly, no hand free to shake. His palm felt stiff against mine, unyielding. This didn't feel like the beginning of a love affair.

'I'm Esther. I was Rachel's au pair, hard as it is to believe.'

I dropped his hand.

'Strictly speaking you were Sophie's au pair,' I said icily, aware that Guy must be thinking I was more unstable by the second.

I took a swig of my drink, aware the room was starting to feel a little blurry around the edges. I should have eaten more than a lone slice of toast for breakfast.

Esther didn't miss a beat. 'Hard to remember now, when you all made me so welcome! Anyway, lovely to see you, Rachel.

Hope we can catch up properly soon. Good luck with the promotion.'

'Bye, Esther,' I said, forcing a smile entirely for Guy's benefit. I turned my gaze upwards towards him as soon as she'd retreated. 'Sorry about that.'

'All felt a bit lipsticks at dawn,' he said, slightly flustered. I took a tiny step backwards.

'She's a stupid bi—' I thought better of it. 'Long story. I won't bore you with it. Thanks for braving the crowds in search of bubbles.'

Bubbles – it sounded so innocuous.

'Your wish is my command,' he said, his smile wolfish now. 'And I can't imagine you ever boring me.'

'Trust me, I can be very, very boring,' I said. The one thing that I excelled at back then was flirtation.

'So, tell me about your promotion,' he asked. 'Is that very, very boring? What is it you do, anyway?'

'I'm a civil servant. I'm about to move into the foreign office. Lots of international travel.' I thought of the pile of papers on my desk, the dense type about urban planning. I warmed to my fantasy job. 'I'll be preparing briefings for the foreign secretary so I'm going to have to have a much higher security clearance.'

'Wow, amazing. I'm just another dullard in the City. I wish sometimes I'd done something more meaningful with my life.'

'There's still time,' I said, allowing my fingers to graze his hand as I raised my glass to my lips. Something complicated crossed his features, but he swiftly wiped it away.

'Now, tell me, is it appalling form if we get a top-up when our glasses are half full?' he asked.

'Terrible,' I twinkled.

For the next few hours I kept us in a bubble of bubbles, refusing to engage with my family. Josh's disapproval radiated off him, but all it did was egg me on. Some part of me wanted to live up to all of their worst expectations of me. To prove them right. The fact that Guy and I had started going out for longer and longer fag breaks kept us out of sight for much of the time, and the discovery of a nook near the loos, complete with comfy velvet sofas, meant we could eventually stage a complete disappearance.

'This has been really nice,' he said, slinging his tree trunk of an arm around my shoulders. 'Getting to know you properly. Not just some little squirt reading *Just Seventeen*.'

'Excuse *me*,' I said, leaning into his chest. 'I'm sure I was reading Proust. I was a teenage genius, I think you'll find.'

He held my gaze, then kissed me lightly.

'You're really fun, aren't you? Really funny.'

'So are you,' I said, pressing my lips against his, closing my eyes. His kiss felt tentative at first, but it rapidly gathered heat. The room started to spin in the darkness. I snapped open my eyes. His eyes goggled back at me, vertiginously close from this angle.

'You're so pretty,' he said quickly. 'So, so pretty.'

'Thanks,' I said, entwining our fingers. Something was off, but I kept pushing the feeling away. I was painfully drunk, painfully disturbed by Esther's presence. I took another gulp of champagne, leaning towards the ice bucket we'd stolen from behind the bar. 'How fun are you feeling?' I said. 'On a scale from one to ten?'

'What do you want me to say?' he enquired, leaning in.

'Eleven?' I shrugged.

'So, what have you got in mind?' he asked.

Another fork in the road. The hubbub of voices had dropped low next door, the party starting to thin out. It was tea time by now, and people needed to hurry home for children's bath times and evening engagements. I had no such responsibilities. Was I really going to do this? It seemed I was.

I reached into my clutch bag, pulled out my coin purse and extracted it. His face stayed immobile for what felt like forever.

'Coke?'

I nodded.

'Here? Really?' A tide of embarrassment started lapping up my body, but then I saw a smile spread across his face. 'I can't believe you. You're an outrage!'

'Believe,' I said, untangling myself from him and heading towards the loos. There were some closer to the bar, so the coast was clear. Soon we were jammed in a cubicle in the ladies, the kissing more intense now there was no danger of being seen.

'Hang on,' I said, dropping to the ground and shaking a dust of powder over the closed seat. The floor felt damp against my bare knees, an unpleasant tangy stench hitting my nostrils now I was out of reach of the elegant reed diffusers that were placed around the bathroom. Shame threatened to engulf me again, but I concentrated on expertly evening out the two parallel train tracks of cocaine, trying not to think of how close to the limit my trusty Mastercard, doing this holy work, actually was. I skimmed the last crumbs of powder off it, rolled up a note and looked up at Guy.

'Ladies first,' he said, and I honked up a line, praying for a bolt of chemical euphoria to sweep away the despair that was hovering, waiting to pounce. A few seconds later it hit, excitement and energy pulsing through my whole body. Guy's sandy head was bent over the seat, the cocaine disappearing swiftly up his nose.

And then we were kissing in earnest, his hands roving my body, slipping inside my dress. Two fingers trapped one of my nipples, his other hand pushing its way up the exposed flesh of my thigh. Even in the throes of my high, it felt pretty grim and tawdry. I looked up at him, but his face was turned away.

'I like you,' I said, squeezing his fingers and looking up at him. 'I really like you. Can we slow down a second?'

His body slackened against mine, all the energy between us instantly draining away.

'Rachel . . .'

I'd got it wrong. Why did I always get it so wrong?

'Sorry, I shouldn't have said that . . .'

'No, no. It's not you.' He sank heavily onto the seat, stared up at me. 'I'm the one who's sorry. I shouldn't be doing this.'

'No, I pushed it,' I said, desperate to reignite the spark that had suddenly been extinguished. 'It was stupid of me to bring out drugs. I don't really do them. I just went to a thirtieth and some girl from school had some—'

He stuck up a hand, waved it in the cramped cubicle. 'Stop apologizing. I need to be honest with you.' He was choking on his words now. 'I'm engaged.'

'What?'

'I know, I know,' he said, his hand now wedged in his thick hair, his head bowed. 'We've been having problems. She's back in New York, but she's moving here soon and I'm . . .' He looked up at me. 'We're really going to try to make a go of it.'

He looked so plaintive, like he wanted me to reassure him.

To congratulate him, even. The shame hit full force now, almost doubling me over. I wanted to rage at him, but instead I crumpled. Of course he wasn't single. And even if he had been, my behaviour was hardly Chapter One of *The Rules*. A man like him wasn't a Tinder hook-up.

'Oh,' I said, my voice as tiny as the space we were crammed in to.

'I'm sorry,' he said, his hands encasing mine. 'I'm a total arsehole, I know. It was such a blast seeing you again, and we were having so much fun.' He smiled at me, forcing eye contact. 'We really were, weren't we? I mean, if my situation were different . . .'

We both knew that was a lie. Suddenly the drink and drugs hit hard, and I lurched backwards.

'Let's get you out of here,' he said, slipping the lock and awkwardly steering me through the cubicle door. I leaned over a sink, retched. I caught a glance of myself in the gilt mirror that ran down the width of the wall. My eye make-up was smudged into inky bruises, my hair tangled into string by our grim clawing. I looked disgusting. I ran the tap, cupped my hand and slurped back some water.

'You shouldn't drink that,' muttered Guy.

I rounded on him.

'Oh, now you're worried about my welfare?' I snarled. 'Now you're not trying to pull my underwear down?'

'I've said I'm sorry,' he said, pink with embarrassment and desperation, fists clenched into tight balls. 'Let me get you into a cab. It's the least I can do.'

I stood up, grabbed the lip of the sink to steady myself.

'Just fuck off. Spare me the chivalry.'

'Rachel . . .'

'Get out!' I was screaming at him now. 'Get away from me.'
A sob erupted out of me and I doubled over. 'I'm so fucking
stupid . . .'

He stepped towards me and my arms windmilled outwards,
keeping him at bay.

'Rachel, I'm going to go and find someone who can help
you,' he said, heading fast for the door. I ran after him, but as I
caught hold of a handful of his jacket, I felt the bile rise again in
my throat. I lurched back to the sink, a thick fountain of vomit
shooting out of my mouth. The door swung behind him and I
lurched after his retreating body.

'Don't!' I shouted. 'I don't want anyone helping me.'

I'd lost all sense of the place, the corridor rotating like a kaleidoscope as I followed him. The distance had shrunk to nothing,
and suddenly I was there, in the room, shocked faces taking in
my vomit-flecked dress. All I could focus on was Mum marching
towards me.

*

Now I was sitting on the tiled floor of the bathroom, my back
leaning against the sinks, willing myself not to vomit. The pity
on Sophie's face was almost worse than Mum's disgust.

'God, how many times do we have to go through this?' Mum
said, standing over me.

Sophie dropped to her knees, pulling a bottle of water from
her handbag.

'Drink some of this,' she said, holding it to my parched lips.
She put her other arm around my shoulders, rubbed my back.
'Oh, Rachel, what happened?'

'That's fairly obvious,' said Mum witheringly, staring down at us on the ground as if we were a pair of squabbling toddlers in a sandpit. 'Rachel doesn't know when to stop. She's incapable.'

'Mum ...' said Sophie, her hand still making comforting circles on my back. Who was the big sister here, really?

'It wasn't just me!' I protested. 'He's a fucking liar. He ...'

'What I saw was you throwing yourself at him,' said Mum. 'He's not the one sprawled on the floor of a public toilet ...' Sophie gave her an admonishing stare. 'I'm sorry, Sophie, I've done nothing but baby her. Tough love is all I've got left.' Two high spots of colour were splashed across her angular cheekbones. 'Today was meant to be a celebration of our family, and you've turned it into yet another disaster.'

'What, is Esther part of our family now?' I snarled. The self-righteous blaze in Mum's eyes started to dim. Was I really going to go there? 'Do the family who cheat together, stay together – something like that?'

Sophie whipped her hand away, and my shoulder blades ricocheted against the hard surface behind us. 'Rachel, stop,' she said, her voice shaking. 'You're drunk.'

Mum's hand sprung out, demanding silence. Her jaw was clenched, her expression fierce. My throat dried, my body shrinking backwards.

'Esther was a very important part of Sophie's childhood. We opened our home to her, and the fact she's still part of our lives is a tribute to our family.' She stood a little taller. 'Now get yourself up, wash your face and we'll walk down the back stairs. Thank God there are some.'

I pulled myself up to standing, as obedient as a child.

Mum shook her head with disgust. 'And once you've slept off the shameful state you're in, we'll go back to trying to sort out the sorry chaos of your life.'

LILY

This idea – this narrative – that I didn't care, that I humiliated and abandoned Rachel, is patent nonsense. As I said to Sophie – not that she'll hear it now – what I was administering that terrible day was tough love. Love was the point; the toughness was a necessary byproduct. It wasn't poison; it was medicine.

I did everything I could to take her home with us once we'd finally found a black cab that would agree to stop. Most of them took one passing glance at her and sailed straight down the Cromwell Road. No amount of cold water and expensive hand wash could disguise the wildness in her eyes or the brittle way she held her body, like she was allergic to me. As soon as some poor fool slowed his cab and the three of us were in the back, the arguing started up again like some kind of Shakespearian howl. Going home with me was the last thing she wanted; she didn't even want me to step over the threshold of the flat. She had some drunken fantasy that I'd called her 'disgusting', that I'd called her 'a slut', and it was impossible for me to defend myself without the very real danger of our cab driver, already stealing nosy glances in the rearview mirror, dumping us on the Westway.

Instead it was Sophie who took her upstairs, giving my hand

a comforting squeeze as she clambered out of the cab, her kind little face telling me how agonizing it was to be stranded between us, the two women she loved most in the world. Not that something like that would ever occur to Rachel of course. *I'll call you later*, Sophie mouthed over her shoulder, and I asked the cab driver to stay put, waiting until I could see the light go on in the middle-floor window, stinging tears pouring down my cheeks.

Was that my mistake? Not treating my emotions like a game of show and tell? Instead I tried to stay strong for her: to be a parent, not an indulgent friend. What I hadn't grasped yet was that parenthood was a job you could be fired from; it was not my primal right.

*

By the time Nick's key turned in the lock, I was an hour into some soporific crime drama with a sage, hangdog detective in a wide-brimmed hat wandering around Italian vineyards. He leaned down to my prone body, slumped on the sofa, and kissed me full on the lips.

'You look like a wife in need of a drink.'

The irony. My hangdog detective could've pointed out the watertight evidence we'd received that seeking relief in alcohol was the last habit our family needed to indulge. He came back from the kitchen with two brimming glasses of Chablis and some salty almonds in a ceramic bowl. I took a deep glug, despite my irritation with him. His unexplained absences, his refusal to metabolize any more worry than the amount I spoon-fed him. I stopped myself. He was caring for me, in his own way, wasn't he? We all have different languages for love: the trick was to appreciate his, rather than complaining about the ones he wasn't fluent in.

'We got her into bed between us,' I said, the lie as light as gossamer. 'It's not nearly as bad as last time. She can sleep it off. I told Sophie to stay, keep an eye on her.'

'Well done, darling,' said Nick, picking up my hand in his. His wedding ring glinted: it felt so progressive that he'd wanted to wear one when we tied the knot. 'She's a fucking disaster, isn't she?'

I rolled my eyes, not trusting myself to speak.

'You'll get her back to see the therapist next week, yes?' he asked, squeezing my hand with his. 'At least we know we're getting her help.'

I thought of Rachel's blazing eyes as she screamed up at me from the cold tiles, Esther's name reverberating around the cramped space. I sat up, almost dizzy, and took a handful of almonds.

'We need to take it one day at a time,' I said. I was the one to press my lips against his this time. His breath had that residual sourness that champagne always leaves, but I overrode the thought. Something I was good at. 'At least the other two are thriving.'

'Exactly,' said Nick, visibly comforted by the thought. It was our constant refrain, a comfort blanket that would one day come to smother us. He pushed me backwards against the cushions, and I allowed my body to yield to him. 'I love you,' he muttered into my hair, as his hand sought out the zip that ran down the length of my back.

'I love you, too,' I said, kissing him back with an impressive degree of fervour.

I think I even fooled myself.

RACHEL

The buzzer was discreet, a small label stuck next to it – 'A. Greville', it said, in courier script. The doorway was at the far end of the Goldborne Road, where fruit and veg stalls and dodgy antique vendors spill out on the street and the nasty, showy wealth of Notting Hill starts to fade. My finger hovered above it for a few seconds, the noise and bustle around me jangling my already shredded nerves. I'd been going over the shitstorm that was Saturday again and again, more repelled by that version of me every time I replayed the tape. I'd made a cautious peace with Mum, all by text – *I'm sorry I drank too much xx* was all I said, knowing that everything I wasn't saying would leave her raging.

She'd tried to call me, then left a voicemail that contained a few of her standard phrases. *We can't go on like this* was followed by a date and time to see Amber. And now, here I was, shivering pathetically on the doorstep, victimized even by the November weather, not sure who I was really here for. Was it Mum? Was it me? Was it even for Amber? I stopped my navel-gazing and pushed the bell.

'Is that you, Rachel?' Amber's voice sounded warm, even via the crackly intercom.

I swallowed, my eyes flicking down the road. There was a handbag shop on the corner, buttery leather sacks stacked up in a tempting pile in the window. It took all of my self-control not to skip away and max out my already groaning overdraft.

'Yes. I'm here,' I said, forcing myself to push the heavy door open when it clicked.

The hallway was cream, fresh red tulips overflowing from a vase on a console table, a silver mirror above it making the space feel welcoming and open. It was warm and cozy, like I'd been wrapped up tight in a John Lewis Christmas ad.

'Rachel?'

There she was, standing at the top of the stairs, gazing down at me. She had an off-the-shoulder black jumper on, pulled down over skinny jeans, her dark hair piled up in a messy bun. I remember wondering inexplicably if she was cold, if those bare shoulders would be pocked with goosebumps when I got up close to her. She felt like a chic, ageless friend, not some proxy parent sent to judge me.

'Hi,' I said, ashamed of the way my voice quavered.

'Come on up,' she said, encouraging me with a wide, red-mouthed smile. 'Sorry there are so many stairs. Bit of an arse, I know.'

She turned quickly on her heel, and I made the climb. Her rooms were two flights up, as elegant and welcoming as the hallway had been. There were two green velvet sofas littered with cushions, a low glass coffee table between them, soft lighting shedding a sepia glow.

'The bathroom's to the left if you need it, and I've made you a cup of jasmine tea,' she said, gesturing to a chunky pottery cup on the table. 'If you think it sounds disgusting, I won't be offended.' She laughed. 'We'll just tip it down the sink and I'll make you a coffee.'

'No,' I said, continuing my run of monosyllables. 'Tea's fine.'

Her bare shoulders sunk back against the velvet, wintry morning sun filtering through the slatted wooden blinds. I thought randomly of those grainy black-and-white photographs of Freud, peering out myopically from behind thick glasses. What kind of Instagram-friendly version of therapy was Amber offering? She smiled at me, head cocked, as if she could sense the defensive questions that were swirling inside my head.

'I just think caffeine ramps up the nervous system, and you look like you need the exact opposite of that.' Her voice was like a caress. 'You need comfort. You need . . . you need to rest, don't you, Rachel? Not sleep – rest. It's very different.'

A lump rose in my throat, but I forced it back down, the memory of the sobbing mess I'd become the last time we met working like a cattle prod on my psyche. I had a budget meeting after this, a detailed discussion about joint ownership schemes in satellite towns. That girl – that pathetic version of me – was not welcome here.

A flash of Guy's face, of my desperate hand clawing for a hold on his suit jacket. I sat down and took a sip of the jasmine tea. It was scalding hot, but I forced myself not to wince.

'It's delicious,' I said stiffly.

'I'm glad,' she said, sinking further into the plump cushions with a confidence that they would melt and mould to meet her. Every particle of her exuded self-belief. Me – I sat up a little straighter, my spine taut. 'How does it feel to be here, for us to be meeting again?' she asked.

'I'm happy to be here,' I said. God, I sounded as unnatural as a politician on the back of a sex scandal, forced to read a prepared statement on the *Six O'Clock News*. 'Thanks for making the time.'

'You don't have to thank me, Rachel. It's a real pleasure to see you again.'

'I know. It's your job. I don't need to thank you.'

She paused, a gentle smile playing across her face.

'I'm going to repeat what I said, but this time I want you to try to actually hear it. *It's a real pleasure to see you again.*'

I tried to smile back.

'Thanks.'

She laughed, but not unkindly.

'Try closing your eyes this time, actually absorb what I'm telling you.' I shut them, feeling idiotic. The words flooded out of her like a poem. *'It's a real pleasure to see you again. It's a real pleasure to see you again.'*

The lump rose again in my throat, and I snapped my eyes back open. She was watching me.

'You heard me that time, didn't you? I saw you start to let the words penetrate.'

I wanted to simultaneously hold her at bay and excel at this. It was exhausting.

'I think so,' I said.

'It's important, Rachel,' she said, intense. 'It's important for you to know that I see you. This isn't a job for me – it's a privilege to be able to help people in psychic pain. To help them stop hating themselves and start letting the love that wants to flow to all of us, start guiding their lives.'

A surge of hopelessness swept across me, Saturday night flickering in my peripheral vision. Love never seemed all that keen to flow towards me. It mostly seemed to enjoy punching me in the face.

'Right.'

Amber laughed.

'Too much? Too much new age bullshit for session two?'

I laughed too, despite myself.

'Well, I like Goop as much as the next person . . .' I said.

We paused a second, eying each other. She spoke first.

'You're smart, aren't you?' she said. 'I bet you did really well academically.'

'I got a First, yeah,' I confirmed. The year of my A levels I'd wanted nothing more than escape, barricaded in my bedroom at the top of the house with a stack of books. Mum and Dad were so proud of my diligence, in denial about the lengths I'd go to to avoid the booby traps that lurked downstairs. Esther kept her Instagram feed open. I hoped she had no means of knowing how often I looked.

'So does your career give you satisfaction now? You're a civil servant, right?'

'Yeah,' I said. I'd told Tim I had a doctor's appointment, which felt at least half true, a fifty per cent improvement on my normal rate of honesty. 'I mean, it's important.'

'That's not the same thing,' she said, soft.

'Everyone's job is boring some of the time, isn't it? Going to an office, seeing the same old people . . .'

'So what *does* give you satisfaction? What gives you joy?' I felt a surge of irritation at her relentless, teasing questions. 'Not much right now, I'm guessing?'

I shook my head.

'Rachel, it's important that we listen to that.'

'I'm listening,' I said, aware of the edge in my tone. I could tell she heard it too: Amber didn't miss a trick.

'What I'm hearing – and tell me if this sounds remotely true to you – is that sometimes you have to go to extremes just to feel something. To fight for that joy that's actually your birthright.'

My head turned away from her, my burning eyes dropped to the ground. Here we were, right where Mum wanted me to be, discussing what a monumental fuck-up I was.

I spat my words out. 'When I'm crying on the floor of a toilet or puking my guts up on the Kings Road with an ambulance on its way – trust me, there's not much joy going on.'

I was shaking now, my face scalding hot. Amber stayed quiet, the few seconds of silence stretching like elastic.

'And I believe you. You're an intelligent, assured woman. I know you don't want to be risking your life.'

'You say that, but the fact is I do it to myself . . .' It sounded tinny in my ears. It was Mum's phrase, that one. Her syntax, not mine, even though I couldn't deny its truth.

'Yes, and I think that's the paradox. A fucking annoying one, I'm afraid.' There was something oddly thrilling about hearing her swear. I raised my eyes, let them meet hers – I stayed staring at her, almost craving what she would say next. 'All you're doing is trying to find comfort, to find connection – what all of us need to survive. But the tragedy is that in trying so hard to find it, you leave yourself more alone than ever.'

And then the tears came – not the kind of sobs that send waves of relief through your body and bring an exhausted peace; these tears felt like liquid rage. A rage that was bigger than the past few months. A rage that could annihilate me if I let it.

'Why am I like this? Why am I like this?' I couldn't stop, the phrase pouring out of me again and again, my head in my hands, sooty tears running through my fingers. Then I felt Amber's hand, warm and steady, land between my shoulder blades.

'Let it come out. Let it out.'

Her palm started to work on my heaving back, circular motions that soothed me, despite myself.

'Do you know what a mantra is?' she said, her voice as soft as a whisper. 'It's a phrase we repeat again and again, until it's part of us. This is yours, isn't it? This is what you're living by. And I want you to know that you can throw it away.'

The rage was for her now, for her stupid, trite little homily. This bawling fuck-up was who I was, not a coat that I could slip out of and fling across the room.

'Yeah, because it's that's fucking easy,' I muttered, jerking my body away from her and curling backwards into the depths of the sofa. She crossed the room, sat back down in her seat, her calm smile never wavering.

'And what if it is? What if the truth you think you're telling yourself – what if it's a lie? What if it's a lie that isn't even yours?'

'What does that even mean?' I demanded.

'You've learnt something very wrong about your value – about what defines you. And I think it's our job to trace that lie to its source and take its power away so you can stop stepping onto the stage that's your life and acting it out. Let's give you a whole new script to work from.'

For a second, I dared to hope. I dared to imagine living without the endless punishing monologue in my head that told me that love was for other people. That happiness was for other people – thinner, nicer people who could say no to a fourth drink. People whose families weren't just pretty on the outside, but all the way through, like the writing through a stick of rock.

'What does that even mean, practically speaking?' I asked.

'How old were you when you started believing this garbage about yourself? Do you remember?'

I thought back. Josh was so golden, so clearly Mum's favourite. And then Sophie came along, all cute gurgles and chubby fists. And then finally – finally she arrived. By then there was no air left for me to breathe. I pushed the complicated explanations, the half-truths of my history, away.

'I'm not sure I ever believed anything different about myself.'

Amber looked almost stricken.

'That makes me sad, Rachel. I'm sad that being part of your family didn't make you feel like you were a gift.'

It was as if my thoughts were subtitles that she could simply read and repeat back to me.

'My family definitely don't think I'm a gift right now.' I gave a mirthless laugh. Would a baby remember, somewhere in their psyche, that their aunt was a drunken, disgusting mess at their christening?

Amber allowed a few seconds of silence.

'Do you think that *they're* a gift?'

'I know that they love me,' I said, measuring out the words carefully, like they were part of a complicated recipe that I'd never cooked before.

'You say that like it's a favour they're doing you,' she said, with that half smile of hers.

'That's not how I meant it,' I said, even though it was. It was too soon for me to trust her with all of me. With all of us.

'I think it's a question that is worth you reflecting on before we next meet.' She gave a self-deprecating shrug of her bony shoulders. 'Sorry, presumptuous. I mean, *if* we meet again.'

'Yes, please,' I said. It blindsided me, how much it sounded like a plea. I glanced down at my watch: the session had slipped by so quickly. A strange desperation overtook me, as if I was in the dark of a confessional box. 'I didn't tell you . . . I promised you I wouldn't drink and . . . I meant it. But instead I got shit-faced on coke and champagne at Nancy's christening. I fucked someone else's husband in the toilets. I'm not . . .' I hid my face from her all-seeing gaze, staring down at the polished wooden floorboards as I gabbled out my confession. 'I'm sure Mum's told you all of this anyway. Let's both stop pretending I'm some-thing I'm not.' My face was wet, my hand grasping for my bag so I could make my escape. 'Something better. Someone who's actually a nice person.'

I ground to a halt, not ready to risk looking up. The atmo-sphere felt oddly, hypnotically calm. I let my eyes meet hers. She was staring at me as if I was some kind of fascinating, exotic wild animal.

'Slow down,' she said. 'Take a big gulp of air.'

I looked at my watch again, pulled my bag onto my knees.

'It's twelve anyway,' I said. 'I should go.'

'I'm not a big stickler for rules,' she said. Wasn't that the truth? But it would be a while before I found that out. 'Feel your feet on the ground, breathe deeply into your belly.'

I felt my body still.

'First of all, yes, your mum did mention there'd been some kind of incident, but I stopped her right there.'

I grinned with a triumphant kind of gratitude.

'What – like attorney/client privilege?'

'Something like that,' she said, smiling back.

'Thank you,' I said, my breath coming less jagged now.

'And if you want to share it – rewind it together – we can. But it's your choice. This is your session. You're in charge. I'm here to help you, not make you feel even shittier.'

It was so skillful, the way her casual swearing helped me forgive myself for all of my messy chaos. We're all trying and failing, it seemed to imply. All a work in progress.

I gave her a garbled account: the humiliation of turning up alone among all of those polished couples, the first drink which morphed into the fifth, the chaotic public mess I'd become, scraped off the floor of a toilet by my horrified family. I almost uttered Esther's name, but it stuck fast in my throat. She made me ashamed for all of us.

Amber was quiet at the end, almost pensive.

'Perhaps it was too soon.'

'Too soon?'

'All I'm hearing is pressure.' Her red-tipped fingers popped into the empty space around her face. 'You're back there, on stage again. All of them wanting you to be well. Wanting you to be happy. Sometimes trying to live up to other people's expectations can be the loneliest place on earth.'

I couldn't accept her compassion, not yet. 'I was a disgrace.' My hands clenched into involuntary fists. 'Why do I keep doing it to myself, when I know—?'

Amber gently cut across me.

'All I'm hearing is what *you* did wrong. You're judge and jury all at once – it's pretty impressive. I'm feeling like there are a few co-defendants here.' She held my gaze in that unnerving, intimate way she had, tapping a finger. 'Firstly, Guy,' she said, voice dripping with contempt. 'He's the one in a relationship, not you. He's the one committing adultery. And by the way, he's not someone's husband, but I'm noticing that you found a way to make your crime – if we can even call it that – sound even worse than it is.'

It's a weird kind of irony, the way she sketched out a court-room. Perhaps she sensed where we were headed, even then.

'You do that a lot, don't you, Rachel?' she continued. 'Find petrol to throw on the fire of your self-disgust?'

I flinched.

'I'm sorry!' she said. 'I work so intuitively, and sometimes I articulate what I'm sensing a little too quickly. Feel free to tell me to shut my mouth.'

'No, no, it's okay,' I said, forcing myself to smile. What hurt was that my carefully concealed acts of self-harm were so obvious.

Amber continued, soft. 'Sometimes, when we do something we can't even explain to ourselves, it's another part of us trying to express a truth we can't bear to consciously own.'

'Yeah, no, I understand about the subconscious,' I said, shame making me pompous.

Amber paused.

'But we can never really understand the subconscious, can we?' She laughed. 'It's kind of its survival strategy! It can be scary when a part of us goes rogue, finds a more extreme way to force us to acknowledge the reality of a situation.'

'So, Saturday was a terrorist attack, is that what you're saying? I'm like – emotional ISIS?'

When Amber laughed, it felt like the most incredible release of tension.

'Perhaps it wasn't just you who needed to hear the message,' she said. 'It can be the truth-teller in the family who's the real hero, even if it doesn't look that way.'

'Do you think that's what I was trying to do? Make my family listen?'

How was she so perceptive when I hadn't even spoken Esther's name? I sat with her version for a second, and my shame started to miraculously recede, to reshape itself into something almost noble.

She gave a sage nod.

'You don't strike me as a disruptor, Rachel, with your A grades and your first-class degree.' I remember being surprised by how thorough Mum must have been, the level of detail she'd bothered to impart. It made me feel instantly guilty for the fact that I was sitting here, slyly sliding blame over to her for my own revolting behaviour.

Then I started to think about the endless boring work meetings that were coming my way, the inevitable chat with Julia about whether or not she should go vegan. I needed to get a grip.

I picked up my bag. 'I should go.'

'Of course,' smiled Amber. 'I'm sorry that I overran.'

'No, it was really nice of you to give me that time . . .' I said. It was harder than I expected to actually leave.

'Just think about what we talked about,' Amber added. She nested her fingers together and stretched them out in front of her, silently acknowledging the session was closing. 'I think you're a very special young woman – a bright spirit that wants to shine – and I'm hoping once we've done our work together, you won't even need me to tell you that. You'll own it.'

Her faith in me – even if Mum had paid for it – made sharp

tears prickle behind my eyes. It was amazing and agonizing all at once.

'Thanks,' I said, standing up so fast that the blood rushed to my head. She must have seen my fingers grasp for the arm of the plush sofa.

'I know you have to get to work, but let's just take a couple more minutes to really close out the session,' she said.

I sunk down heavily: suddenly the outside world felt like way too much. Amber reached under the coffee table and pulled out a black box. Inside was a huge lump of pink crystal which she planted ceremoniously between us.

'Forgive me the hippy dippy stuff, but this is a piece of rose quartz. A shaman who . . .' her voice had a tremor to it. 'He's been life-changing – he blessed it in service of all my clients.' Her eyes were bright, as if the very thought of him was over-whelming to her. 'Let's just place our fingers on it.' I stretched out a tentative hand. As the pads of my fingers settled on it, something unquiet inside me settled too. 'That's it. Let it heal you,' murmured Amber, her lids heavy, eyes half closed.

Now she was emitting not words but a tone, a sound that was somewhere between pain and ecstasy. Her face was turned upwards, towards what – a god that only she could see? I looked away as the noise she made filled the room: it was too intimate, like I'd caught her with a hand surreptitiously stuffed down her knickers.

Then her eyes sprung open, her hands moving to prayer position at her heart. Her eyes were shining, her laser focus back on me. I checked myself. Was joy really that hard for me to contemplate? Was it somehow dirty to me?

'The light in me honours the light in you,' she said, bowing deeply towards me. 'Namaste.'

'Namaste,' I said, copying the gesture, familiar from the yoga classes I'd occasionally manage when my hangovers allowed.

'Until we meet again . . .' she said.

I booked to come back the following Monday before I'd even left the room. It was five days away – I couldn't even wait a week.

LILY

When I look back, it's hard not to curse my own naivety. The fact is, I wanted to believe that I'd solved the problem. After all, I'd solved bigger, darker problems before. Perhaps by then I believed I was invincible.

When Rachel called me, the apologies that I'd been angrily craving finally erupting out of her, I let myself feel the relief. When Amber – the self-appointed queen of patient/client confidentiality – told me that their session had been a 'deeply healing experience', I forgave her the Californian syrup and celebrated the good news.

My self-belief wasn't narcissism – it was the absolute opposite. Everything I did, I did for my family. I sacrificed every last vestige of my own peace of mind so that they could sleep at night.

How was I to know that my 'solving the problem' was me simply seeding the ground for far bigger issues to grow?

No one ever acknowledges that it was unadulterated love that drove me to do what I did.

RACHEL

It was me that arrived at the restaurant first. Mum's shock was visible when she came through the door – she was used to my trickle of texts – *sorry, sorry, sorry* – which would start to arrive ten or twenty minutes before we were due to meet. I'd find a distraction – an urgent piece of work, a sweatshirt with a slogan on it in the window of a shop – and somehow the time would slink away, and I'd arrive to find her with those pink splashes on her perfect cheekbones like two red flags marking danger.

I stood up to greet her, my heart unexpectedly mulching inside my chest at the sight of her smile – genuine, unguarded. For once I had made her happy.

'Hi, darling,' she said, her eyes flicking across the white tablecloth. A single bottle of San Pellegrino, a full glass. The most daring thing was the slice of lime floating across the surface. More happiness. Could it really be this easy to make our relationship work?

'Hi, Mum,' I said, hugging her properly. She hugged me back, tightly.

'Nice place,' she said, looking around. It was a basement Italian in Marylebone, tables close together, waiters rushing between them with plates precariously balanced. It wasn't fancy, but it was atmospheric. I'd booked it for us, and I was paying the bill. 'Dad would like it,' she added, then paused. 'He wanted to crash, but he's stuck on a contract negotiation call. He might make dessert.'

Was she wondering if that contract call even existed? I squeezed her hand, pushing away all the dark thoughts that could tank our evening. 'He's not invited. This is a girls' night.'

'There isn't really room, anyway,' she said, ignoring any subtext. She signalled for a passing waiter who stopped immediately, despite the full plates he was balancing. Mum had that effect on people, the confidence of a woman who'd grown up unarguably beautiful. 'Can we have another water glass please?'

The waiter twinkled at her, his dark hair falling in a floppy cow lick over his face.

'No wine for madam? Really?'

Mum hesitated.

'Go on Mum, have a glass of white. It's fine.' I patted her hand. 'I'm fine.' I looked up at the waiter. 'She'll have a glass of Pinot Grigio.'

'And nothing for you?'

'Nothing for me,' I said smugly. 'I don't drink.'

I'd seen Mum once since the christening, stopping by for a hastily drunk latte when she and Sophie were having breakfast in Clapham one Saturday morning. It had done what I'd hoped, successfully decompressed the building tension between us, and a couple of weeks later, I'd come up with this plan.

'Do you really have to do that?' Amber had asked me when I'd told her at our fourth session. 'Does it truly feel like what *you* need?' I'd felt grateful and irritated all at once. She treated me like a precious glass ornament, as if keeping me from breaking was the most important thing in the world. But sometimes it felt like that world she was inhabiting wasn't the real one. I knew it would be more trouble than it was worth to keep Mum at arm's length for too long.

And now we were here together, I was happy to find that I was actually glad to be with her. I wanted to share my newfound clarity. My lightness. It wasn't all lightness though: my emotional weather was changeable. I cried at odd times – brushing my teeth, my morning face make-up free and vulnerable, or at a child straining for their sister from their pushchair at a next-door lunch table. 'You're coming back to life,' said Amber, when I told her how delicate I felt. 'You're not numb anymore. And I'm awe-struck!'

Mum was considering me from behind her raised glass. The waiter seemed to have brought her a bucket of wine to make up for my disappointing lack of interest.

'You look well, darling,' she said. 'Your dark circles have gone.' She laughed. 'You're not my little raccoon anymore.'

I bit back my irritation at how every compliment she ever gave me came with a 'PS'.

'I'm sleeping properly. Working hard. Doing lots of yoga. I feel great, actually,' I said.

'Tell me about what's going on at work,' she said. 'Have you closed on a site now?'

This was one thing I did have in common with my parents: a career around housing and property. Mum had her own business, an upmarket rental company that put stressed-out tenants with too much money and not enough time into homes around West London. Dad's law firm exclusively dealt in property, devising deals for multi-million-pound transactions. Both of them had done so well, particularly Mum, who'd herself grown up in a council flat in Hounslow that she'd never dream of stepping foot in now. Still, sometimes I felt like their proximity to the super rich left them feeling like they'd somehow failed by being merely wealthy. Mum's drive had got her a long way, but it didn't necessarily give her peace – you could apply that statement across the sweep of her life.

'Yeah, we're going for this repurposed industrial estate outside Letchworth,' I said, relaxing again. She remembered what I was doing. We were talking about normal things, like a normal mum and daughter on a normal night out. For a second, I almost flagged down the waiter for a glass of wine, to add another layer of normal, but it was too risky. Meanwhile, Mum was running on.

'With architects, the first month is critical. You've got to make sure they don't start overthinking it and get behind. You need to be on their case every day. Out there in your hard hat!'

'Don't you worry, neon really brings out the colour of my eyes,' I said.

'Orange gilets are so this season,' Mum shot back, and we giggled. It was nice.

'I'm enjoying it,' I said, which was weirdly true. The rigour of trying had become addictive. It was like I was back to my stack of A level textbooks, order restored.

'I'm really pleased,' said Mum, and I could see in her eyes that she meant it.

'Thanks for helping me get myself . . .' these were hard words to find. A part of me didn't want to offer them, but I resisted being stingy. 'Back on track. I appreciate the support.'

'And you're still seeing Amber every week?' said Mum. 'I just got her invoice.'

'Yes,' I said, an involuntary smile spreading across my face like I was in the first flush of love – which I suppose I was. When I'd seen Amber at lunchtime, she'd helped me prep for tonight. In fact, she was the reason I hadn't reacted to being compared to a four-legged creature that buried its own shit. 'She's really . . .' I searched for the right adjective. 'She's just really wise. But she's also no bullshit.' I paused. 'Thanks for her, most of all. I know you went to a lot of trouble to find out about her. She's amazing.'

Mum's smile was more guarded this time.

'That's alright,' she said. 'We all knew that you desperately needed help. We're just so glad it seems to be working.'

I took a breath, a shard of glass piercing my heart. *We*. The shiny clean, sober members of the family. And then there's *you*. I summoned Amber up, a genie with great skinny jeans. I wouldn't allow myself to feel bad. I shouldn't have risked being vulnerable with Mum. I always paid for it.

'Thanks for giving me the sessions, but I'll take it from here,' I said, my words flat. 'I can pay my own bills.'

Mum looked down, then cocked her blonde head. How did her hair always stay so perfect, even after a day in a hot car showing spoilt people soulless penthouses?

'Darling, it's great you want to, but . . . Amber's actually very expensive. And we really want you to get the treatment you need. Dad and I are happy to keep footing the bill.'

The rage that was suddenly building inside me was out of proportion to the situation. A blowback of grief followed it: if only everything was as easy as smiling a pretty smile and obediently swigging my San Pellegrino.

'I've got a *job*,' I said, my voice rising. Right at that moment I'd have done anything to have a gulp of her wine, take the edge off. 'I'm in charge of that whole project. It's a major government project.'

I was bigging myself up, and we both knew it.

'That's wonderful. I'm proud of you. But ...' She put down her glass, waved a dismissive hand. 'Trust me when I tell you that you can't foot the bill. Let us take care of you.'

There was something so smug about her in that moment. She was so proud of how far she'd scrabbled up the ladder of achievement. How perfect it all looked. No wonder she was so thrilled by Josh's triumphant days in court. Of Sophie's ability to land a romantic catch.

'Okay,' I said, my cheeks burning. 'Thanks, then.' I wanted to throw the offer back in her face, but the truth was, my Mastercard had almost five grand on it, and I was still using it to buy tampons in the week before pay day. I felt pathetic, a teenager with wrinkles. I needed Amber, and I needed Mum to keep my grip on her.

'Say thank you to Dad, too,' she said, lightly cupping my hand. 'He'll appreciate hearing it from you.'

My heart sank even lower now, a dead weight inside a hollow shell.

*

My spaghetti pomodoro kept falling off my fork, slithering away before I got it into my mouth. Mum was elegantly impaling ravioli, telling me about the latest series of a twisty crime drama – corrupt cops with beady eyes and too many implausible motives – that everyone at work seemed obsessed with too. My joy had gone, her words just noise.

'I'm not really watching much TV at the moment,' I said. 'I'd rather read.'

It was true. Amber had given me a stack of books with dreamy covers to immerse myself in. *Love Your Inner Child*, a blonde-haired angel on the cover with clouds floating above her. *The Alchemist* – ancient wisdom packaged for a Western audience. They comforted me. They made me feel Amber was with me, even when she wasn't. I think I read them looking for clues to who she was, behind that messily glossy facade. I even kept *The Alchemist* in my handbag, revelling in how dog-eared the pages were. It made me feel like we were reading it together. Any questions I asked about her were batted away, so those little moments of false intimacy I created were all the more precious. 'You'll feel safer if you don't have to worry about me,' she said. 'Our time together is all about you.'

'It's one of the only shows Dad and I can watch together,' Mum said. 'He actually wants to be home in time. It's a miracle!'

'Big time,' I said, immediately regretting it. She raked me with her eyes, took a forkful of salad from the bowl between us.

'He works hard. He always has. I admire that about him.'

'Yes, no,' I said, scrabbling for safe ground. 'We all do.'

'You can obviously choose what you want to watch, living on your own,' she said coolly. 'But I do hope, when you're really through all of this, you'll meet someone too.'

Every time, that little postscript. That little reminder that I was the one lagging behind. The problem. Something dangerous spiked inside of me.

*

Amber had been so calm when I told her, her steadiness giving me strength. I rarely spoke about it in those days. Even when I hated them, they were still my family and I didn't want to give anyone else the chance to judge them. To judge me: I was them and they were me, and I'd been burnt in the past. I'd told a boyfriend who I believed I loved at university, and later, in a row about a girl in the bar wearing a tight rugby shirt who I knew fancied him, he threw it back in my face. 'Just because your family fuck the staff, there's no reason for you to be such a psycho about us.' I felt like he'd slapped me round the face, and yet I stayed with him for another whole year. In fact, he was the one who dumped me.

Amber had asked me to map out my family for me, to describe how we all related to each other. I'd described for her how Sophie was the precious afterthought whom we'd all adored. The five-year gap between us made her more like a beloved doll than a rival, so different from my combative relationship with Josh, the brother who I swear hated me on sight at six hours old.

'Why am I sensing sadness?' asked Amber, as I described how Sophie would toddle into my bedroom every morning shouting, 'Raach-el, Raach-el,' when dawn was barely breaking. 'It's a happy story, no?'

I'd looked down at the floor, my cheeks starting to flame. Could I really tell her? Could I really not?

'It wasn't Sophie who made us unhappy,' I whispered. 'It was what it meant for my parents.' She'd left a long silence, waited for me to find the words. 'She's why Esther came.'

'Who's Esther?' she asked eventually. 'And if you're not ready to tell me, please don't force yourself. We have all the time you need.'

I looked up at her.

'Sophie's au pair,' I said. I felt nauseous. 'And then Dad's girl-friend. Maybe she still is. Why else was she at the christening?'

Amber's face was suffused with empathy. It was beautiful to watch: she saw me. She honoured my pain – she made it sacred.

'Oh, Rachel.'

'I was the one who walked in on them together.'

*

'Who invited Esther to the christening?' I asked, keeping my voice deliberately light.

'Josh, I imagine,' said Mum, giving a brittle wave to the waiter. 'That was so delicious that I'll have another glass,' she said, despite the pool of wine still sitting at the bottom of the current one.

'Really?' I said.

'For a time, she was a member of our family,' said Mum. 'She was a very important part of Sophie's childhood.'

'Yeah, that's one way of putting it.'

Mum's jaw was rigid, her eyes cold. *Why was I doing this?*

'I'm surprised you want to talk about the christening at all,' she said. 'I thought we'd made a collective decision to leave it behind us.'

'I just want us to start being honest with each other,' I said. 'Even if it's uncomfortable.'

'Is that the therapy talking?' she spat, making angry quotation marks in the air.

'No,' I said, infused with an unexpected calm. 'It's me talking. Rachel. Your daughter. You know, the other one.'

The waiter reappeared; Mum's wine glass balanced on a tray.

As she looked up at him, her poise was all but gone, her hand shaking as she reached for it. It turned out she really did have a lot invested in me burying my own shit.

'Let's not do this to each other,' she said, voice tight. 'I thought things were getting easier.'

'I want it to be easier too, Mum,' I said. 'I just want to understand you.'

'Maybe there's not all that much to understand,' she said, her tone a full stop.

I couldn't help myself. 'Why do you put up with it?'

'Don't you think there's something rather icky about prying into your parents' marriage?' she said. 'Most children would run a mile in the opposite direction.'

'But it's affected me,' I said, my voice starting to rise. 'These problems I've had, they're not some kind of freak accident. They came from somewhere.'

'Oh, it's *my* fault?' she said. Her tone was piercing; heads were discreetly starting to turn in our direction. 'What an appalling cliché, Rachel. Take some responsibility.'

I stood up, legs shaky. I wasn't going to be victimized by her a second longer.

'I'm sorry you've made the choice to be angry. I'm just trying to make our relationship better. I wish you could be brave enough to see that.'

She snorted, looked up at me with something close to hatred. 'Which just goes to show how pitifully little you know about any kind of relationship.'

I pulled out as much cash as I could find from my purse, threw it down. There was a crumpled up ten-euro note in the pathetic pile I left.

'I'm sorry, Mum, I can't do this anymore,' I said, shoving my way through the tight tables before she could get up and follow me.

LILY

The hallway light was on as my taxi pulled up. I stared at the glow, as transfixed as a moth, my hand refusing to dig into my handbag for the fare. I took a breath in, tried to reset.

'Hi, darling,' I trilled, as I finally stepped inside.

Nick ambled down the hall towards me. His shirt was untucked, a couple of buttons undone.

'Hi baby,' he said, leaning down to kiss my mouth. 'How was she? I got stuck on the call until nine, so I just got some Deliveroo with Martin. Thank fuck for the mute button.' He gestured at a grease spot on his shirt. 'Noodles. Disaster.'

I smiled, the blackness of my mood momentarily lifting. He always made me laugh. Rachel did, too.

'Don't worry,' I said, following him down the hallway to the kitchen. 'We had fun without you.' I hit the button on the filter tap. I hoped he didn't see the way the water splished and splashed in response to my shaky grip on the glass.

'How'd she seem?' asked Nick. 'She doing better?'

My eyes prickled with tears, and I kept my face turned away. I hit the button again, filled the glass right to the brim.

'Lily? Are you alright?'

I stood there a second too long, holding tight to all of it. To everything that Rachel had said to me. Then I turned, a smile fixed in place.

'Oh, I think I'm a bit drunk!' I said, manufacturing a giggle. 'It was actually really lovely,' I said. 'She's doing much better at work.' Nick nodded approvingly. 'And she was drinking San Pellegrino all night.'

He exhaled, a broad grin on his face. 'What, like it was vodka?' I made a face that told him it was too soon for a joke like that. 'And it's okay with the two of you now?'

Humiliation twisted inside of me.

'I just said it was lovely,' I replied tartly. I softened my tone. 'It's cramped in there, cozy. It was embarrassing actually – the next table kept staring at us because we were laughing so much. She was telling me all about her big project at work, all the fools she has to tolerate to make it all work.'

He didn't hear the edge to my voice. Only I did.

'Thank Christ she's back on track,' said Nick. It was illogically irritating how easy it was to lie to him. It suited him, my version of events. He had the supreme luxury of believing me. 'Let's just hope it lasts. So, this Amber woman's worth all the cash we're throwing at her?'

I nearly broke then. I nearly threw myself at his grease-smeared chest, let the tears, which were so ready to flow, wash the stain away. But the thing was, Rachel was right, even though I couldn't have admitted it yet. Truth was the most expensive luxury of all in this family.

'Definitely,' I said, squeezing his hand, already on the move. 'I'll see you upstairs.'

I was the biggest liar of all of us, of course, but it would be a while until any of them found me out.

RACHEL

The breath honked out of my nostrils like I had some kind of disgusting flu.

'That's it,' said Amber. 'Puff it out. Faster! Expel that rage from your body.'

We were sitting cross-legged on the floor of her treatment room, cushions spread out all around us. I'd arrived half an hour ago with tears streaming down my blotchy face, trying to avoid the nosy looks from the market traders setting up their stalls for the day. I'd called her the night before in desperation, and Amber – caring, kind Amber – had carved out an emergency appointment for me at 7.30 a.m. It was two days since my dinner with Mum and the emotional rawness that I'd been feeling before it was now more like an open wound. I had to work. I had to live. I couldn't afford to bleed out.

I collapsed back against the bank of cushions, exhausted. Amber smiled down at me from above, her dark fringe swept across her high forehead, her lips smudged with a sticky red gloss. She looked so beautiful and fierce.

'Your body was holding on so tightly, wasn't it? You did so well, expelling that rage. Pushing it out of your cells.'

If only it were that easy, I thought. Of course, she knew that's what I was thinking.

'What's she talking about, right?' she said, eyes dancing. 'Trust me, I know how hard it is unravelling the bonds of a toxic relationship with someone you love.'

The words were like an electric shock.

'I don't think ...' My thoughts were scrambled, impossible to order. 'Do you really think that's what it is with Mum?' I said. 'Toxic?'

Amber looked down at the woven ethnic rug we were sitting on, her fingers playing with the fringing.

'I'm sorry, that was me going too fast again,' she said, her gaze coming up to meet mine. 'Sometimes, when I can feel your pain in my own cells so acutely – it makes me try too hard to help you heal. I've been tuning into you since you called. It's been agony, hasn't it?'

Everything she said made our bond sound so tantalizingly intimate. It was food for my unhealthy craving to know her better – to understand *her* pain, to be more than just another name on her fat roster of paying clients. I'd tried a deep-dive online, but nothing had come up – no Facebook account, no Twitter. I'd had high hopes for an Instagram account stuffed with inspirational quotes and photographs of her pretzeled into complex yoga poses against Ibizan sunsets, but there was nothing there either. If I was really devious, I could use the servers at work to penetrate way further than Google could, but so far I'd resisted the urge.

A backdraft of defensiveness swept up. 'I haven't always described her right,' I said. 'She can be the most amazing Mum, too.'

And she could. I thought about that little island in the midst of our dinner when it was the two of us against the world, her delighting in my progress. But the truth was that it was only ever an island; it was never a continent. I kept going, nevertheless.

'She's never boring, like some people's parents are. She's funny. She sees through people.'

'Does she?' said Amber, her half smile telling me she heard something in my words I hadn't intended to be there. The pesky subconscious up to its old tricks.

'Yes,' I said firmly. Why was I sitting here defending her, when this whole emergency appointment was about how much being with her had hurt me? 'And she does love us. When she's being difficult, I know it's also because she wants to keep us safe. She can't always control Dad . . .' I faltered a little there. 'So controlling us is second best.'

Amber's smile was wider now, kindness in her eyes.

'Do you think it's possible both things are true?' she asked.

'What do you mean?'

'It's hard to accept that two things that seem to conflict can both be true. She does love you, no question, and that's a precious thing. But what I'd ask you to reflect on is the fact that so many of your interactions with her – with both your parents – leave you feeling like this.' Her voice rose as she warmed to her theme. 'Fragmented, ashamed, no longer sure where your sacred ground is.'

I swallowed, a boulder sitting low in my stomach. My eyes skimmed the mantelpiece of the elegant fireplace that dominated the left side of the room. Amber had strung some fairy lights over it – tiny white hearts, bohemian and chic – and a row of Christmas cards were lined up across the marble top. This was the worst possible time of year to feel so alone.

'All I was trying to do was make it better.' Tears started their inexorable roll down my chapped cheeks. 'I wish she could understand that.'

There was a long pause.

'I don't know if you can make it better right now,' said Amber, almost under her breath. The silence stretched out again, a void. 'I saw you looking at the mantelpiece. What does Christmas mean to you, Rachel?'

Her words were still worming their way around my brain. *I don't know if you can make it better.*

'Christmas? Oh, it's great,' I said petulantly. 'Josh has got his 2.4 children lined up behind him in formation, Sophie's not even just got a boyfriend now, this year she's got a fiancé, and . . . I've got a five-grand overdraft and a profile on Tinder where I knocked three years off my age. And I won't even be able to drink my way through it.'

The thought of enduring Christmas sober, of the pantomime my family would stage every time a cork popped, was horrific. Amber laughed, but not in a mean way.

'So you just need to swap them over, right? Knock three grand off your overdraft and make your Tinder profile truthful?'

'Exactly,' I said, grateful for that incredible talent she had for breaking the tension.

'And what about your parents? Where do they fit into this charming nativity scene?'

'I catch them staring at me, when we're all chinking our glasses. Then they look away, like I won't see the pity. Like I won't see them silently asking themselves why I went so wrong. It's like I was a discount item in the sales and now they wish they could swap me for the full-price version.'

'Maybe you're not the one who needs pitying!' shot back Amber. 'From what you've told me, you're the only authentic person in the picture you're painting.'

Unease began to creep up my spine. I shouldn't have told her. It was meant to stay inside the picture, not seep out of the frame and into the world where it could stain us all.

'Not Sophie,' I said. 'She doesn't even know.' Sophie was everyone's favourite Christmas present. Pristine, unbroken. That was why we fought over her so fiercely.

'But *you* do.' My head was bowed, but I could feel Amber's eyes trained on me. 'I know it's hard to talk about, but a part of you brought it here. When one part of us fights another, it can paralyze us.' Tears prickled behind my eyes. 'Let's try to make a step forward together, take a look.'

'I don't know . . .'

'Rachel, if these secrets are left to fester, they just find ways to repeat. Families play out their traumas again and again, the same pain rippling through the generations. Personally, I think they move through the ages, but not everyone believes in past lives.'

'Past lives?' I said, thrown.

Amber's eyes were blazing, her focus on me absolute. 'Don't think about that right now,' she said. 'Let's just try to set you free in this incarnation.'

'Okay,' I said, two whispered syllables.

'What would that part of you say to me if it could speak? What would it say about Esther?'

It felt dangerous, her name in somebody else's mouth.

'I hate her,' I said, my heart drumming in my chest. 'I know I'm meant to be a feminist and I should just blame Dad, but I feel like she came into our house and destroyed everything. And somehow she still won't fuck off.'

Was it disgust that crossed Amber's face? To me – in my flayed and vulnerable state – it felt like a slap.

'I *can* hear myself,' I added hurriedly. 'I know how young she was. I know it's unfair of me, and he's the shit-bag cheater. But . . .'

'You're allowed to feel your feelings, Rachel,' said Amber, her expression restored to soft compassion, but by now I'd lost my footing.

'I shouldn't be telling you this. I don't even know for sure. Mum's always denied it and I'd never ask him . . . Perhaps it is just me, looking for excuses for why I'm such a fucking disgusting mess.'

I was staring at the ground, my body hot and shaky, but as the silence stretched into elastic infinity, I was forced to look up.

'Slow down, Rachel, okay? Don't abandon your own knowing to preserve the status quo.' Her eyes blazed. 'The status quo has been killing you.'

'They weren't actually . . .' I'd lost all articulacy, the memories too harsh for me to be able to neatly package them up into clear sentences.

'They were in your parents' bedroom together.' She was doing that thing again, striking off the facts with her fingers. 'You said your father was actually in bed.'

My voice wobbled. 'That's how I remember it, yeah.'

It was more than my voice; my whole world was wobbling with my profound feeling that it was me who was the real betrayer here.

Amber's eyes didn't leave my face. 'And your mother still wouldn't believe you,' she said, making the words come slow and weighty. They were like a wrecking ball.

'I can't do this, okay?' I was almost shouting. 'I'm not ready. I don't know for sure.' My face was buried in my hands, tears trickling through them onto the worn velvet. 'They do love me. She loves me so much, that's why she's so controlling!'

Amber's face was pure kindness when she replied. 'I know that, Rachel, and of course we should honour it. What's so sad is that it doesn't make it any easier for you.'

That was it: I gave way to the sobbing, my body shaking and heaving with dirty, complicated grief.

'Do you need some physical contact?' whispered Amber, and I gave a muffled grunt of permission. Soon her arms were ringed around my shoulders: gradually I let myself sink into her, my tears soaking the stylish black silk shirt she wore, decorated with tiny white question marks. She was so chic, so pretty. Sometimes it was almost like a crush, the way I felt about her. I wondered idly how old she was, relieved to momentarily devote my thinking to something trivial. I had no idea. My sobs started to subside.

'You're such a brave young woman, Rachel,' she said, the words whispered into my hair. 'You're doing so, so well.'

'Am I?' I said, looking up at her. 'Look at the state of me. I'm going to roll into the staff meeting looking like a panda that's been sent from China to mate in London Zoo.'

A joke was always my get-out-of-jail-free card in those days. Amber accepted it, laughing down at me before we pulled apart.

'There's your bravery, right there,' she said, narrowing her eyes like she was gazing at a far-off star. 'You've just gone headlong into the biggest, most painful trauma of your life, and you're already looking for the light.'

I grinned, delighted with her assessment.

'I'm trying,' I said. 'I really am.' I paused. 'I want this to change me.'

Amber cocked her head. 'You're perfect now, Rachel.'

'Jesus, hardly . . .'

'You're perfectly imperfect, like all of us. Some of your behaviours are problematic, but you're working on the reasons why, and shaming yourself won't get you where you want to go.' She smiled. 'It's time to stop listening to other people's voices in your own head.'

It was almost spooky, the way she seemed to know me better than I knew myself after a few short weeks. She'd nailed it: all day, every day, I converted Mum's judge-y commentary on my life into a hateful inner monologue.

'You're right,' I breathed.

'Life doesn't have to be about what anyone else wants you to be,' she grinned. 'And how liberating is that?'

'Sounds like the fucking dream!' I said.

Amber's moods – reflective, exuberant – every single one of them was as infectious as chickenpox. In that moment, I felt as if I was going to slay Thursday. That none of it mattered. I neglected to think about the fact that the parents I was happily throwing on the emotional scrapheap were footing the bill for my triumphant self-actualization. I looked down at my watch. 'Shit, I've got to go.'

Amber looked over at me. 'I shouldn't offer – I'm sure it's breaking every boundary there is – but do you want to borrow my make-up bag before you leave? I hear they shoot pandas in the wild.'

'Could I?'

'For one of my very favourite clients? Of course you can.'

I tingled when she said that; I lit up like that string of Christmas lights she'd slung so casually over the fireplace. She knew it too: nothing Amber did was casual, however much she faked it.

She reached into a stylishly battered brown leather bag that was slotted behind the sofa. The make-up bag itself was black vinyl, decorated with extravagant red hearts. For me, so hungry to vault the boundaries that stood between us, it felt like a precious piece of evidence. When I came back from the loo – having raked through every product in there, trying to assess what they told me about who she was in real life – she was staring out of the window onto the market. I handed the bag back to her as she turned to me.

'Thank you,' I said, the word too full. The day that stretched out ahead was starting to feel real. I froze. 'I'm sorry if I couldn't . . . if I wasn't . . .'

My words faded again.

'Don't apologize,' she said, fierce. 'I'm not here to judge you. Don't add any more inner critics to the list. I'm Team Rachel – I hope you know that by now.'

'I do,' I said, my voice twisting with emotion.

'The fact is,' she added, 'and I hope it's not weird me saying it – I think we'd be friends if we met in real life. I can't say that about many of my clients.'

'Me too,' I said. I was surprised how it felt hearing that: it was thrilling and intimidating all at once, like a sixth former smuggling you into the pub and plying you with vodka. 'I'm so lucky to have you,' I said, my eyes drawn back to the row of cards. 'If it wasn't for you, the prospect of family Christmas would be basically killing me.'

How long would she be away for? The very thought of it was making me panic: these weekly sessions of ours were my lifeline. Amber contemplated me for a second.

'You know, Christmas is a prime example of a time where you don't have to sacrifice yourself for what other people want you to be.'

'What do you mean?' I asked uncertainly.

'That long break can be incredibly healing, rather than some-thing that we have to dread. I rarely spend it with my family. This year I'm leading a retreat, scooping up a few Christmas orphans for something genuinely healing and peaceful.'

I couldn't tell if it was an invitation or not.

'But I have to be there for Christmas . . .' I said. 'I mean, it's Christmas,' I added stupidly.

Amber smiled gently at my naivety.

'You don't *have* to do anything,' she said. 'You don't have to be anyone, either. You can just be Rachel.'

It was a typical Amber statement: profound and meaningless all at once. To me, right then, it was a precious jewel, and I would take it away and treasure it. Polish it until it became so valuable to me that it was dangerous, a talisman to guide me.

LILY

Rachel was obviously being impossible, but I kidded myself that Christmas would fix it. She'd be under my roof for days on end, not flitting in and out like the other two. She'd be able to see how much I loved her, even if we exasperated each other along the way. That was our dynamic, our seamless two-step. I felt sure she hadn't forgotten the moves. How could she, when we'd practised tirelessly for so many years?

It wasn't like I hadn't been thinking about Esther since the christening, wondering whether she was going to need dealing with. But it still didn't lessen the shock I felt that night. With Rachel out of the picture, I had leftover love to give, and on this particular evening it took me to his office after hours, like some kind of demented 1950s housewife. Obviously I hadn't cooked the chicken fricassee myself – I'd picked it up from an overpriced French deli next to the final viewing of the day, a family home in Ealing which a visiting American couple were going to be paying top dollar to rent after I'd told them they'd likely be camping in Hyde Park come January if they didn't make a snap decision. People ultimately benefit from clarity, even if they don't appreciate it in the short term.

The deli had a blue-and-white checked awning, stacks of Christmas treats piled up high in the window. I queued impatiently behind well-heeled locals grabbing a bottle of Beaujolais to get them through the night, then picked out a few glistening chicken thighs on top of a bed of potatoes. I even threw in a bottle of wine of my own, just in case Nick had time for an office picnic between his endless calls.

The security guard waved me upstairs without bothering to call to announce me. I swept through the corridors unimpeded, the reception desk deserted. When I got to his office, Nick was bent over his computer, eyes narrowed in concentration, his aquiline profile illuminated like a pencil sketch by the light it was giving out. I watched him for a couple of seconds before I made my presence known.

'Surprise!' I trilled, pulling the plastic boxes out of the carrier bag, adorned with pretentious twirly writing. 'Extra surprise!' I said, reaching back in for the bottle of wine. 'Oh God, do you even have a corkscrew?'

He gave a quick, tight smile.

'Not in my top drawer,' he said. 'We've reached our quota of drunks in this family.' I didn't smile. 'There's probably one in the kitchen,' he added.

He didn't immediately move to go and get it. 'This is amazing, Lil!' he said, but his tone wasn't selling it to me. I was still standing, the two boxes marooned forlornly on his wide desk, the twinkly lights of the city a backdrop to the whole strange tableau. I pulled up a chair so we were sat opposite each other.

'I know you're busy. Wine was a bit of a wild card. There's some plastic cutlery in the bag.' I reached down to find it. 'I just wanted you to know I appreciate you – *we* appreciate you – and we know how hard you're working to get everything done before Christmas.'

Nick's mouth was ajar, like a sentence was waiting to be born, his eyes elsewhere. I turned around, and there she was, standing awkwardly in the doorway. She was wearing a grey skirt suit, the fabric crumpling unattractively around her hips, the size she'd picked off the rack clearly far too optimistic.

'Hi, Lily!' she said, a toothy grin splattered across her round face. 'What a treat!'

'Esther!' I said, forcing my voice to sail upwards like hers had. 'Come and join us. If you get a fork from the kitchen, I'm sure this chicken will stretch three ways.'

The silence stretched out for a couple of seconds before she shook her head. I like to think she blushed, but it's probably wishful thinking.

'I'm just leaving, actually. I've only got a couple of weeks here, but hopefully you'll be in again before we finish up for Christmas.'

We.

'Or come and see us over the break!' I said. 'The kids would be thrilled. We can definitely promise you a mince pie or two.'

'I'll be back with my folks,' she said, wriggling in the frame of the door like a specimen on a slide. They were in Barnsley or somewhere. I could still hear that Northern lilt in her voice. 'Definitely in the New Year, though!'

'Esther was a bit short of Christmas cash,' said Nick, jumping in. 'So I said at the christening we could do with an extra pair of hands here. Better than a temp agency.'

'Good thinking!' I said. Every utterance I forced out of my mouth came with an exclamation mark.

'It was a fab day,' said Esther. 'The baby's a proper little poppet, isn't she?'

A flash of Rachel, her cheek pressed against the cold floor of the toilet like it was home.

'I know,' I said. 'We're very lucky.'

*

'So, are you going to get that corkscrew?' I asked Nick once she'd finally disappeared.

'Coming right up,' he said, popping up from his chair like a sweaty jack-in-the-box.

Once he'd come back and opened the bottle, I slugged back a plastic cup. It was expensive Chablis, but it didn't taste that way: it was warm and sweet, a soupy mess. I still went in for a second 'glass', poking at the chicken with my plastic fork. It was hard to force a mouthful of it down my tight throat.

'Esther looks well,' I said casually, even though I thought she looked like an extra from the Australian soap operas the kids used to crowd around after school. But then, I'm sure part of her charm was her lack of sophistication.

'Yeah, I'm glad to be able to help her out,' said Nick, taking a more modest sip from his own cup. 'She's been teaching English as a foreign language in Spain. She's come back here, and the only place she could afford sounds more like a doss house than a flat share. It's in Turnpike fucking Lane.'

'It's been a while since we saw her,' I said, my tone as light as I could make it.

'Yeah, it has,' he agreed, his tone kept equally weightless. 'It was nice that Josh invited her after all that time.' He glanced down at his watch. 'This was great, Lily.'

I threw the remains back in the carrier bag, all gristle and bones. 'Duty calls, I know,' I said, tying up the top of it. 'You keep fighting the good fight, and I'll see you back at base camp.'

He smiled up at me from behind the desk. 'Thanks for this . . .' – he stumbled for a second – 'unexpected pleasure.'

'I like to keep surprising you,' I shot back.

We both stopped dead.

'Let's get all the kids round this weekend,' said Nick, recovering. 'Do a Sunday roast. Family time.'

'That's a great idea,' I agreed. I moved towards the door, carrier bag clutched in my left hand, the wine sloshing around in my right.

'Love you, Lily,' he called after my retreating back.

I didn't turn around.

RACHEL

Sophie clutched the red silk scarf to herself anxiously, pulling it up towards her face.

'Are you planning on eating it?' I asked her. 'I know you're dieting for the wedding, but . . .'

'I'm worried it's a bit scratchy,' she said, rubbing it against her skin. She held it out towards me. 'The colour's perfect for her, but it feels a bit nylon-y, I don't know.'

A young male assistant was poised nearby, waiting for the right moment to come and up-sell us. I turned my shoulder away from him, building an energetic wall that told him we didn't need him swooping in.

This wasn't about whether the scarf was the smoothest satin or the nastiest polyester. I felt pleased with my observation: this was the kind of nuance I'd only begun to appreciate since I'd started working with Amber.

'We've been doing this every year since you were pretty much a foetus, Sophie.'

I handed it back to her ceremonially, high on my own righteousness.

'Doing what?' she said, worrying the scarf through her fingers.

We were in one of those mid-level boutiques on Marylebone High Street, almost designer, but not quite. More expensive than it should have been, trying to prove its credentials with the reed diffusers that sweetened the air and the 1920s French prints that lined the walls in weather-beaten wooden frames.

'Agonize over what to get Mum. Every Mother's Day card. Every birthday. Every Christmas. And it *is* only Christmas. She's not the actual second coming.'

Sophie didn't crack a smile, her face wrinkling with upset instead, and I felt a stab of shame. I shoved it away. I was being honest. I was nurturing our relationship, even if she didn't yet understand it.

'She's our mum, Rachel. Don't you like it when we find her something she loves?'

'Don't tell me you're enjoying this,' I said. 'It's stress on a stick, because she makes it so impossible to find her something perfect enough. And the truth is, perfect doesn't exist.'

Good enough is enough. It was the second half of the sentence, but I managed to hold it in. Amber had given me so many mantras to follow by then that it was almost as if she was my invisible shadow. I snuck my hand into the pocket of my jeans and massaged the tiny chip of rose quartz she'd given me. I believed it gave me courage in those kinds of situations. It reminded me that my essence was pure love.

'Fine,' said Sophie, rolling the scarf up into an angry ball. 'This is fine. I'm going to buy it. It's up to you if you want to go halves. I don't know what kind of state your finances are in, anyway.'

We glared at each other before she stalked off towards the till. My heart pounded in my chest, the rose quartz leaving a painful indentation on my fingertips. I looked at her rigid posture as she earnestly tapped her pin number into the keypad. My little sister. Why was it so hard to be me and simultaneously be a part of *them*?

*

We sat in the bakery opposite, nursing big pottery bowls of coffee in stony silence. Sophie broke first.

'I'm sorry, okay? I shouldn't have said that about your finances. It was rude. I was just frustrated—'

I cut in. 'And I'm sorry too,' I said, 'if I upset you.'

Her eyes glinted for a second, the distinction between our apologies not lost on her, but she was too much of a peacemaker to kick off round two.

'Are you okay, Rach?' she said. 'I feel like you've been a bit AWOL since . . .'

The christening. Neither of us wanted to go there. It was six weeks ago now, but it still hung between us like a stained sheet on a washing line.

'We've had breakfast,' I said quickly. 'Twice.'

'Course we did!' she agreed brightly. 'And you had dinner with Mum?'

Mum hadn't told her, then. I made a split-second calculation: we'd be there in an hour. There was no need to guarantee it would be a disaster by forcing Sophie to pick a side. 'Yeah. We went to this Italian up there on the left. I think you and Toby would love it. It's romantic. Well, I imagine it's romantic,' I added, a drop of acid.

Sophie flushed – it's one of the most charming things about my little sister, the way every emotion plasters itself across her face like it's a billboard. She was feeling bad for me – bad for us – that she'd bucked birth order and found commitment first, while I was still acting like the slutty girl with a bad rep at the sixth form prom.

'Talking of which,' she said, 'Toby and I really wanted to ask if you'd like to be my maid of honour.' She smoothed her fringe out of her eyes and smiled nervously. My heart leapt upwards with uncomplicated happiness.

'Of course,' I said, reaching across the table and taking her hand, squeezing it in apology. *Sometimes I hate myself, and it makes me mean* was what I was trying to say, but all she felt was the blood being squashed in her veins. I would wonder back then if everyone had an internal life as dark as my own – was it better if they did, or better if they didn't? The first meant I wasn't alone, the second meant there was no hope for humanity. 'I'd be honoured. Literally.'

'Good!' she said, her face lighting up. Her expression dimmed a little as, I imagine, she ran a silent film of the worst potential version of events through her head. I tapped my bowl of coffee.

'This is the hard stuff for me now, I promise. You don't need to fret about it.'

'I know,' she said, her smile a wobbly line. 'Of course. I'm really glad you're up for it.'

*

Sophie swung the car off the Westway and onto the backstreets of Shepherd's Bush, her neat VW Polo never nudging its German nose above the 30mph limit. Being good wasn't even a decision for her, just a fact. A few turns later she pulled up outside our parents' house.

'Did you bring anything?' she asked.

Of course I hadn't.

'Don't worry, I've got a bottle of rosé in the boot. It can be from both of us. I wonder if they invited Esther?'

'Esther?' I said. My voice sounded like broken glass.

'Yes, she's working with Dad at the moment. Sounds like she's been struggling, not found a real career yet. He's helping her out.'

'Helping her out?' The shock was too great. All I could do was parrot her.

'Yeah . . .' Sophie looked at me owlishly. 'Why are you being so uptight about it?'

That was what she told herself, that it was a weird kind of jealousy I had. I'd never been able to bring myself to tell her the whole story – it felt like I'd be mugging her of her childhood. And it certainly wasn't the official version.

'Sophie . . .' I tailed off. 'Actually, forget it.'

I froze, my body resisting going inside, my seatbelt staying strapped across my body.

'Come on, lazy bones,' said Sophie cheerfully.

She'd clambered out of the car by now and was looking at me expectantly. There was no escape. I followed her up the path, each step a miniature internal war.

Dad opened the door, his face flushed from cooking, a grey marl T-shirt clinging to his worked-out chest. He was holding a meat skewer, thrilled with himself. He dropped it on the hall table.

'My girls, present and correct!' he said, throwing his arms open and crushing us into a group hug. I felt myself stiffen as Sophie moulded herself against his bulk.

'Daddy!' she said.

I stepped backwards out of his embrace.

'Hi, Dad,' I said. 'Are we the first to arrive?'

'You are,' he said. 'Which is a first in itself for you, right, Rachel?'

I refused to smile back at him.

'So, who's coming?' I said, my heart pounding. My moments of stability were so fleeting back then, archipelagos in a stormy ocean.

'Josh and his girls.'

'Chloe's a grown woman, actually, Dad. So are we.' He and Sophie both stared at me, their bodies still squashed close. 'So that's it, then?'

'Rach ...' said Sophie, reaching out a hand and nervously skimming my bare wrist. 'Esther's not coming? Mum said she ...'

'No,' said Dad, blue eyes narrowing with annoyance. He strode away down the corridor. 'It's just your perfect, happy family, Rachel, no need to panic.'

Sophie shot me a look, hurrying after him.

'I'm not trying to be difficult ...' I hissed, but she didn't turn back.

Mum was circling the kitchen table, laying out the cutlery like it was a geometry exercise. She deliberately kept her back to us, and I could feel the anxiety start to steam and bubble inside me. Even massaging the chip of rose quartz didn't produce any reduction in my heart rate. Eventually she straightened up and crossed the room, reaching me first and giving me a staccato kiss on each cheek like a bird pecking for worms. Sophie got a hug – a real one that meant something to both of them. I felt the hurt ripple through me, the fight draining away in its wake. It wasn't worth getting in the ring with her. She always won.

'We've been tramping up and down Marylebone High Street, haven't we?' I said, forcing brightness into my tone. 'You're going to love Sophie's present.'

Dad was at the hob by now, poking at the pans and refusing to speak.

'I always adore Sophie's presents,' said Mum, back at the table now. 'And your presence too, darling!' she added, laughing at her own pun. 'That's a given.'

'You'll love Rachel's, too,' said Sophie, eyes darting between us. 'She just couldn't find anything chic enough today, but you know she's going to end up winning hands down.'

'I'm sure,' said Mum tartly. 'Sophie, darling, can you get the water glasses out of the cupboard?'

I couldn't help it; I raced over to the dresser before Sophie could react. My hand shook as I held the wobbly stack of tumblers – I looked down at the Spanish tiled floor, willing myself not to drop them. 'Here you go,' I said, crossing towards Mum and touching her arm, forcing her to turn her head towards me, her perfect weekday blow-dry still falling elegantly around her shoulders. 'Is there anything else I can do?'

'You could pour us all a lovely glass of sparkling water,' she said. 'I ordered a whole box of San Pellegrino from Ocado. I dumped it in the basement I think.'

Deep underground, where everything in our family was meant to go. I wonder if she's yet forgiven me for breaking our silent pact?

*

Josh's two boys were rampaging around the garden, swiping at rose bushes with sticks and rugby-tackling each other. It looked violent to my fragile gaze, but no one else seemed remotely worried. Chloe seemed more concerned about me, if anything. She kept throwing me looks and bundling Nancy to her chest, or maybe that was just my paranoia. They'd just arrived, and Dad and Josh were having a scandalized conversation at the other end of the kitchen about some lawyer who'd been struck off for squirrelling client funds.

'She's getting so big!' said Sophie, reaching tentative fingers out to stroke Nancy's head. I desperately wanted to ask to hold her – this little being whose life I'd been given a role in – but the words choked in my throat.

'Tell me about it,' said Chloe, grinning at her. 'My arms are killing me – do you want to take her?'

No wonder, I thought meanly, when your arms are as thin and brittle as stale Twiglets.

'Of course I do!' said Sophie, reaching for the baby. Nancy immediately started to grizzle and twist.

'Step away from the baby, Sophie. Give her back to Chloe,' said Josh, striding across the kitchen. 'We all know you're trying to practice on her! Where's my soon-to-be brother-in-law, anyway?'

He walked straight past me, reaching for Nancy as if I wasn't there. He'd said a clipped hello when he arrived, but he was making his feelings about my behaviour at the christening abundantly clear.

'He's working today,' said Sophie. 'Gave me a chance to hang out with Rachel.' She was almost vibrating with her need for us to connect. 'Coffee, shopping – sister stuff that your inferior male mind couldn't compute.'

Josh finally deigned to look at me.

'Hopefully not the Irish kind of coffee,' he said, smirking. My brother had always been relentlessly cruel. I secretly gripped my crystal.

'I haven't drunk for over a month,' I said. The silence curdled around me. 'And I want to say – in person, to all of you – how sorry I am about the christening.'

'Thanks, Rachel,' said Chloe awkwardly. 'And thanks for your email, too. We appreciated it.'

'Guy's fiancée's mum's got cancer!' said Josh, flushed with self-righteousness, as if I'd personally blown smoke rings into her mum's face until her lungs had given up the ghost. 'Trust me, it didn't exactly help.'

'Did he tell her?' I said, heat rising up through my body. How were we having this conversation in everyone's earshot? How was it that some things in our family could never be spoken of and other things demanded a virtual megaphone? And why was it that I never got to decide which was which?

'Honesty's really important to him,' said Josh. 'I mean, they *are* getting married.'

Honesty definitely seemed like one of Guy's key values, judging by the way he'd dragged me into the toilets without mentioning his betrothed. I risked glancing around the circle of stricken faces. No one else seemed to register this as fake news.

'Okay,' I said. 'Well, I'm very sorry, like I said.'

I started to falter. It was repulsive, what I'd done. No wonder they were looking at me with such obvious disgust.

'Let's just forget about it,' said Josh, swinging Nancy above his head. 'Your daddy's the one who needs a drink,' he said. She giggled at him, gleefully reaching her pudgy hands for his hair. 'Yes, he does!'

And I needed to step out of the toxic circle. Without even thinking about the irony, I crossed to the fridge, poured a glass of Chablis from the open bottle in the door and served my brother and his wife like I was their butler.

Mum's cool gaze tracked me throughout. She didn't utter a word.

*

I chewed my lamb again and again, trying to force myself to swallow. By now the practicalities of Christmas were under the microscope.

'Just don't get them too much, Lily, honestly,' Chloe was saying. 'You're always so generous ...'

'We're just thrilled you're with us this year,' Mum was saying. It was always a passive-aggressive fight to the death with Chloe's parents for who got the precious gift of the grandchildren. 'Come on Christmas Eve if you like. I'm hoping the girls will.'

Christmas was less than a month away now and my dread was starting to feel more like a tsunami than a lapping tide.

'Yeah, Toby's parents are going away this year, so I don't see why not,' said Sophie cheerfully. 'Are you up for it, Rachel?'

How could she be so oblivious to how hard it was for me?

'Um, I don't know yet. I'm just working out my schedule at the moment.'

My family looked at me with pity in their eyes, a collective thought bubble floating above the table wondering what a single woman of my age could possibly have to 'schedule'. Amber's words roared up inside me. They didn't own me, and they didn't own Christmas.

'I might actually be away for it,' I added airily.

'But, darling, it's Christmas!' said Mum. 'And you're meant to be saving money, don't forget.'

'You still paying interest on your credit cards?' said Dad, stabbing at his meat. 'It's a crime if you are.'

The fact that they were still paying the bill for Amber and the subsequent prying rights it seemed to give them over my finances was truly infuriating. And it was true that my credit cards had hit dizzying new heights, as I treated myself to massages and green juices to try to soothe myself in new, virtuous ways between our precious sessions. I felt so raw these days – my skin flayed, my energy wide open. Being honest about how bad it had been was making me feel worse than ever, but I trusted Amber when she promised me it was a profound emotional detox that I'd emerge from with new strength.

'I'll keep you posted once my plans firm up,' I said, inwardly revelling in their irritation.

'It's three weeks away, Rachel,' snapped Josh. 'Mum and Dad need to be able to make arrangements.'

'I'm sure they can figure out how fat the turkey should be without having an hour-by-hour agenda for me,' I snapped back.

'You need to learn how to make a commitment and stick to it,' said Josh. He gave me a patronizing smile. 'I've seen it when people are trying to get sober. You'll thrive on calm and order.'

'He's right,' said Chloe, who was always looking for ways to prove she was his loyal lieutenant. My brother's a bully; she'd worked out long ago that it made her life a whole lot easier if he knew she was in his camp. 'And I'll be really disappointed if you're not here,' she added disingenuously, spooning a mouthful of food towards the baby, who was wedged into a high chair next to her. 'So will Nancy. You'd miss your godmother, wouldn't you?' she cooed.

Humiliation felled me. I looked across to Sophie, who smiled nervously, then looked down at her plate without saying a word.

'Of course she'll be here,' said Dad dismissively. 'Anyone need more meat?'

He stood, ready to get the tented rack of lamb from the counter.

'Why don't you just invite Esther instead?' I asked him. 'I'm sure she'd love to spend some extra-curricular time with you. Shame to limit it to the office.'

'Rachel!' said Mum, her face splashed red.

'Jesus, don't start this again . . .' said Dad.

'I just find it weird, the way she's suddenly reappeared,' I said. I wasn't going to be silenced. 'Where exactly did she crawl out from, anyway? Does anyone actually know?'

'Don't talk about her like that!' said Sophie, her voice catching.

'Sorry, Sophie,' I said. 'But you don't know the whole story.'

'Shut the . . .' Josh stared at me with something that looked like hatred. 'My children are playing twenty feet away,' he hissed. 'Whatever fantasy you made up when you were even more of a manipulative little bitch of a teenager, you don't need to keep banging on about it. Hurting Mum and Dad. Hurting all of us.'

'It hurts me, having it shoved in our faces,' I said, aiming my words at Dad. He'd crossed the kitchen, busied himself with the meat. 'It makes me feel like I'm going mad, even though I'm the only one telling the truth.'

Something stopped me forming the words. Something stopped me saying 'Dad's mistress' out loud. It was still too dangerous.

Mum was studying me, her face a blank mask. I faltered: would she really be this calm if my darkest suspicions were right?

'I think you should go home now, Rachel,' she said evenly. 'You're under a lot of personal stress right now, we all appreciate that. You need plenty of rest. Time to recuperate.'

'Your mother's right,' said Dad, crossing back to the table, holding a platter of meat aloft like he was Gordon Ramsey himself. 'I'll call you a cab.' He sat down, glared at me. 'Maybe one day you'll stop ruining every family occasion you bother to turn up for.'

His casual scorn pushed me over the edge.

'Let's start with Christmas,' I said, standing up, my chair screeching against the Spanish tiles. 'You can all have the perfect fucking family celebration you're dreaming of without me.'

'No, Rachel,' said Mum. 'Christmas is precious. You just need to take some time to calm down . . .'

'What I want to know,' I said, heading for the door, 'is how many other Esthers there are out there? It's not a good look these days, Dad.'

I risked a final look back at the tableau of the table. Mum didn't look quite so calm anymore: I didn't know whether to be triumphant or heartbroken by the fact.

*

I rang MBNA first. Perhaps it was too close to Christmas, and they had a policy about naked desperation. Either way, they wouldn't give me a cash advance. I googled frantically, finally calling a supermarket credit card line and lying in response to every question the kind-sounding man in his call centre on the other side of the world asked me. I had a flatmate, apparently, who paid their half of the rent in cash, and my glittering career involved generous bonuses that hadn't yet appeared in my bank account. As he went away to process my credit score, every fibre of my being churned with tension. Escaping family Christmas was feeling like life or death. He sounded genuinely happy for me when he gave me the good news: perhaps he could sense that I was lightheaded with relief.

I texted Amber immediately, fat tears falling onto the screen of my phone, blurring my words.

I wish I could call you. Today was worse than my worst nightmare. I hate my family. Coming to the retreat, if you'll have me. R xx

Nothing came back. There was one bottle of wine in the back of the cupboard, my 'break glass in case of emergency' option, and I sat it on the coffee table with a corkscrew, simultaneously comforted and devastated by the knowledge that there was no one to stop me opening it.

The shrill ring of the phone broke the silence. I looked tentatively at the screen: Amber.

'Hello,' I said, my voice unsteady. 'I didn't think we were allowed to speak outside . . .'

'Rachel,' she said. The warmth of her voice turned on the tap of my tears. 'Rules are made to be broken, don't you think?'

They certainly were.

'Thank you,' I said. 'It was so awful today, they—'

'Let's not get into the details now, Rachel. Let's explore it properly when we're together. Just know that I understand, and that I'm holding you in my thoughts. I'm sending you healing right now.'

'Thank you,' I breathed.

'And of course you can come at Christmas, I'd be honoured to have you. I've even managed to swing you a little discount. It's not much, but hopefully it goes some way to telling you how much you're wanted.'

Wanted. The word was like a hot bath I could sink in to.

'I'm so grateful!' I said. 'Thank you.'

'Transfer me £1,500 if you can, by the end of the week. And just get the last £750 to us by Christmas Eve.'

Questions started to whirr. Who was the 'us' she was referring to, and how was it so much? I shoved the thoughts away. I was lucky she'd got me the discount – just imagine if she hadn't. She was so kind, so caring.

Questions were too dangerous. They would stay that way for a while yet.

LILY

It disgusted me that I'd been reduced to this. Amber simply refused to see me, willfully disregarding the fact that it was our money that allowed her to work in this expensive enclave of west London. I say that; she somehow seemed to have chosen the most down-market pocket of W11 possible. I elbowed my way through the great unwashed that thronged the market, squashed in close enough to smell them. The stalls sold a mishmash of unrecognizable fruits and vegetables from far-flung places and the kind of overpriced old tat that had been optimistically rebranded as 'antique'.

Eventually I found the tall townhouse that she practised out of. I ground to a halt on the doorstep, momentarily losing my nerve. What if she recognized my voice, refused to let me up? I'd made the appointment via a phone I'd bought from Carphone Warehouse, the kind of basic lump of plastic teenage drug dealers probably used to arrange drop-offs of molly.

My rage propelled my finger to the bell. Rachel was point-blank refusing to speak to us now, adamant that she wasn't coming for Christmas. She was refusing to tell us what glorious festive plans she'd made instead: *It's something I need to guard for myself* was all she'd said in her text.

Of course, my instinct was to turn off the tap, put an end to the relationship that had kickstarted this whole new phase of difficulty, but I couldn't quite risk it. When I came close to doing it, I would see her face down on the floor of that loo, or, worse, hooked up to that drip, and a flickering future memory would fell me: a coffin lowered into the ground, a mortuary drawer, my daughter's name scrawled on the label. How could she put me through this when I loved her so deeply? If she ever became a mother, I felt sure she'd beg my forgiveness, but for now, she was a selfish child who needed her own parent to stay as solid as a rock.

When Amber answered the buzzer, I tried to disguise my voice a little.

'It's Becky Friedman,' I said, realizing as I said it that my alter ego appeared to be Jewish. She'd also paid for the session in advance.

'Come on up,' she trilled, and I pushed open the door. Even if this was as far as I got, I thought smugly, at least I'd won round one.

How stupid I was. We were at least three rounds in, and I was already on the ropes.

I climbed upwards determinedly, just as she must have started down. We almost collided on the landing. I waited for the shock to land on her, but she either hid it masterfully well or experienced something else entirely.

'Lily,' she said. 'You know you can't be here. I've been crystal clear with you.'

I hated the fact that I couldn't hit back. I took a deep breath, thought about those stubborn clients who don't initially want me to be the one to rent their house, even though

I know the market better than they know the alphabet. They always cave.

'I understand,' I said, forcing a warm smile. 'I really do. But we both care deeply about Rachel.' *I'm her mother!* I wanted to scream. *You're just the latest hired help, and trust me, I've fired plenty of your brethren over the years.* 'If you'd just let me have ten minutes, I think we could help each other – help her – without in any way breaking her confidence.'

Amber paused. I looked at her properly now, trying not to let her see my eyes raking over her. Was it professional to wear those snug black jeans to work, a long-sleeved Breton T-shirt slung casually over the top to complete the look? I looked at her plump skin, the suspicious absence of lines that rendered her undeniably attractive face an ageless mask. I know how subtle filler can be: I wasn't fooled for an instant. She could well have been only five or six years younger than me once you'd leeched the chemicals out of those firm cheeks.

'You're way out of line here. You know that, though, don't you, Lily?'

I gave her a level stare. I wasn't going to be ticked off like some schoolgirl caught with a crumpled packet of fags in my locker. After a couple of seconds, she gave a sharp little nod of her chin.

'I've got professional boundaries. They protect my clients, including your daughter. Ten minutes, that's it.'

I tried to keep the triumph out of my face. Come to think of it, maybe she did too. From where we stand now, even the smallest, most insignificant truth is impossible to track back and verify.

Her room was as artificially casual as her outfit. The cushions on the velvet sofa were ever so slightly balding, like the weight of all the grateful patients' bottoms had left them battle-scarred.

The round brass base of the table lamp had visible scratches and dents. She would have picked them up at the surrounding antique shops I was sure, the shabby chic aesthetic designed to put desperate millennials at their ease. I found it faintly repellent – when you've known real shabbiness, the artificial version just seems grubby. My mother would have got to work on her room with a mop and a bucket of disinfectant.

An uneasy silence festered. It was me who broke it: if she really insisted on imposing her ten-minute countdown, I couldn't go away with nothing.

'I'm desperately worried about my daughter. So is my husband.'

Amber sat there meditatively, taking her time to reply.

'That's why you came to me in the first place, wasn't it, Lily? Because you were so worried about her?'

'Well, yes, but I don't think she's getting any better.'

She cocked her head, ruminative.

'Look, Lily, I've made it clear I can't discuss the specifics, but, the binge drinking for example . . .'

It was infuriating, the way she kept using my name.

'Obviously we're thrilled she's sticking to the sparkling water, and trust me, we're all really supporting her efforts.' A look of doubt, or amusement, crossed her face, clearing so quickly it was impossible to call out. 'But she seems so angry. So hateful . . . when all we've ever tried to do is love her.'

Amber's steady gaze bathed me in silent judgement.

'I hope you don't mind me saying this.'

I braced myself.

'But it seems like you're here to soothe your own pain, not Rachel's.' She smiled without warmth. 'Sorry, I know that might sound like I'm overstepping the mark, but I wonder if you need someone to talk to yourself? This is about your whole family system, not just Rachel.'

'My other children are thriving.'

She took another infuriating pause, as if she was mentally leafing through the files on our collective dysfunction.

'Just a suggestion, Lily. And as I say, I can't talk specifics, but what I *can* say is that I think your daughter's a wonderful young woman who is wrestling her demons with a lot of courage.'

'I didn't say she wasn't wonderful,' I snapped. 'I love my daughter very much.'

'I'm sure you do,' she said.

She was like some infuriating troll in a fairy tale, refusing to let me cross a bridge until I solved some impossible riddle. I tried to breathe, to calm my mounting fury.

'I just don't know if this ...' – my hands flung out into her ridiculous room unbidden – 'if working with you, is actually helping her get happier. That's all I want. For my daughter to be happy. My feelings – my *emotions* – are irrelevant.'

'Right.'

'A world in which she doesn't want to spend Christmas ...' – I could hear my voice rising, sharp as a knife, and I tried to blunt it – 'with her own family, I just don't see how that can be right.'

Amber's look of sympathy – or was it pity? – was more than I could bear.

'Christmas is such a triggering time, isn't it?' she said. 'All those expectations we have about it. Wanting it to be perfect. *Look* perfect.'

That sly suggestion of my superficiality – I hoped my expression told her I hadn't missed it.

'I want my family to be together, under the same roof, where they belong. Like any mother would.'

A horrible thought occurred to me: did this appalling woman know what roof my daughter was spending Christmas under, when I didn't? She continued in her infuriating sing-song drone.

'It's hard sometimes, isn't it, to accept the fact that what our children want – what they need – is different from what we want.'

I forced myself to take a breath.

'Do *you* have children, Amber?'

Something crossed her face, disturbed that implacable calm she'd so carefully cultivated. Of course it did – even Amber wasn't made of stone. It didn't worry me then, it simply gave me a nasty jolt of satisfaction, like a rat in a lab successfully nudging his furry nose against the cocaine lever.

'I can't reveal personal information to you, Lily. I'm sure you know that.'

'What – is it the first rule of therapist's club?' I shot back.

She refused to smile.

'It's one of the many ways I keep my clients safe.'

'So you think it's right what she's doing? Rejecting us?'

She placed her hands deliberately on her denim knees, as if she was trying to push down the rising tension.

'It's not about what I think. My job is to support her.'

'What, so if she was about to hurl herself off Hammersmith Bridge, your job would just be to support her? That's a ridiculous statement!'

'No. If I think a patient is in physical harm, I will, of course, take the necessary steps to protect them. What Rachel's doing is making a life choice – an emotional choice – that you're not happy about.'

'Thank you for stating something so utterly obvious,' I said. 'That's most definitely worth ninety pounds.'

Her jaw pulsed, her cornflower-blue eyes flashing like twin lasers.

'I don't think this is getting us anywhere, Lily,' she said sharply. 'And that ninety pounds? We both know it landed in my account under false pretences.'

Note that she didn't offer to return it. 'Unlike the rest of it . . .' I muttered.

'My care for Rachel is real,' she said. 'And I want to keep working with her. She wants that too. You may not realize it now, but it's actually providing healing for your whole family. So I think for her sake – and maybe for all of your sakes – we should agree to cut this conversation here.'

It was infuriating. She was so patronizing: like a nursery teacher with a fetish for crystals and jangly brass bangles.

'Don't worry,' I said, 'I've got to be across town in half an hour anyway.'

'So, let's say our goodbyes . . .' she said, eyeing me in a way that told me I was being evicted. I slumped internally. The truth was, I wasn't ready to leave. I wanted something from her that I couldn't even name. I paused, considered my next utterance. It would be expensive.

'I've got some idea what she will have told you – told you about us – and I just want you to know, to help you more than anything, that Rachel can be something of . . . not quite a fantasist, but an exaggerator.' I laughed. 'She's had a gift for storytelling right from when she was a little girl. Dragons under her bed, fairies waving from the trees – that kind of thing.'

Amber stared at me without a shred of warmth. 'The fact

you're paying doesn't give you a right to the tapes, even if there were any.'

It was nasty, her tone. Her vowels had lost their smooth glide, had been replaced with something more savage.

'And on that note,' I said, getting to my feet, 'I have to give very serious consideration as to whether we continue funding this – this healing process. Is that what you'd call it?'

Amber had recovered her equilibrium, staying neatly perched on her ghastly velvet sofa, as if standing up were too great a trial.

'I would, yes. And the truth is it's not a quick fix. When a client's suffered years of trauma, I don't have a magic wand that can spirit it away.'

My stomach clenched. *Years of trauma*. I smiled at her.

'There are so many clever phrases for it all now, aren't there? You can be *traumatized* or *triggered*. You can need a *safe space* or a *safe word*. It's what we used to call being wrapped up in cotton wool.'

Amber's stare was intense.

'When you hired me, you seemed genuinely scared for Rachel's physical safety. And I think you were right to be. I'd just bear that in mind, Lily.'

It sounded like a threat. It wasn't the words themselves; it was the way she uttered them. She was warning me.

'She's my flesh and blood,' I said, picking up my bag and turning on my heel. 'Not yours.'

I should have listened. I should have listened to her warning.

RACHEL

It was Christmas Eve. Paddington Station hummed with kinetic energy – hundreds of people were crowded around ticket machines and departure boards, rushing for platforms with their huge suitcases dragging behind them, all manically focused on reuniting with their families for the Christmas break. I seesawed between loneliness and relief as I wheeled my own case – feather-light from the lack of presents – across the concourse. How many of them were silently dreading the drunken Brexit disputes and petty rows over the remote control? But how about the others? The parents looking forward to constructing their kids' Christmas stockings, or people kept apart from far-flung, beloved siblings all year long? How could I not envy them?

I blinked away the tears that prickled behind my eyes, joining the long coffee queue that snaked its way across the station floor. Amber was always encouraging me to choose acceptance. This was my life: all I could do was carve out the best possible choices from the circumstances that existed. And spending Christmas with my family was a total non-starter.

I'd started to fire up a spark of triumph by the time I was asking for my double-shot latte. Mum had been convinced

I'd break, that I'd come crawling back for her hulking organic turkey and excruciating selection of Christmas mocktails (San Pellegrino with a twist for our little alcoholic?). Instead I was running free. Amber knew where I was, and Mum didn't. I was my own woman; an emotional orphan, in charge of my own destiny.

*

The station I got off at was deep in the Devon countryside, the platform dark and deserted. I pulled my ugly, warm coat a little tighter around my body, remembering Amber's airy suggestion that I just 'grab a cab' when I arrived. I headed for the ticket office, but it was shuttered closed, and the tiny car park was a ghostly garage, no cab rank in sight. Something stopped me from simply calling her, demanding help as part of the pricy package I'd paid for. Now I marvel at how much I was prepared to put up with in order to kid myself that I was a friend or an equal, something more to her than a mere client.

After some frantic googling I found a firm who promised a cab in half an hour. I shivered on a bench inside the tiny entrance hall, my hands plunged deep in my pockets. Eventually a battered Vauxhall Astra pulled up, the cheery driver heaving my case into the boot. 'Last Christmas' blared from his radio, approximately the nine millionth time I'd heard it that month. The cab smelt of fags, a tinsel tree swinging jauntily from his mirror while the heater blasted out noisy air.

'So, you're going to Holcroft, are you?' he asked as I swung the seatbelt across my swaddled body.

'Yes, that's right.'

'Buckle up, then,' he said, laughing to himself. 'Your family rented it for Christmas?'

'Yeah, they have,' I said merrily. Lying still came so easily. And besides, Amber sort of was family in my mind. 'We've been planning it for ages. What are you up to?'

As his car zoomed down pitch-black lanes as narrow as spaghetti, twisting and turning around hairpin bends, 'Gavin' gave me the full rundown. His daughter had got divorced, taken up with a fella he didn't think much of, but he was at least getting to spend Christmas with his two angelic grand-daughters. His wife had died two years ago, and Christmas made the loss particularly savage, but he knew she was watching over them all, giving him marks out of ten for his gravy. I sat there, letting his monologue wash over me: I couldn't imagine my dad ever talking about us with the same easy warmth. Sometimes it felt more like we were prizes than offspring, and I was definitely the booby of the bunch. Waves of nausea got progressively worse as the journey refused to end, but eventually we drew up to a pair of high, wrought-iron gates. Gavin leant out of his rolled-down window and pressed the buzzer, the gates parting slowly like the wings of a bird of prey, to reveal a forbidding grey pile.

'Wow,' I said.

'Addams Family Christmas?' Gavin said, turning his ruddy face around to grin at me. Suddenly I didn't want him to leave me here. Surely he had a couple of beloved brothers he could describe to me for an hour or two?

'It is a bit,' I agreed.

As the cab crunched to a halt, the door was flung open and I saw Amber framed perfectly in an oblong of light. It was almost like a snatched paparazzi shot – her beautiful face lit up by her wide lipsticked smile, her lithe body sculpted and kissed by a long jersey dress in a deep red. Gavin didn't even attempt to hide his gawping.

'Rachel!' she cried. 'Here you are!'

Gavin busied himself pulling my case from the boot as Amber enveloped me in a tight hug. Her perfume was so familiar to me by then: it seeped into my nostrils, and I felt my whole nervous system start to loosen and relax. It was the kind of subtle change in emotional temperature I'd never have been able to detect before she came into my life: I could have stayed there forever.

'Have a lovely Christmas, ladies,' said Gavin, heading back around the car to the driver's seat. He gave a mischievous smirk as he climbed in. 'And may I say, you don't look old enough to be her mum.'

I flushed scarlet with shame, but Amber didn't skip a beat.

'Why, thank you,' she said playfully.

As Gavin drove off, I tried to cover my tracks.

'I don't know where he got that idea from,' I said, grabbing the handle of my case, hiding my flushed cheeks behind a curtain of hair.

'I'm flattered!' said Amber, peeling my fingers off and gripping it herself. 'And please, let me; you're a guest.'

'Thanks so much for inviting me,' I said gratefully, point-blank refusing to engage with the large bank transfer that was a condition of said invitation.

'Thanks so much for trusting me with your Christmas,' she said, as if I'd had a glittering selection of options – St Barts put on ice in favour of rural Devon. 'I'm honoured, I really am. Come and meet the rest of the gang.'

The gang. I jacked a smile across my face, even though I was feeling an odd sort of jealousy. Amber was mine, wasn't she?

Or at least more mine than this 'gang' she was about to reveal. I tentatively followed her into the house, guilty about the way the wheels of my case scraped through the gravel as she awkwardly dragged it for me.

'Everyone's in the kitchen,' she said, swiftly abandoning it at the bottom of a long wooden staircase. It all smelt a little bit musty, the hemp rug that ran down the hallway threadbare and stained. Still, light from a burning candelabra made it all glow prettily, and the dark wood furniture felt old and stately. I felt a stab of shame – I needed to purge myself of Mum's ability to deliver a sniper stream of sneering judgements. That was what Amber was offering me – a chance to grow myself towards the light.

Amber pushed open the kitchen door. A group of five people sat around a large pine table, wine glasses and beer cans littering the surface. A jolt of anxiety hit me. Why had I assumed that no one would be drinking? A girl a good ten years younger than me with pink streaks through her hair picked up a bottle of white to top up her glass, and I could almost feel its cool progress down my own throat. All I wanted, when faced with a room full of strangers, was a way to take the edge off.

'Everyone, this is Rachel. Rachel, this is—' She giggled, more girlish than I'd seen her before. It made my anxiety spike even more. Was this social Amber? Would this be more like a house party than a retreat? I'd asked so few questions before I'd jumped off the cliff feet first. '. . . well, everyone.'

'Hi, Rachel,' they chanted. A guy in his early twenties, cropped dyed blonde hair framing a Peter Pan face, pulled out a chair. 'Come and sit down,' he said, a European lilt to his voice. 'I'm Marco.'

131

'I'm Hannah,' said the pink-haired girl, sticking out a hand. Her nails were grubby and bitten. 'Sorry, bit formal!' she added, coming over to give me a hug. I awkwardly hugged her from my seated position, my spine jammed upwards, her embrace too close. Her organic deodorant was nowhere near as effective as the health food shop had promised her.

Ugh – it was like Mum was in my head. Even though I despised her sly monologue, missing her felt so unexpectedly visceral that my body almost jackknifed. Can we ever truly exorcize the people who made us, or will they always haunt us, their ghostly voices ventriloquizing out of our throats, or sending up thought bubbles from our fevered brains? Even now – even after everything that's happened – I still wrestle with that question every single day.

'I'm Arthur,' said the older man sat on the other side of the table. He had a grey-flecked beard, slightly bushy, that made him look more distinguished than homeless. It was the elegance of his clothes too – their studied casualness undermined by the thick luxury of the dark denim and soft cashmere hanging off his solid frame. There was a hole in the elbow of the jumper, and I wondered if he'd secretly scissored it into existence. He had a presence, a confidence, that immediately drew me.

There was another man, Tim, closer to my age, who was tall and balding, his long body hunched back down over the table like a giraffe trying to take a drink. He wiggled his fingers companionably in my direction, nervy but warm. The last happy camper was a haunted-looking woman in her late forties, Joanna, who struggled to raise a smile when I said hello. Her ringless hands were wrapped tightly around a chipped mug, the steam condensing on her narrow, black-framed glasses. It was as if she was surrounded by a forcefield of misery. I swallowed down another wave of trepidation.

'Joanna's having lemon verbena tea,' said Amber. 'Would you like one too, Rachel?'

I felt a flash of irritation. *Way to broadcast to the group that I'm an alcoholic.*

'I'll just have water, thanks,' I said, and Marco carefully poured some from a smudged glass jug that sat on the table, his burning eyes telling me he'd taken on board my 'problem'.

Amber walked to the head of the table and clapped her hands.

'Welcome, everyone,' she said, laying a hand on her heart. A gold star was hanging around her neck, dipping down into her cleavage, which led the eye to follow. I noticed Arthur's eyes already seemed to be taking the hint. 'I want to tell you how honoured I am that you're all trusting me to take you on this healing journey.'

She bowed to us, and we spontaneously bowed back, our eyes darting towards each other and back to her. I felt a little firework of jealousy go off as I saw their rapt expressions – did they carry Amber around in their heads the way I did, always leaning on her for a snippet of silent advice? I needed to purge this negativity.

'Let's close our eyes and breathe together, take a moment to set an intention for the days ahead.'

The darkness was quickly broken by a snuffling sob. I let my eyes blink open. Eyeliner streaked Hannah's plump cheeks, her broad shoulders heaving. Amber rushed to her.

'My brave girl,' she said, enveloping her in a hug. 'It's taken a lot for you to get here, hasn't it?'

Hannah gave a desperate nod, her sobs getting even louder.

Everyone stared at the tableau of the two of them, their faces earnest. I looked down into my water, willing it to honour Jesus and turn into wine. Why the hell was I here? My eyes grazed Hannah's sobbing form, and suddenly she was my little sister, my Sophie. We'd never spent Christmas apart before. We'd met last week, but I almost wished we hadn't, the air so thick with mutual resentment that our Christmas presents felt more like unexploded bombs. I'd still brought hers with me, carefully wrapped with silky ribbons the way she always did them. It was swaddled in my jeans at the bottom of my suitcase.

'Thank you, Amber,' managed Hannah eventually, unbinding her arms from around Amber's torso.

Sophie had got it out of me eventually, her hurt at my secrecy like an open wound. I'd admitted to Amber's retreat as we'd said our goodbyes, pretended it was no more than massages and Christmas carols, and made her swear not to tell Mum. It was feeling way more complicated than that right now.

Amber stalked back to her position at the top of the table.

'The fact is, we're all going to cry this weekend,' she said, eyes resting benevolently on Hannah. 'I've got many clients, many people I could have invited, but you lot – you're my warriors.' She grinned at us, almost triumphant. 'You're the ones who are ready to walk through the darkness, wade through the shit and honour your own precious hearts.'

Marco gave a spontaneous cheer.

'We're very lucky Arthur agreed to join us,' she continued. 'He's a master practitioner in past life regression.' A pulse of anxiety spread through my body. 'He and I have worked together before, and ...' – her hand fluttered upwards – 'well, it's literally life-changing. That's all I'm saying for now.' Arthur

gave a wide grin of appreciation. 'When we find those lost fragments of our souls, it gives us permission to step fully into this
incarnation.'

I glanced around the table, hoping some of the others were
finding the prospect unnerving, but their faces were rapt moons.
I can always go home, I told myself, but the thought of throwing
myself onto the mercy of someone else's family or spending it
alone in my poky flat, only the 7/11 on the corner open for business, was too much to bear.

I was doing it again – removing myself, like I always did –
feeling inadequate and superior all at once, loneliness the only
constant. I forced myself to merge with Amber, to inhale her
words. I was here for a reason. I was ready to be transformed.

*

Hannah's enormous rucksack landed on the single bed with a
heavy thud.

'Do you mind if I go next to the window?' she asked anxiously. 'I get a bit claustrophobic.'

I looked around the tiny space, the narrow landing strip between
the tiny beds. Why hadn't I asked about the sleeping arrangements? But then, as it wasn't a Brownie camp, it would never have
occurred to me that I'd be sharing a room. It was bare and white,
with a scratchy beige carpet. We each had a bedside cubby, but it
didn't look like there was anywhere to hang our clothes. A single
light burned harshly from the centre of the low ceiling.

'If you're claustrophobic, this is going to be some serious
aversion therapy,' I said.

'Amber says it's really important,' she said primly. 'It's part
of the whole healing journey, sharing our space.'

'Yeah, no, it's great,' I said quickly. I didn't want her sneaking to Amber, telling her I was undermining the retreat. 'I was only joking.'

'This is a whole healing immersion, Rachel,' she said, staring intently at me. She sank down on her bed. 'I'm not ashamed of being emotional downstairs. I was honouring how deep we'll go, the places Amber's already taken me.'

Tremors of unease ran up and down my limbs.

'Sure, but it's Christmas,' I said lamely. 'She told me how relaxing it would be. We'll have fun too.'

Hannah gave a slightly knowing laugh.

'I'm really happy to be sharing with you,' she said. 'I felt a connection as soon as we hugged.'

A lump closed up my throat, her not Sophie-ishness almost too much to bear.

'Yeah, me too,' I said.

She gave an odd little namaste bow.

'It's an honour to spend Christmas with you, Rachel.'

I froze a second, forcing my face into submission. Then I bowed back.

'The light in me honours the light in you,' I said, and Hannah beamed.

'We should go downstairs for supper,' she said happily.

*

Amber was ladling a brown, sludgy concoction out of a huge saucepan.

'I bet this is your first vegan Christmas,' she said to me, handing me a steaming earthenware bowl.

The heat was searing, but I forced myself to hold onto the

bowl. 'Yeah, not really Mum's scene,' I said. Amber grinned at that. 'Can I do anything to help?'

'Absolutely not,' she demurred. 'How many times do I have to remind you that you're a guest?'

Apart from the fact that my fingerprints were close to being burned off – a gangland hit via the medium of lentil stew – I wanted nothing more than to stay glued to Amber's side. Instead I reluctantly retreated to the kitchen table, plonking myself down next to Marco.

'*Salute*,' he said, chinking his water glass against mine supportively, while Tim watched our little exchange.

Hannah smiled gently across the table. 'How long have you been . . . not been drinking?' she asked.

Ugh. I really didn't want to go there, but they were all looking at me expectantly. Arthur's spoon had paused en route to his bearded mouth and even Joanna seemed to have been shaken out of her cocoon of misery at the prospect of my big reveal.

'Um, about three months. Well, I started trying not to drink three months ago – had a bit of an epic fail – and then, since then, it's been eight weeks and three days.' Amber was hovering behind me, my sobriety angel. 'Obviously I couldn't have done it without Amber.'

'Ob-viously,' laughed Marco, and everyone looked up at her with adoration.

'It's all you, my darling,' she said. She'd never called me darling before – I fondled the word internally. 'Rachel's been incredibly brave and determined, against some tough odds.' Her voice dropped low. 'People haven't been as supportive as she's deserved them to be, but she's . . .' – she paused, gazing at me meaningfully – 'well, it's been humbling to watch.'

Murmurs of congratulation bubbled up from the group, and I flushed, pleased now that I'd been brave enough to be truthful with them. Arthur cocked his head, contemplated me with something that looked like admiration, and I blushed even more, noticing how handsome he was. He glowed somehow, the flickering from the lit candles giving him a soft warmth. His face was lined and weather-beaten, but it looked distinguished in this light, his soulful eyes like melted chocolate. He felt like an anchor suddenly, a point of safety. I forced myself to look away.

Everyone tore into the stew, dipping hunks of bread into their bowls and throwing more compliments at Amber. She nibbled at hers, birdlike, deflecting the praise. Once the meal was over, she clapped her hands and stood up.

'It's great news that you're all getting on so well, but I'm afraid it's time to say goodbye.' We all looked up at her, confused. Hannah's bottom lip began to tremble. 'Don't be sad!' laughed Amber. 'It's the first part of the healing journey we're taking together. You're going to shed your names for the next few days, try out a new one.'

'Call me Romeo,' said Marco, and Hannah giggled. My eyes flicked between them. Were they flirting already? It was unnerving to me. I trained my gaze on Amber, made sure I didn't look at Arthur.

'I don't understand,' said Joanna sharply. I'd learnt over dinner that she was a corporate lawyer and her tone suggested that this particular contract was faulty.

'Let me explain,' said Amber, her tone honeyed. 'As I've explained to each of you in the work we've done together, each of us develops a shield very young, a core wound that imprisons us and steals our joy.'

'What like?' said Hannah.

'Well, for me,' said Amber, 'I've always been a rescuer. When I was a little girl, my parents asked way too much of me, and punished me when I . . .' Her eyes flashed with anger. A wave of fear washed over me, the earth unsteady. '. . . failed to meet *their* needs.' The twist in her face smoothed away to nothing, and I wondered if my fragile state was making my mind play tricks. 'It's typical of alcoholics. So, my name might be, say, "Little Lost Rescuer".'

'But how does it help us?' demanded Joanna, showing scant interest in Amber's awful childhood. Amber was next to me, and I lightly touched the crook of her elbow to let her know that I, at least, had heard her. The move felt like a risk, so when she gave me a soft, almost imperceptible smile, I felt another wave of pride at my courage. Everything was starting to feel heightened, like the first lapping waves of MDMA. I breathed in, let myself trust it.

'By confronting our key issue, by witnessing each other's deepest pain, we can throw away the lies we've believed all our lives, and finally see ourselves – and each other – for the radiant beings we really are.'

'It's a Christmas miracle!' said Marco, ever the joker.

Joanna continued to look unconvinced, narrowed eyes peering out from behind her glasses. Arthur looked calm. Calm and sure of his place in the world. I tried to inhale some of his surety from across the table.

'I don't know how I'd ever pick my name,' whimpered Hannah.

'I'll help each of you,' said Amber. She turned towards me, eyes fixing on my face. 'Let's start with Rachel. You up for that?'

Fear began to lap up again, but I refused to drown in it. She was choosing me. She was declaring me her equal, up to the task of showing this broken gang how to heal.

'Definitely!' I said. Could they all see it? How special our bond was? It was bad in a way, that she was making it so obvious.

'Good girl,' she said. She cocked her head and stared into my eyes with a loving intensity. 'Stand here next to me.'

I got to my feet, standing opposite her. I could feel the energy between us.

'So, Rachel, tell the group a little bit about your place in the family.' She giggled. 'Not this family. Your *actual* family.'

'I'm the middle child. I've got an older brother, Josh, and a younger sister, Sophie. My mum and dad are still together.'

Amber gazed at me, almost pitying. Then she gave me an unexpected hug.

'Rachel, darling, you sound like you're on a French exchange. Do you want to tell us how many pets you've got? Any stray guinea pigs we should know about?'

Marco and Hannah tittered, and I felt myself cringe.

'We don't want facts,' she said. 'We want feelings.'

'Right.'

I wanted to please her, but the words were jammed in my throat, choking me. Why had I volunteered for this? I wasn't strong enough. Tim gave me an encouraging smile, his long fingers steepled in front of him.

'Sharing your story isn't a betrayal,' said Amber softly. 'How does it feel to be their sister, their child?' She paused a beat, waiting for me to speak. 'Tell us about Lily.'

Something tore a little inside.

'My mum is – she loves me, but it's hard.' I paused. The silence felt too full. 'She won't let me tell the truth. In big ways and

140

small ways.' I heard my voice crack. 'It's like she loves the idea of me more than she loves *me*.'

'And love is a verb,' intoned Amber. 'If someone tells us they love us, but they're not loving – well, is that even love? It's deeply distressing for a child.'

'She does love me, she's just … she's a complicated person. She had a really hard childhood herself, she …' Amber watched me, letting me peter out.

'Maybe it is love,' said Amber, 'but I don't think that love should make you feel this sad. This shitty about yourself. Do you? Do you really think you deserve that, Rachel?'

I was crying now, standing up in that grubby kitchen, the pile of lentils I'd failed to eat congealing on my plate in a grey pile. I let the stinging tears roll down my face like a window pane battered by a storm. I felt utterly desolate.

'No, I don't!' I said, suddenly galvanized by a surge of righteous rage. 'I fucking don't deserve to feel like this.'

'Too right,' agreed Amber, flushed with indignation on my behalf.

I should have seen it. I should have detected the triumph that shone out of her eyes.

'Your mum constantly manipulates you. She *tortures* you.'

'Fuck her,' I sobbed. 'Fuck my fucking family.'

'That's it,' said Amber. 'Let it out. Connect with that pain you've spent so many years numbing away.' She looked around the group. 'You're safe. You're held. We're all here for you.'

I risked a look around the room. All of them were smiling at me, even Joanna. Arthur's handsome face was almost split in two by his grin.

'Thanks,' I said in a small voice. 'I'm sorry to be such a cry baby.' Then I felt bad about Hannah, my proxy baby sister. 'I mean, obviously I'm just being incredibly brave, being this vulnerable.' I smiled at them, and they took my cue to laugh. I felt like Arthur was drawn to me, intrigued, admiring of my spirit. The high came back, kicking in just as hard as the low had done a few minutes earlier.

'So, there we have it!' said Amber, beaming. 'We've got to your issue. Let's try out a phrase or two for size. Give me some words.'

'Toxic. It's fucking toxic,' I said, filled with righteous energy.

'You're right,' agreed Amber. 'It is. So let's name it. Toxic Mummy's Daughter?'

I stared at her. *Could I do this?*

'Yes. Okay. Yes!'

'So, there we have it,' she said. 'Rachel's left the building, and in her place we have Toxic Mummy's Daughter. Let's give her a clap and decide who goes next!'

I collapsed heavily into my seat, the applause reverberating through my body. I had committed.

*

It was late now, and Amber had gone to bed. I'd lost track of time, my hands waving above my head as my body swayed and dipped in a vague approximation of dancing. The wailing chorus of 'I Feel Love' kicked in, and we all sang along at the top of our voices, tuneless and blissful. Our fingers, freezing in the draughty living room, touched and grasped, our eyes locking with a warm sweetness.

'Happy Christmas, losers!' yelled Marco, pointing at his watch.

'Happy Christmas, Abandoned Peter Pan,' I yelled back, hugging him. If love was a verb, our hug certainly felt like it, and so did all the others I shared. I didn't want to be anywhere else but here, with these precious people. My family threatened to lurch up, but I forced down any threatening emotion. My happiness was too hard won to let them rob me of it.

Arthur's hug came last.

'Happy Christmas, Toxic Mummy's Daughter,' he said, directly into my ear.

How could such a ridiculous phrase feel like a come-on? I felt his lips brush my skin, and an unexpected tremor shot through me. I peeled my neck backwards to look up at him. Was this dangerous? A stab of desire as strong as this almost always ushered in disaster, but maybe I was a whole new person now.

'Happy Christmas,' I said. It felt mean not to use his name. His pain needed acknowledgement too. 'Never Good Enough.'

He grabbed my hand, entwined his fingers with mine as the opening chords of an Adele ballad kicked in. I stood on tiptoes so I could get close enough for him to hear me.

'Are you married?' I regretted the question as soon as I'd asked it. The lights were as bright here as everywhere else in this house, so there was no hiding my embarrassment. 'Sorry, it's none of my business. Scrub that.'

A slow smile unfurled across his face.

'I'm flattered you want to know,' he said, his dark brown eyes intense. 'No. Not now.'

'Right. Sorry.'

'Don't ever apologize for being open-hearted,' he said, pulling me closer to him, and moving me to the music. His firm fingers played scales on my ribs. 'I love that about you.'

He loved that about me: it sounded like something you'd whisper after five years of dating. But that was the funny thing about this whole situation – time had started to warp and melt, dangerously fluid. By now it was almost impossible to believe that I'd only known my fellow warriors for a few short hours.

I leaned into Arthur, allowing his arms to snake their way around my waist, letting the bass line seep through our melded bodies. Then I saw how Marco's elfin face was scrunched up in cheeky amusement, and immediately I came crashing down to earth. I'd be a fool to trust myself: when had this kind of situation not ended in disaster? I was a disgusting mess who just happened to be sober.

I stiffened, slipping out of the circle Arthur had woven around me before the next song could draw us back together.

'I should go to bed,' I said. 'No one wants panda eyes for Christmas.'

Arthur considered me, his handsome, grizzled face suddenly hard to read.

'Get some beauty sleep,' he said, almost as if it was a command. 'Not that you need it. Tomorrow will be quite a trip.'

*

When I got back to my room I sank onto my thin mattress, trying and failing to make sense of the past few hours. All that fizzing energy had drained from me now, my body limp and useless. I eyed the solid black oblong of my suitcase, torn.

After a few minutes I crossed to it and yanked the zip, rootling through the layers of jeans and jumpers until I felt the silky sheen of the ribbons that encircled Sophie's present. I sat cross-legged on the hard floor, gently teasing out the knots. I pulled back the paper with reverential care, as if Sophie would be able to feel the soft murmur of my attention through the ether.

A long scarf unfurled itself in my hands, soft and yielding. It was far more stylish than the ones we'd looked at for Mum in the shop in Marylebone, chunky and thick, a vivid emerald green that she knew I'd love. A card fell out, a line drawing of a mouse in a Father Christmas hat.

I don't know exactly where she's taken you, but I'd hate it if you were cold. Love you always, your sister Sophie xx

I buried my face deep in the wool, inhaling the faint trace of Sophie's perfume. My tears left it sodden. 'Happy Christmas,' I whispered under my breath, almost convincing myself I heard her repeat the words back to me, a sisterly incantation, unbound by time or space.

LILY

I've never stopped making my children stockings. Even now, if this whole situation was miraculously transformed, Rachel would find her polyester stripy sausage, with its scratched plastic Santa face stuck to the front, leaning tipsily against the end of her bed on Christmas morning, stuffed fat with presents.

I crept out of our bed in the darkness of Christmas morning, my body vibrating with a humiliated anger that had kicked in as soon as my eyes opened. Nick gave an angry grunt at being woken, a trail of drool garlanding his pillow.

'Happy Christmas,' I said softly.

'You're not still doing this, are you?' he hissed. 'No one wants their mum in their bedroom when it's still dark.'

'It's important,' I said.

'You realize they could be fucking?' he said with a grim satisfaction. 'They're adults. Hate to break it to you, Lily, but those grandchildren didn't come down the chimney.'

He knew I hated that kind of coarseness. 'Locker room talk' should be kept in the locker room – our marriage certainly survived best that way.

'I need this,' I said, teeth gritted. 'There's enough missing for me as it is.'

He had the good grace to look sheepish, pulling himself upright and leaning back on the bank of satin throw pillows that I decorated our bed with. His chest was still taut, but the skin looked grey to me, like a plucked chicken. In a way, every day was Christmas for him, always gifted the powerful man's privilege of wildly overestimating his own attractiveness.

'Darling, she's just having a hissy fit,' he said, reaching a half-hearted hand out towards me. 'She's probably in her flat with her phone switched off, bingeing shit on Netflix. I wouldn't be surprised if she turns up for lunch, all sorry for herself.'

'She won't,' I said. 'I know she won't, I can feel it. She could be anywhere. With anyone.'

I hadn't told him about ambushing Amber, because it had left me feeling like I'd failed. Nick's confident grin didn't waver.

'I'll drive round and check if you like. She's not too big for a fireman's lift.'

My teeth ground almost as far down as my gums. Another privilege he greedily took: letting me do all the parental worrying for both of us. Or was it more than that? I watched him taking a slurp of tepid water from the glass on his bedside table. Was he looking for the perfect alibi for a morning flit?

I'd retrieved the two stuffed stockings from the wardrobe by now, the absence of the third a lightness that felt more like a weight. It weaponized me.

'You know, if someone heard you talking about your first-born daughter – the daughter who doesn't even want to spend Christmas Day with you – in the dismissive way you just did, they might think you're a long way off father of the year. They might even sympathize with her decision.'

Nick's grin reversed into an expression of slack-jawed hurt. I almost felt sorry for him.

'Don't try and blame me for all this shit,' he spat. 'Your brilliant solution's not working out so well, is it? Turns out you can't pay someone else to do what you're too selfish to do yourself.'

'What, clear up your disgusting mess?'

'No. Be a mother to your own child,' he said, his voice pure venom.

Now it was my hurt that was agony. It made me lash out in a way that was dangerous.

'You have no idea the mess I've cleared up for you,' I said. 'No idea the damage you've done to all of us. I've spared you because you're too weak and pathetic to survive the truth.'

Nick was red in the face now, mouth gold-fishing as he searched for the right comeback to an insult he didn't entirely understand. I was skirting too close to the edge of the precipice. I'd come too far to lose everything for the petty satisfaction of getting the last word. I knew, with a lurching dread, that it would be more than the last word. It could spell the end of everything.

I turned on my heel before the skirmish could turn into all-out war.

'Just get in the shower and start making today feel like Christmas,' I hissed. 'Your family need you more than ever. Maybe for once, you could try not failing us.'

RACHEL

I sat up, my breath a foggy cloud that furled outwards into the freezing bedroom. It took me a second to remember where I was, but the biting chill soon reminded me. So, too, did the sight of Hannah, who leapt from her own bed and crossed the room, flinging her arms around my shoulders.

'Happy Christmas, lazy bones!' she said. The relentless intimacy was a bit unnerving, almost as if I'd adopted a rescue dog who'd expected to live out his days in a damp kennel. 'I waited to go down to breakfast so I'd be here when you woke up.'

'Right, thanks,' I said, forcing my body not to turn rigor-mortis stiff.

'I know how weird it must be for you, not being with your family, so . . .' She looked down at me with blazing eyes. 'They sound like total fuckers, Toxic Mummy's Daughter. You've done the right thing coming here.'

I reached up a hand unconsciously to fondle Sophie's scarf, which was still looped around my neck – I'd fallen asleep in its embrace. I could smell the mustiness of Hannah's morning breath, her lank, dyed hair curtaining my forehead.

There I was, dodging intimacy again.

'Happy Christmas!' I said, injecting cheer into my tone. I hugged her back properly, then swung my feet down onto the sticky carpet. 'And thank you for saying that. You're brave, too, taking a risk on this whole thing.'

We'd established last night that Hannah was adopted, had never felt her adoptive parents loved her as much as her high-flying siblings. There was a suicide attempt that she wasn't yet ready to talk about: instead she'd taken on Amber's suggestion of Little Lost Lamb as her name and promised to get courageous enough to share more today.

'Nothing's a risk if Amber's with us,' said Hannah, her expression as dreamy as a lover.

*

Amber was back at the stove, her big orange tureen now filled with steaming porridge. Her dark hair was pulled back in an elegant chignon, a woollen dress skimming her body, the scarlet bow of her mouth as festive as a Christmas decoration. My eyes flicked to the kitchen table, unconsciously searching for Arthur. Why had I brought a suitcase full of jeans and tracksuit bottoms? I chided myself: I was falling for the biggest con in the book: comparison – something Amber herself had taught me to reject as I'd sat in her room wailing about all the milestones I'd failed to achieve. What an irony that I was now comparing myself to my liberator. I'd brought the warm, comfortable clothes she'd advised us to pack, whilst she was expressing herself in her normal, vivid way.

Meanwhile, there was no sign of Arthur. I tried not to overthink it.

'Here's your Happy Christmas breakfast!' Amber trilled, holding out a bowl for me. 'Made with almond milk and water. There's maple syrup on the table.'

'Thanks,' I said. I couldn't help feeling like every meal had the same mulchy quality you'd only fully appreciate if you had false teeth. 'Are there are any eggs I could boil?'

She cocked her head, looking slightly disappointed.

'Eggs aren't strictly vegan, Toxic Mummy's Daughter.'

'No,' agreed Hannah, coming up behind me. 'The hens get really mistreated actually – I can send you a link about it. Amber, can I have a big bowl of the yummy stuff?'

'Of course you can!' beamed Amber, and I retreated to the table, feeling stung. Everything still had that heightened quality, emotions so close to the surface that the slightest touch triggered an electric reaction.

Tim picked up a big cafetière of coffee as I sat down next to him.

'Want some?' he said. 'I guess you're not suffering like the rest of us. Oh yeah, and Happy Christmas.'

Tim was gay, an A&E doctor, and he'd been having an affair with a married male colleague for the past three years. He was illegitimate, too, and Amber was convinced it was all part of the same internal story.

'Certainly do, Shameful Secret.'

I caught his eye, wondering if we'd smile at the ridiculousness, but we didn't. It was yet another reminder that I needed to fully commit. As he poured a hot stream of coffee into one of the tannin-ringed mugs, Arthur ambled into the room, scuffing his beard with his left hand. He surveyed the room, then crossed directly over to me.

'Happy Christmas, you,' he said softly, leaning downwards so that his lips almost grazed my earlobe.

'Happy Christmas to you too,' I stuttered, willing my cheeks not to flush.

Amber was watching us from the stove, the wooden spoon static in her hand, her gaze steady and unwavering. Was it pity or contempt I could see in her eyes?

A shudder of self-disgust ripped through my body. She was my focus. She was my protector. I needed to stifle this crush before it ruined everything I'd worked so hard to gain.

LILY

The pop of the cork sounded more like a bullet to the head than a celebration. We always have champagne on Christmas morning, our flutes chinking, our little family circle something magical and precious. Of course there had been absences in the past – triumphant in-laws who've made off with my babies, claiming it's 'their' Christmas – but there had never been an absence as agonizing as this one.

'Cheers!' said Sophie, smashing her glass against mine.

'Careful,' I said sharply. 'These were your grandmother's.'

I could feel how eager she was to please, how determined to fill the space of two, and it irritated me. What an ungrateful fool I was back then.

'Sorry, Mum,' she said, her body imperceptibly shifting towards Toby's soft bulk. He was built for comfort not for speed, my son-in-law, but maybe that was a good thing. Maybe, despite her outward naivety, Sophie had listened more carefully than her sister to the cautionary tales that her father and I had silently taught them about love.

'Happy Christmas, everyone!' said Josh, a self-satisfied grin splitting his face in two. He seemed genuinely unconcerned about Rachel's absence.

He must have seen my face. 'Come on, Mum, it's fine. She's sulking. Do her good to miss us. It'll remind her what she's actually got.'

His dreary wife nodded her agreement like a little china dog, ignoring the black look I gave them both. Rachel was always brighter than him: they both got As, but hers were effortless. He'd never quite forgiven her for that – her absence was probably a Christmas present in itself, or so he'd thought. 'Let's go and get some unwrapping on the go,' cried Nick, and my grandchildren began their relentless sugar-revved screaming. It was only 11 a.m.

As they tore towards the living room, the adults in tow, Sophie hung back.

'You okay, Mum? I miss her, too. It's so weird without her. I keep looking round, and she's not there, rolling her eyes at me.'

'I don't know how to feel, quite frankly,' I said. 'I'm angry, of course, but most of all I'm hurt.' My hand went unconsciously to my heart, encased by a black crepe dress which could've just as easily done for a funeral. 'I ache, Sophie.' It was true; my body throbbed with the kind of pain that no amount of paracetamol could take away. 'That's what she's done to me.'

Sophie's round, expressive eyes moistened.

'It's making me feel like total poo, too, Mum.' Her inability to swear was normally endearing. Not today. 'But . . .' She froze, framed by the French windows that opened onto the bare winter garden, the light grey and low. 'I think she needs this.'

'Needs what, exactly?' I said witheringly. Why could I summon no warmth for the children who had actually deigned to spend Christmas with me?

'To be in a different space this year,' stuttered Sophie. 'To try to heal. She's trying really hard to change.'

'The most healing thing is to be with the people who love you, not to be alone.'

'She's not ... I mean ...' Sophie blushed crimson, her feet starting towards the door. I'd grabbed the flesh of her upper arm before she could make her escape. Everything sped up in that moment, inside and outside my body.

'She's with that woman, isn't she?' I demanded. 'She's with Amber.'

'I don't know,' said Sophie.

'Don't lie to me!' I was shouting. I couldn't help it. There was a whole river of pent-up rage that was bursting its banks. I could see Sophie quaking, and I used it to my advantage. It's hard not to hate myself for that now. 'Tell me the truth. Where is your sister?'

'I don't know!' she said, tears starting.

'She's with her, though, isn't she?' I thought about her smug smile as she sank into her flea-bitten sofa, refusing to help me. 'That vile bitch is spending Christmas with my daughter. Your sister, Sophie! Why did you let this happen, when it's the absolute opposite of what Rachel needs?'

Nick and Toby were in the kitchen now, Josh and Chloe following behind them. I let go of Sophie's arm and flung myself down at the kitchen table, giving way to the sobs that I'd been holding in since dawn. All of them looked at me as if I was some kind of grief sideshow. Nick eventually put a hand on each of my shoulders.

'Let me call her again,' he said, useless as ever. 'She might pick up this time.'

Was this my punishment? Was this my punishment for what I'd done? I raised my head an inch.

'If you want to call anyone, call that *cunt*,' I hissed, too quietly for any children to hear. I hadn't lost all sense of common decency.

At least not yet.

RACHEL

The living room had a static chill to it, partly from the temperature, partly from tension. The five of us – Amber's tribe – sat on the two floral sofas opposite one another, while she and Arthur ruled over us from high-backed wooden chairs. I felt anxious and trapped, consumed by the sagging sofa with its sharp springs that poked up through the threadbare cushions, Tim and Hannah either side of me. I couldn't help feeling as if Hannah was using the sloppiness of the soft furnishings to slide into my personal space. Right now we were taking a 'deep, centring breath', our eyes closed. Hannah's was warm on my neck.

'Lovely!' chirped Amber, calling us back to full consciousness. 'And before the day begins in earnest ...' – she cast a significant look at Arthur – 'what delights we have in store ... I wanted to appoint myself Secret Santa.'

She crossed to the sofa opposite ours and pulled out a cardboard box from behind it.

'Someone might have to clarify the concept for you, Amber,' said Arthur, in his deep, sonorous voice. God, he was posh. 'I don't think you're all that undercover.'

'Point taken,' giggled Amber, handing him a package

wrapped in shiny red paper. She continued on to Marco. 'No opening these until everyone's got one.'

People were already starting to pipe up with thanks and appreciation. 'Your present's upstairs,' said Joanna and, while Amber protested, I could tell she was delighted. I cursed myself for not bringing her a gift – why had I taken her at her word when she'd said not to bring anything but myself? Of course, my gift was my maxed-out credit card, but it was still too early in my relationship with Amber for me to admit that to myself.

I slipped my fingers under the sellotape. Hannah, a few seconds ahead of me, was already bouncing with delight beside me.

'Thank you, thank you, thank you!' she said, holding up the bubble bath we'd both received. Hers was lemongrass, mine was sea kelp. 'You know I love lemongrass, don't you?'

'I certainly do!' Amber confirmed. I couldn't help noticing they didn't have labels, just red for the men, blue for the women. Her response was a kind indulgence, giving the painfully inse-cure Hannah a chance to feel special.

'Thanks, Amber,' I said, squirting a bit onto the back of my hand. It was a wobbly blob, sticky and synthetic. 'Smells delicious.'

'Mine's liquid fags,' muttered Tim, showing me the tobacco label on the brown bottle of shower gel, and we both laughed. Amber's eyes grazed us, and I beamed at her. I'd appreciated the moment of silliness, but now I had the feeling I was doing some-thing wrong, failing at healing. I redoubled my vow to spend the day demonstrating how much I valued her.

'Right,' said Amber, circling the room with a frayed wicker bin. 'Paper in here, and then we'll get started.'

Was it excitement or dread that was curling its way upwards through my body like a plume of smoke?

*

Marco was eager to go first, his hand waving above his head like a victory flag when Amber asked for a volunteer. He was an acting student, his rich Milan family paying for him to study in London: he had sweetness, but also a craving for the spotlight that you could see even when he was just pouring milk over his cereal or lighting a sneaky cigarette.

'Brave boy,' said Amber, as he took a comedy bow and crossed to the massage table that she and Arthur had wheeled into the centre of the room. 'Make yourself comfortable.'

Marco took off his expensive white leather trainers and lay down on the bed. He rolled his eyes upwards towards Arthur, looming above him.

'Now do you saw me in half?' he said, making Hannah guffaw. It was nervous hysteria, I could tell from the way that her limbs were compulsively twitching. I laid a calming hand on her knee and as I tried to take it away, she trapped it under hers.

'No, Abandoned Peter Pan. But we might cut away your past,' said Amber smoothly. She was subtly turning the energy, forcing a crackly kind of calm on the whole room.

'Okay,' said Marco, subdued now.

'I want you to move backwards in time,' intoned Amber, while Arthur laid two firm hands on Marco's thin shoulders. 'Take us back to a moment when you felt that abandonment, when you felt that deep sense of being alone.'

'I don't know . . .' said Marco.

'We're all here with you, Marco,' said Amber. 'It's safe to

go on this journey. Just let your subconscious lead the way – it knows where you need to go.' There was a pause. Then Arthur started to emit a deep hum, his hands working Marco's shoulders through his grey jumper. 'Arthur's performing some reiki on you now, Marco,' said Amber. Marco's body jerked, and then his internal motor seemed to kick in.

'I was nine,' he said, his Italian accent suddenly much more pronounced, his eyes firmly closed. My body prickled with unease: it felt as if he really was spiralling backwards in time, to a place where we might not be able to reach him. I longed now for one of his stupid jokes: it made me grateful for Hannah's clammy palm, sitting heavily on my hand.

'I *am* nine,' whispered Amber.

'I am nine,' he repeated. 'I cannot sleep. I come down the stairs, and my father is in the lounge. He tidies them away, but I know there are drugs on the table, even if I don't know what they are called.'

'And where's your mother?' asked Amber, her focus on him absolute.

'She is working. She is in America. I have nobody but him.' Marco's body juddered. 'She's been gone for so long. I am scared.'

'Of course you're scared,' said Arthur.

'I am so scared,' said Marco, starting to cry. 'I know I need to be his little man.'

'So of course you never grew up,' said Amber triumphantly. 'You never had the chance to be a child.'

'You're our child today, Marco,' said Arthur.

I looked around the room, trying to catch someone's eye, but everybody was staring intently at the tableau unfolding in front of us. Only Hannah responded, her flushed face full of emotion. 'I love you,' she mouthed. I smiled weakly back.

'I ask him what he's doing, and then I say I won't tell Mummy. He is my best friend.'

'My poor little boy,' said Amber, her voice soaked with sympathy. 'You have to try so hard, don't you? You have to work so hard to survive.'

'It's so *fuck-ing* hard,' yelled Marco, fists balled up like the frustrated child he once was, tears spurting. 'He takes out a card, he lines up the drugs and I'm ... I'm just waiting to see what he will do. It looks like sugar ... from when we make the biscuits at school.' The petty innocence of that detail pierced me, dragged me inside of Marco's story and out of my own head. 'But I know it's something bad.'

'So what does he do to you, Marco?' hisses Amber.

'He ...' Marco's profile was white, tears cascading down his cheeks. 'He leans down, he snorts some up and then ...' Marco shuddered to silence, the whole room rigid as we waited for him. 'He shows me how to do it.'

Our collective shock felt as though it curdled the air around us. It was me who squeezed Hannah's hand this time.

'Oh, Marco,' said Amber, loving and wise. He looked up at her through wet eyes, gratitude and vulnerability shining out. 'You're safe now. We've got you. You're not Abandoned Peter Pan anymore.'

My heart filled up watching them, watching all of us. I was part of something that felt so pure and primal. It wasn't just me, inside my own painful thoughts, hating myself for every petty thing from the sneaky packet of Marlboro Lights at the bottom of my handbag to the crinkly line that ran below my left eye. All of my loneliness, the petty 'crimes' I pinned my self-hatred on, felt like they were being burned away in this blazing circle of love. Tears were rolling down my cheeks now, and I momentarily took my hand away from Hannah's, grinning at her with the open warmth I should have had from the first second I met her. I mopped them away with Sophie's soft scarf, then pushed the thought of my sister aside and let my hand cover Hannah's again.

'We're going to try and reach back now, Marco,' said Arthur, his voice low and calm. 'We're going to try and reach back to where you and your father first found each other.'

Marco looked crumpled and exhausted, lying prone on the couch.

'We're with you, Marco!' shouted Hannah. She giggled. 'Is that allowed?'

'We are, though!' I added, and Amber smiled over at us both like an indulgent mum.

'Okay!' said Marco, some of his familiar cheekiness poking through again.

Arthur began his strange, guttural humming as Amber stalked around the couch, her gaze far away. She owned that room. She owned every single one of us.

'Let yourself move backwards, Marco,' she said, intense and focused. 'Time is an illusion. It's a construct. You can move beyond it. You can move beyond anything. You know that now.'

I watched Marco's olive-skinned profile, the way his eyelids were flickering with deep internal effort. Was it as simple as that? Would I never again stand outside Londis with my credit card slicing into my palm, hating myself in advance for the sour-tasting Rioja I knew would be sluicing down my throat until the bottle was empty? Amber had urged me to be compassionate with myself, told me that all I'd been doing in those moments was self-medicating. Would today be the final dose – all the medicine I'd ever need?

'I am muddy,' he said eventually. 'I am in the mud.'

'You're in the mud?' said Amber. 'How does it feel in your body?'

'I am wet. I am cold.'

I could see his thin frame was starting to shiver. Tim was watching intently, his bald head cocked to one side. I tried to smile at him, but his gaze was unwavering. Was he professionally fascinated by the way Marco's body was mirroring the memory?

'Where are you, Marco?' said Arthur. 'Tell us what you see.'

'I am ... it's a field.' His shivering grew more pronounced. 'It's dangerous!'

'Is anyone with you, Marco?' said Amber. 'Is there anyone you can ask to help you?'

He paused, breath heavy and laboured, and then a smile spread across his face.

'I am a soldier. But he is with me. We are together.'

Amber and Arthur locked eyes above his prone body, their satisfaction tangible. Marco's eyes were still closed, but I registered their look for him, basking in the beautiful reminder of how much they cared about every one of us.

'Who is he, Marco?' said Amber. 'Is he your best friend?'

'He is,' said Marco, starting to cry again. The tears were different this time, infused with more love and less pain. 'He is my best friend.'

'Your best friend,' said Arthur. 'Guys, I think we've found him!'

We all laughed, but then Marco's face contorted with a new agony.

'Don't leave me. Don't leave me behind!' he wailed.

'What's happening?' hissed Amber. 'Where is he going?' Marco's body began to jerk around, and Amber laid her hands on his legs as Arthur encased his shoulders.

'Keep talking, Marco, keep telling us where you are. We're here with you.'

'I am . . .' Marco's words were getting stuck in his throat. I could hear the terror, and I gripped Hannah's hand again. Safety and terror were fighting for me, too. *Could I really do this?* 'No!' he wailed, thrashing about. 'He's . . . he's gone from me.'

'He died, didn't he?' said Amber, quiet and sombre, as if it really was a funeral. 'You lost your best friend, at least for a time. And then he came back to find you.'

She grabbed a handful of tissues from the nearby box, handing them to the sobbing Marco.

'He was shot!' said Marco. 'He died there, in the mud. I couldn't save him!'

'You've carried a great deal, Marco,' said Arthur.

'It's no wonder life has been so hard for you,' said Amber softly, stroking his blonde crop. 'You've carried so much, this lifetime. And I think he came back to find you.'

'He did,' agreed Marco fervently. 'He came back for me.'

'But he was too young a soul to be a father,' she continued. 'He should have just been your friend.'

Marco's whole body visibly relaxed, stretching out on the couch like a cat in the sunshine. His eyes opened, a peaceful smile wrapping its way across his pretty face.

'Thank you,' he said, utterly sincere. 'You are . . .' His hands went to his heart. 'You will be here with me forever.'

Amber smiled down at him, her face pink and glowing. She wiped a tear away, gazing at Arthur with so much emotion that it was almost as if Marco was their newborn son.

'No, Marco, thank *you*,' she said. Everyone in the circle looked deeply moved. I slid across the floor towards the box of tissues: Hannah was crying in earnest, scrubbing at her cheeks with her sleeve. I landed almost at Amber's feet. She looked down at me, eyes searching me, and just for a second, I couldn't read her face.

'Toxic Mummy's Daughter,' she said. 'Are you volunteering?'

'Um . . .'

She laughed.

'Either way, I think the universe just volunteered you.' She clapped her hands authoritatively. 'We'll take a break now, discharge some of that beautiful energy. Then it's back here for Toxic Mummy's Daughter's liberation!'

Everyone cheered and grinned, and I tried to return their enthusiasm. I wanted this, I really did, but a worm of fear was crawling around my stomach, eating me from the inside. Amber would keep me safe, though, surely?

LILY

'Where did you even find Amber anyway, Mum?'

Josh's pomposity was unbearable. Once he'd realized he couldn't keep pretending the situation with Rachel was no more than a minor festive blip, he'd decided it was time to 'take control'. He was pink in the face, demanding answers, his face not unlike the one that used to look up at me as he strained on the potty. He'd insisted on ringing Rachel himself, personally outraged by the way her phone went straight to voicemail, just as it had for the past forty-eight hours for the rest of us. 'Rachel, you need to call home right now,' he'd snarled. 'Where the fuck are you?'

It was funny how easily my pride in my son – in his confident masculinity, the way he'd cut a swathe through the legal profession without breaking a sweat – had curdled into something close to repulsion. Like his father, he was so ill-equipped to find a path when life didn't cleave to his will. I'd made both of their lives far too easy for them – now we were all paying the price. Nick had driven to Rachel's flat to 'double check', even though we all knew perfectly well she wasn't there.

Sophie was still snivelling into a Kleenex, and I absently rubbed her broad back.

'Stop shouting at people, Josh!' she said. 'It's not helping. She needs us to love her. How can you still not understand that?'

I was grateful for the distraction. I was tracing back in my mind how I actually had found Amber. It was as if her name bubbled up from the ether, passed from mother to mother as the last resort. It was one of the old school mums, Deborah Madden, who'd ultimately given it to me.

Josh snorted.

'Tough love, not fucking handouts and aromatherapy. Amber must have a fucking website; she's a therapist.'

He jabbed angrily at his slab of an iPhone as I turned my attentions back to Sophie. I knew already the website wouldn't yield much. I'd tried to find her address that way, back when I'd sprung my surprise visit on her, but social media of any kind was not her style.

'Sophie, Rachel must have said something to you – anything – that gave you a clue as to where she could be.'

Sophie eyed me nervously.

'But Mum ... she's not a child. I don't know, but even if I did ...'

Rage flamed up inside me.

'Your sister is having a breakdown! Do you not understand that? She needs us – she needs her mother – more than she ever has.'

Something crossed Sophie's face – was it pity for my self-delusion? – that made me imagine my hand cracking itself hard across the soft pillows of her cheeks.

'It's a retreat, I think. They're going to work on their problems together, as a group. But I don't know where it is.' Her chin tilted upwards, defiant. 'And even if I did, I wouldn't betray her like that! She doesn't want you to know – can't you get that, Mum?'

I waited for a long second before I deigned to respond to her.

'Do you have amnesia, Sophie? Some kind of head injury you haven't told us about?'

She was wrong-footed, groping for a response.

'Mum . . .'

'Have you forgotten the past few years? What we've been through? If your sister ends up dead – choking on her own vomit or stuffed full of pills – you'll remember this moment. You'll remember choosing her delusions over my mothering. And you'll have to ask yourself, are you the reason she's in the ground?'

How quickly I could alchemize my hurt, transform it into anger and weaponize it against my own flesh and blood. I used to think it was a skill, a useful way to shepherd them through a messy, dangerous world without scaring them with my own vulnerability. With everything that's happened since, I have to wonder if it was always a curse.

RACHEL

It wasn't exactly a coffee break. Instead I took a warm, sweet cup of herbal tea from Amber and sipped it, letting it heat me from the inside.

'You've got such a deep sensitivity,' she said as she handed it to me, eyes full of concern. 'I don't want any caffeine triggering your nervous system before we do this piece of work together.'

I luxuriated in her attention, in feeling like a fragile and precious artefact that had to be handled with the utmost care.

'Thanks, Amber,' I said softly. There was a queue of people behind me waiting for their own hot drinks, and I couldn't simply stay there and bask. Instead I backed away. My heart was beating fast, even without caffeine to drive the tattoo.

Marco sat alone at the table, his eyes almost hazy. He grabbed my wrist a little too tightly as I approached.

'Get ready!' he said. We were like a circuit now, his excitement sparking through me. 'I feel incredible.'

'Do you really?' I said, keeping my voice low. I didn't want anyone to think I was being critical, but I wanted to know what I was in for. 'You seemed pretty devastated for some of that.'

'No, no,' said Marco. His words felt too loud, too quick – I could imagine exactly what he was like when he was high. 'I feel like it's all gone. It's just gone. All that, that' – his hands karate-chopped the chilly air around him – 'that shit! Just gone. My life is beginning again, just like yours will. Lucky you, Toxic Mummy's Daughter.'

A beatific grin spread across his face, like sunlight glinting on water, and hope began to flood me. Maybe what I thought was fear was pure bravery. We were Amber's warriors, and I was riding into battle. I was fighting for myself the way my family had never bothered to fight for me. They might not know my value, but here – with this random, beautiful new family I'd just discovered – I could find the unblemished me, the pristine version that existed before their twisted take on love scarred and mauled me.

I reached over, hugged Marco so tightly I could feel his heart beating against mine.

'I think you're incredible,' I whispered into his ear, as intimate as a lover.

*

'Welcome to your turn!' said Amber, as I stood by the couch. The rest of the group watched intently, their focus lifting me skyward. 'Why don't you lie down?'

'Sure,' I said, hopping up and peeling myself backwards. Arthur's dark eyes unexpectedly bored down from above.

'So!' said Amber, almost playful. 'Here you are, Toxic Mummy's Daughter. Ready for your release.'

I was shaking with fearful anticipation, my limbs quivering against the rough towelling fabric that covered the couch. I tried to reply, but the words stuck fast in my throat. I looked up at

Arthur – the face I'd decided was wise and kind – and tried to find my focus. There was a haziness that I put down to resistance. To my misplaced loyalty.

'I'm ready,' I said. Frustration welled up inside me. How incredible would it be to be free of that nagging voice, constantly telling me I was a piece of shit? 'I'm so fucking ready!'

'Amen to that!' whooped Amber. 'And are we ready to support Toxic Mummy's daughter? Are we all here beside her?'

Their voices bubbled up from the surround, full of care and love and blessings and I let myself bask in it, hot tears already starting to streak my cheeks, pain and happiness made liquid.

'Let's begin,' said Amber. Her voice dropped, her words a low incantation. 'Tell us where you're going to take us.'

Marco's story had been so dramatic, so rockstar. Drugs and danger. Would my own trauma seem pathetic and suburban by comparison? Amber picked up on my hesitation.

'Arthur. Some reiki would help here.'

And then his strong hands were cupping my head, fingers on my neck, unexpected waves of trance-like relaxation spreading through my body and giving me a burst of clarity. My reticence wasn't about whether my story was dramatic enough – it was my reluctance to betray my family, to unlock the box. And all the time I was betraying *me*. I still hadn't told Amber the whole story, because I could barely tell it to myself. The time was now.

'I was thirteen, and I was in the drama group,' I started. Drama was everywhere it seemed. 'We were doing *Top Girls*. I was the lead, Marlene.' I laughed nervously and everyone supportively laughed with me. 'Sorry, that's not really the point of this story.'

Amber stroked my arm supportively while Arthur's hands

were still wrapped around my head. Was it wrong how much I liked the feeling? How much I didn't want him to stop? My eyes met his for a split second and I glanced away.

'Mrs Farrell, our teacher who was directing it, was ill and she had to leave the rehearsal. She was pregnant and it was making her sick.'

Amber's fingers exerted a microsecond of pressure on my arm.

'So I came home. It was the middle of the day. I remember it was January and I'd borrowed Mum's leather gloves without asking and I'd lost one. I was trying to work out if I should fess up or try to find a way to replace them, but I knew I'd never be able to afford to.'

'You see', said Amber softly, 'how your mum is always your internal anchor? But all the stories you tell about her are studded with these tiny, painful battles.'

'I know,' I said, my voice high and tight now, all too aware where it was I was heading. I never spoke this out loud. 'I could hear someone was upstairs,' I said, 'even though I'd thought the house would be empty and it'd just be me, watching TV.'

I stopped again, and this time it was harder to find the path back.

'Here,' said Amber. 'Take a sip of tea. It's warming. It'll bring you back into your body.'

I sat up for a minute, reluctantly breaking the contact with Arthur. Amber held out an aluminium flask, and I took a gulp. It tasted more bitter than I expected, unlike the comfortingly sweet brew I'd had earlier. Tim grinned at me, catching my face scrunching up at the taste, and I smiled back at him, comforted by his easy warmth. I lay back down again, relieved to feel Arthur's hands wrap themselves back around my head. My focus softened and sharpened all at once.

'So I go upstairs,' I said, my voice loud in my ears now. 'And I'm thinking, she'll shout at me, but at least we'll get it over with. And anyway, there was a weird kind of satisfaction in annoying her, and not respecting all her – stuff.' A sob escaped. 'I wasn't a very nice teenager to be honest.'

'You were doing your best to navigate a deeply disturbed family,' said Amber, cutting in. 'We can all see that, even if you can't see it quite yet.'

The answering chorus of support from the circle was my rocket fuel. I was on a roll now, words tumbling out.

'I get to the landing, get to their room, and I think she must be watching TV in there. There's noise. And I don't know why, but I just open the door.' Even then, nearly twenty years later, the shock still reverberated through me, time sliced thin. 'And Dad's in the bed, and she's in there, and she's got this little blue wool dress on, but I can tell she's just pulled it over her head. I'm thinking, *You've got no knickers on, have you?* She was blushing bright red. And Dad starts covering, saying how he's got flu and Esther's brought him Nurofen, but I just ran out of the room and down the road. And . . .'

My gaze caught Amber's, the naked fury on her face catching me off guard. Her blue eyes were like chips of ice, her jaw clenched tight as if she was swallowing down something disgusting. At first it frightened me, but then I reframed it, just like she'd taught me to do. Her twisted face was a snapshot of how much she cared for me, how much my pain had become *her* pain. And that, I believed, was love.

'So I go to the Starbucks on the Uxbridge Road, and I'm

retching in the toilet, and I don't want to call anyone and tell them my dad's a bastard. And Esther's only four years older than me, and she puts my little sister to bed every night and reads her stories like she's her mum. I'm so ashamed it feels like I'm dying, like it's my sin. And then I think – I have to call Mum. And we've been fighting all the time, and I've lost her gloves, but now we're going to need each other. So . . .'

And then the sobbing overtook me, my body wracked with all of the pain and the betrayal.

'Sip some more tea,' said Amber, rubbing my back as I sat up. The group sat in the circle, eyes wide and loving. 'Tell us what happened next,' she said once my sobs had subsided. 'We're all here for you.'

I lay back down, the room slightly hazy, the woodchip wallpaper moving around like tiny, crawling bugs. Being this emotional, this bare, was a drug all of its own, it turned out.

'I don't even have a mobile phone. I have to go to this phone box that tramps piss in and hold my nose and call her. And I tell her, and I'm sobbing, and she tells me to wait, and she'll come and get me. And then . . .'

More tears – a torrent that made Hannah's squalls of emotion from the night before seem like a passing cloud. Arthur's hands cupped my head again, and for a second I sank into his touch. It was an effort to pull myself back into my story.

'I was there for two hours! She just left me there. And then she came through the door in this camel coat she had – she was so proud of that fucking coat that autumn – and even though I'd been waiting all that time, I couldn't be angry, I was just so relieved . . .'

I paused, and Amber's soft voice cut in.

'What happened, Rachel?'

'I saw her face.' I was whispering now. 'It was *me* she was angry with. It was *me* who'd done something wrong. How could I say that about Dad? How could I disrespect their marriage? But I knew.'

'Yes, you did,' agreed Amber. 'You knew the truth. And so often the truth-teller is the one that gets cast out.'

'And I had to live in that house with that stupid little bitch; it was months till she left. And all I wanted to do was get away.'

Amber's face had relaxed for a while, but now it returned to that furious twist of rage.

'She was only seventeen,' she said, her voice like a knife. 'Basically a child. You were only thirteen. Both of you needed a mother, but she just couldn't do it, could she? She couldn't show up for *either* of you.'

I knew in my heart that it was right, the sympathy that she was doling out for Esther, but I wasn't ready to share her compassion. She'd been a villain for too long for the #MeToo truth that Amber was telling to puncture my narrative. And besides, I was greedy. I wanted to suck up all the love and sympathy that was on offer.

'She just left me with it,' I sobbed, my hands intertwining with Amber's ring-laden fingers.

'And the pain had to go somewhere!' said Amber, loud and firm. 'So you turned it on yourself.'

'Dad just pretended nothing had happened,' I wailed. 'He never mentioned it again.'

'But it was your mother who actively rejected you,' Amber said. 'Who you went to for comfort, and who rejected and punished you.'

'I was so alone,' I said, the pain overwhelming me now. My

vision was blurry with tears, Amber's other disciples no more than fuzzy shapes. 'She just punished me for telling the truth.'

'I know, I know,' intoned Amber, 'so let's find out where this toxic bond first started. Then we can break it. You're doing so well. So, so well.'

Arthur started up with the soft ululating sound that came from the back of his throat, his strong hands working the bones of my shoulders.

'Where is the spirit taking you?' said Amber. 'Follow its guidance. It knows where to lead you, Rachel.'

The room was spinning again, my thoughts wisps of energy that I could barely catch. It was hard to get air deep in my lungs, my breath shallow with shock and fear. It made it so much easier to slip down the path into an imagined past, just as Marco had.

'I'm wearing a long dress,' I said, pictures starting to swim up in my brain.

'I bet,' said Arthur. 'My intuition is that you were very high status.'

'Was I?' I said, trying not to be gratified. Amber laughed indulgently, and I let myself sink deeper into the experience. 'I'm in a big room. There's a long table.'

'Who's there?' whispered Amber. 'Who's there with you, Rachel? Look around and tell us.'

The intensity of that day makes the memories indistinct, a camera flash too bright to leave a clear picture in its wake. It wasn't all suggestion, but I must have known what she wanted to hear – and she in turn must have known how well trained I was to silently intuit another person's needs and obediently fulfil them. Even now, with everything I've learnt, that knowledge still chills me to my core.

'It's a dressing table,' I said. 'I'm brushing her hair.'

'Whose hair?' said Amber, urgent.

I could almost feel the cool metal of the brush's handle in my hand, the texture of her long tresses responding to my strokes.

'I'm her lady-in-waiting,' I said.

'Lady-in-waiting?' said Amber. 'That sounds about right.'

Laughter bubbled up from the group, propelling me forwards.

'I'm scared of her,' I said, a wave of terror sweeping through me like an unexpected tide. 'I'm so scared,' I added, grabbing tightly to Amber's hand. The room was spinning again, a kaleidoscope of images.

'You're safe, Rachel. We've got you. Keep telling us what you see. What's she done to frighten you? To make you feel so vulnerable?'

'I made her angry . . .'

Amber's voice was an intense growl.

'Why is she so angry, Rachel?'

Tears were streaming down my face again, my breath tight in my throat. I was lightheaded. I tried to feel the solidity of the couch beneath my shaking body.

'I wronged her.' My language was changing. 'I betrayed her trust.'

'How?' demanded Amber. 'How did you betray her, Rachel?' Her voice dropped lower. 'And how is she going to punish you?'

A moan escaped from my mouth, my limbs thrashing around on the couch. This time Amber didn't move to comfort me.

'She betrayed him. Then I betrayed her.' It felt so real, my mind a cinema screen. I could see her eyes in the mirror, the rage that burnt in them. 'I told him. I forsook her.'

'And then she destroyed you!' said Amber. 'My own body's

burning up now.' She looked out to the group. 'I can feel it right through me – your fear, your rage.' I could hear her above me, taking great big gulps of air. 'It feels like I'm choking.' A strange howl came from her, almost animal. 'Don't hurt her!'

My body felt like it was nothing more than a streak of fear. I didn't know who was howling now, me or her.

'I think she hurt you very badly,' Amber said, voice low and guttural.

'I died at her hand,' I said. It was so strange, the way my syntax was changing without any effort from me.

'I can see it,' said Amber. 'You're in darkness, *so cold*.' Her whole body was swaying now, like branches buffeted by wind, her voice a piercing sing song. 'It's a dark cell, and you're all alone.'

As she said it, I started to see it, her stories becoming mine. Her hands dove for my heart, kneading my trembling body. Arthur's hands were around my head again.

'I don't want to die,' I wailed, not sure where the words even came from.

'Leave her now!' she demanded. 'I command you to leave her.'

My sobbing had reached fever pitch, my whole body convulsing. Was this why my life had been so hard? Some twisted sacred contract with the woman who was meant to love me more than anyone, but hated me on some level too deep and primal for either of us to even know about?

The pain welled up, exploded, and finally enveloped me in its blackness.

*

I could hear sounds, but it was hard to identify them. My eyelids reluctantly strained open, Hannah swimming into vision above me.

'Where am I?' I said.

'You're tucked up in bed,' she said, smiling contentedly. 'Amber says you need to rest. You were so brave – I was really proud of you.' She ducked down to floor level. 'Here, I brought you a cup of tea. Builders, two sugars. I thought you needed something stronger than chamomile!'

I sat up in bed, my head knocking against the cold wall, and took the mug from her hands. My temples were thudding with pain.

'How did I even get here?' I asked. Outside the small window above my bed, the sky was inky black.

Hannah paused a second, nervously licking her cracked lips, and then recovered herself.

'You . . . I think you tried so hard it got too much. Everything just had to be purged, Rachel! Amber says we can call you that again, because you've shed it all!'

She flung her hands up as she said it, the phrase so clearly Amber's, not her own.

'What do you mean, too much?' I said, my body spiky with panic. 'How long have I been out for?'

Hannah hesitated again.

'You kind of . . . it was like you needed to rest. And then you did. Your body had so much wisdom!'

'I blacked out?'

'Kind of.' She lunged towards me, gripping both my hands in hers. 'You went on the most incredible journey.' Her eyes were wet with tears now. 'I was . . . I was humbled, watching you. And now you're free!'

It wasn't just my head that throbbed; my left side felt bruised and tender. The story was starting to come back to me in fragments – the raging woman, the dark, dank cell that I'd perished in, a shape-shifting version of my own mother responsible. I think I must have made a lightning decision in that moment, lying in that tiny bedroom – a cell of another kind – that I'd paid so much to lock myself into. I couldn't afford to burn down another structure. To leave myself all alone in the wreckage. For now, I had to believe that this was home. That these were people I could find shelter with, a family I'd chosen at least for now. I smiled back at Hannah.

'How about you?' I said, squeezing her hand. 'How was your turn?'

Her eyes shone brightly.

'Oh my God, it was amazing. I feel amazing!'

I can barely remember the details of Hannah's story, only my sense of shame that she – and the others according to her garbled account – had all managed such ecstatic rebirths whilst mine had felt like something closer to an exorcism. As her words washed over me, I had a visceral image of my siblings, of Sophie most of all, ringed around the kitchen table with our parents, wine glasses brimming and paper hats wonky and crumpled, Christmas gently seeping away. Would it always be me who prowled the edges of any group, pitiful and difficult?

How easily I tortured myself back then; it's not surprising that I'd conjured up a cell when I'd been invited to let my imagination run riot. It would take a long time to set myself free.

LILY

Two hours elapsed before Nick finally came back through the door. We were trying to vaguely approximate Christmas by then – I was stirring gravy and drinking more white wine than was strictly advisable, all the time being sickly sweet to the children that I still had some modicum of control over to try to redeem myself for my earlier behaviour. *Was this what it was like for Rachel?* I thought, tipping another generous measure into my glass, hidden behind the door of the fridge that was so big it wouldn't have been out of place in a morgue. I giggled to myself, unsure if it was funny or morbid, then emerged with a respectable inch left in the bottom. It turned out taking the edge off wasn't such a bad option.

'Where were you?' I said as Nick stepped into the kitchen in his excessively youthful yellow puffer jacket, grim-faced. Lucky for him, my blunted edges were preventing me from imagining any lurid crimes he'd committed, the kind that would require silent punishment. Which came first, the chicken or the egg?

'She's not there,' he said.

'I think we've already established that, haven't we?' I said, looking at Sophie, who had been nervously circling me all afternoon, finding jobs to do. Currently she was scoring a mound of sprouts like it was an Olympic sport. Josh had lost interest and retreated into his own nuclear family, who were gathered around the TV, watching ear-shatteringly loud American cartoons. At the sound of his father's voice, he strode back through.

'Yeah, I got that,' Nick said tersely. I'd sent him an update after Sophie's confession, but I hadn't told him how low a blow I'd struck. It wasn't as if I was without shame: I was aware of my own bad behaviour, not the psychopathic monster that I've been made out to be by some parties. 'So I looked around the flat to see if I could find an address for where that silly cow's taken her . . .'

'Dad!' said Sophie sharply. 'Rachel's not been abducted. She's an adult. Why do you even have a key? You don't have the right—'

I held up a hand to silence her.

'Did you find anything else?' I asked. Sophie was looking livid now. 'Darling, we're the parents of a sick child,' I said, laying that same hand on her arm in an attempt to calm her. 'Of course we have a key.'

'Just these . . . lying on the table.' Nick pulled out a sheaf of papers from inside his jacket. I could see they were credit card statements, row after row of purchases running down the pages. 'Flat looks like a jumble sale too, clothes all over the floor.'

'Hardly a news flash, Dad,' said Josh, with a patronizing laugh. 'She's always been a disaster with money.'

'Christ, Josh, stop digging at her!' said Sophie, flushed with anger.

'I went through them,' said Nick. In the pub, I assessed – I was close enough to smell the sour undercurrent of whisky on his breath. But then, who was I to judge? He paused a second, his usual confident ease drained out of him like an empty juice carton. 'This woman – who the hell is she, Lily? Look at this.' He thrust the top page towards me. 'Two thousand pounds to Wild Swan Health – that's got to be this fucking retreat, hasn't it? And she owes two hundred quid in interest, just this month alone.'

'Jesus,' said Josh. 'Where did you find her, Mum? We might need to start getting legal. It's fraud, isn't it?'

Sophie looked stricken, but this time I held my tongue, avoided pointing out that everything I'd presumed about the healing properties of this 'retreat' was proven true already.

'Enough is enough,' I said, righteous anger restoring my clarity. 'She's underestimated our family, the strength of our bond.' I gripped hold of Sophie's hand, then took Nick's. 'She's underestimated how much we love our daughter. If she wants to fight us, she's a fool. We'll destroy her.'

Josh and Sophie had joined hands too now, the circle complete but for one vital link. I couldn't let another woman win.

I never had before.

RACHEL

The atmosphere was different that night – almost febrile, the kinetic energy of our sessions translated into something more bacchanalian. The pine table was already littered with half-empty bottles, music pumping out of tinny portable speakers.

'Rachel!' cried Amber, as I tentatively pushed my way into the kitchen. She rushed over to me, enveloped me in a fug of smells – perfume, alcohol, tobacco. She felt off duty – for all my fantasies about us being best friends, it made me prickle with unease. I banished the sensation, doubled down on its opposite, leaning my body into hers. I was starving, ravenous for comfort. It's funny how our addictions shape-shift, leave us just as craven but for a different kind of drug.

I could sense Arthur even when I couldn't see him – right now he was sitting at the table, deep in conversation with Joanna. Sometimes I felt like he didn't look at me on purpose, let the tension build up before allowing it to break at a time of his choosing. I gripped the top of one of the hard wooden chairs, trying to conceal how shaky my limbs felt.

'Welcome, *bella*!' said Marco. 'Come and sit with me.' I gratefully sunk down into the seat next to him. 'You okay?' I nodded, not quite trusting myself to speak. 'You did . . .' He kissed his fingers, grinned. 'You are an amazing person; I have to tell you this.'

I couldn't help but preen a bit.

'Thanks, Marco.' It was me who enveloped him this time: the chain of endless physical intimacy, meaningful and meaningless all at once, could not afford to be broken. Over his shoulder, coming into the room, I spotted Tim. The look on his face brought me up short, drained away the warm glow of congratulation that I'd been basking in. What was it I could see etched into his expression? Was it disapproval or something worse? He must have seen the flash of shame in my eyes, because he hastily rearranged his features and gave me a smile that didn't catch light. My body was cold now: I felt as if I'd seen a ghost, and perhaps that ghost was me.

Amber tapped on a wine glass, breaking the moment. Once we were silent, she left a dramatic pause.

'*Well* . . .' she said eventually. 'Today was . . .' Was she choking up? 'You were there, guys, you don't need me to tell you. You were like, like . . . a firework display!' She was flushed, her hands whirling, eyes alight. 'You shot up into the universe, transcended every fucking thing that you've been put through and claimed your new lives. And I . . .' She put a hand on her heart, thin fingers splayed across the pale flesh that was left exposed by the low scoop of her black dress. I looked at Arthur unconsciously – he wasn't looking at her, his eyes were instead trained on me. 'I am so honoured to have played a small part in each of your liberations. Let's drink to that!'

As the table erupted into a noisy toast, Marco leapt to his feet.

'I looove this woman,' he declared. He looked around at all of us. 'Guys, we love her, right? Time for a standing ovation!'

Now everyone was on their feet, roaring and thumping the table. I stood too, legs shaky, the noise reverberating through my bruised body. When I felt a strong hand on the small of my back, I gratefully leant into its pressure.

'It's too much for you right now, isn't it?' said Arthur, his voice low and comfortingly authoritative. 'You went deeper than anyone, I think. Come and sit in the living room and catch your breath before supper.'

*

'Heroin,' said Arthur cheerfully. 'I don't recommend it. I easily lost a decade.'

We'd been sitting in the lounge for twenty minutes now, the conversation flowing with an ease I hadn't necessarily expected. The massage table had been cleared away, a few scattered cushions the only remnants of the traumas of the day. Arthur had found a scratchy blanket and put it around my shoulders. Did I imagine it, or had his hands lingered longer than necessary as he swaddled me in it?

'Heroin?' I repeated.

'Have you never tried it?'

It was quite nice, not being the biggest sinner for once. It was also nice to be distracted from my gnawing dread at the prospect of real life imminently smacking me in the face once the retreat ended. There was only one day left.

'No!' I said. 'I don't mean to be insulting, but it's kind of a posh boy thing.'

Arthur roared with laughter, then fixed me with a twinkly gaze, the laugh still dancing across his handsome face.

'You're probably right. Jesus, I'm such a cliché. Brought up by nanny, sent to boarding school as a snot-nosed eight-year-old, and then I'm shooting up when I'm barely out of short trousers.'

'I don't mean to take the piss,' I told him. 'You did really well. Surviving it, kicking the habit. I hope ... well, I hope I manage it.'

I could feel it for a second, my cheekbone on the cold London pavement back in October, the paramedic kneeling on the ground, his face swimming into vision. Then my eyes locked on the thin beige carpet, where my body had slammed to the ground earlier. I couldn't remember much beyond that moment – the moment when the darkness of what Mum had done to me fully eclipsed the light. My breath jammed in my throat, panic building. Was this really what liberation was meant to feel like?

Arthur didn't seem to notice; there was a faraway look in his eye as his chunky fingers played with the neck of his wine glass. I forced a gulp of air into my lungs.

'You can only attend so many funerals before you start doing the maths,' he said eventually. 'Besides, by the time I got clean I'd left quite the trail of destruction.' He counted down his crimes. 'I'd been disinherited, divorced, I was unemployable ... It's a sorry old laundry list, Rachel. If you don't mind, I think I'll stop there.' He gave that smile again, the smile of a man who'd spent a lifetime revelling in the effect he had on women. 'The fact is, you're far too good at drawing out my most grisly secrets.'

'Just to be clear, I charge eighty pounds a session,' I said, holding his gaze and flipping my palm outwards. This was another kind of muscle memory for me. It was probably the most dangerous addiction of all, but its ability to numb the pain, even briefly, was second to none. Arthur leaned forward, his fingertips momentarily spiralling across the circle of bare flesh I'd offered up to him.

'You're selling yourself short,' he said softly.

There was truth to that statement, and we both knew it. Neither of us spoke, both of us waiting for the silence to break.

'There you are!' said Amber, the sharpness of her tone puncturing the quiet. She'd crept into the room, was watching us. How long had she been there? I slid my body backwards across the sofa, instantly guilty.

'Well, hello!' said Arthur, with none of my unease. 'We were just about to come and hunt down supper. This one needed a moment to clear her head after the emotional marathon she ran earlier.'

Amber didn't speak immediately, too busy scanning the picture that we painted together. I cringed under the weight of her gaze, the disappointment she must surely be feeling in me. I was here to be healed by her, not to trash her generosity of spirit by indulging my very worst impulses.

'It's on the table,' she said, clipped. Then she crossed to the sofa, unexpectedly wrapping my head against her belly. 'If you were struggling, you only had to come and find me, you silly girl,' she cooed, her fingers tangling themselves up in my hair. 'I'm the one you should come to when it hurts too much. I thought you knew that by now.'

'I'm sorry,' I muttered, my words lost in the cocoon of fabric and flesh that she'd pushed me into, my face suddenly wet with tears. My nostrils filled with the smell of her – not with that familiar, sophisticated spritz of rose that she always wore, but with something more primal, more dangerous. A musk that was entirely Amber's own.

*

Dinner was full of predictable compliments and toasts. I surfed the warmth of it, gratefully let the group energy carry me, but I didn't have the spirit to jump in feet first. 'Are you alright?' mouthed Hannah, my faithful companion, and I nodded a solemn yes. She was sitting further up the table, snuggling close to Marco, failing at any kind of romantic subterfuge. I couldn't help fearing for her – her appeal here, in this febrile intensity, would be very different when it was transplanted to a Eurotrash bar at the far end of the Fulham Road. Or maybe it wouldn't; maybe I was simply a cynic.

Meanwhile I'd gone back to avoiding Arthur's gaze, determined to eat a respectable amount of my vegetarian chilli – the hard kidney beans like lumps of shrapnel – and take my thumping head to bed. Why couldn't I inhale the fairy dust of the day that seemed to have left everyone else so gloriously high? They all felt brimming with festive cheer, what with their overflowing glasses and euphoric chatter, whereas I was truly the grinch that stole Christmas. I got up and walked to the far end of the kitchen, intending to brew myself another cup of ginger tea. As the kettle dinged, Tim appeared beside me.

'Are you okay, Rachel?' he said, face serious.

'Yeah, no. I'm fine, just tired,' I said, trying for breezy. 'It was a big day for all of us.'

'Yeah, but . . .' He watched me, some internal struggle taking place. It was starting to irritate me.

'What is it, Tim? Did my head spin on my neck or something? It's all a bit blurry at the end. What happened?'

He raised a smile.

'It was just – I was worried about you, Rachel. Medically. I actually put you in the recovery position when you were on the ground.'

'What do you mean?' I asked, panic starting to rise back up.

Tim cocked his head, his eyes kind. I could tell in that second how lucky his patients were to have him.

'It didn't feel right . . .' he started, but before he could finish Amber had sailed up behind us.

'Rachel's the queen of secret squirrel huddles this evening!' she said, putting an arm around each of us. 'Come back and enjoy the party. The family's missing you!'

I grabbed at the scarf around my neck, a little piece of my sister. Perhaps if I wandered every corner of the house, I could find a glimmer of signal and send her a text.

'I'm going to go to bed, I think,' I said, smiling an apology. I couldn't let Tim's words sink in too deeply – perhaps sleep would erase their ability to permeate. A flash of annoyance crossed Amber's face. 'I'm exhausted,' I said apologetically. 'I want to really enjoy our last day. Our last chance to all be together.' How seamlessly I rolled it out – not people-pleasing, but mummy-pleasing.

She gracefully smiled her assent. 'You do that, darling girl,' she said.

'Night, everyone,' I said, avoiding Tim's gaze and risking a tiny smile in Arthur's direction. His look back at me lingered, but I turned away before it could start to spark.

*

I brushed my teeth methodically in the tiny shared bathroom, taking comfort in the mundane familiarity of the task. There

190

was a vaguely sewage-y smell which I could only endure so long, and I crossed the narrow corridor to mine and Hannah's monastic cell, goosebumps covering my naked flesh as I pulled on my pyjamas. I put the light out, waiting for sleep to blanket me, but instead I simply lay there, my heart beating too fast, my brain swirling with images. It was like a strange kind of vertigo – Mum's face merging with the queenly tormentor of my fantasy, who according to Amber wasn't even a fantasy. Loneliness delivered a gut punch. Who would ever sympathize with this terrifying hall of mirrors? If I told Sophie that Mum and I had travelled through time, her torturing me through the ages, she'd think I'd completely lost it, but the absurdity of it didn't make it feel any less visceral: if anything, it made it feel more real, harder to dispute with cold logic. The only person who could possibly understand me now was Amber.

When the light tap on the door came, I was lost in a spiral of anxiety about the debt mountain I'd been ignoring. What if Mum's newest strike was to take away the life support of Amber? Would I even survive it?

'Hello?' I called, and Arthur poked his head around the door. I sat up in bed, hugging my knees, a wave of self-protection sweeping over me.

'Sorry, sorry, did I wake you up?' he said, smiling down at me, his chiselled features illuminated by the yellowy light from the hall. I prayed he wouldn't put on the main light and see my puffy, make-up-free face under the harsh glare of the bare bulb. Jesus – how was it that, even in the midst of a transformational retreat, I was still hanging onto my desire for a man to only see me at my most perfect? Would I be applying an extra layer of lipstick in a nuclear apocalypse?

'Nope,' I said, unwinding myself and smiling back at him. 'I couldn't sleep.'

'Thought as much,' said Arthur, crossing the threshold and landing heavily on the end of the saggy single bed. 'I didn't want to abandon you.'

'You didn't abandon me,' I said. The verbal volley was so seamless between us.

'So, how's Rachel?' he said, putting a hand on the mound my calves created under the thin duvet. I paused for a second, resisting the desire to trot out another slick reply.

'Terrible? Wonderful? I'm not sure I can tell anymore,' I said, my teeth starting to chatter. It wasn't the cold, or at least it wasn't *only* the cold.

'Oh, sweetheart,' he said, his hand stroking my legs through the fabric. I couldn't tell if it was the comfort you'd give to a frightened animal or the first move in a seduction. My bare face combined with the bare room made the second option seem almost outlandish. Neither of us spoke, each assessing the other's state of mind in a sticky kind of silence. There was a second where I was ready to pull back, the moonlight illuminating the deep lines on his face, telling part of the story about how predatory this was, how inappropriate. Eventually I let my eyes meet his, holding his gaze, and he accepted the invitation. Or at least that was how I interpreted it in the moment – now I wonder how much choice I had in any of it. His mouth was on mine in a millisecond, his beard rubbing my raw skin. I clutched at him, craving another heartbeat now the choice had been made, my body cleaving against his. After a couple of minutes, he broke away.

'I don't know about you,' he muttered, 'but my patience for

getting amorous in single beds wore rather thin after my first year at university. Would you be open to taking this upstairs?'

'Upstairs?' I said, unwilling to let go of him now the space between us had been breached. It was always like that back then – ambivalence would turn to obsession in the blink of an eye.

'Yes. Without meaning to throw shade on your digs, my room's a smidge more palatial than this,' he said, casting a look of wry amusement around the grim bedroom.

'Okay,' I said, swinging my bare feet down onto the carpet.

Arthur grinned. 'Hold your horses, partner,' he said. 'Let's employ a bit of subtlety. I'll go first. Give it five minutes and then take the stairs at the end of the landing. I'm the first door on the left.' He must have sensed my unease. 'Don't worry, Amber's sleeping in the stables in the grounds. They're even nicer.'

How subtly he made off with all the power, and how easily I gifted it to him. It still gives me a shot of shame, even though intellectually I know I did nothing wrong.

*

The truth is, most of that night remains a blur, despite the police reports that lay out the facts. I remember that the sense of shock far outweighed the sense of pleasure when I first felt him inside my body, his bulk pressing down on me. I remember, too, how little of the shock I let him see – my priority was making him feel like a conquering hero. I conjured up the right noises, the right dialogue, that completely obliterated my authentic experience of being with him. It wasn't even that he was unskilled as a lover, but I was in no fit state to receive his well-practised moves. It's funny how I simultaneously knew everything and nothing about how to handle men. The truth is, I knew everything about how to squeeze the most out of men who had nothing to give.

When I woke, the early morning sky was the colour of sour milk. Arthur was sitting on the side of the large, ornate wooden bed, his bare back and butt crack exposed to me. I felt a reverb of shock at his nakedness, at the memory of everything that had happened to me in the past twenty-four hours. He stood up, not looking over.

'Arthur?'

He turned, his smile on a slight time delay.

'Good morning, angel. I'm just going to hop in the shower.'

He directed an awkward thumb towards the en-suite, then crossed the room, everything exposed. I lay there, pulling the sheet around my own nakedness, unsure whether to scramble into the checked pyjamas that were strewn across the floor. I decided against it – surely I wanted him to come back and be overcome with lust, not blindsided by the knowledge that drunkenness meant he'd accidentally seduced Paddington?

I needn't have worried. He came back in with a towel around his waist and began pulling on his clothes. He cast a rueful glance in my direction.

'I'm sorry to have to rush off like this,' he said. 'I mean, it's hardly the venue for it, but I'd love nothing more than to spend the day with you.'

I sat up against the bank of plump pillows, the white sheet forming an odd kind of bridal gown.

'Where are you going?' I asked, trying to prevent my voice morphing into a whine.

'Didn't I tell you yesterday? I'm taking my sons skiing. I've got to pick them up from their mum's this afternoon.'

I wasn't even aware he had sons, and I knew it was the kind of detail I'd have retained, even in my fragile state. After all, I'd been compiling an internal dossier on him ever since we'd met. It was one of my romantic tics – knowledge was power, and my power was always in short supply.

'No, you didn't,' I said flatly.

Arthur paused. He had his jeans on now, his broad chest still bare. He came towards me, leaning down to kiss me. I kept my mouth firmly closed, scared of my morning breath destroying any scrap of attraction he might still feel. My warped thinking meant that, despite all the indicators that he was more than wrong for me, I had to keep him locked in at any cost.

'You're so lovely, Rachel. Thank you for last night. It was . . .' His dark eyes stared down at me. 'It was incredibly intimate, wasn't it?'

Yes and no.

'Yes,' I agreed, holding his gaze.

'And I'd very much like to see you again. I'll call you when I'm back from Val D'Isere. Make a plan.'

'Okay,' I said, smiling back at him. 'Have a fantastic time.'

Within a few minutes he was gone. I lay there, marooned in the wide bed, weaving myself an elaborate fairy tale about him. About us. And I almost believed it, because I had to keep running now. Looking back was way too dangerous.

LILY

Boxing Day felt almost respectable – a hint of desperate, but not too exposing for us. I closeted myself away in Rachel's bedroom, long since repurposed. I had an exercise bike in there by then, shelves full of box files and oatmeal-painted walls, but I imagined I could still see the shadow of the Blu-tack she'd used to stick up her endless Spice Girls posters. It used to infuriate me, the way it left greasy marks on the paintwork, but now she was out of reach, every aspect of her, every memory, seemed like a precious artefact.

I shook myself out of my pointless reverie and called Deborah Madden. We were school mum friends back in the day, now relegated to the occasional 'girls night out' as our gang still tragically framed such things, despite the fact we were well into the age of HRT cream and compulsory Spanx.

'Are you okay, Lily?' she asked after the opening niceties. Something in the lilt of her voice infuriated me, made me feel I'd given my distress away. Was I imagining it, or was the implied question whether or not I was treating myself to a post-Christmas divorce? Nick and Josh had headed out first thing for a game of squash. I knew exactly where my husband was.

'We're great,' I said firmly. 'More grandchildren than we know what to do with, and the whole house still reeking of turkey. How was yours?'

'Oh, you know,' she said, weary. 'It's hard work, isn't it?'

'It is,' I agreed, 'but so nice to have an excuse to have the whole family together.'

'Yes.'

The pause stretched out elastically down the phone line. I had to dive in.

'I wanted to ask you ... Do you remember, we were having a few problems with Rachel?' Deborah's daughter Olivia was a contemporary of Sophie's, so Rachel was less familiar to her. 'And you passed on a number for Amber Greville, that therapist?'

'Oh yes, of course,' she said. 'How *is* Rachel?'

'She's great,' I said, words almost overlapping hers, then instantly regretted the way I'd boxed myself in. 'But we wanted to learn a little bit more about Amber. Qualifications, you know.' I gave a brittle little laugh that rung in my ears like I imagined tinnitus might. 'I mean, you wouldn't buy driving lessons for your kids from a random bloke in a Skoda. I just want to reassure myself she's the real deal and she doesn't have much detail on her website.'

'But Rachel's doing better, it sounds like?'

'Yes.' I stared at the willow tree that grew outside the square window, its branches blowing about in the wind, trying to force down my impatience. 'I just wanted to know where you found out about her. Do you know anyone who's actually been treated by her?'

Deborah gave an irritating laugh.

'Trip Advisor reviews, that kind of thing? I don't think Amber quite works like that. You're lucky you got Rachel in to see her. She's pretty selective. I nearly didn't even bother giving you the number.'

'Have you, or any of your family and friends, ever been treated by Amber Greville?' I said, my words staccato.

I heard Deborah inhale. There were a couple of years we were on the PTA together – she was hopelessly indecisive as I recall, always leaving me to steer the ship while she flapped about 'considering all angles'. Stay-at-home mothers are woefully inefficient in my experience.

'My niece was struggling with anorexia,' she said. 'I'd say Amber brought her back to the light. She's thriving now; she'll be graduating from Exeter this year.'

Back to the light. Somebody had most certainly drunk Amber's sickening Kool-Aid.

'Right. And would her parents agree with that assessment, do you think?'

Another testy pause.

'What are you actually getting at, Lily?' snapped Deborah. 'I'm happy to help you, but you have to tell me what it is you need. We all like Amber very much – she actually saw Olivia briefly too, after she graduated – but she's unconventional. Maybe you'd be happier with someone who's more by the book.'

So, it was my lack of bohemian free spirit that had landed me in this mess?

'Forget it,' I snapped. 'You've been very helpful already. Thanks again.'

Before I hung up, Deborah got in her parting shot.

'Amber might not be right for you, but it sounds like she's right for Rachel. Don't you think that's what matters, Lily?'

The two things were one and the same, but no one gives me credit for having known that. Not even now.

RACHEL

Eventually I got myself out of the wide bed, treating myself to a hot blast in Arthur's en-suite shower, then crept downstairs, thinking about what was I going to say to Hannah. I needn't have worried. Her clothes were still strewn across her bed, muddy trainers upside down on the carpet where they'd lain the night before. As I pulled my jeans on, she reappeared. She was pinker than ever, a coy look on her face.

'Sorry, roomie!' she said, giggling. 'I got a bit distracted last night.' Then her expression turned serious. 'Were you worried about me? I'm sorry, Rachel, I should've been more thoughtful.'

Her intensity was infuriating and endearing in equal parts. How much did she really think I cared about her, forty-eight hours into our relationship?

'I did at first, but then I figured you were probably having fun. *Were* you having fun?'

Hannah flopped dramatically onto my bed like a Victorian wench with a fit of the vapours.

'Rachel, everything Amber said is coming true! I know it sounds ridiculous, but ... I know you'll understand.'

'Tell me,' I said, turning towards her. I felt very old in that moment, my body still bruised and sore, the sources multiplying.

'New me. New life. I don't know. I just felt these incredible connections from when I first got here. You, Marco.' Uttering his name triggered a whole new crimson bloom in her cheeks. 'Last night was – I don't think I've ever made love before, you know? Not truly.'

'Wow, things are moving fast,' I said hypocritically.

'Are they, though?' said Hannah, dreamy. 'We know from yesterday that time's just an illusion. I wouldn't be surprised if Marco and I have known each other through many, many lifetimes.'

A flash of Mum's face in that nightmarish incarnation. It was too visceral, too real. I couldn't stay there.

'So, do you think it's your diamond anniversary?' I asked.

Hannah looked put out. 'He *is* a diamond, I know that. I think I had my first ever full-body orgasm last night.' She giggled again. 'Is it okay that I'm telling you this?'

Why was I judging her? Which of us was really the fool?

'That's amazing,' I said, the hug I gave her a real one. 'Now go and brush your teeth. You're definitely in need of breakfast.'

*

'No Arthur today, I'm afraid,' Amber announced to the break-fast table. 'He's got a family emergency.' Was it my imagination, or was she watching for my reaction? I kept my face deliberately neutral. Surely skiing wasn't an emergency? Perhaps he'd lied to her. 'This last day should be all about relaxing,' she continued. 'Our very own family Christmas! Board games. Country walks. Let's give all your hard work a chance to process and embed.'

I joined in the cheers and thanks that greeted anything Amber said or did and tried to give myself over to the day. At least now I wasn't constantly monitoring the state of play between me and Arthur. Of course I would have liked a 'morning after' text from him, but even if he had sent one, the terrible signal would probably have stopped it arriving. It was a useful excuse to give myself; he'd made it quite clear he wouldn't be bothering to get in touch till after his trip. It should have told me everything – it probably did – but there was only so much truth I could handle.

The day slipped by easily enough. A late breakfast morphed into lunch, and a game of Monopoly stretched into the afternoon. Around three we went for a long walk in the nearby woods, my trainers quickly turning out to be more suited to the London streets than a rural mud bath. As I scraped them against a tree, Tim caught up to me. I'd been semi avoiding him, still embarrassed about how out of control I must have been for him to react the way he did, but now he was apologetic.

'I'm sorry, Rachel,' he said, winter sun illuminating the bald dome of his intelligent face. 'I was overthinking it.'

'Don't apologize,' I said. 'I appreciate you caring.'

'No, no,' he said, frustrated. With me? With him? 'It sounds stupid, but I'm so used to being treated like this wise guru at work. I need to learn to let go. Give myself over to spirit.'

That phrase really didn't sound like the Tim I'd got to know these past few days. I chided myself – that was the point. He was allowing himself to be transformed.

'Yeah, me too,' I agreed. 'I really need to get better at surrendering.'

'I don't know about that,' he said, 'you did pretty well

yesterday', setting off a new wave of paranoia about what I'd been reduced to. I pushed it away, linking my arm through his.

'So did you,' I said, giving my muddy trainers a scrape through the thick carpet of leaves that we were standing on. The sun was getting lower, the day closing in around us like a dark cloak. I shivered. 'Let's keep moving. I'm freezing.'

*

'Come with. Please come with!'

It was the next day, and Hannah and I were packing our bags, readying ourselves to leave. We'd had a final, centring chant around the kitchen table and already said our goodbyes to Joanna and Tim. I should've booked my cab ages ago, but it was as if my feet were submerged in glue.

'Don't be crazy,' I said. 'It'll be romantic, that whole long drive home. Just the two of you. Singing Christmas songs, snogging at the lights.'

Hannah giggled, flushing.

'You're so funny, Rachel. I'm really going to miss you.' Her expression turned earnest. 'Not that I'll have to. We're all a family now. We'll see each other all the time, won't we?'

'Of course,' I said. The word 'family' made me shiver. No wonder my feet were stuck to the ground.

'And we're all in it together,' added Hannah. 'So you don't really have a choice!'

I didn't want to be alone, it was true, and soon I was squashed in the back of Marco's sporty little Alfa Romeo, our piled-up luggage holding me fast.

'Are you sure you're okay in the back?' said Hannah, swivelling her face around to look at me.

'I'm fine, it's great,' I said, and I wasn't lying. There was something so comforting, so childlike, about being stowed away like this. It was almost as if Marco and Hannah were my new parents.

I'd clung to Amber when I'd said goodbye, suddenly overwhelmed with guilt about my secret night with Arthur. I felt like I'd abused her trust, damaged the sanctity of what she'd created. It didn't make sense, particularly considering how open Marco and Hannah were being, but then, nothing made sense. 'Darling girl,' she'd said, wrapping me tightly in her arms. 'You did so well. I know you're hurting, but I promise we'll keep unlocking you from her now.' Her voice dropped low. 'You're free,' she whispered, intimate. 'If only you can start believing it.'

'Okay *bellas*,' said Marco, starting the engine with an extravagant flick of the key. 'We're heading back to the future.'

Could I? Could I start believing it? Hannah started cheering, still high on life, and I added my own more muted round of applause. Then I tucked my knees up on the seat beneath me and looked out of the window, distracting myself with the bleak winter beauty of the countryside. It wasn't long before the beeping began, my phone throbbing with messages as soon as signal crept up on us.

'Remember, you don't have to look if you don't want to,' commanded Hannah from the front, but I could only ignore the relentless alerts for so long. Besides, I wanted to know if Arthur had missed me enough to message me. Nothing from him of course, just endless messages from my family. I tried to concentrate on the communication from Sophie, but the chain of texts from Mum was too awful to swerve.

They started out sweet – *We miss you, please come home*

xx type vibes, but then the anger started to build. *We KNOW you're with Amber. We need you to come back. This cannot continue,* read one. I felt sick to my stomach – had Sophie really betrayed me like this? I yanked off her scarf, which was still wound around my neck like it had been all of Christmas, and carried on reading. *How can you let me worry about you like this? If you were a mother you would never do this to me.* On and on they went, blaming and angry, full of poison. There were multiple messages from Sophie too – Mum had forced it out of her, she claimed, but please could I ring home? I read the final text from Mum, even though I knew it would fell me. *Your relationship with Amber is over,* it said. Nothing more.

'Sorry, guys,' I said, the hand that was holding the phone to my ear shaking uncontrollably. 'I have to call my sister.'

She answered on the second ring.

'How could you tell her?' I demanded.

'Rachel I'm sorry, but . . . we've all been so worried. I couldn't keep lying to her. You know what she's like.'

'So you lied to me instead? I trusted you!'

'Rachel,' she said, voice sharper than I could ever remember it. 'We've all had a shitty Christmas because of this. I'm sorry I told her, but if you'd been honest with them in the first place, it wouldn't all be such a mess.'

'This isn't a fucking Christmas film, Sophie. It's not like if I'd been honest, she'd have waved me off with a box of crackers. It's Mum. She's a bitch.'

I'd surprised myself with my own venom. I guess I was practising radical honesty, just like Amber counselled. I could tell Sophie – my sweet, soft little sister – was too shocked to reply right away.

205

'A bitch who's been bankrolling you while you have some kind of self-inflicted breakdown?' she said eventually. 'I don't know – why don't you try thinking about the way you've been treating all of us, rather than dishing it out?'

'So you're taking her side now?' I said.

'You're the one who's turned it into a competition,' Sophie snapped.

'You don't understand . . . I've been protecting you,' I pleaded. 'Because I love you so much. But it's not helping any of us. You need to hear the truth now.'

'I can't do this again,' she said, voice breaking, and then there was silence. She'd hung up.

I sat there for a few seconds in shock, the phone still held to my ear as if she might ring back and apologize, before bursting into noisy tears.

'Oh my God!' wailed Hannah, gesturing to Marco to pull the car over. 'Your family are so horrible to you.'

Soon she'd wedged herself alongside me in the back, luggage piled so high around us that Marco could barely see to drive, staying there with me most of the way home. 'This is why we need each other,' she said solemnly. 'We have to be each other's mirrors, the way Amber is for all of us.'

I let my head rest against her broad bulk, the odd sob erupting unbidden. Hannah stroked my hair, made soothing noises: it was a reversal of roles that the superior version of me from Christmas Eve would never have believed possible. Eventually I let myself feel safe enough to fall asleep, leaning heavily against her, the real world temporarily blotted out.

*

It was gone nine by the time Marco pulled his car to a stop outside my flat. I looked up with trepidation, jealous of the fact that the two of them would be curled up like one life form as they came down from the intensity of the workshop. But then trepidation gave way to something far worse.

There was a light burning brightly in my living room. Someone was waiting for me to come home.

LILY

I know I did the right thing that night, whatever anyone says. The right thing isn't always the popular thing.

Ask anyone who's fought as hard as me for justice.

RACHEL

Hannah and Marco insisted on coming upstairs with me. 'What if it's burglars?' said Hannah, but I knew it wouldn't be. Was an emotional terrorist better or worse than someone rifling through my unimpressive collection of high-street jewellery? I led them up the two flights of stairs and turned the key, an embarrassing whiff of kitchen bin invading my nostrils as soon as I opened the door. It was the least of my problems.

Mum was standing there, shoulders squared for a fight.

'How dare you just let yourself in?' I was screaming at her, right from the off. 'How have you even got a key?'

Hannah stepped forward protectively, my familiar.

'When your daughter's a drug addict you have to make provisions for the worst,' she said, deliberately calm. She looked at Hannah – her straggly hair pulled back from her pink face with a rubber band, her days-old tracksuit bottoms crumpled and stained – with utter contempt.

'I'm not a drug addict!' I said. 'I haven't even had a drink for nine weeks.'

'The fact you're counting says everything, darling.' She took in both Hannah and Marco now. 'I don't know who you both are – I suspect other unfortunate acolytes of Amber Greville. This is a family matter now. I need you both to leave.'

Marco was looking a bit unnerved by the whole situation, body turning towards the door, but Hannah was blazing with loyal outrage.

'We're her family now!' she shouted. 'Not you. And we're not leaving. We know all about you, and your horrible behaviour towards Rachel. You don't deserve such a wonderful daughter.'

Mum's eyes flashed with something dangerous, her jaw rigid with fury. There was no good option here. I put a hand on Hannah's arm.

'Thank you – let me deal with this. You don't need to protect me.'

Her eyes were beseeching.

'Are you sure? Are you sure you want us to go and leave you with …' – she looked over at Mum, who returned her gaze through narrowed eyes – '… this witch?'

I could tell Hannah was enjoying this, in a strange kind of a way. She was like a superhero at the height of her powers, all her intensity brought into glorious focus. She didn't need Mum destroying her warm righteousness; I wanted her to have her moment. I nodded, hugging her tightly, her sweet, sweaty smell comforting by now.

I felt so weary.

*

'Good decision,' said Mum as the door closed on Marco and Hannah.

I looked at her in disbelief.

'Decision? You really do live in your own fantasy world, don't you?'

Mum had been standing, but now she sank down on to the sofa, covering her eyes with her hand. The pull was so strong – to fling myself down beside her, to try to fix her unhappiness. I forced myself to stay upright, looking down at the slivers of grey that poked through her honeyed highlights. She was older now. She wasn't invincible. I couldn't decide if it made me feel stronger or more scared.

'I'm sorry,' she said, a sob choking the words. 'I didn't think you'd be like this. I thought by now you'd understand how much you're hurting all of us.'

I backed away from her and leant against the wall, the acrid stink of the week-old bin making the atmosphere even more toxic than it already was.

'But, Mum, you've hurt *me* so much,' I said. 'I'm only just starting to realize how much everything that happened back then destroyed my self-esteem.'

Real agony, not pantomime pain, registered in her face, but then it turned flinty. That was her dance move – her two-step – I realized, with blinding clarity. If only clarity offered the instant relief that the word seemed to promise it would.

'Started to realize?' she hissed, sitting up straight. 'And why the sudden epiphany? We both know the answer – Amber. Dripping poison in your ear. Stealing you away from me.'

I was shaking now, barely able to string a chain of words together.

'She's saved me, Mum! I was pretty much killing myself, and now . . .' An anxious kind of euphoria rose up in me, almost as if I was still lying spreadeagled on that couch, surrounded by my fellow warriors. 'Now I'm starting a whole new life.' The image of Mum in her robes swum up inside me, and I nearly blurted the story out, but I managed to keep it inside. 'I'm a different person now.'

'Some days I blame myself,' she continued, ranting as if she hadn't even heard me. 'I'm the one who brought her into your life. And no one even really knows who she is. No real information on her website.' She was ticking off Amber's crimes with her fingers. 'She's not registered as a therapist with the BACP – I checked. She's nothing but a charismatic fraud who's destroying my daughter's sanity.' She stared at me. 'I was desperate when I called her, Rachel. You'd made me desperate.'

This was awful. I had to make her see sense – I couldn't afford for her to stop paying for my sessions, not with that credit card bill breathing down my neck and rent due in five days. I forced softness into my tone.

'Mum, I'm so much better for seeing her – I am grateful to you. I feel wise; I feel grounded. I've actually got a new boyfriend.'

She visibly flinched at that: the sight of her instinctive reaction made shame flood my entire body. That was how radioactive I was when it came to men. No wonder Arthur hadn't even bothered to text.

'Rachel, you're in no fit state to start another affair.'

'It's not an affair! He's available. He's great, he's a ...' What was Arthur, really? Certainly not my boyfriend, and 'reiki practitioner' would send her sky high. 'He's a filmmaker,' I said randomly. Most men in West London claimed they were Scorsese, cruelly undiscovered. 'He's really successful. You'd like him.'

'Did you meet him on this transformational retreat?'

'Yes, but ...' Why was I so incapable of lying to her face? Time squashed flat and I was a child again.

'Right,' she said, that contemptuous sneer back on her face. She looked out of the window, as if she had to find a distraction to prevent herself from telling me the hard truth about how unlovable I was. How only *she* could love me, doomed by biology to take me on.

'Oh right, so you're the expert on relationships, are you?' I said, a dangerous amount of rage coursing through my veins. I was still wearing my coat, and I flung it on the ground. 'You know what I've learnt – what Amber's made me see – is that you and Dad are the whole reason I'm so fucked! You let him cheat on you in our house, and when I found out, you fucking gaslighted me, like *I* was the problem! No wonder I've gone for men who confirmed all my worst fears about how unlovable I am. It's textbook – and you're the one who taught me all my lessons.'

Mum stood up, her ivory skin splashed red. Her finger jabbed at me.

'You have no idea what I've sacrificed to keep this family together.'

'Yes, I do! You ignored him fucking the nanny. And probably, like, a thousand assistants. Well done. You're a hero.'

She wouldn't meet my gaze, staring blankly out of the window, even though there was nothing to see but the sodium glow of a streetlight.

'You're not the queen!' I continued, on a roll now. 'No one cares if you're divorced. You're a grown woman with a career. You've chosen to stay in that marriage, and it's not just you that's paid for it.'

'No, it's not that,' she said, her voice low and quiet. It was disturbing. 'I did everything I could to protect you. A mother's love. You can't understand it, but you have to trust me.'

When I look back now, I curse myself for not pushing harder on that door, but perhaps on some level I knew I was too fragile to let it swing open just yet.

'So, you admit it?' I shouted. 'Just admit you knew about him and Esther all along. And she's back now? What the fuck is that about?'

Her calm was starting to infuriate me.

'Marriage is hard, Rachel. Hopefully one day you'll have the chance to find that out firsthand.'

There it was, her sugar-coated spite. Rage charged through me like a power surge. Why couldn't she tell me she was sorry? Why did she have to keep hurting me instead, making herself into the heroine of her own twisted narrative? And how many lifetimes had I let her abuse me? I was free now. Amber had shown me the road out.

'Just go, okay?' I said. 'Just leave. Get out of my house.'

'You don't mean that, darling,' she said, stepping towards me. 'I love you!' I stepped backwards, putting my hands up to protect myself as if she was poised to strike.

'I do. I really do. This – this is toxic. *You're* toxic for me.'

She stopped in her tracks, face hardening, eyeing me like I was prey. A camera flash: those same eyes in the mirror, the silver-backed brush shaking in my hand, running through her hair. I almost screamed.

'I went to see her recently. Amber.' Mum's mouth curled into a smile, like she was enjoying my distress. 'She clearly thinks you're a total mess.'

'She cares about me,' I said, my voice shaking. 'She loves me!'

She gave a humourless laugh.

'No, darling, she cares about the money. And there won't be

any more of that coming her way. Not from us, anyway. The Bank of Mum and Dad is shutting up shop. After all, you'll be middle-aged soon. It's about time you learnt to stand on your own two feet.'

'I'm thirty-one!'

She shrugged on the elegant berry-coloured coat which she'd left slung on the sofa like it was her own home, belting it decisively.

'You let me know when you're ready to talk. When you're ready to accept some responsibility for your behaviour. And call your sister if you care about her at all. She's in pieces.'

'Mum ... I need her.' Why had I let my rage get the better of me? I was pleading now, snot and tears streaming down my face – it was gross. 'I need Amber. To stay well.'

'Amber's certainly going to be hearing from us, but not via any more bank transfers,' said Mum, that cold smile still dancing across her face. 'She's the one that's toxic, Rachel. And trust me, I'll do whatever I have to do to make you see that for yourself.'

A few seconds later, I heard the door click shut. I sunk to the ground, my back against the sofa, too emptied out even to cry. A thin stream of cold air snuck through the rickety, rental windows, but I couldn't find the juice to go and get a jumper from my bedroom. Eventually my phone beeped, and I grabbed for it. It was, of course, Hannah.

Your mum is HORRIBLE, she wrote. *Are you okay? I could come back?? xxx*

I stared at the bright square of the screen, then typed a message back.

Don't worry, I survived! I think you must've scared her into submission xxx

I could almost see Hannah's round face lighting up, the pride she'd feel at how she'd protected me. But how could anyone protect me from her if she'd stalked me through centuries?

I dropped the phone, sunk to my knees, and howled into the empty darkness.

LILY

It took all my strength to walk out, all my strength to try to force Rachel to witness her dangerous obsession with that manipulative bitch for what it really was. She hated me for it in that moment, but I know that it was an act of pure love.

And as for that girl she had in tow, that grubby follower: I think Rachel was secretly grateful that I dispatched her. She seemed like the kind of character who would've had a ratty old sleeping bag stowed in her rucksack, all ready to set up camp on the sofa for the next ten years, not a penny paid in rent.

My composure dropped the second I got into the car. It was a stupid white SUV that Nick had bought us, the driver's seat high up off the road as if that somehow made us all powerful. I dropped my head to the steering wheel and gave way to the sobs I'd been holding in for the past hour. The horn tooted as my head hit it, and I had a weird solitary laugh at the unbridled tragedy of my life. I looked up at the yellow glow of Rachel's window, desperate to race back up the stairs and hold her in my arms, share the laugh with the funniest of my children. But this was like the naughty step – a necessary evil. She needed to feel the chill to come back into the warmth, once and for all. I hoped so, anyway. The anguished twist of her face when I'd left her had torn at my heart.

I had to do this. She was skirting far too close to the truth.

I wasn't toxic, but our secret certainly was.

RACHEL

It was four in the morning by the time I fell into a sweaty, nightmare-ridden sleep, the alarm simply part of the hideous dreamscape. I punched it off, waking again at ten, and sitting bolt upright in horror. It was my first day back at work, and I was in my pyjamas mid-morning like a student. I took the world's briefest shower, threw on a skirt with a crumpled shirt over the top from the bottom of the wash basket, and raced for the tube.

No one was in our section when I walked in, and I fantasized for one glorious moment that I had the day wrong, could turn around and go back to bed. But then I saw through the glass into the conference room. Heads were bowed, papers strewn across the table. Duncan looked up and saw me, his familiar look of disappointment replaced by something more worrying. Was it resignation? I half sprinted across the floor, my chest so tight I could barely breathe.

'Sorry, sorry,' I said. There was no chair for me, and I had to wheel one in, everyone stopping what they were doing to watch me, sweaty and stressed. Julia at least smiled at me, but it felt guarded, like she didn't want to damage her own reputation by coming out as my friend. 'Sorry again,' I said, once I was sitting in the circle. 'I had a family emergency. What have I missed?'

'The chance to hit the ground running?' said Duncan. I smiled pleadingly, trying to find that relentless kindness that normally undid any of his attempts to exert authority.

'I'm running now, Duncan!'

'We can all see that,' he said coldly. My shirt was untucked from my waistband, my cheeks scarlet. I wanted to die. 'As we agreed before the break, we're spending this first morning reviewing our ongoing projects. Why don't you take us through the state of play with the sites you're overseeing?'

He was right, we'd all been told about this on our last day in the office, when he was full of praise and enthusiasm, even with me. Especially with me – I knew he'd been relieved by how more visibly stable I'd been. How had I totally failed to remember?

'But I haven't ... I haven't printed off any notes.' I looked around at the flurry of documents splayed across the table: everyone else had meticulously prepared.

'Well then we'll just have to settle for broad brushstrokes,' said this new, authoritarian version of Duncan that I barely recognized. Everyone turned to look at me as I made a stammering start.

'Letchworth is ...' A flash of Mum's face, the cold curl of her lips as she told me how determined she was to destroy my relationship with Amber. 'Letchworth is progressing well now.' My voice was swooping and diving. It was the other version of her I could see now, the cruel, ancient one. My hands were shaking, and I held one steady with the other under the table. 'If everything goes according to plan, tenants should be able to start moving in March. No – April.'

'And how do the projected costs look against budget, considering there's been a delay?' asked Duncan.

'Um, they're quite steady.'

'What do you mean by steady? Steady as in there's already an overspend, but it's not rising, or that the costs have been contained?'

This was like some kind of horrific courtroom cross-examination. My face got even redder, my eyes trained on the table.

'Yes, there is an overspend . . .' I trailed off. Sophie's fury with me, a fury I'd never heard in my life, before the phone clicked to silence. When I managed to speak, the words felt thick in my throat. 'But it's not out of control.'

'What does that even mean, in concrete terms?' demanded Duncan.

'I'd need . . .' I took a gulp of air. 'I'd really need my notes to be able to answer that accurately, Duncan. Can I go and print—'

'No,' he said, cutting across me. 'We don't have time to wait for you. You'll have to report to me individually later today.'

'It'll only take two minutes,' I begged.

'You're done, Rachel,' said Duncan, already looking to Jim, who worked in procurement, and was practically straining out of his seat with readiness.

You're done.

*

I sat on the closed seat of the loo, my head leaning against the cool surface of the door. I was dizzy with distress, the anxiety so extreme I couldn't even cry. I wanted to call Amber, but I was scared to. What could I say? I'm desperate to see you, but I'm so

221

broke that I'm buying toilet roll with a credit card. Of course she was part of the reason for that, but I couldn't ever say it. The fact she'd let me spend Christmas with her, had helped me so much, was such a privilege.

My phone seemed to taunt me. The person I most wanted to call – Sophie – would have all her worst assumptions confirmed by the state I was in. How could I call my 'normal' friends and tell them my mum had haunted me through the ages, plotting my destruction? Besides, they'd only suggest drinking through the trauma, and I couldn't risk trying to socialize with only a Diet Coke to prop me up. I nearly called Hannah, but I'd told her I was okay, and there was no way that would be a five-minute call. I had to return to my desk before Duncan got back on the warpath.

I don't know what twisted logic allowed me to think messaging Arthur was the answer, but I suppose that was my sickness. *Ugh*, I wrote, *back to work and all I want is to be cocooned with all of you in deepest darkest Devon. Hope you're having fun on the slopes!* Oh, the painful, jaunty exclamation mark, a transparent stand in for a kiss. It made me cringe as soon as I'd sent it, along with the knowledge that I was now dangling from a noose of my own making until he replied. At least the fact that I had to get back to my desk meant I couldn't simply sit there watching my phone, hating myself until he gave me cause not to.

Julia was staring determinedly at her monitor as I crossed the office, taking a second too long to look up as I slipped into my seat. At least I'd tucked in my shirt and slapped on a layer of tinted moisturizer.

'How was Christmas?' she asked, painfully cheerful.

I thought of Arthur, pressed down on top of me. The bulk of him. Addictive. Obliterating.

'Eventful,' I said. 'I was away with friends.'

'Right,' she said, looking at me a little too hard. She clearly thought I'd spent a week caning drugs and drinking before crawling back to work on a monumental come-down. 'You're so glamorous, Rachel. Fred and I are just boring, middle-aged old farts compared to you, and we're like, what, two years younger than you?'

It wasn't even January. Another year of this stretched out in front of me like a life sentence.

'It was Devon, not the Bahamas,' I said, swivelling around to switch on my computer. 'And it was pretty small and intimate. I'm seeing someone, so . . .'

Why did I keep doing this? Was I willing it to be true – for my phone to give that reassuring chirrup that would restore my self-esteem at a stroke? Julia clapped her hands like it was her third birthday and it was time to blow out the candles.

'Oh, Rachel, that's so exciting! What's his name? Who is he?'

I gave a garbled response – Arthur was a doctor this time, a devoted father with an impressively civilized divorce – already regretting my haphazard lie. Julia was rapt.

'I've got news, too!' she said, when I'd run out of imaginary heroics. 'Hobo's going to have a sibling!'

'What, you're adopting another dog?'

'No,' said Julia, with a twee little giggle. 'I'm only ten weeks in, so I'm not really meant to tell anyone, but considering how much I've been throwing up, there's no point hiding it from my desk buddy.'

'Oh wow, congratulations!' I said, struggling to make my voice match up with the sentiment.

It was stupid how crushed I felt. Maybe Mum was right about

me; maybe she was being cruel to be kind. I would be forty before I knew it, with nothing but a debt mountain and an imaginary boyfriend to show for it. I had to call Amber. I had to see her and get back some of that pioneer spirit that had surged through me when I'd been with the others, all of us brave outliers. Now I was stranded in the fish tank of my normal life, comparison sending me insane. Perhaps she'd let me pay by credit card?

As I stood up, phone stuck in my sleeve, I spotted Duncan striding towards our bank of desks.

'Rachel, can we talk in my office?'

This didn't feel like a promotion.

*

The picture of Hayley and the twins on Duncan's desk wasn't angled outwards – he wasn't the kind of person to use his family as a status symbol, a reminder of how much he was winning at life. Instead it was turned towards him, next to his ancient, standard-issue computer – something that he glanced at almost unconsciously for comfort, to remind himself of who he was, outside of being a cog in the wheel of government. His soft brown eyes were darting towards it now: it made it inconveniently hard to hate him.

'The thing is, I've protected you, Rachel. I know you don't even understand it – and in a way I blame myself for being underhand . . .' *God, he sounded like Mum.* I was like some kind of stealth missile, making people self-implode. I clenched my fists as tightly as I could, trying to force myself not to well up. 'But I've always known how bright you were, ever since you joined the team. I've always wanted to keep you.'

'I want you to keep me . . .'

How was this the straw that broke the camel's back?

'But your frequent absences, the lack of doctors' notes – it's been flagged by HR before. Lydia pushed me to give you a formal warning last September. And then you were hospitalized the next month.' He stared at me intently now. 'It's not as if we haven't privately asked questions about your ... your lifestyle, Rachel.'

I smoothed down my shirt, tucked it into my waistband yet again.

'Duncan, I haven't had a drink since October.' His face shifted. Too much truth. 'I mean, it's not like I ever had a problem,' I added quickly, 'but I've been on a serious lifestyle audit ever since I was hospitalized. I've tried to show you how committed I am.'

Duncan nodded.

'And your mother explained very clearly about the gastro-enteritis.' She saved me. He would have been no match for that smooth patter of hers: my mum could rent a flea pit in Acton for double its value without breaking a sweat. 'And after a few weeks, you're right. You did seem quite transformed.'

The word was like nectar.

'I was,' I said, filled with a sudden surge of love for Amber. 'I was transformed. Which is why I can't understand why you're making such a big deal about me being late today. I'm sorry, Duncan, I really am. I don't know how to apologize any more than I already have.'

His jaw was rigid beneath his pallid winter skin, his eyes flashing with anger.

'This is where I have serious worries about you. How do you not see the problem?'

My heart was racing now. Thinking of Amber had loosened me up, made me too authentic. It was almost as if part of me was still in Devon, the edges between all of us blurred and soft. The sharp corners of London life were cutting way too deeply.

'I . . . I do see . . .'

Duncan cut across me.

'To turn up for a cross-departmental audit almost two hours late, utterly unprepared, without any kind of attempt to message your line manager or your colleagues. On day one back in the office!' He thrust a frustrated hand through his wiry, dark curls like he wanted to yank them out at the roots. 'It's beyond belief,' he said.

He slumped backwards in his chair while I desperately scrabbled around for something – anything – to make things better. It was completely impossible to tell if radical honesty or radical dishonesty was the best route out of this.

'I've had some very serious problems with my family over the break . . .'

Duncan looked baffled.

'What, with your parents?'

God, I sounded so juvenile. That was still what 'family' meant to me – it was almost as if some part of me was still that thirteen-year-old girl, sobbing in Starbucks on the Uxbridge Road in my navy uniform, skirt shortened above regulation length with a sneaky row of safety pins. I had to keep breaking free of them. I couldn't afford to lose this job.

'My mother's got some mental health issues that we've been grappling with.' It felt true as I said it. The problem was he'd been on the receiving end of Mum's silken authority so recently. I had to keep going now. 'It all came to a head last night. I was up until God knows when dealing with it, and – I know it's no excuse, but I wanted to be honest. I will do better.' My voice was cracking now. I had so little left that I could lose. 'I promise you that.'

Duncan stared into space for a long minute before his gaze came back to rest on me.

'I'm sorry things have been difficult, I really am. But all of us have personal stresses to deal with. I'm not going to take drastic steps, but I am registering today as a formal warning. HR will be in touch to confirm it in writing. I have to warn you that if we reach this point again, your role here will become untenable. I hope for both of our sakes it has the desired effect.'

'Thank you, Duncan,' I stammered, pushing my chair back abruptly and getting to my feet on shaking legs. I backed out of his office as fast as those wobbling splints could carry me.

*

The day was a con merchant – the sky cobalt blue and bright, the wind so vicious it could slice a layer off your skin. It was lunchtime, so I could finally risk leaving my desk without setting Duncan off again. *Formal warning.* The words kept reverberating through me, impossible to quiet.

I'd supposedly gone in search of a sandwich, but really I'd gone in search of Amber. The Westminster streets were peppered with grumpy workers on their first day back, resenting the fact they'd swapped their midday pyjamas for uncomfortable suits. I battled my way through them towards Pret, trying to compose my opening gambit. I can't come tomorrow? Please can I come tomorrow? I'm so desperate that I *have* to come tomorrow, but even that kind sucker at Barclaycard has given up on me?

I thought she'd be in a session, but she picked up on the second ring. She has to eat lunch too, I thought, gratitude and trepidation flooding me.

'Hi, darling,' she said, warm and kind. 'How are you surviving the real world?'

That was it. I pushed my way out of the crowd and leant against a wall, the last twenty-four hours spilling out of me in a painful torrent. How determined Mum was to destroy our relationship, even though it was the most precious thing I had. How appalled my family, and my boss, were with me. How fragile and yet how alive I felt – thanks to her – and how hard it had made it to slide back into the grey, hollow routines of the 'normal' life I was supposed to want. I'd obviously forgotten about the dank cold of my shared bedroom by then. In my memory, it felt like the Ritz.

'My love . . .' said Amber. 'Sometimes things have to burn to the ground before they can be rebuilt. It's never easy.'

I looked up into the infinite blue, searching for the right words for what I needed to ask her. Normally I had a trick – a back route to get around any situation that I knew the other person wouldn't have a map for – but there was no fooling Amber.

'Amber, I don't think I can come this week. I've got like, eighty-two pounds left of my overdraft limit.'

The pause felt infinite.

'Mum means what she said,' I added. I started crying, ducking my wet face against the loop of Sophie's scarf and ignoring the nosy stares that I was getting from the stream of passers-by. 'I need you, but she doesn't care. She only cares about herself.'

Amber exhaled.

'I'm so glad that you said that. I'm so proud that you're

at the point where you can acknowledge the truth of the relationship.'

My stomach dropped. Did she mean that her work was done?

'Thanks . . .' I said nervously.

'Just come along tomorrow as planned,' she said. My knees buckled, and I leant more heavily against the wall for support. 'I'm not going to abandon you, Rachel,' she continued. 'Don't worry. You're safe now. You know that, don't you, darling?'

My heart was pounding with relief. *Safe now.* She'd saved me.

'Thank you. Thank you so much,' I said. I thought of Mum's smug face. *She only cares about the money.* She knew nothing about who Amber really was. What we meant to each other. I was gabbling now. 'I'll pay you back. I promise you, I'll pay you back!'

'I know you will,' she said crisply. I liked the way the words sounded in her mouth. It was definitive, like she believed me, not like I was some overgrown child that she had to indulge.

She certainly did believe me. I just didn't know why yet.

LILY

Nick's striped shirt was erupting from his waistband, his blonde hair tousled in a way that made his thinning patches a little too obvious. I chided myself. I was only stripping him down for parts because I felt so wretched.

'Coercion!' he said, leaning over his desk and jabbing at the computer's keyboard. 'I've been researching it properly and I spoke to a mate at the CPS, too. The law's changed a lot in the last couple of years. Trust me, it's going to be our friend here.'

Sophie, sat in the grey B&B Italia sofa that stretched out across the length of the wall, pulled up her knees and looped her arms around them, making herself into a little cosmic egg. It looked so infuriatingly childish.

'Are you sure it's right to get legal?' she said, nervously twirling her fingers in her frizzy curls. 'So she didn't spend Christmas with us, and Amber's fees are greedy: is it really enough for you to start suing her? I just don't want Rachel to take herself even further away from us because she thinks we're tormenting this woman she worships.'

To my relief, Nick jumped in before I had to. It wasn't just me playing the Big Bad Wolf with our snowflake offspring.

'For Christ's sake, Sophie, this woman's taking the piss. Did you hear what your mother said about the state Rachel's in? Ranting and raving, talking about suicide.'

Had I really said that? I was in such a state when I'd arrived home the night before that it was hard to remember. The large gin and tonic I'd poured myself before I went upstairs and found him had certainly helped to take the edge off, but its after-effects also seemed to be blunting my memory.

'But it's Rachel!' said Sophie, flushed and pleading. 'She's still just Rachel. I'm as pissed off as anyone with her, but she needs our love to get better. I hung up on her yesterday, even though she sounded completely desperate.'

'Yeah, tough love,' grunted Nick, studying his computer. 'We go to the police first off, lodge a formal complaint.' I studied Sophie's face, the contempt that was blooming there as she watched her father's narrowed eyes scanning his screen. 'We tell them how she's been manipulating Rachel when she's at her most vulnerable, stealing from her and alienating her from her family. Coercive control. That's what this is – mental abuse.'

Was it enough? It certainly wouldn't be enough if the suicide angle was exposed as a stretched truth, and Sophie's contempt for his argument was all too obvious. I couldn't lose her. I couldn't lose either of my girls – I needed them too much, even if they chose not to appreciate it. Perhaps there was a way to take out both problems with one round of ammunition?

'Sophie's right,' I said, smiling over at her. It was like flicking on a light switch, so grateful was she for my approval. This was going to be even easier than I'd hoped. 'Rachel needs our protection, our love. But you're right too, darling. With the state she's reached, tough love's part of the package.'

Both of them were fixed on me now.

'We need to know . . .' I was starting to shake, my calm evaporating. That appalling encounter in her ratty treatment room, the look on Rachel's face last night as she rhapsodized about her. 'We need to know what Amber's capable of. What her methods are. Trust me, that Christmas retreat was more than just foot massages and supermarket Prosecco. It's broken Rachel.'

Sophie looked stricken.

'Oh God, Mum . . . what do we do?'

'And who are these people? The state of her little friend – she looked like a traveller.' Righteous anger was lighting me up from within by now, as I thought of how that greasy-haired child had torn into me. 'I'm surprised she didn't have a mongrel trailing behind her on a string.'

'Probably a druggie. What are you actually suggesting here, Lily?' said Nick.

Esther crossed my eyeline, visible through the glass wall behind Sophie, and I faltered for a second. She was holding a sheaf of papers, walking purposefully, with the air of someone who was fully confident in their own domain. I'd let it go too far this time.

'You're up next, my darling,' I said, pointing to Sophie. 'You need to go and find her. Find out what that terrible woman put her through at Christmas, so we've got the full picture.'

Sophie looked uncertain.

'I don't want to spy on her, Mum . . .'

I crossed over to her, enveloped her in my arms. Soon I could feel her tears soaking into my cream silk shirt, her body moulding against mine.

'You're not betraying her, Sophie,' I said, gently rocking her solid frame. 'You're just making sure she's alright. You said your-self you should never have hung up on her.' A little sob escaped at that. 'You're being the best sister you could possibly be.'

As I hugged my innocent girl, my eyes kept roving the space. I was like a sniper, waiting for the next target.

How arrogant I was to believe I was invincible.

RACHEL

Amber's faith in me gave me a pepped-up courage that carried me through the rest of the day. From where I am now, it's hard to understand how I failed to witness the pattern – the fact that the highs and lows that used to arrive chemically, via a furtive late-night drop-off on a scooter, were now arriving with equal ferocity via different means. I even managed to turn the feeble text I received from Arthur into a positive. *Ha!* he wrote – nothing else – in the late afternoon. Then a few minutes later, another bubble appeared on my phone's screen. *Stay strong! Catch up with you when I'm back x.* It was hardly a sonnet, but somehow I managed to transform receiving a kiss into a romantic triumph. I hadn't sent him one – he was clearly upping the ante, making it clear he wanted our relationship to be ongoing, and definitely more than friends. I shut off my computer at seven, well after Julia had left and twenty minutes after Duncan, and headed to the lift with a stubborn optimism. It was a fresh start in every possible way.

The end of the day bustle was long over as I swiped my pass on the turnstile. The row of leather chairs in the lobby were left exposed, so I saw her immediately.

'Sophie!' I said, rushing towards her, my voice cracking. She took a few seconds to stand up, the easy smile that normally lit up her face at the sight of me failing to ignite. At least she was here. That meant everything. 'I'm wearing your scarf,' I said, hugging her unyielding body. 'I love it so much.'

'I liked the cookbook too,' she said, words muffled by the long hug that I was refusing to quit.

'I'm so happy you're here!' I added. My voice had developed that watery uplift that Hannah's so often had, neediness turned into a lilting chime.

'I needed to see you,' said Sophie, almost businesslike. She paused. 'Do you want some supper? My treat.'

It was so humiliating how much of a bonus it was that she would pay.

'I'd love that,' I said, awkwardly threading my arm through the crook of her stiff elbow.

*

We ended up in a dim sum place, all low lighting and intimate velvet booths. Had she lined it up beforehand, picking some-where where there would be no easy distractions? I let her order for both of us, a cover for my self-consciousness about the fact she was paying. All I asked for was a bottle of sparkling water.

'You can get a drink,' I said to Sophie, but she shook her head, her face shut tight. 'Just because I'm not drinking, doesn't mean you . . . or are you practising for dry January?'

'I just don't want one,' she said, shutting the menu firmly and handing it back to the waiter. 'Thank you,' she said to him, raising her first smile of the evening.

'Sophie,' I said, once he'd retreated. I grabbed for her hand across the table. 'Can't we just have a nice time together? Sister Act?' It was a silly way we sometimes used the phrase, a little nod to our special bond within our family. We were the sister act. Or at least we always had been.

She stared at me searchingly.

'I wish,' she said softly. 'I wish that more than anything.'

'So ... I'm still me, Sophie! I'm me, without you having to worry that I'm going to sink two bottles of wine and do something totally inappropriate and possibly naked.'

She refused to laugh – instead she somehow managed to look even more pained.

'Why aren't you happy for me?' I said, anger building now. 'Everyone wanted me to stop being so self-destructive. To get a life. And now you're all still judging me. I can't win, can I?'

Sophie snatched her hand away.

'I'm happy you're not drinking, I really am. I'm proud of you for that. But I don't know why you have to be so horrible to Mum. To both of them. She's in bits, Rachel. I've never seen her like this. Why didn't you just tell her where you were? I know you're angry I told her, but you put me in an impossible position. And then last night all she was trying to do was make peace, and you were awful to her again.'

My rage was like a tidal wave. I forced myself to stay silent until I could trust myself to speak. This wasn't Sophie's fault: she'd been indoctrinated too. But before I'd formulated a reply, she changed tack.

'How was it, anyway?' she said, lighter suddenly. The waiter delivered our bottle of water, and she busily rearranged our glasses to make it easier for him to pour. 'Mum said you met someone?'

'Yeah, I did,' I said.

'So – gory details?' she asked, perky.

Something jarred. Something didn't sound like Sophie. But the chance to pretend that we were back to normal was too alluring, and soon I was blabbing away about Arthur like he was my one true love rather than a grown man who thought 'Ha!' was a coherent sentence. My sister's smile felt too persistent, too glazed, and I checked myself.

'God, listen to me wanging on.' I laughed. 'What about you? I can't believe it's only two months until the wedding. How is Toby?'

'Yeah, no, he's fine,' she said. 'Busy at work.'

'I am still your maid of honour, aren't I?' I said. My hand hovered above the table like a UFO: I wanted to grab hers, but the airspace felt hostile. 'I know Kitty's organizing the hen night, but I want to help in any way I can.'

That pained look again. How could she – the functional, together sister – possibly need my so-called help? Shame washed through me like a mouthful of acid.

'Just say if you don't want me there,' I snapped. 'It's fine.'

The waiter was returning with a towering plate of dim sum. Sophie looked outwards into the buzz of the busy restaurant, playing for time.

'Of course I want you there!' she said. 'You're my sister. You're you.' The way that those words cracked her voice, cracked me. 'But I can't choose between you and Mum. I can't choose between you and enjoying our wedding day. You must understand that.'

'Of course I do!' I said, my hand flying for hers across the food. She let me take it now: there was hope. I had to make this right. Mum's cold, vindictive stare as she left the flat was still boring into me. I'd have to match her to survive – maybe that was my twisted genetic inheritance. I took a breath.

'Sophie, I know how it looks. Like I'm this self-indulgent, unstable nightmare who went off the rails when I was a teenager and never came back. But you were too young to understand, and I've wanted to protect you from the truth. Because you're my baby sister, who I love more than anyone.'

Sophie's wide brown eyes were watery behind her glasses. I kept going, pressing hard against the chink in her armour.

'I didn't want to destroy your childhood. You've always been so . . . so fucking happy! And I love that about you. It makes life easier . . .'

'My life isn't some permanent sodding picnic, Rachel,' she interrupted, but I squeezed her hand and carried on talking. I couldn't afford to look down before I'd walked the full length of this particular tightrope.

'Mum and Dad – I'm not saying they don't love us, or they haven't tried to be good parents, but . . . that marriage isn't what it looks like. How they want it to look. And I was too young . . .' A sob rose up, but I forced it down. 'I know how much you loved Esther, and I've never wanted to tell you this, but she was definitely Dad's mistress. In our house. And when I found out, when I walked in on them, Mum punished me for it. I needed her so badly, and she just – she just chucked me out, emotionally, like I was rubbish. You know how hard on us she can be. It was that times a hundred till I went to university.'

Sophie was pale now, her face pinched tight with shock. She didn't say a word: I couldn't work out if that was a good or a bad sign. All I could do was carry on.

'And it kind of broke me. Home wasn't a home anymore. I didn't trust anyone. I didn't trust myself. And if you don't trust yourself – if you don't *like* yourself – then it doesn't really matter what you do to yourself, does it?'

'Esther?' she said, the name uttered with such disbelief that it sounded like an unfamiliar foreign word that she couldn't pronounce. 'Our nanny – Esther?'

'Yes. I know it's hard to believe, but ... that's why it was so impossible for me to survive intact, Sophie. It took me apart.'

I could say it now. Being surrounded in Devon by all those warm, kind faces as I shared the darkest truths of my family had finally let me own the trauma of what had happened on my terms. But then I thought of what I'd seen next – who Mum really was for me – and my clarity was overwhelmed by shaky terror. I took a long gulp of water and a mouthful of food, trying to steady myself. Perhaps I could text Amber when I got out of here, let her be the one to steady me the way she always did. I was so lucky that she didn't even restrict my contact to sessions anymore.

'Rachel, are you sure?' pleaded Sophie. 'I mean – Dad? Is he really capable of that?'

'Do you really think they're happy?' I said.

She paused, her bottom lip pinned tight by her teeth, the way she used to hold it when she was first learning to colour inside the lines. Love rushed up inside me, but I didn't say a word.

'I mean, I don't think they're love's young dream,' she said eventually. 'They bicker, but then, they're both strong characters.' Her voice was rising with distress, and I felt a stab of guilt at smashing her pretty picture to smithereens, but then I thought of Amber. The way that she'd taught me to value truth and integrity above the numb comfort of lies. 'I've never had to think about it. They've just been Mum and Dad.'

'I'm sorry—' I said, but it was her turn to cut across me.

'Tell me properly, Rachel,' she said, eyes blazing. 'I need to understand this properly.'

And I told her the story of that day, and how it had allowed me to put together all the strange inconsistencies of the months leading up to it. The way our workaholic Dad had started regularly 'working from home', his eagerness to pick up our au pair from late nights out. And the phoney war of the weeks that stretched out afterwards, before Esther's abrupt and unexplained departure.

'I remember I cried night after night after she left,' breathed Sophie. 'It was so sudden, wasn't it? I was really pleased when she got back in touch all that time later.'

I allowed myself to feel some hope. Perhaps someone in my family could believe me – could understand how hard it was to keep hold of all of this and also stay part of them.

'Yes, it was!' I agreed.

'But you can't be sure, Rachel,' she said. 'You could have misread the situation. It's not like they were . . . like you saw them.' She flushed, the horror of the idea painted on her face.

'Mum's virtually admitted it to me!' I said. 'She almost said it last night, in fact.'

Sophie looked doubtful, like a doggedly honest juror who took 'beyond reasonable doubt' to the nth degree.

'Really?'

'Yes!' I said, my voice so shrill that a nearby table swivelled their heads to look in our direction. I was desperate to win her back – too desperate. In retrospect, I can see what a fatal mistake that would prove to be. 'Not in so many words, but yes.'

'But, Rachel . . .' said Sophie, struggling with something.

'Just say it.'

'I saw Esther. Today. She's still working in Dad's office. Mum was there – we both know what she's like! There's no way she'd let him have a mistress right under her nose. She'd – she'd cut his balls off.' I could see from the way her face softened that the thought comforted her.

'But . . .'

'I'm not saying you're wrong, but you must admit it's possible she was telling the truth.' Now it was her who reached across the table for my hand. 'I couldn't bear it if you cut yourself off because of some stupid misunderstanding. We know what she's like – she could be an utter cow to me when I was a teenager too. It doesn't mean Dad cheated with our nanny. It's a big accusation.'

I snatched my hand away. I was struggling to compute everything at once – how painfully easy it was for my sister to dismiss me, and the fact that Esther's cancerous presence was buried so deep in our family that it was still eating away at the flesh.

'A misunderstanding?' I exploded. 'Is that what you think this is? Me and Mum having a misunderstanding? Jesus!'

'Rachel . . .'

In my defence, I was splintering apart.

'You're totally brainwashed, and you don't even know it!' I said, angry tears coursing down my cheeks. 'The way you're talking about her – "she'd cut off Dad's balls", "she's been a bitch to us". You know exactly who she is, but you're so fucking used to making excuses for her that you can't even hear the doublespeak.' I looked at my sister's stubbornly innocent face and, for the first time in my life, I wanted to slap it. 'I wish it was you

241

seeing Amber, not me. Then you'd have to grow up and face how fucking toxic our family really is!'

Sophie's eyes flashed with fury.

'Seeing Amber? Looking at the state she's got you in, I can't think of anything worse.'

'She's saved me!' I wailed. 'Sometimes things have to be burnt down so they can be rebuilt.'

Sophie shook her head.

'That's not you speaking, Rachel; that's her,' she said, waving an angry hand for the bill. 'There's only one person here who's been brainwashed.'

It jolted me, the realization that my sister knew me so well that she could trace the hidden contours of my words the second they left my mouth, almost as if they were braille beneath her fingertips. The twin realization – comforting and terrifying all at once – that my connection to my family ran so much deeper than mere DNA.

'That's not true!' I said. 'That retreat healed me. It healed all of us.'

'What, all three grand of it?' she snapped, handing her credit card over to an understandably nervous waiter. 'She charged three bloody grand for you to all sit around talking about your own navels in the arse-end of nowhere.'

'How do you even know that?' My whole family, even my beloved Sophie, were plotting against me. Spying.

'Oh, don't you worry – Mum's all over it,' she said ominously.

'It's none of your fucking business, but it was an incredible, healing journey that she took us on. She gave everything to us. Arthur too. We went back into our past lives, and I can tell you that Mum's vendetta against me started way more than twenty years ago.'

Sophie angrily keyed in her pin, then grabbed for her coat from the seat next to her.

'What are you even *talking about*, Rachel? If you could hear yourself! You're not making any sense.' She abruptly stood up.

'Sophie, don't go,' I pleaded. 'We can't leave it like this. You're my sister! I love you – you know how much I love you.'

'I don't not love you, Rachel,' she said, her voice breaking in a way that tore at my heart. 'But I can't talk to you when you're being like this.' She paused, staring down at me. 'It's as bad as … It's as bad as it's ever been. Maybe worse. I don't know how to even find you this time.'

'I'm right here.' I grabbed for her sleeve, but she yanked her arm away as if my fingers had burnt her.

'Don't, okay?' she said. 'I'll call you.'

'Don't bother,' I snarled, humiliated and ashamed. 'Just think about what I told you instead. Ask yourself – why's Esther come back now? Because we both know it's not to read you bedtime stories.'

I saw her stricken profile as she swept out of the door into the cold London night: I took a grim satisfaction in the fact my words had cut like a knife.

LILY

I directed Nick to park on a side street I knew behind Shepherd's Bush Green – a row of squat little houses that can fetch a small fortune, despite the constant flow of takeaway chicken boxes flung into the gardens like they're plastic gnomes – and we climbed out of the aggressively heated car into the January chill. As he reached the pavement next to me, I took his hand, even though we'd barely spoken during the drive. I'd been running through my scripts – all my scripts – and I wondered if he'd been doing the same.

'We can do this, darling,' I said, squeezing his fingers through the black leather of his gloves. They were so thick, with their plush sheepskin lining, that it was hard to know if my touch even registered. 'We're good parents, even if she doesn't know it right now.'

'Yeah, obviously,' he said irritably. 'We've given those kids everything.'

'I'm not sure if it's about that,' I said.

'Wow, Lily, you sound just like I reckon she does,' he replied, pulling his hand away from mine to pull out his phone and pay for our parking. Ostensibly at least.

For a brief second, I suddenly envied Rachel her relentless freedom, her utter inability to commit. There was a certain self-destructive honesty to it, a bonfire of norms. Whereas me – I was welded to someone and entirely alone, all at once. Some people would say I'd chosen that, but I'm not sure that making choices is the same as choosing their eventual outcome – we humans are often too blind to work out even the simplest of sums.

*

The police station was red-brick and Victorian, a thin ribbon of scrubby grass ringing the exterior. I faltered at the bottom of the steps for a second, but Nick's determined stride forced me forward. He marched up to the desk. There were people hovering in front of it, but he cut through them, speaking directly to the uniformed female PC behind the desk in a voice that carried across the noisy chaos.

'We're here to report a crime,' he said. 'Coercion. Is there a detective available to take a statement?'

I've loved that about him from the very beginning of our relationship, his innate ability to slice a path through the world. He even had it as a sixth former, his choice of university – his choice of girlfriend – perfectly mapped out. I was grateful for the reminder. I needed it right then.

Soon we were in a blank box of an interview room, a callow young detective listening intently to our story. I let Nick speak first, his lawyer brain ordering the facts into a coherent narrative.

'So your daughter's a drug addict?' asked the detective, scribbling notes.

What a repulsive statement.

'No, I wouldn't say that,' I said, too quickly. Nick squeezed my hand, hard. It was the opposite of a gesture of solidarity.

'Yeah, she's got a real problem,' said Nick. 'Alcohol too. This woman's exploiting that to extort money.'

'But she's a therapist, right?' asked the detective, his pale, pasty face twisting up with concentration. 'Like a shrink?' He looked like a man who didn't put much store in Freud's insights on the human condition. 'That's her job? So it makes sense she charges for it.'

'Supposedly,' said Nick. 'But we can't find any sign of her qualifications.'

'But aren't you the ones who hired her?' said the detective, his large palms turned upwards in resignation.

'My wife . . .' started Nick.

I cut across him.

'Detective, can I stop you there? I was desperate. My daughter was lying in a hospital bed having had her stomach pumped, after countless incidents of bingeing on drink and drugs. This last time, she was found lying unconscious on the street. I love my children with all my heart, and I couldn't let it continue. Amber Greville felt like my last hope.' I let my voice crack. 'My only hope.'

Detective Maron's shoulders, encased in a nondescript navy suit, dropped a little. He looked too young to be a father, but recently everyone looked young to me. Age was creeping up on me, enveloping my perceptions. Maybe he did have a little girl of his own at home, toddling around, all innocence. I could take him on a journey now.

'We let Amber into our home, let her into Rachel's life, but soon after she re-payed our trust by drip-feeding poison about us into her ears.' My voice was rising now. 'Manipulating her vulnerability. Plunging her into debt for a so-called healing retreat, where she was sexually exploited and abused . . .'

Nick's gaze was fixed on me – was it admiration or fear I could see in his eyes? I let myself believe it was the former. Meanwhile, Maron was scribbling notes.

'Hang on, hang on,' he said. 'We need to go through these incidents properly, have each of you write a statement.'

My whole body tingled with triumph. I had his buy-in, and the information Sophie had telegraphed back to me was more than enough to make a charge stand up. I could do this.

*

I hadn't lost my touch with daughter number two. She'd been reticent when we met up yesterday morning, wary and monosyllabic. I'd expected it, her loyalty to Rachel was almost forged in the womb. I'd deliberately suggested breakfast at Delilah's, a brunch spot we often visited – the familiar whoosh of the coffee machine and the smiling waitresses lulled her into a feeling of ease, made the occasion seem ordinary. When I'd planned it, I'd had no idea how much I would need the camouflage. Rachel was clearly spiralling out of control, downloading her spiteful stories about the state of her parents' marriage with no thought for how hurtful it was for all of us. How destructive. When Sophie – poor, stricken Sophie – told me what she'd said, I let silence settle over us before I deigned to respond.

'Your sister's always struggled with her mental health,' I told her calmly, one hand gripping the other under the table. 'I've always done everything – *everything* – to protect you from it, but you're a grown woman now, Sophie. I need you. So does she.'

'She seemed pretty sure, Mum,' she said. Another pause: I watched her start to crumple under my gaze. 'Or ... she believes it. She's not just saying it.'

I let my eyes fill.

'We had so much to deal with back then,' I said, my voice a hoarse whisper. 'You probably don't remember how she'd starve herself, how unreasonable it made her. How much she fantasized.'

'God, she didn't eat, did she?'

'She was a rake, Sophie – there was nothing of her! I was terrified of what she was doing to herself.'

'Mum ...'

'That was her addiction back then,' I said. 'And now her addiction is Amber, the most dangerous addiction of all, it turns out.' I reached across the table, caressed her arm. 'She needs you, darling girl. She loves you more than anyone else in the world.'

Sophie began to cry, all of Rachel's confidences starting to tumble out of her, like coppers shaken free from a child's piggy bank. Soon I knew all about Arthur, all about the weird hands-on healing they'd subjected my daughter to, all about the accusations Amber had levelled about my lifetimes of abuse.

It was chilling, but I forced myself to hear every word. It was my duty. There was only one abuser in this scenario – one person who was endangering my daughter – and I was going to make sure she got exactly what she deserved.

*

'Say that to me again,' said Detective Maron. We'd been in that interview room for almost two hours by then. 'She's told her that you tortured her in other lifetimes. I don't mean this as a joke, but – like Doctor Who? Like you're a time lord?'

Nick snorted.

'It's fucking absurd, isn't it?' he said.

'And she's got other clients?' added Maron. 'This lady needs stopping. I want to make sure I've got everything in here. Tell me the suicide part in a bit more detail please.'

Nick slumped forward, head in his hands.

'Tell him, Lily, tell him what she said.'

'She just . . .' I hesitated. 'I was concerned when she came back from the retreat that she was so distressed she might be suicidal.'

'No,' said Nick, banging his fist on the Formica table. 'You're soft-soaping it. She threatened it.'

'Well . . .'

'She said if we stopped paying for Amber, she'd be a suicide risk. That's what she said, Lily! That evil bitch clearly told her to use that line on us – blatant extortion! That grunge girl she was with backed it up, didn't she?'

That awful, insolent friend of hers. I felt a new surge of rage thinking of the way she'd spoken to me, like she was the one who was Rachel's blood.

I certainly tried to tone down Nick's interpretation, but neither man chose to hear me. Soon Maron's versions of our statements were complete, ready for us to sign. He passed us a tired-looking biro, and each of us scribbled our names. All the triumph had drained out of me as I passed over the pen. I was crashing now.

We gathered up our things, Nick holding up my cashmere coat for me to thread my arms into. I saw Maron clock how gentlemanly a gesture it was, how lucky I must be.

'Thank you both for coming in,' he said. 'I promise you we'll do everything we can to get the CPS to take this seriously. Even getting the letter asking her to come in for an interview is going to make her think twice about how she's operating.'

'I hope you're right,' I said.

'Thank you,' said Nick, leaning in to give him a firm handshake. 'We appreciate it, we really do. I've got to get back to work now, but we'll keep in touch.'

Back to work. That was another situation that needed my attention.

'It might be a week or so before you hear from us,' said Maron, 'but I'm personally going to drive this investigation, get some answers. These people should be properly regulated.'

'We're so grateful,' I told him. 'And I'll just keep reminding Rachel how much we love her, even if she doesn't reply.'

The detective looked thoughtful, almost pensive. It had been clear to me that he was the sensitive type from the moment I first drew him into our plight. This was either the perfect job or the worst possible job for our Detective Maron.

'If you don't mind me asking, when did your daughter first start going off the rails? Was there something – a trigger, perhaps?'

Nick and I locked eyes for a second, something passing between us.

'No trigger, I'm afraid,' I said, my tone gossamer light. 'If only life really did work like that, we'd know what to do.' I smiled into his troubled expression. 'Besides asking you for help, of course.'

When we finally stepped back out of the police station, the frigid January air was like a slap around the face. Some might say I deserved it.

RACHEL

'Espresso?'

It took a second to remember where I was. My eyes blinked open, taking in the unfamiliar room. There was a weird combination of tired Ikea bedroom furniture and ornate floral wallpaper, punctuated by a series of grand oil paintings. Right now, I seemed to be being eyeballed by a witchy-looking woman in a bonnet, who definitely disapproved of my nakedness. I pulled the duvet around me like a shroud. It smelt lived in – more man than Persil.

'Straight espresso's a bit strong for me,' I said, looking up at Arthur. 'Can I have some milk in it?'

'It'll put hairs on your chest,' he said, grinning and putting the tiny cup down on the messy nightstand. There was a stack of battered paperbacks with broken spines – *On the Road*, *Crime and Punishment* – a university reading list, frozen in time.

'Is that your thing?' I said, trying for playful. 'A werewolf fetish?' Jesus – I was failing miserably at hard to get.

'You'll have to wait and see,' said Arthur, smirking down at me, and reaching a questing hand under the duvet.

Yesterday had felt Arctic on every front. It had started with the official letter left on my desk, confirming my formal warning in black and white beneath a raised government seal. I shoved it in my drawer, but I could see from the way that Julia spent the day observing me that word had already reached her pregnant ears. Duncan was certainly making it pretty obvious how much shit I was in, his withering attitude showing no sign of thawing.

Meanwhile, there was no reply when I texted Sophie a pleading message – instead I just got a stomach-churning email from Mum mid-afternoon, reminding me how much my selfishness was tearing our family to shreds. It sent me back into my favourite, familiar toilet cubicle, my sobs swallowed down and silent so no one could add another crime to my rap sheet.

My loneliness felt absolute, so when Arthur texted, I was vulnerable. It was gone ten o'clock by then, and I was in my pyjamas, zoned out in front of a reality show stuffed with twenty-somethings in bikinis hoping to get it on. He'd just got back, he said, and I was on his mind. Would it be ungentlemanly to ask if I fancied a nightcap? It was sexy, I told myself, a mark of how much he liked me that I was the first thing he'd thought of when he'd touched back down on British soil. I didn't want him to step into the messy chaos of my real life, so instead I decided his offer to pay for an Uber was pretty much the equivalent of a nobleman sending a horse-drawn carriage. And now, here I was, naked under the covers, while his hand made determined progress across the bumpy terrain of my body. There hadn't been much deep and meaningful conversation last night, either.

'Slow down,' I said, smiling at him to soften the words. 'I mean ... obviously it's lovely, but I've got to go. I'm seeing Amber before work.'

His hand stopped dead, withdrew. He stood up straight.

'Right. Of course. Do you see her every week?'

What to say? He knew so much about me, and also almost nothing. He'd heard me vomit out my deepest secrets and most painful vulnerabilities, yet I still felt too awkward to insist on milk in my coffee so it wouldn't taste like tar.

'Yeah, I have been,' I said. 'I hope I still am.' I wanted to blurt it all out, tell him how agonizing it was not to be speaking to my beloved sister, but I didn't want him to think I was draining. 'It's complicated. It's been pretty awful with my family since I got back to be honest.'

Arthur looked visibly worried – maybe he did care about me, about my welfare. He paused, running one of his strong hands through the rumpled mess of his salt-and-pepper hair. I sat up and leaned back against the headboard.

'Rachel . . . I don't know about you, but I'm loving this.'

I could feel myself blushing, excitement coursing through my body at this handbrake turn. My whole consciousness was a trick mirror in those days, the warped reflections I saw so much more bearable than a clear image.

'Yeah, no. Me too,' I said. 'Last night was really fun.'

'I just want to protect it for now. Don't you? The two of us watering it, and letting it flower.'

The words landed like a dead weight, but I pushed the feeling off.

'Absolutely,' I said brightly. 'It's just ours, isn't it? That's what makes it special.'

Arthur grinned, visibly relaxing. I'd made myself unhappy to make him happy, which in a twisted way made me happy.

'Exactly!' he agreed. 'Just ours for now. I'll make you some toast. I'm guessing you're far too sophisticated for marmalade?'

'I'm not Paddington!' I shouted after his retreating back.

Arthur Montague – the consummate host.

*

The shape-shifting unhappiness came back as soon as I saw Amber, but there was enough other trouble going on to ensure that she didn't identify the source. My tears soaked into the worn-out velvet of her sofa – I stroked its damp, piebald surface, the feel of it as familiar and comforting to me by now as a toddler's favourite soft toy. I couldn't bear the idea that Mum had sat on it, invading my sacred space. Now I couldn't help but see this room through her narrowed eyes, the ugliness she'd have found where to me there was only beauty.

'Why did you let her in?' I demanded. 'And why didn't you tell me?'

Amber tucked a handful of dark hair behind her ear, revealing the gorgeous little track of silver studs that brought out the intense blue of her eyes.

'Look at you, Rachel. Look at what even the *thought of her* does to you.'

'I'm okay,' I said, my voice muffled by snotty distress.

Amber's smile was kindly disbelieving. 'It's my job to protect you, to let you feel safe so you can heal. The last thing you needed was knowing that your parents were trying to destroy that.'

A moan of fury erupted out of me, the sound almost a surprise. The truth was, I didn't feel entirely in control anymore.

'Fuck them. Fuck them! All that shit they talked about wanting me to get better – it was only for them. I can't heal without telling the truth. And she'll never let me have that because it doesn't fit with her fucking narrative. And now she's taken Sophie away from me, too.'

Amber continued with quiet intensity. 'And she won't even let you have peace. She's never let you rest, has she? She's always been too busy trying to mould you into the doll she ordered.'

I doubled over with sobs, my chest landing on my knees.

'I'm so exhausted. I'm so fucking tired.' A night of Arthur mauling me probably hadn't helped, but I wasn't going to admit to that.

'I hear you, darling girl,' said Amber softly. 'There have been lifetimes of this. We know that now.'

That image of Mum – from long, long ago – swooped upwards and enveloped me, like a bat's wings wrapping themselves around my face. My breath was ragged in my throat.

'Stay in the room, Rachel. Take a sip of water,' commanded Amber. 'Feel your feet on the floor. I know it's taking everything you've got right now, but all of this ...' – she paused, eyes full of feeling – '... I promise you it's the darkness before the dawn.'

'Sophie!' I wailed, paranoid thoughts assailing me in random configurations. 'What's Mum said to her? I thought she'd believe me. I've protected her for so long – I never thought she'd think I was lying when I finally told the truth.'

Amber was the calm within the storm that I was kicking up.

'Your mother is a very powerful woman. Not everyone in your family's as strong and far-sighted as you. You've changed; they haven't. And that's lonely.'

'But she must see how weird it is that Esther's just appeared again. It *is* weird. Fucking slipping around in our lives, all sickly sweet. She's revolting. There's something about it that—'

Amber abruptly shook her head, cutting across me.

'Don't think about that now, Rachel. Besides, that girl deserves your pity.'

'She can look after herself,' I spat.

Amber's eyes flashed with unexpected anger. 'You're going down rabbit holes – trying to control things you can't control, when you should be using that energy for your healing. For protecting yourself.'

'But what if I have to stop coming?' I said, my distress a rising tide. 'You're the one who's taught me to protect myself. It sounds fucking stupid, but I don't know if I'll survive.' I was sobbing even harder now. 'Jesus – what's wrong with me?'

I'd shredded the damp tissue I was clinging onto, the remnants drifting down like a snowstorm onto the green velvet.

'I'm not going to leave you, Rachel,' Amber crooned. 'You're too dear to me. You know that. And it's healthy that you feel that way – you're attached to me, and that's going to help you learn to trust in other healthy bonds. Find love that's nothing like the twisted version you were forced to witness. Forced to collude with.' Her expression was fierce, her face both beautiful and ugly, in that unique way that it could be. 'It makes me so angry when I think about what you went through.'

I could barely speak through my tears. 'Don't leave me with them. Please.'

Amber stood up and quickly crossed to the sofa, her arms wrapping tightly around me like a warm net. I huddled my body against hers, shaking.

'What if I lose my job? What if I lose everything?'

Amber cupped my face in her hands, as intimate as a lover.

'Bag lady fantasy? Everyone has them.'

I laughed despite myself, and in the process I remembered how to breathe. Amber ran a thumb down my cheekbone.

'This level of trauma,' she said, blue eyes searching my face, 'it's unsustainable. You need to be selfish now, protect what *is* working.'

I thought of Arthur: his lion's grin, his mane of curls. Was that working?

'I know I do,' I said, guilty about my secret.

Amber was looking thoughtful.

'There's another way of looking at all of this, Rachel. You could choose to see it as your liberation. They're not paying, and I'm not leaving. Simple maths.'

'What do you mean?' I said. 'I got a C for GCSE, just FYI.'

Amber grinned at me indulgently, and I loved her for it. 'You could leave them. Cut contact. Look at how they make you feel. Would that be so bad?'

My head was shaking almost involuntarily. 'I couldn't. I don't think I could do that to her. And even if I could – she'd never let me go.'

'Why? Why couldn't you?' said Amber. 'Try and wrap words around it.'

'I . . .' I couldn't speak, words as sharp as glass in my throat. 'It would kill her.'

'What does that even mean, Rachel?' she said. 'Do you actually think it would make her suicidal? Give her cancer?'

'No . . .'

Amber looked at me so intensely that it felt as though she was X-raying my soul.

'You know what this sounds like to me – a pact you made as a child, to protect Mummy. It probably made you feel safe, gave you

257

a job to do, when in reality everything was so scary and out of control.' Her voice dropped low. 'Who knows how many lifetimes you even made it in, but I promise you, it's a delusion. It was never your job to take care of her. *She should have been looking after you.*'

I sunk backwards, my sadness suddenly a dead weight that felt like it could crush me into dust. I forced myself to rally.

'Anyway, her fucking ego wouldn't allow it,' I said. 'She can't bear people thinking we're not the perfect family. It's pretty much part of the business plan.'

Amber laughed. 'And – newsflash – you're not a commodity. How many messages has she sent you in the past twenty-four hours?'

'Five texts and two emails.' I shuddered. 'That email yesterday afternoon really felt like a threat.'

'What made it feel that way?'

Amber was so focused – as energized as she'd been on each of our sessions in Devon, but now her attention was all mine. It made me feel unattractively smug.

'The way she talked about you. I'm sorry . . .'

'It's okay. I can be strong for both of us,' said Amber, with that mischievous smile of hers. 'I don't scare easily.'

'She talked about not letting you take me away from her. That she was taking steps. She doesn't say that kind of thing unless she means it.'

A shiver of fear whispered across me, like someone had walked across my grave, and I leaned into Amber again. She took my weight, stroked my hair. It didn't seem strange to me at all back then. Now when I conjure it up, it's like an ancient snapshot from a time so different that I'd have to study my face to truly swear that it was me.

'And you've asked her, when she's texted, to stop, haven't you? More than once?'

I nodded assent. 'Totally.'

'So, she's ignoring that, and continuing to make threats. In fact, those threats are escalating. Becoming more sinister.'

'Yes,' I said, my voice barely audible.

Amber looked down at me, her eyes as clear and bright as stars.

'You're going to struggle with what I've got to say, but try to hear the words and feel how your body reacts. Your body will always tell you the truth if you choose to hear its messages.'

'I'm listening,' I whispered.

'Think about what it would mean to be free of all this guilt, all this shame ... all of the shit, Rachel! All of the shit that isn't yours, which was dumped onto you and is still being used to control you and destroy your life.'

Lightness overtook me, like I was a helium balloon, disappearing into infinite sky.

'I'd be free.'

Freedom or annihilation? Hard to call.

'Exactly,' said Amber triumphantly. 'And I've got a plan to get you there.'

LILY

I dropped by in the morning with two steaming lattes that I'd picked up in an unexpected gap between viewings – an entirely self-created one – and flattered Nick into taking an afternoon off.

'You did so well to research all of that legal stuff,' I told him. 'We've got a way forward now the police are involved. It's good for you to have the time with Josh. Let's keep hold of the other two as tightly as we can. We can't let Rachel's state of mind poison any more corners of our family.' I'd kissed him lightly on the lips, his stubble grazing my cheek. 'It's too precious.'

He seemed happy with that: a Friday afternoon on a squash court with our son was never going to be unwelcome, and the level of deals he'd been overseeing recently meant that he could hardly worry about leaving the fort for a single afternoon. It was an ancient mini iPad that I slipped down the soft depths of the plump sofa cushions, one that I hadn't used in years, but no one other than me needed to know it wasn't a vital piece of equipment.

*

I got back there at four, sliding the Golf I used for work into Nick's empty parking slot. I swept through the office like it was my fiefdom, finding Esther diligently typing behind a monitor in the open-plan area.

'Hi, Esther,' I called out. Her face betrayed a tremor of unease before she swiftly rearranged it into a wide grin. The teeth it displayed had a yellowish quality, which made me wonder if she still sneakily puffed on roll-ups the same way that she did as a teenager, the flakes of Golden Virginia getting trapped in the weave of her baggy jumpers. The thought of it was winding, a prickling sensation stinging the back of my eyes. I turned the pain into fuel.

'Lily!' she cried. 'Nick's not actually here.'

'I know. I'm the one who gave him the afternoon off!' I said, my laughter jarring in my ears. 'I think I left my iPad here and I didn't want to put him off his game. Will you come and help me check his office?'

Her momentary hesitation flooded me with satisfaction.

'Of course!' she said, jumping up and heading down the corridor. It was her who opened the door, and me who shut it firmly behind us. I hoped the click sounded like a gunshot to her. It wasn't friendly fire.

'Doesn't look like it's on his desk,' she said, stepping behind it like it was her own. A spurt of bile shot through me, and I decided to cut to the chase.

'No, I don't think it is,' I said, standing stock still and contemplating her. The tight little office shift dress that looked like something aspirational from a 90s car commercial. The court shoes with their sloping, flattened heels, as if it was too big a hassle or expense to replace them or find a cobbler. Her unease was palpable now. I gave it a few more seconds.

'I'm not quite sure why you're still here, Esther.'

'Hasn't Nick told you? I was teaching in Spain, and then it just seemed to dry up, and he was kind enough . . .'

I ignored her, instead looking out of the window at the Friday afternoon traffic streaming towards the Hammersmith flyover.

'I know the bare facts, but you and I also know that we've got an agreement. I've ignored your presence up to now, because I assumed you'd honour it.'

She reddened, looking down at the desk.

'I'm sorry, Lily, I promise I'll be gone soon.' I could hear the Northern lilt in her voice, the way the 'I' lazily stretched itself out like a stray cat in a patch of sunlight. She really hadn't learned that the first rule of moving up in life is to paper over the cracks – no wonder her heels were worn down to wafers.

'I kept my side of the bargain before Christmas,' I said.

'Yeah, I know you did. I'm really grateful,' she said, stumbling over her words.

'I want you gone,' I said. 'It's not a request.'

I kept staring at her, wondering if my gaze could actually succeed in reducing her to tears: I was a Jedi warrior with a very specific set of skills. Then I turned on my heels and slipped a hand down the side of the sofa, pulling the iPad out like a magician performing his final trick.

'There it is! I don't know how I managed to leave it in such an unlikely place.'

Esther's shoulders slumped, her body registering defeat. Certainly, that's what I put it down to at the time.

'At least you've found it now,' she stammered.

'Absolutely. I got what I came for.' I pushed the iPad into the deep recesses of my black leather tote and swung the door wide. 'Have a lovely weekend, won't you?'

It's galling to think, from where I stand now, that there's every chance she actually did.

RACHEL

It was far too early when I left my flat, the yellowish, sodium glow of the streetlights only just breaking through the darkness. I splashed out on an Uber to the police station, even though my overdraft limit was now so close that I could smell it. The station was at the tip of Kilburn High Road, a low, grey concrete box, surrounded by iron railings. I stared at it from the pavement, feeling almost as if I was having an out-of-body experience. That airy feeling in my limbs, that fizzy lightheadedness – it reminded me of the first stirrings of a pill on a messy night out, even though this moment was diametrically opposed to that. I checked myself – I needed to ground. I needed to find the quiet authority that Amber had coached me to project, so that this decision didn't end up making my life even worse, even more disastrous, than it already was.

*

It had been surprisingly easy to get this far. I'd wondered if they'd react with disbelief, or leave me waiting for hours like in an overstretched A&E. Instead, when I'd simply told them calmly that I wanted to report a case of harassment, they'd ushered me through to this comfortable room, all pastel walls and soft furnishings, and found a thoughtful female detective to take a statement. Was this all life really was? An elaborate confidence trick? I felt another surge of rage towards Mum. Why had I been robbed of the ability to believe in myself, to instruct the world to believe in me, for the first thirty-one years of my life? Thank God I had Amber: she'd be so proud if she could see me sitting here, handling all of this.

'So, take me through it properly, Rachel. I want to make sure we've got enough details.' The detective must've seen me unconsciously glance up at the clock. 'Do you have time?'

'I've got about half an hour. I've got a 9.30 team briefing, and I really can't miss it.'

Detective Williams smiled approvingly. She looked late forties to me, smart enough but with a comforting air of someone who was more interested in doing a good job than in attracting attention to herself. She was dual heritage, dark hair trapped at the back of her head by a plastic claw, polished beige nails chipped at the edges, as if she hadn't had time to re-paint them or strip the colour away, and thought the neutral tone was keeping her secret.

'Working for the government – no rest for the wicked, eh?'

'Exactly!' I said. I'd made sure to flag my job early, making it clear that I was a responsible member of society, not some druggie flake.

'So, tell me again about how your parents became suspicious of your relationship with Ms Greville. How it has played out in their treatment of you?'

Their treatment of you – the words felt like nectar.

'Like I told you, I was definitely struggling with . . . alcohol.'

I couldn't bring myself to say drugs out loud, not to a police-woman. 'And I'm grateful they helped me get treatment: after I collapsed on the street, I was determined to get sober. But the thing I know now, thanks to Amber, is that it was all a symptom. I was trying to blot out anxiety and low self-esteem that I've been fighting since I was a teenager, thanks to my parents. And as I started to change, my family couldn't handle this – this new version of me . . .'

'Right,' said Detective Williams, looking thoughtful.

'I'm so much better now. I haven't had a drink for three months, I'm running a huge infrastructure project at work, I've got a wonderful new boyfriend. I don't know why my parents can't just be happy for me.'

That statement was so very nearly true – the tiny gap with reality was a gully that pulled me down into a slipstream of sadness. I didn't let the mask slip.

'But give me the facts,' said Williams, her concentration intense. 'Why, in your opinion, is this harassment?'

Colour rose to my cheeks, my heart beating like a piston in my chest. I needed to pitch this next shot carefully.

'The fact that I chose not to spend Christmas with them sent Mum over the edge.'

'And you spent it with Ms Greville? At her home, or . . .'

'It was a healing retreat.' A flash of memory. My face, rolling fast towards the carpet as I came off the couch. I felt my body contract with residual shock. 'It was amazing, it was such a privilege to be a part of it.'

'So that frustrated your mother?' said Williams, her expression hard to read. My gaze surfed her hands again – two bands sat firmly on her wedding finger. Was she imagining her own child rejecting her for the most wonderful time of the year, wondering how I could be that selfish?

'More than that. When I got home, she'd let herself into my flat. It was terrifying – I thought it was a break-in.' My voice wobbled a little. 'I'm a woman living alone. It's a vulnerable feeling.'

'So, she has a key?'

'Apparently. I didn't know that.'

Williams industriously scribbled a note. 'So, you hadn't given permission for her to enter your property or hold a key?'

'Absolutely not. And then she was verbally abusive, not just to me, but to the two friends I'd brought in for protection. I mean, there was no burglar, but it turned out I needed protection anyway.'

Williams nodded with what looked like sympathy. 'And how did that night end?'

I took a second to remember the phrase that I'd practised so diligently with Amber.

'With threats and verbal intimidation. She maligned Amber and her work, and made it clear she was out for revenge.'

Williams took that in.

'Why do you think she feels so protective towards you around Ms Greville? Is there any logic to her behaviour?'

'She's jealous!' I said, the words coming out a little too fast, a little too hard. I took a breath. 'She feels threatened by our relationship, like Amber's taken me away from her. When the truth is, Amber saved me. I ... I'm not sure I'd even be here without her.'

Williams looked slightly unnerved, and I subtly rearranged my expression. I'd been shocked sometimes when I'd seen the look my fellow disciples had when they spoke about her – the one I knew I had, too, but never saw in a mirror. It was lovestruck.

'So now I need you to be precise about the subsequent events. You say that she's refusing to leave you alone, so I need you to share all of the text and email exchanges which demonstrate you asking her to desist from contact, and her overriding it.'

'Absolutely,' I said, forcing my voice back to the calm glaze that had impressed her at the start of the interview. 'I've printed off all of the documentary evidence and brought it with me for you.'

It turned out to be the perfect gift to win her over – she reached eagerly for the clear plastic wallet, thumbing swiftly through its contents like it was an airport thriller.

'I can see that her tone is intimidating, Rachel,' she said, looking up. She paused, cocked her head. 'If you don't mind me asking, has your relationship always been difficult?'

My eyes suddenly filled with hot tears. I scrubbed at them with the dark sleeve of my work jacket, embarrassed.

'Sorry . . .' I said. 'I'm so sorry.'

'Don't apologize,' said Williams kindly. 'Do you want a cup of tea? This is the suite for people reporting – the nasty stuff – so we've got our own kettle.' She mimed a little cheer. 'Yay!'

I laughed, grabbing a tissue from the box I'd just spotted on the windowsill. She was an empirically nice person.

'Yes, it has always been difficult,' I said. 'My parents have quite a toxic relationship, my dad's not been entirely faithful, and I've had to . . .' Words defeated me, but I could tell that, in this case, silence really was the louder option. 'It's been really hard,' I said eventually.

We sat there for a second, the energy settling.

'Okay,' said Williams, looking at the clock and giving another warm smile. 'We need to get you to work. If you want to fix your face, there's a bathroom through there. I've got enough here that I think I can go for a Section Five.' She looked at my baffled, streaky face. 'Sorry, too much jargon. It's a harassment order. Means your parents can't come within 250 yards of you – so no more unwanted keys turning in the lock, and she certainly can't send any more of these frankly nasty emails . . .'

I took a gulp of air. This was all feeling very real – almost *too* real. Amber had been so confident, but I realized now that on some level I hadn't believed the authorities would take me seriously. Would take *us* seriously.

'Thank you,' I said, the tears returning as I thought of Sophie. Would this force her to believe me – to turn up on my door-step full of love and apologies – or do the absolute opposite? I couldn't kid myself it would be the result I wanted and now it was too late to turn back.

'Don't cry, Rachel,' said Williams, handing over a fistful of tissues. 'You were incredibly brave to come in and do this.'

'I don't feel brave,' I said through my tears. 'I feel like a bitch.'

She watched me kindly.

'They're your mum and dad. I'm sure you love them, too.'

Now I was sobbing, any vestige of calm having well and truly left the building. Of course I loved them: it wasn't something you could simply carve out of yourself like a tumour caught early. But I hated them, too, and, unfair as it was, it was her that I reserved the blackest feelings for. How was it possible to feel both emotions so intensely and not crack in two?

Williams reached over and handed me another handful of Kleenex. 'It might not feel like it right now, but the worst is over.'

As if.

*

The pub was in Kennington, books and pictures lining the walls, a blackboard listing chi chi comfort food hung next to the bar. I looked around the room, finding Hannah and Marco huddled in a corner, fingers entwined on a table that was illuminated by a dripping candle. I didn't have time to start feeling like a gooseberry before Hannah's arms were wrapped around my body, her wet mouth on my neck.

'Rachel! Darling Rachel! We're so happy you're here!'

The royal we, less than a fortnight in. I wasn't the only one who was hopeless at playing hard to get. I was happy to see her, though, hugging her back with fierce need.

'Hey, honey,' said Marco, unfurling his lithe body from the seat and giving me a double kiss on the cheeks. His smile was comfortingly warm and familiar. I squeezed into the corner nook, grateful for our tiny circle being redrawn.

'How *are* you?' said Hannah, eyes stretched wide with worry. 'How are you surviving your mum?'

I hesitated for a second, part of me desperate to block out what I'd done today. Every time I thought about it – thought about them opening a letter or taking a call from the police – my stomach dropped earthwards. Had I really done the right thing? When I'd called Amber afterwards she'd been almost celebratory, like it was a birthday with a zero in it, but it was hard for me to feel triumphant.

I gave myself a virtual slap, reminding myself how lucky I was to have her. It was a mark of how much she cared about me that she was so proud, so pleased that firm boundaries were finally being built. And the fact that she was seeing me for free was the most incredible act of love. But then, was it free, or was she deferring the cost? I realized I didn't really know, and, much like a credit card with a 0% limit that expired in India at some mysterious point in the future, I had no desire to clarify it.

'You don't have to talk about it,' added Hannah, 'but I got the feeling from Amber it was bad.' I felt a flicker of betrayal, then pushed it away. We were our own raggle-taggle family now: she obviously wanted me to feel their support outside our prescribed hours together. It was another indication of her love for me. Now I understood why Hannah had been so insistent we meet tonight.

'Did she tell you . . .'

Hannah silently nodded, concern etched into her face. She must have seen how sad I looked, because her arms octopus-ed their way back around my shoulders.

'You're amazing, Rachel. So amazing. Isn't she, Marco?'

Marco grinned.

'You're a legend, *bella*!'

'You're taking no shit,' continued Hannah, gabbling with excitement and pride. 'No fucks given. You're telling your family who's boss. You're choosing yourself. You're choosing all of us, and Amber and your brand-new life. It's going to be amazing. This is just the darkness before the dawn.'

Had Amber told her to employ that phrase to comfort me, like a benign form of group hypnosis, or was it something she trotted out to all her clients as they plumbed the depths? Another stab of unease that I squashed as quickly as it arose. I leaned into Hannah, thanked her, and found my hand unconsciously reaching towards the wine bottle. Surely today of all days it would be acceptable to afford myself a little comfort?

'Stop there, missy!' said Marco, standing up and playfully slapping my hand away. 'I'm gonna get you something delicious with no booze in sight.'

Hannah smiled goofily at his retreating back as he loped to the bar. He was wearing slim-fitting sand-coloured chinos, a thin cashmere V-neck slung over the top. They still looked completely incongruous together to me, but no one would appoint me a relationship expert.

'He's so amazing, Rachel,' she said, voice low with awe. 'I mean, I can't believe how many gifts Amber's given me. And it's not just him – it's you, too. You're a precious gift in my life. And we've invited Tim as well.'

'Great!' I said, not quite selling the enthusiasm. It wasn't that I disliked him, it was just that I couldn't bear to think again about how out of control I'd been at the end of my turn. It had never felt quite right between us since then.

'Shame he's gay or else we could double date. Have a double wedding!' said Hannah, flushed with giggly enthusiasm. With a few days grace, I'd forgotten how simultaneously lovely and exhausting her earnestness was. Was this my reality now? It was a million miles from the witty, cynical girls I was used to sharing a pub table with. Or – or my sister. The sadness was too acute. I needed to distract myself.

'Can I tell you a secret?' I said.

'We have secrets?' said Hannah, clutching her heart, mock offended. She was wearing a baggy grey sweatshirt with a picture of an elephant – trunk aloft – on the front.

'I've been seeing a bit of Arthur.'

'Arthur, Arthur?' said Hannah, looking flummoxed. 'Right.'

I felt a surge of irritation.

'Yes. Arthur.'

'Wow,' added Hannah, her verbal diarrhoea all cleared up.

Now, I could see Marco extravagantly greeting Tim across the room, their faces lit up with pleasure at being reunited.

'Don't you like him?' I said, wanting to finish the conversation before they came over.

'You know I'll always support you, Rachel. Whatever you choose to do.' She spoke as if we'd shared a friendship that had lasted through the ages. It was sweet, I insisted to myself. 'I suppose – I mean, he's quite old.'

'Age is just a number,' I declared airily.

Hannah looked unconvinced. 'What does Amber think?'

Before I could craft a reply, the boys were approaching the table, Marco holding a tall purple drink with a sprig of mint poking out. He placed it in front of me ceremoniously.

'For the lady – a cranberry royale. Very exclusive artisanal recipe.'

He was relentlessly fun – I felt like he'd make me laugh in a nuclear apocalypse. Which was lucky, as that was roughly what my life had become by that point.

'Hey, Rachel,' said Tim, awkwardly folding his bald head downwards to kiss my cheek.

'Hi,' I said, equally awkward. 'Lovely to see you.'

Hannah had sucked Marco back into the vortex by now, their bodies a tangle of lips and limbs.

'Likewise,' said Tim, before both of us ground to a conversational halt.

Hannah eventually emerged. 'Tell us about how real life's been, Tim,' she said. 'Are you coping without us?'

'I'm not going to lie, it's been pretty hardcore coming back,' he said, smiling ruefully. 'A week of night shifts in A&E isn't the ideal way to come off a workshop like that.'

'We're all just so open now, aren't we?' enthused Hannah. 'So sensitive. It's easy to bruise, but it's just because we're so alive to our experience!'

'Yeah, I think it did really help me,' said Tim. 'I've kicked Dan to the kerb, he's just going to be Dr Rogers from now on.'

His married lover, a thing of the past. More evidence of Amber's power to change our lives for the better.

'Good for you!' I said.

'How about you, Rachel?' asked Tim carefully.

Hannah's eyes were trained on me like she was my support animal. I took a second to reply.

'Oh I'm . . . it's been pretty bad with my parents to be honest.' I waved a dismissive hand. 'It's got legal. I'll be okay.'

'She's been really brave,' intoned Hannah.

I gave a brief smile, my guts churning. I wished I could find a way to align how I felt inside with all of their cheerleading. I glanced down at my phone, balanced face upwards in my bag. Nothing from Sophie, even though I'd texted her twice today. I needed to reach her before the news broke.

'Let's talk about something else,' I said, taking a big gulp of my purple drink. 'Marco, you should be a sobriety coach!'

'My true calling!' he said, grinning, and the conversation mercifully moved on.

*

We somehow stayed until closing time, although a late night was the last thing I needed, what with Duncan's beady eyes trained on me every second at work. The truth was, I didn't want to go back to my empty flat and I didn't have the energy to turn up on Arthur's doorstep and fake 'cool girl, no commitment necessary' vibes. Eventually we were all on the pavement, goodbyes reluctantly being said. They were warm and sweet, and I was glad for all of them in that moment, grateful to Amber for bringing us together.

'You're going north, correct?' said Tim. 'Do you want to share a cab?'

I couldn't afford one. And in that moment I realized I also didn't want to: I was wary still.

'Thanks, but I'm just going to take the tube,' I said. 'I need to read something for work.'

Lying was my second language, and I was most definitely bilingual. Perhaps I still am.

'Let me walk you to the tube, at least,' he said. 'It's late.'

'Thanks,' I said reluctantly.

I turned to finish my goodbyes.

'Are you going home, home?' whispered Hannah after I'd hugged Marco, and I nodded my assent. 'Call you tomorrow,' she said, conspiratorial, and released me into the night.

Tim and I walked a hundred yards in silence, the awkwardness returning now we were alone. There weren't many people around, so we lacked for convenient distractions.

'I'm glad you're doing so well,' I ventured.

'Thanks,' he said, thrusting his hands into the pockets of his long wool coat. Silence settled like snow, but then he swept it aside. 'I wanted to talk to you actually.'

'Right,' I said. The tube was only three minutes or so away now. I could get through this.

'I've been thinking about it – medically – what I saw. You know, cold light of day and all that.'

He was so fucking doctor-ly, like a visiting physician in a black-and-white film.

'We don't need to talk about it,' I protested.

He turned to look at me, his serious expression spotlighted by a streetlamp.

'Please, just hear me out. I know you're working with Amber because you've had problems with addiction, and if you'd taken something to take the edge off the anxiety, I get it. It was scary for all of us to go that deep with our traumas.'

'Of course I didn't,' I snapped. This new family was turning out to be exactly like my real family, judging and mistrusting me. 'I wouldn't come to a healing retreat and then get fucked up on drugs.'

'Rachel, please . . .' said Tim, his hands held up in surrender. 'I'm not trying to insult you. I know how that probably sounded. I'm just worried.'

'Why do you keep going on about this?' I said, pulling ahead of him, my head dropping against the cold and his continued assault.

'Because if you didn't *take* it, who *gave* it to you?'

'What?'

'That wasn't just reiki, or the power of the emotional release. You were on something.' He had good enough manners to look embarrassed. 'I could see there was something building up with you and Arthur. You don't think he'd have done that to you, do you? I know it sounds crazy but – I care about you, Rachel. You're vulnerable.'

My heart was pounding in my chest. The illuminated sign outside Stockwell tube was yards away from us now. I took off, half running.

'Goodnight, Tim,' I shouted behind me. I whacked a credit card down on the barrier and threw myself onto a Northern Line train, music pounding through my headphones.

That night I had my first drink.

LILY

I was optimistic; Nick less so. The letter arrived in a crisp, official envelope: could we come and give an interview connected to an ongoing investigation?

'It's a different police station,' said Nick, jabbing at the paper with his finger. We were both starting late that day, and we had newspapers splayed out across the kitchen table, a cafetière of coffee sitting between us. It was like a still life of contented middle-aged coupledom.

'Yes, silly, it's Rachel's local police station,' I said. 'They must have spread the web, expanded the investigation. She's a different council from us, so if they want to involve mental health services . . .'

'Lest we forget how good my wife is at telling a story,' said Nick, with a mirthless laugh, which succeeded in making his remark sound like the exact opposite of a compliment. 'Mark my words, we need to be prepped for this one.'

*

I hate Kilburn: I'd begged Rachel not to move there when she'd first rented that nasty flat. It borders the leafy environs of Queens Park, an area I'm happy to cover, but even a couple of streets across takes you into a subterranean hinterland. The police station was no exception, the pavement outside littered with takeaway cartons and dog mess. We picked our way through the debris to the door and asked the clerk on the desk for the Detective Williams who'd written the letter.

We waited at least ten minutes before a dishevelled woman shoved her way through the crowded waiting area towards us.

'Mr and Mrs Appleby?' she said.

I sprung to my feet, stuck out a hand.

'Yes!' I said. 'Detective Williams? It's a pleasure to meet you.'

She took a beat before she responded, eyes subtly flicking up and down. I'd come from a viewing and was wearing a new pair of black wedge heels with a fitted aubergine dress that skimmed my Pilates-toned body before falling to the knee. I knew in an instant – particularly looking at the way she was futilely pretending that her bobbly black jacket matched her shapeless trousers – that I should have made myself less threatening.

'Do follow me through,' she said with a smile that failed to reach her eyes.

My skin began to prickle. I'd been anticipating sympathy and vindication, but perhaps Nick was right to be on high alert. I comforted myself: in a way, it confirmed that we were a good team, filling in the gaps for one another.

She led us to a windowless interview room, a white Formica table like a butcher's slab dominating the space. We sat down opposite her, but she didn't utter a word for a few seconds. Ordinarily I'd have grabbed the bull by the horns, but I knew enough from my lawyer husband to know that we shouldn't speak first. It was more than that, though – she was somehow owning our collective silence.

'Sorry, I should have offered you water,' she said.

'I'm fine,' said Nick, just as I responded, 'That would be great.'

A faint smile played around her lips, as if our opposing replies confirmed all her suspicions. She was starting to enrage me, and we were only five minutes in.

Water was fetched, and after another artificial silence, she finally deigned to start.

'Mr and Mrs Appleby, I've asked you to come in on the back of a complaint made by your daughter, Rachel. She—'

'No,' I said, cutting across her, my heart pounding. 'That's incorrect. *We've* made a complaint about Amber Greville, her therapist. Or *so-called* therapist.'

'Yes, I heard that from Shepherd's Bush. But Rachel's complaint was formally registered first, by me. It's against you. And I take it very seriously.'

I could feel the blood draining from my face. I grabbed for Nick's hand, which was stiff with barely contained anger.

'Our daughter's a mess,' he said. 'You can't trust a word she says. That woman's treating her like a puppet. She's got no mind of her own right now.'

Williams's gaze was cool. 'That really doesn't match up with my impression of your daughter, Mr Appleby. She was composed, articulate. The only point where she was obviously distressed, or lost her train of thought, was when she talked about the harassment she alleges she's suffered from her family.'

For a second it was though I was watching the scene from above. It felt like a dream, or that supposed moment between life and death when you float untethered from the material world and your whole miserable existence flashes before your eyes.

'But it's all lies!' I wailed. Nick's palm pressed down on my hand, but I was too far gone, the stress of the past few months erupting out of me. 'She's got her involved in a sex cult. She's pushed her into thousands of pounds worth of debt. She's told her I'm some kind of medieval torturer . . .'

Williams's face was impassive, cold. Nick squeezed my hand, hard.

'Lily!' he said, sharp.

'Do not speak to me like I'm a dog you accidentally let off the lead,' I said, more venom in my voice than I intended. We needed to wrest back control, and Nick knew it.

'Our daughter is a very ill girl,' he said. 'Addicts are manipulative, and she's doing exactly that to you, if you don't mind me saying. And we've lived with it for thirty-one years.'

'She's not a girl, she's a woman,' said the tiresomely politically correct detective. 'And as I've stated, my impression was that she was a woman entirely in control of her mental faculties. That's why I've referred this case to the CPS.'

It was as if all the blood had drained from my body. I felt weak.

'The CPS?' I said. 'What, as if we're criminals?'

Williams didn't respond. She didn't have to. Nick was puce with anger.

'This is f—' he stopped himself. 'If my daughter tops herself because you didn't take us – her parents – seriously, you'll have blood on your hands. And I will sue you into oblivion.'

Williams stayed infuriatingly calm, a grim little smile of contempt on her face.

'From my impression of Rachel, I don't see that as a likely outcome of us pursuing this case. As I said to you, the only point at which she displayed extreme distress was when she talked about the treatment she claimed she'd experienced at your hands.' Her eyes bored into us. 'You're now legally obligated to stop contacting her, and to go no closer than 250 yards from her person. Those are the terms of the temporary harassment order we've got as an interim measure.'

'What?' I said. It was more a sob than a word, the walls of the drab, dark room closing in on me.

Nick was jabbing his finger at her as if he wished it was his fist. 'So, what, our complaint against that fucking woman counts for nothing because you got in there first?'

Williams gave a smug little shrug, like she was deflecting his praise for winning the race. 'Your statements can certainly form part of your defence.'

'Our defence?' I croaked. 'Why do we have to defend ourselves, while that b— That *woman*, is out there in the world ruining other families' lives?'

'Do you know of anyone who can verify that accusation?' said Williams, quick as a flash.

Could I force Deborah Madden to back me up, the way I'd led her by the nose on the PTA? No – this situation was way beyond a gluten-free bake sale. And besides that, I felt so broken.

'I'm working on it,' I said pathetically. I wanted to go. I wanted to lie down and cry, all alone, and then regain my strength for the fight of my life. This wasn't meant to happen. My family was supposed to stay intact – that was the whole point of what I did. Maybe the fire-and-brimstone God of my Catholic childhood really did exist. Maybe he'd been keeping score all this time.

'You're wrong about the suicide thing,' said Nick. 'She threatened it to my wife when Lily told her we weren't going to pay for Amber Greville anymore. I guarantee you she manipulated Rachel into that state so we'd keep chucking money at her.'

Williams remained untroubled. 'Rachel told me that Ms Greville is seeing her for free, because she's so concerned about the stress she's under, so that argument really doesn't hold any weight.'

'For free?' I said, the words landing like a punch in the solar plexus. 'That's worse! She's literally trying to replace me. To destroy me! I'm Rachel's mother; not her.'

I was weeping uncontrollably now. Nick stood up, leaning over me and putting an arm around my hunched shoulders.

'Lily, come on,' he said, his voice gentler than earlier. 'Let's go. This is pointless.'

I reluctantly let myself lean into him. 'Okay,' I said, my voice small, scrubbing at my eyes with a tissue that I'd found in my bag. I hated what a state I must look. How stupid I'd been to set a viewing for after this. How arrogant.

Williams watched me gather my things, that half smile still playing across her face, like every move we made was a scene from a play that she'd already seen. I stood up.

'Is Sophie part of this harassment order of yours?' I said, standing up and forcing steel into my voice.

'Sorry?'

'Our other daughter.' I was the one to smile without warmth now. She didn't know quite as much about our family as she thought she did. 'We have a son also – Josh.'

'No, it's only you two,' said Williams. 'I rang Rachel before you came in to tell her it was in place.'

The phrase was like a burning match flying through the air – she and Amber could just casually pick up the phone to my daughter, but I was deemed to be some kind of dangerous stalker. Rage was starting to overtake distress now, fuel flooding back into the tank.

'Thank you, Detective Williams,' I said. 'This is a dark moment for our family, but we'll heal from it.' I glanced to Nick. 'She's trying to destroy us, but most of all she's trying to destroy Rachel, and I will not let that happen. You think you're helping her, but you're just part of the abuse now.' I smiled sweetly before Nick could bundle me out. 'I know your intentions are good. You're simply deluded.'

RACHEL

I paced up and down the street, my hands balled up into fists. Sophie's desk light was shining in the living room – she often worked from home on Fridays, sketching out plans and assembling mood boards for the interior designer she worked for. All of those soft swatches of fabric and delicate lines perfectly suited my sister's gentle character. The green scarf she'd given me for Christmas was wound tightly around my neck.

I'd risked telling Duncan that I had a doctor's appointment, and I didn't have long before Mum and Dad would be out of that interview and straight on the phone. I half walked to the pathway and then turned back, for what must have been the third or fourth time. I pulled out the gum that I'd been chewing and balled it up in the silver foil it had come in, paranoid she'd be able to smell last night's gin on my breath. I was drinking away Tim's intervention, I knew that, but I couldn't yet face engaging with why I was willing to risk everything to blot out his words. A woman who'd already passed me once, her black dachshund trotting next to her on its lead, threw me an odd look: to be fair, my manic pacing didn't exactly suit the quiet gentility of the Chiswick street. It was now or never, and I knew I couldn't bear never.

I marched up to the door, burying any emotion until my finger had pressed the bell. The ringing sound sent a reverberation of dread through my body.

'Rachel!' Sophie said, as the door swung wide. I could see from her expression that my carefully applied foundation and ironed work clothes weren't fooling her for a second. 'Come inside,' she said, a quaver in her voice, standing back so that I could pass her. 'I'll make us some coffee.'

I sank gratefully onto one of the two padded benches that ran down the sides of her pine kitchen table. Their little flat was so cozy: evidence of their shared life was stuck to the fridge like a loving collage – a jumble of photos and optician's letters and invitations to other people's weddings. Just for a second, I let myself relax enough to feel the exhaustion. It made me long to curl up and sleep right there, like I was their child or their beloved pet.

Sophie came in after me, barely turning to look at me at first. Instead she methodically poured water from the filter into the kettle, reaching up into the cupboard for a packet of chocolate biscuits.

'There we go,' she said, with false brightness, depositing it all in the centre of the table.

'Earth to Sophie . . .' I said, waving a hand in her direction.

'Don't do that!' she said, eyes narrowed with anger. 'We're not joking about any of this, Rachel.'

'Is "we" you and Mum, or you and me?' I said.

'Just stop it, okay? I'm not playing that game with you anymore.'

I took a sip of my coffee, trying to ignore how fast my heart was beating. 'It's not a game anymore,' I said quietly.

Sophie stared at me, so much pain in her eyes that it made me want to cry. It was as if her pain was my pain, like I was feeling its tremors and ripples in my own body. I almost said it to her, but I knew she'd think it was no more than a tactic.

'Go on,' she said eventually.

'I've taken out a harassment order so they can't contact me anymore.'

Sophie jumped up, tipping the bench she was sitting on backwards. It clattered loudly to the floor.

'Why the hell did you do that?' she shouted.

'I didn't have a choice!'

'Yes, you did. You really did,' she said, her face flaming with anger. 'Stop playing the fucking victim. They went to the police because of *Amber*, not because of you. Because they're frightened for you!' She sank back down onto the bench. '*I'm* frightened for you.' She wiped her hand through the air. 'I mean, look at you.'

There was almost too much to react to. I sat there a second, words dry in my throat.

'Sophie . . .'

'I asked Mum about Esther, and she said it wasn't true. That you were paranoid, borderline anorexic. But you're not that now. You've just got to pull yourself together and stop acting like this . . .'

'No, Sophie, *you* stop,' I shouted. 'What are you talking about? *I* went to the police, not them.'

Sophie's shoulders slumped with sadness. Rage never suited her: even as a toddler, her tantrums would melt to a whimper within minutes.

'They went last week. They reported Amber for coercive

control.' She looked at me warily. 'I probably shouldn't even be telling you this.'

'Yes, you should! *Coercive control*? For fuck's—'

'No, I mean it!' she snapped. 'You've made it that way. Picking sides, making accusations. I hate it – every time I speak to one of you I feel like I'm telling tales. I'm trying to plan my hen night, my wedding – this should be a happy time for me, but you've hijacked it . . .'

'When last week?' I demanded.

'What?'

'What day did they go?'

Sophie looked confused. 'I don't know . . . Wednesday? Why does it even matter? The whole thing is completely effing ridiculous.'

Her words were drifting in and out – they went on Wednesday, and I went on Friday. Thursday was when Amber had brought up the whole idea. She was the one who said it first, wasn't she? My thoughts were hard to marshal, blunted by sleep deprivation and alcohol.

'Definitely Wednesday?' I demanded. Sophie's nod felt like a trap door opening, a hatch into a dark underworld I couldn't yet explore or even acknowledge existed. Besides, I didn't have time to engage with the implications: this could be my final chance to save my relationship with my sister.

'I've been thinking about what you said, about Esther.' I was aware I was spitting out my words too fast to sound like I was wholly in control of myself. 'What if Mum wants her where she can see her?'

'What?'

'What if Mum and Dad have an arrangement? She accepts

he's never going to be faithful, but at least she knows who it is. Maybe she's got someone, too.'

'Don't be so ridiculous,' snapped Sophie.

'Is it? Do you think Dad's faithful? Do you think they're happy?' Sophie reddened.

'I don't spend much time thinking about our parents' sex life, to be honest.'

'All the times he'd flirt with waitresses, or with our teachers at parents' evenings. All those work trips that stretched into the weekend. It was just normal for us, wasn't it?'

Sophie took a slug of her coffee, turning to look out of the window.

'Dad's Dad. He likes turning on the charm. It's what makes him so good at his job.'

'Keep telling yourself that, Sophie,' I said. 'Keep telling yourself it hasn't affected us, how toxic an environment we grew up in. Just because it's been our normal life doesn't mean it's normal.'

'Me and Josh are fine,' she retorted.

'Josh's marriage is a 1950s nightmare – I don't know how she stands him. And ...' I stopped myself. 'I hope you and Toby will be really happy.' She was marrying her first proper boyfriend – chubby, unthreatening, slightly dull – the complete opposite of Dad.

'Because you're such a fucking expert!' she said, standing up and slamming her mug into the sink.

I stood too, my whole body shaking.

'Don't do that,' I said. 'Please don't do that. It hurts me how hard it's been. I know you all pity me, or make a joke out of it, but what I saw – what I soaked up over all those years – it made it really difficult for me to trust in any man, in any relationship! And I hated myself, because I was the easiest person to hate. When you say *pull yourself together*, don't you think I haven't said that to myself a million times? And then I haven't, and I've kept on racking up lines or having another fucking glass, because I'm so ashamed of how weak I am. But I couldn't stop until I understood what really happened to us all. And if my family don't want to admit the truth, then ... then right now I can't know my family.'

Sophie stared at me, her face frozen with sadness. 'But you haven't stopped, have you? I can tell.'

'What? No! I haven't drunk anything since October.'

'I know you,' she said simply.

I could feel my face crumpling. I looked at the old-fashioned wall clock, the hands closing in on 11 a.m. I adjusted my expression as best I could, the lie cutting deep into me. 'I'm really sad you think that. I've got to go now, anyway. I've got a major meeting about my building project at midday.'

It was Sophie who crumpled now. 'Don't leave, Rachel. Let me help you. We're all so worried about you.'

Little spikes of adrenaline were sending me skittering off in different directions, grabbing for verifiable facts. I paused, eyeing her. I was unravelling it now.

'That's what she said to you, isn't it?'

'What?'

'Mum. She went on and on about how worried she was. And then you told her everything I said! I've been sat here trying to work out how they could accuse Amber of coercion. It's bullshit, but if they twisted what I told you ...'

'We love you,' Sophie wailed. 'We're all just trying to protect you. Why can't you see that?'

I yanked on my coat, deliberately leaving her scarf lying discarded under the table. I would yearn for it later.

'That's why you came to see me on Monday, isn't it? You're not my sister; you're just Mum's spy.'

'Rachel, listen to yourself,' she said, pulling at the sleeve of my coat. 'You're so paranoid! I really think you're having a breakdown.'

I turned on her.

'You're the one who should listen to *me*. There's more to all of this than either of us understand, and Mum's playing you. You need to learn to protect yourself when I'm not here to protect you anymore.'

I was heading down the hallway, Sophie running after me. I opened the front door.

'Rachel, wait,' she said, tears streaming down her cheeks. 'Please!'

My brain was simultaneously fuzzy and sharp, like an instrument I hadn't yet mastered. I looked at Sophie, refusing to let her tears melt me the way they always had. I'd reached the doorstep now.

'In the end, you'll know who was telling the truth.' I froze a second. 'Maybe it's not Mum who's got the power. Maybe it's Esther – maybe she's got something over her. You watch what happens next.'

With that, I retreated down the stone steps, ignoring my sister's sobs until they'd faded away into almost nothing.

LILY

Nick pulled the car up next to Holland Park, a couple of streets from my viewing. We'd barely spoken during the drive from Kilburn, with only the warm air that pumped from the heating system for background noise. The engine stopped, and he twisted his whole body towards me.

'I'm sorry,' he said, his voice flat and sober. It made me realize how often it was layered, one meaning blanketing another, my ears perfectly attuned to the duality.

'For which part?' I said. I sounded brittle. I *was* brittle: I could snap in two, or I could do damage.

He gave a hoarse laugh and shrugged.

'Take your pick, Lily.'

I looked out towards the grand black iron gates that ringed the park, the tall, strong trees that lay beyond them. The houses that lined this street, that overlooked this view, were so imposing. It was odd, sometimes, up-selling something to goggle-eyed Americans that I could never afford myself. If they balked at the price, I knew exactly how to subtly make them feel cheap, how to send them scuttling for their self-worth via an eye-watering deposit. I always buried the discomfort, the way it took me

292

back to a time I'd worked so hard to leave behind, when it was my own nose pressed up against the glass. Staying quiet in the changing rooms while other girls casually described unimaginable luxuries – a microwave, a Biba skirt.

'I've always known who you are,' I said, my eyes staying trained on the trees. 'And vice versa, don't you think?'

'What do you mean?'

I looked back at him, weighing up how truthful to be. He'd never been as bright as me – it had been lonely and reassuring, all at once. I'd never wanted to be my mother, trapped with my father, no agency. At least in a sense I'd chosen this.

'We both knew what we wanted,' I said.

Nick's eyes narrowed. 'I'm not sure how to take that.'

'I think we've been a good team,' I said. My eyes raked over him, taking in the way the bulge of his belly was pressing against his white work shirt. He needed to go up a size. Perhaps I'd just switch them out in his wardrobe without his knowledge. 'Filled in for each other's weaknesses.'

Nick looked slightly helpless.

'It's not just been about money, though, or lifestyle?' he said. 'We love our kids. We've been good parents.'

His voice was a pleading whine, a cry for my reassurance. I could tell he was as baffled by how we'd got here as I was, a couple of would-be criminals in a flash car. Every time I remembered where it was we'd just come from, I wanted to disappear, to evaporate.

'Of course we have,' I said firmly. 'And Rachel will come back to us – she can't survive without her family, whatever she's believing right now. I will not let that bitch win this, Nick.'

'I know you won't,' he said, putting his hand over mine, his scratched wedding ring chafing my skin. 'You brought her into our lives; you can get her out.'

All the rage I'd been mutating into false calm surged up, overwhelming. I pulled my hand away and reached for my bag on the floor, flicking open the lock on the passenger door.

'You're every bit as responsible,' I hissed. 'If anything happens to our daughter, it won't just be the police with blood on their hands.'

Anger was making me sloppy. The truth was beginning to erupt, however much I fought to contain it.

RACHEL

My eyes tracked Arthur as he leaned over the bar, effortlessly charming our drinks out of the barmaid as other customers jostled for service. For a horrible second, his resemblance to my dad – the particular way they swung through the trees in the jungle – was too acute to ignore. I pushed the thought away – there wasn't time for it. I already had an agenda for this evening: I had to know if there was any truth to Tim's horrible, torturing suggestions.

Arthur came ambling back to the table, a drink held in each of his gnarled hands. He put down my white wine and raised a bushy eyebrow.

'Are you sure you're alright with this?'

My hand moved towards the glass a little too fast, a bandit reaching for a gun.

'Yeah, honestly, I'm fine now. Me and Amber agree on that. The binge drinking was really just a symptom – a way of making my unhappiness visible.' Arthur looked slightly glazed over. 'But I'm *so* much better now!'

I took a gulp of my drink, waiting for the internal equation to kick in – a starburst of pleasure followed by a pleasing numbness. How had I survived without this sensation for all those months? I hoped it would give me the courage to find the words I needed.

'As long as you're sure,' said Arthur, taking a long mouthful of his Guinness. We were in a west London pub around the corner from his flat, which did a bad impression of a spit and sawdust boozer. The Chablis by the glass and the plates of charcuterie, reluctantly picked at by skinny blondes on Tinder dates, told a very different story.

'Definitely,' I gabbled. 'I mean, everything's going so much better. I've finally set appropriate boundaries with my family, work's stabilizing and the depth I'm reaching with Amber . . .' I unconsciously touched my heart through my jumper, the way Hannah would. 'It's really changed me.'

It seems incredible to me now, the way I could simultaneously live in multiple realities. No wonder the questions I had to ask were still too mangled to pass my lips.

'That's great, Rachel,' said Arthur.

Silence stretched out between us. My mouth was dry, and I took another greedy gulp of wine.

'Have you got your boys this weekend?' I asked, still playing for time.

His face melted in a way that it never had for me. 'Yeah, they're coming Friday. Little terrors. Anyway, talking about how good you're feeling . . .' He gave a wolfish smile. 'Shall we go back to mine soon?'

I hesitated. I couldn't simply fold.

'Arthur . . . I wanted to ask you something.'

'What's that?'

I forced clarity. 'Um, with reiki, do you ever use anything to relax the – what, patient?'

He looked confused. 'What do you mean?'

'Like, I don't know. Hallucinogenics or – you know, like how everyone's going on about mushrooms these days.'

'Absolutely not,' he said irritably. 'It would be completely unprofessional. It's a hands-on healing; it's not about other substances.'

'What, never? So, there was no way, on the retreat, you'd have given us something for – energy flow, or something?'

'Of course not,' he barked. 'Anyone who does practice that way should be barred.' Fear prickled through my body. His professional affront was real: I felt sure that, if anyone had drugged me, it wasn't him.

'Right, it's just something Tim said. About how I was at the end of my session.'

Something different crossed his face now, something complicated, but he wiped it away so swiftly that I could kid myself I imagined it.

'I'd ignore him if I were you,' he said. 'Conventional medicine breeds hysteria. I'll go to the bar and settle up. Do you want to give me your card, and I'll just tap it for you?'

'Here you go,' I said, pulling out my radioactive Amex out of my purse. I kept my focus on following his progress back to the bar, refusing to let my mind roam to the places it would soon be forced to travel to.

*

It was barely sunrise as I approached Amber's treatment room the next morning. It was kind of her to see me at this ungodly hour, I told myself, still refusing to unravel the implications of what Arthur had said to me. Some part of me was wary, though, judging by the way my finger hovered over the buzzer the same way it had that first time I came here. But this was *Amber*, I insisted to myself, firmly pressing. She was my protector. The saviour of my sanity.

I felt it the moment I walked into the room. If she'd had an aura, it would have been an icy blue, the chill in the room tangible enough to make me shiver. She was sitting on the sofa, one leg folded underneath her like a ballet dancer. She didn't get up to hug me like she normally did; instead she slowly raised her head, allowing our eyes to meet only when she was ready.

'Hi,' I said uncertainly, my stomach churning with a seasick dread.

'Hello, Rachel,' she replied, clipped. 'Sit yourself down,' she added, as if I should be asking her permission.

I sat down opposite her, waiting for her to add something, but nothing came.

'I've been really looking forward to seeing you,' I said. 'The whole thing with Sophie . . .' I waited for my inevitable tears, but it seemed I was too tense for them to flow. Who knew that grief could be constipated? 'It was so awful. I just wanted to hug her, to force her to see that we're still *us*, despite all the horrible stuff with our parents, but she was so angry with me.'

Amber's face remained a rigid mask.

'And, Amber, she said they went to the police. Separately from me. Like, two days before. You didn't know that, did you? The police didn't contact you? I know how sometimes you've tried to protect me from the way they bully me, but . . .'

I petered out, waiting for her to come back to life, but she simply stared at me blankly. It wasn't safe here now, which made all the questions I was refusing to speak shout so loudly I knew

I couldn't block them out much longer. Still, I tried to bring her back to me.

'Have I done something?' I stammered.

'I don't know, Rachel. You tell me. Tell me about your week in a little more detail.'

Ice slithered down my spine. I knew where this was going.

'Have you seen Hannah?' I asked, as if I didn't already know the answer to that question. I was as angry with myself as I was with her. Of course she'd run straight to Amber.

Amber cocked her head, giving nothing away. 'Why do you ask?'

'I just ...' My heart was fluttering like a trapped bird, my teeth chattering. I was irrationally terrified. 'I just ... I wondered what she'd said.'

'What do you think she might have said?'

'I wanted to tell you – I just ... I didn't know if you'd approve, and your approval means so much to me. *You* mean so much to me – you know that, don't you?'

Amber held up a slim white hand, the rainbow of stones in her rings catching the light.

'Slow down, Rachel. Spit out what it is you want to say so we know we're on the same page.'

I was trapped now. What if she didn't know, and I was unnecessarily dropping a bomb? A bomb Arthur had specifically asked me not to detonate.

'Me and Arthur ...' The words were thick in my throat, hard to put together. 'We've been seeing a bit of each other.'

Amber steepled her elegant fingers, pausing before she deigned to reply.

'As friends?'

Was it a genuine question? Her expression was inscrutable.

'N-no.' I stammered. 'We've been seeing each other – romantically.'

I sounded like a Mills and Boon novel. A deluded one at that – even I couldn't kid myself that the series of secretive booty calls I'd signed up for were textbook romance.

'Romantically?' said Amber, with a ghost of a smile. 'And do you think that's a good idea, considering the fragility of your mental health?'

'It just happened,' I said pathetically.

Amber's gaze flitted away, as if she couldn't quite bear to lay eyes on me, her failed experiment.

'You do realize how early you are in the recovery process? How quickly the drink and drugs could become a life-threatening problem again?'

I nodded guiltily. At least she hadn't guessed that I'd been tempted back already: how was it that Sophie simply knew? The thought of that innate closeness made the missing of my sister so visceral that I almost doubled up in pain. I could feel in that moment that, the way things were evolving, soon I would have no one.

'I don't take many patients on,' Amber continued. 'I'm very discerning, because when I do invest in rebuilding someone's life, I need to know they're really up for it.'

'I know, and I'm so lucky—'

She cut across me. 'But that requires total trust, total transparency on both sides.'

'Of course!'

Amber almost sneered. 'Of course?'

I paused, searching for the most authentic truth inside myself.

The transparency she was demanding. Despite everything I half knew, I still wanted her to be the one to put me back together again. It was too precious to give up on without a fight.

'I just – I miss it. The attention. Sex. All of it. He initiated it, and I wasn't strong enough to say no to him.'

Not once did I think to say that it was her who had thrown him in my path. Who had created that messy sexual breeding ground for all of us.

Amber shook her head sorrowfully. 'Everything you just said – they're the words of an addict. As we know, sex and love addiction are a major part of your profile, unsurprising with parents like yours. But that's why I've been here. To give you the guidance to stop using these vices to numb the pain.' Her eyes flashed with anger. 'And I can only do that if you don't lie to me.'

'I didn't . . .'

Her voice rose. 'A lie of omission is still a lie. And a deeply destructive one in the context of the therapeutic relationship.'

'I'm sorry, I really am sorry,' I said, pleading.

Her expression remained cold.

'You are not well enough for this, Rachel. Who knows when you will be? I suspect this addiction is more destructive for you than any of the others. It speaks directly to the twisted, abusive family that tried to mould you in their image.'

Her words were like bullets. Now I was sobbing, my face buried in my hands. Would I always be defective – nothing more than a broken branch of a rotten tree?

'I'll end it . . . I'll end it today,' I told her. 'I know I'm not ready. I'm so glad I told you.'

Her face slightly softened.

'I'm glad you know that,' she said.

I smiled through my tears, pathetically grateful for this chink of light. Perhaps I could just forget about what Tim had said. Perhaps it was life-threatening to do otherwise.

'Look at you, though,' she said. 'Do you really need more stress? Right now you've got to go to work and show Duncan that you're his star staff member. His number one girl. That's going to take a lot from you.'

The ground felt unsteady again, the prospect of the day ahead a dark tunnel. I gasped for breath, my throat constricting with fear.

'I don't know if I can do it ... I can't.'

Amber crossed the room, sinking down next to me on the sofa and putting her arms around me.

'You can. I know that you can. Don't ever forget how brave you are. How far you've come. This is a bump in the road, but you're still driving the car.' I could feel her lips moving against my hair. 'I'll call Arthur – you don't need any more drama put on you right now. He should have recognized how vulnerable you are – I'm going to make sure he thinks long and hard about his behaviour. And you can have an extra session this week; you need the support.'

I wanted to protest, to tell her it was obviously me who should speak to him, but it felt too risky to go up against her. Besides, I was already skating on thin ice – it wasn't like I was paying for all the love and care she was lavishing on me to get me better.

I must have known, too, that if I saw Arthur, I'd never have the strength to end it.

'Thank you,' I breathed. 'I'm sorry I fucked up so badly. Thanks for not giving up on me.'

I was searching inside for those questions I'd arrived knowing that I needed to ask, but every time I grasped for them, they swam away from me. Eventually I gave up, letting my body slump against hers.

'You're welcome, precious girl,' she said, stroking my cheek. Her voice was an equally soft caress. 'You know I'll never give up on you. Never ever.'

LILY

The lights were on and I wasn't about to give up. I was the same with my own doorbell, convinced an unexpected afternoon chime meant Jehovah's Witnesses or recent prison releases – all tattoos and broken teeth – with those brimming plastic crates of overpriced dishcloths. Eventually I heard the patter of footsteps.

'Lily.'

Deborah didn't look exactly thrilled to see me. I leant in for a double kiss, nevertheless. I'd brought a box of cakes from the Gail's on the corner, and I thrust them into her hands.

'I thought we left things a little oddly on Boxing Day, and I wanted to apologize in person,' I said. 'It's been a bit of a stressful time.'

'Right,' she said warily, not stepping aside. She was wearing a pair of wrinkled green tracksuit bottoms that screamed 'working from home', and I wondered if she was weighing up the time commitment. She stared at me, birdlike. 'Are you okay, Lily? You look a bit . . . not quite yourself.'

It took all my wherewithal not to look her up and down and make a joke about 'casual Tuesday'. Instead I pressed home the advantage.

'Not entirely,' I said, my voice shaking. 'That's why I need to talk to you. Can I come in?'

Deborah's face melted and she stepped aside. I hadn't lost my touch with everyone, it appeared.

RACHEL

Cubicle two was becoming my home away from home. I would go for a pee, and then lay my face against the wall, calculating how many minutes I could afford to be away from my desk before it became a hanging offence. That afternoon I'd clearly taken my vice too far, because when I swung open the door, I found Julia standing on the other side, looking worried.

'Hi,' I said, crossing purposefully to the sink and turning the taps on full blast.

'Rachel,' she said hesitantly, her anxious face reflected in the smeared mirrors. 'Are you alright? You seem so quiet today.'

The truth was, since my morning session with Amber, I'd lost all of my remaining ability to pretend I was handling my job. Emails swam in front of my eyes like they were written in Chinese, and I'd dumped every single incoming call, even though there were urgent decisions on the project that needed my input. I'd been watching my phone all day, but there'd been nothing from Arthur. Perhaps Amber would leave it alone. Or perhaps he cared so little that he'd simply slink away into the shadows like we'd never been a thing.

'I'm okay,' I said, leaning over the sink, trying to keep my face hidden.

She considered me – my hunched shoulders, my puffy eyes.

'I know we're not, like, *friend*, friends – but I do care about you,' she said. 'I know it's not been easy with Duncan, but is everything okay with your new guy? It sounded really exciting . . .'

I felt my face flush with humiliation.

'Julia, trust me, I'm fine,' I said, sharp. 'I don't need anything from you.'

'Fine,' she said, equally sharp. 'I was just trying to be a human being.'

'Julia . . .'

I turned, but the door was already slamming behind her. Why had I been so unnecessarily rude to her? It was shame, pure and simple, but there was no way I could humiliate myself by telling her that. Now all I could do was hope she didn't revenge herself by dripping poison to Duncan.

*

I pulled off my usual trick, staying an hour past home time to try to convince Duncan that I was a reformed character. Julia had barely looked at me for the rest of the day, rejecting every conciliatory cup of tea I tried to make her and leaving without so much as a goodbye. Eventually I gathered up my things, already bargaining with myself about wine. Red was less toxic than white, I told myself, and if I bought a bottle, I'd only drink half of it before I stuck the cork back in the neck and went to bed. It was fine – I needed something to sip with a Netflix binge. Something that would ultimately help me sleep.

Arthur rang me as I was almost at the tube. Ironically it was the first call he'd ever made to me: up to that point, it had all been game playing, non-committal texts. I snatched up the call before I could think too hard about how angry the contact would make Amber.

'What the fuck, Rachel?'

'Hi,' I said, my voice shaking. In that moment, all I wanted was comfort. Any kind of comfort. Even this counted.

'I thought we agreed we weren't going to talk about it?' he said. 'And now you're making out to Amber I'm some sort of fucking abuser?'

'I didn't say that to her, and I swear to you I didn't tell her. She guessed.'

Arthur snorted with frustration.

'Arthur, can we talk about it properly? I can come and find you now.' It makes me shudder, remembering how low my desperation took me. 'Please!'

'I'm not sure that's a good idea,' he said, sounding incredibly pompous. 'I don't really like the version of me that's been painted.'

'That's exactly why I need to talk to you. Face to face.'

With the dating history I'd had, I knew enough to know that a man like Arthur was far too opportunistic to resist a woman offering herself up to him on a plate.

*

Soon I was back in his local, a large glass of red in my hand that I'd paid for, a stream of apologies pouring forth.

'I'm sorry, okay? All I did was tell Hannah, and that was only because . . . I was excited.'

Arthur refused to look at me, his face still set with anger. I reached a tentative hand out and stroked his forearm through his jumper. It was pitiful.

'We agreed it was private,' he snapped. 'I don't like my business being discussed, let alone with her.'

There was venom in his voice that I hoped wasn't meant for me.

'I know,' I said. 'It was stupid and disrespectful of me. I'm really sorry.'

Arthur finally turned to look at me, his expression black.

'I'm not sure we should carry on. I mean I really like you, Rachel, but ... it's not like either of us are in the space for a relationship right now.'

I interrupted him.

'That's not true! I know Amber thinks I'm too vulnerable, but – it's really helped me get stronger, beginning to date again. You're so different from the kind of men I was with before I started healing ...'

Arthur had a strange smile on his face.

'What?' I said, unnerved.

He waved a hand. 'I shouldn't. It's not for me to ... The therapeutic relationship has to be sacrosanct.'

'Arthur?'

He gave me a long look, his anger eventually getting the better of him. 'I just don't think her motives are quite as pure as she's making out.'

'Please stop talking in code!'

'It's totally inappropriate for me to tell you this, but ...'

'What are you saying?'

He paused.

'She was my girlfriend at college. She was at the poly, couple of years below me. We lived together for a year or two. I mean, it's aeons ago now, but ... I know what she's like. She can't bear to feel like she's lost a battle, even if she hasn't.'

I could barely form a sentence.

'Amber was your girlfriend?' I could almost feel him inside me now, the sense memory of it. It was enough to make me retch. 'Amber? But – isn't she way younger than you?'

Arthur snorted. 'I'd say she's no stranger to a needle. What is she now – early fifties?'

I sat there trying to absorb what he'd said, my world spinning another revolution. I pushed my chair backwards, the wooden legs screeching loudly against the pub floor.

'You should've told me,' I said, standing up. 'Both of you should've told me!'

'It was years ago,' protested Arthur. 'Come on, Rachel, calm down.'

'No!' I said. 'It's gross. I would never have done that if I'd known ...'

Darkness descended on Arthur again. 'You were hardly fighting me off,' he spat.

'Fuck you,' I said, pulling on my coat. He reached for me, but I shook him off.

'Rachel, I'm really sorry if you feel like I deceived you,' he said.

'I don't *feel* like it – you *did* deceive me.'

'Look, I promised I wouldn't talk to you again,' he said, wheedling now. 'Can you not—'

'Just fuck off,' I said, gulping the dregs of my wine. 'I never want to see you again.'

I left him beached at the table, vain and hopeless, and stepped out into the night.

It felt as though there was no one left.

No one but me.

LILY

Deborah led me down into her kitchen in the basement. It looked like a bomb had hit it – opened post and abandoned mugs strewn across every available surface – with a distinct whiff of cat litter, to add to the overall ambience.

'It's ages since I've been here,' I said. 'It's so cozy, isn't it?'

'Coming from a property expert like you . . .' she said, looking pleased. She was holding an old-fashioned kettle in her hand, which was designed to sit on the big metal range. 'Tea or coffee?'

I paused.

'Oh, I could almost handle something stronger. Couldn't you?'

She grinned her assent and pulled a half-drunk bottle of white out of the fridge. Her whole personality was coming back into focus – it was all about making her feel like she was in the cool gang, like she was bunking off maths to flirt with boys. Then she'd do anything required.

Soon we were sat opposite each other with brimming glasses, a look of earnest concern plastered across her face.

'So, Lily, what's been happening? Is Rachel still struggling?'

I took a slug of my wine – I had to admit to myself, as it slid down my throat, that my request for booze had come from more than just a desire to make her relax.

'It's been a nightmare,' I said. I paused, forcing her to study me. 'I know how you feel about Amber, but we have a responsibility to make sure no more families go through what we've been through.'

'Tell me,' she said, glass left suspended in mid-air by her desperation to know, and I laid out the last few months for her, watching her bulging eyes almost goggle out of the sockets as she struggled to compute it all.

'But Rachel *has* stopped drinking?' she asked, once I'd finished. 'So she has at least got her back on the straight and narrow?'

I snorted.

'Even that small mercy was short-lived. Sophie saw Rachel this week, so she could plead with her to come to her senses, and she was reeking of booze first thing in the morning.'

'Oh, Lily,' said Deborah.

'You see now why I was so desperate for information when I called you? At least then . . .' My voice splintered, emotion overwhelming me now. 'At least then I could still talk to her. Hold her. You have no idea how hard it is to be physically separated from your child.' Pain and anger were flooding me now. 'When I saw her after that terrible retreat, I tried to take her in my arms, to hug her back to her senses, but it was like she'd been possessed.'

I could see Deborah wrestling with what I was telling her.

'Lily, I'm not dismissing what you're saying, but so many of us have seen such good results. Anorexia, cutting, depression – all these things this generation of girls seem to suffer from the way we suffered with acne! Amber seems like some kind of whisperer for their neuroses.'

My heart was pounding in my chest, my eyes narrow. 'The police can arrest me for calling my own child – my broken, beloved child – and telling her how much I love her, Deborah. How can a person who has done that to a mother be anything but evil?'

Deborah looked helpless, clinging on desperately to her narrative. 'She must think that she's helping! I'm not saying she is, but . . . I do believe she's a good person.'

I felt my skin flush, then bleach, my right hand held tightly between my knees to stop it reaching across the table unbidden and dashing itself across her weather-beaten face. A mangy ginger cat unfurled himself from a rattan basket, and I dropped my fingers down, making a chirruping noise.

'What a beautiful moggy!' I said, feeling the tension drop.

'Isn't he handsome?' Deborah gratefully agreed, an eternal optimist in all possible areas. 'He's a rescue.'

'So there are others?' I said, lightly, stroking the piebald fur on the top of his head. One of his ears was missing its pointy tip. He pushed his weight against me, purring as needily as his hopeless owner. 'You know plenty of other people who've encountered her, it sounds like?' I dropped to my knees, so I was level with the cat. This was what we needed – corroboration. I couldn't let righteous fury destroy this opportunity. 'What's he called?'

'Mr Stuffins,' said Deborah, face wreathed with smiles, like he was her firstborn, receiving his doctorate from Oxford University. 'And yes. I mean – you've been quite out of touch with all of us St Johns mums the past few years.'

'Have I?' I said, sharper than I intended. 'I feel like we've all drunk our fair share of Sauvignon Blanc on the Askew Road?'

Deborah looked shifty. 'Yeah, no, of course. But you've built such an incredible business, Lily, while we've all just been bobbing along.'

I could just imagine it – their 'Tipsy Mums W12' WhatsApp group that they'd made a collective decision not to add me to. I didn't care. Listening to them all droning on about whether *Teletubbies* was hilarious or rotting our children's brains had been dull enough back in the day – God only knew what passed for stimulating discourse by this point.

'Yes, the business has rather run away with me the past few years,' I said airily. 'It's not like I ever advertised, but even just the word of mouth . . .'

'Well, quite,' agreed Deborah, a little too quickly. 'We're all in awe! And Nick, too. The Applebys are clearly property geniuses.'

I smiled icily. 'So have quite a few of the St Johns gang ended up with Amber in their lives?'

Deborah was thinking. 'Yes, yes they have.'

I was trying not to sound vindictive. 'Surely other people must have seen how manipulative she is? How controlling?'

She was still hesitant.

'I mean – I know she's a strong character. No one would deny that she's very forceful about her advice. But . . .'

'What? What are you trying to say, Deborah?'

Deborah's gaze was suddenly intense. 'Did you ask anyone else about her before talking to me?'

'No, I didn't. I remembered you'd mentioned someone . . .'

'Definitely?' she said.

'Yes!' I said, irritated with her. 'It's really not the point here, Deborah . . .'

She waved a hand to silence me.

'It's just . . . I felt like when I asked Amber if I could give you her number, she already knew who you were. But that doesn't make any sense, does it?'

RACHEL

It was two days later, and I was back sitting on Amber's sofa, playing for time. She'd given me a cup of chamomile tea, and I dragged the bag back and forth through the yellowing hot water, trying to steel myself for what was to come.

I could feel Amber's eyes on me. 'It can be like this, when there's been a rupture in the therapist/client relationship,' she said eventually. 'But if we can unpack what's happened between us, we'll find the gold.'

'What *has* happened between us?' I said.

She smiled at me. 'Our first conflict. But conflict is part of healthy relationships. And learning to navigate it well will help you when you're out in the big bad world. Healthy conflict brings people closer.'

I stared at her, fighting an internal battle. Either route felt deadly to me. I had to speak now.

'Arthur was your boyfriend,' I muttered.

'Sorry?'

I looked up, the words ringing out on their second airing. 'Arthur was your boyfriend.'

Amber's eyes flashed with rage. 'Rachel, I told you to leave that relationship alone. I handled it. I was protecting you – from yourself, as much as anyone.'

Nausea rose in me again, made me bold.

'It made me feel completely sick when he told me. Like I should've known.' My voice was shaking. 'I would never have done it if I'd known.'

'There was no reason *for* you to know,' she said. 'It was none of your business.'

My own anger was flaring now. 'Why did you even bring him on the retreat?' I demanded.

'I'm disgusted with him, but I also never would have predicted something like what happened between the two of you. I thought you were . . .' She stopped. 'I didn't think you'd put yourself in harm's way like that, after all the work we've done together.'

Why wouldn't she take any responsibility for it? And what did 'harm's way' even mean?

'You shouldn't have brought him, not without telling us who he was.'

Her smile didn't reach her eyes. 'Arthur is a colleague now, nothing more. It would have interfered with the healing journey for all of you if you'd known our history.'

It was dangerous, the way my fury was rising. 'I feel like every time you say you're protecting me, it's to explain away a lie.'

Amber raised her palm up like a stop sign.

'This is classic transference, Rachel. *You* lied, by omission, about Arthur, and now you're struggling with the aftermath of your own dishonesty. The impact on our bond. So you're twisting the story to make me – your protector – the liar.' Her voice got softer. 'I appreciate how frightening it is to need someone as much as you need me, but you trusting in our connection is the key to your healing.'

We sat there for a few seconds on our opposite sofas, staring at each other. Was I really going to risk pushing this?

'I don't know if I *do* trust you right now,' I said, my voice hoarse.

'What are you trying to express to me, Rachel?'

I was beyond her therapy-speak now, the way it drained meaning out of hard truths, all the while pretending it was digging deeper.

'Did you know?' I asked her. 'Did you know that my parents had gone to the police?'

I saw it: a flicker before she recovered herself. I knew those tiny tells from Mum: Amber had got herself back under control, but I'd seen it. My stomach dropped away.

'What?' she said, feigning confusion. 'I remember you mentioned something last session ... something Sophie said? But there was so much more that we were dealing with that we never got time to unpack it.'

'I don't believe you,' I said, some part of me still desperately hoping I was wrong. 'You did know. I think you found out, and then you sent me to make a complaint of my own. It's too much of a coincidence otherwise, us going two days apart.'

'Rachel, now you really are being paranoid.' Amber leant across the coffee table and tried to take my hand, but I wrapped myself up tightly, pulling away. 'Do you think I've bugged your parents' house? Or what, I'm tracking them with drones? Do fill me in!'

'I don't know,' I said. I wrapped myself up more tightly. I was rocking myself now, but it was providing scant comfort. 'I don't know.'

Amber watched me, her face neutral. Winter sun was shining feebly through the window, surrounding her with soft light. She looked almost too beautiful, her youth extended by any means possible. Was there any part of our connection that wasn't a lie?

'Rachel,' she said, her words a gentle lullaby. 'You're not well. You know that. Your damage makes you deeply self-destructive. And now you're trying to destroy the one thing that's saved you out of, what? Some twisted loyalty to your parents? I can't let that happen. Not after all we've been through together.'

I hugged my knees under my chin, shock and confusion buffeting me. I had to try to stay clear – be the woman who could build a career or stand up to her family's relentless bullying, not the girl who sobbed and heaved on this sofa until my face was red raw.

'No. No, no, no. It's not that!' I said. I felt a creeping nausea, a mixture of shock and the after-effects of the bottle of cheap red I'd drained last night to knock myself out, the tannin still sharp in my dry mouth.

Amber stayed hypnotically calm. 'Just sip your tea. Put your feet on the ground. Let your nervous system re-set.'

'I don't trust you anymore.' She heard me this time, the words like a blade cutting through the space between us. 'Tim thinks someone drugged me on the retreat.'

Her eyes flashed black with a rage I'd never seen before, and a small, soft part of me reflexively wished I'd never started this. That I could step effortlessly backwards. But I also knew it was far too late.

'I think we need to stop for today, Rachel.' Her tone felt off, less controlled. 'These baroque accusations would be funny if they didn't make me fear for you so much. For how close you are to breaking point.' Her face shapeshifted from beautiful to ugly before my eyes, the automatic dismissal of my truth shatteringly reminiscent of Mum. 'I've always known your family were toxic, but I don't think I appreciated quite how deep the poison ran.'

And then I suddenly saw it, her rotten face as telling as a crime scene photograph. The realization sent my blood to ice. She didn't hate them on my behalf: her hatred was her very own vendetta.

'I need to go back to Detective Williams,' I said, words tumbling out of my mouth too fast now. 'I need to talk to her again. I need to say it's not as simple as I said it was. She needs to back off from my family until she's got all the facts—'

'Rachel!' Amber was shouting. 'Stop it. Stop talking. You're not going back to the police. There's something I need to tell you – something you've needed to know for a very long time – that will change everything. So please just shut up and listen to me.'

LILY

Nick was oddly upbeat when he got home from work. He called out to me as he slammed the door, then bounded through to the kitchen, where I was stirring a pasta sauce on the hob, a glass of red wine at my elbow.

'Something smells good,' he said, leaning in to give me a kiss, his tongue unexpectedly slipping into my mouth. I could taste the whisky on his breath. 'What we having?'

'It's Bolognese,' I said. I'd squeezed it out from a pouch I'd bought at the deli: since Christmas, I hadn't really felt like cooking. It spoke of hearth and home, of family. If I risked roasting a chicken, I'd inevitably end up salting it with my tears. 'You seem chipper,' I said, trying not to sound judgemental about the fact.

'The Hutton deal closed today,' he said. 'That place is off the scale. It's not just the house. Acres of land, workers' cottages. It should complete next Friday. Serious pay day.' He squeezed his body next to me and I dropped the wooden spoon into the pan. 'I was thinking, why don't we fuck all this off and go to Paris for the weekend? Celebrate?'

'Nick ... It's Sophie's hen night that weekend.'

'You invited?'

I took a sip of my wine, feeling myself flush. 'Not as such, but I don't think she's really thought it all through yet.'

His face crumpled up with sympathy. I suspected he was thinking back fondly to Josh's three-day extravaganza in Amsterdam, where he'd been the star guest, but he at least had the good grace to keep it to himself.

'Hear me out,' he said. 'Right now, we need to be invincible. That woman's trying to destroy our family, and we can't let her. We need to double down. Rachel needs to see us as a unit. We're her stability – she'll come back to us, I know she will. All this shit is going to blow over.'

'But they're treating us like criminals!' I said, both exasperated and comforted by his blithe confidence.

'It's a bullshit case, and we're gonna fight it. And then we're going to destroy that fucking charlatan. How'd you get on with Deborah?'

I felt my body shrink away from him. I picked up the spoon, running it through the bubbling sauce.

'She was as dull as ever,' I said. 'But she did admit that Amber's seen a lot of those St Johns girls. Called her a "strong character". And ...' I was hesitant about the next part, but before I'd eked out any words, Nick was crossing to the fridge, pulling out an open bottle of Sancerre.

'That means there'll be others, Lily! All we need is to get some of those families corroborating the manipulation, and we're back in business to get her for coercion.' He let a torrent of wine waterfall into his glass. 'I was thinking we should look at getting a private detective onto her, and I've definitely found us the right lawyer. She's a fucking bulldog by all reports.'

I was desperately grateful for his energy – for the slipstream it created, sweeping us forward – but I was barely listening to the plan he was laying out. I kept thinking about what Deborah had said: *she already knew who you were.* Something stopped me confiding what she'd said to my husband, some sixth sense as to where this was taking us. I picked up my phone, googled Amber's website, even though the mere sight of her made me cringe. I held it out to him.

'You don't recognize her, do you?'

He batted it away, grimacing. 'I've seen quite enough of that fucking woman's ugly mug the last few weeks.'

He pulled a ridiculous 'listening face', a parody of hers, which would have made me giggle in a parallel universe. As it was, I could barely remember the last time I'd laughed.

'Not from the website! I mean – you don't think we knew her, do you?'

I stared at my phone, transfixed by Amber's photograph. The cobalt-blue eyes, the half-smile that played across her rosy lips. The barely-there make-up that made her look simultaneously beautiful and wholesome. That agelessness of hers had always unnerved me, and it did so more than ever now. It provided cover.

'I've never clapped eyes on her, Lily.' Nick kissed me again. 'Just stop thinking about her, okay? Let's just try to have a nice evening. I think you need a top up.'

As he reached for the bottle, I kept staring at her picture. How could it be that she was familiar and unfamiliar all at once? Was it just my fevered mind, playing horrible tricks on me?

Or was it something far, far worse?

RACHEL

I studied Amber's face, waiting for her next move, my heartbeat reverberating through my whole body. She took her time.

'What I've known about you, since the first day we met, is how bright you are,' she said eventually.

'Thank you,' I said uncertainly.

'But in a way, that's the tragedy. Such wasted potential, Rachel! The way your family have treated you. You hating yourself, every single day. All that potential's been sucked down the drain.'

I couldn't let her words slip inside and destroy me, even though they were so perfectly judged. She knew exactly where my bruises lay. 'What are you trying to say?'

She studied my face. 'That my investment in you – my love for you – it's completely genuine. What I'm about to tell you doesn't take away from that. I truly believe your family are toxic, and what you need more than anything is to liberate yourself from them at any cost.'

'Just say it, Amber, please,' I said, willing the desperation out of my voice. 'Whatever it is.'

Amber paused, a faraway expression on her face as she looked out of the window. 'Please try to just hear this, Rachel. Don't go straight to betrayal. I've taught you so much about how complex it is to be human. How nuanced.' She was staring into my eyes now. 'It's not just your life that your parents have destroyed. It's also mine.' She paused. 'And my child's.'

'Your child's?' I said, blindsided. 'I didn't even know you had a child.'

She looked stricken. 'There's been times when it's felt as though I didn't. When our relationship has been so broken – thanks to your parents – that it almost died.'

'My parents? What the hell have my parents got to do with your child?'

And then, as I stared at her – as I looked into the twin sapphires of her eyes – it felt as though the earth was cratering beneath my feet. My hand was over my mouth, a sharp tang of vomit in the back of my throat.

'Esther. Esther's your child.'

Amber nodded slowly, a slow smile spreading across her face, as though order had finally been restored. 'My baby,' she said.

LILY

I barely slept that night, and for once it wasn't down to Nick's snuffling, piggy snores. Instead it was Amber, stalking my personal darkness. Invading every crack and crevice of my life, past and future. I was back in a PTA meeting, but now no one would listen to a word I said, even when I banged the table. Deborah's upturned face melted horribly into Amber's. I was trapped with that smug policewoman, in a cell this time, and before I knew it, her mask of judgement and condescension had also transformed into Amber's face. That dinner with Rachel – my precious, beautiful girl – suddenly became dinner with Amber, her searching blue eyes staring at me across the white tablecloth.

I would never be free of her – that's what the dream was telling me. No tiny sliver of my life would be safe from that penetrating gaze.

I'd never been more grateful to see the dawn.

RACHEL

'But ...' The past twenty years were speeding through my memory, garbled, like a tape on rewind. 'But no, her parents are in Bolton. She always went to stay with them.' I looked at Amber, elegant and poised in a black cashmere turtleneck. Her sophistication was a million miles from Esther's chaotic Northern sexiness, all chipped red nails and boobs on display. And could Amber be old enough to have given birth to her, even allowing for Arthur's sneering aside about her real age? 'She's not ... you're not ...'

Amber's eyes narrowed. 'Exactly,' she said, icily calm. 'You would never know that my own child is mine. My life – and her life – were stolen from us.'

'I don't understand ...'

Amber leant towards me across the coffee table, and I instinctively drew back. 'I had her very, very young,' she said. 'I came down here for Drama College, got involved with one of my tutors.' She silently shook her head at the memory. 'Oldest story in the book. He didn't want to leave his wife, I didn't want to ...' She paused a second. 'Our family are Catholic; I would never have got rid of her.'

Shock had frozen me now. I just needed to hear the truth; I could allow myself to feel the feelings later. 'Of course,' I said, and let her carry on.

'So, I had her, but my mum said I couldn't possibly look after her. I was only seventeen. They'd bring her up instead.' Her face was set, the blazing rage of earlier drained away, replaced by something far more chilling. 'She was the first one to take my child from me.'

'That must've been agony,' I said. I couldn't think about the whole picture yet, the torture she'd devised for us. I had to wait for her to lay out the whole sorry map.

Amber gave a terse nod. 'It was like I was in the way, whenever I went back home. She didn't know I was her mum; I was just some interloper she had to give up her bed for.' Her blue eyes flashed with that potent, controlled fury. It was so unnerving, the way Esther's face seemed to layer over hers as she talked about her now that I knew the truth. 'I just had to stay away. I wasn't wanted.'

My anger – my fear at where we were headed – got the better of me for a second. 'So it sounds like it was *your* parents who stole her away from you?' I said.

Amber looked at me with pure contempt. 'Unlike your parents, with all of their money and their status, they didn't have many choices. They did what they thought was right to protect us.'

The room hummed with silence. She knew exactly how to take the power back, even now.

'I'm sorry,' I said, the words like glue in my throat. I knew, even in my profound shock, that I had to get us to the end.

'I tried to kill myself, Rachel,' she said. 'That was what my

329

pain drove me to.' Her gaze settled on me, almost affectionate. 'You'll understand that. You came so close to doing yourself serious harm until I intervened.' Her self belief was cast iron – how stupid I'd been to fall so hard for her. 'But ultimately it taught me how much I needed to survive. For my child. I needed to build a life for us.'

'So what did you do?' I said, my voice a whisper. It was getting harder and harder to endure this.

'I went to Oxford Poly and did psychology. I waitressed the whole way through to make ends meet.' She smiled coldly. 'Unimaginable to a girl like you, I should think.'

Her bitterness towards us was so profound, so far-reaching. How deep had it taken her?

'And then what happened?' I said, keeping my voice deliberately gentle. It gave me a horrible feeling of vertigo – me sitting here in this room coaxing and luring out her confessions, the way she had mine for all these months.

'It took a long time, but I was ready. I was ready to take her back. To tell her the truth. And . . . all she wanted to do was go to London, just like I had.' She looked at me. 'She was still my little girl, even if she didn't know it consciously.'

Despite everything she'd done, the tragedy at the heart of this story was real.

'It wasn't like my mum wanted her to know the truth; she still thought it was some shameful secret.' Her face looked as though she'd taken a gulp of sour milk. 'So, I let it happen, I let her go. I kidded myself the shock might be less once she'd lived a bit of life. And then . . .'

'And then she came to us,' I said, the pieces of the story starting to coalesce.

'She was seventeen, too,' said Amber, her eyes boring into me. 'I've told you so many times, haven't I? How history repeats itself in families?'

'Yes,' I said, my voice tiny. There was something worse coming – I could sense her closing in on it, my body tingling with a sickening dread.

'And it did, Rachel,' she said, almost triumphant. 'Pregnant by a man more than twice her age who thought she was shit on his shoe.'

The world went dark momentarily, the shock almost forcing me out of my physical form. Again I felt that childish desire to reverse time, to close the lid on a box of horrors I wasn't sure I was strong enough to stare into.

'Amber . . .' I said, my hand splayed across my mouth like I might vomit. Her face was alight now, her power absolute. Some sick part of her was enjoying this.

'I know it's a shock,' she said, leaning across to gently touch my hand, her old persona flooding back suddenly. Her shape-shifting was terrifying to me. 'But some part of you knew, I'm sure. Some unconscious part of you had to grieve that lost sibling.'

A sound that wasn't quite a word escaped from my lips. Memories were flinging up, shape-shifting the same way that Amber was. That day I found them together: was a baby already forcing its way into existence as I backed out of the room? A secret presence, hidden deep inside? I saw Esther's face now, a snapshot in time. She didn't look sly anymore; she looked stricken.

'I'm so sorry . . .' Shame flooded me, my family's sins a single, crushing weight. All those years that I'd hated Esther – it was nothing but that trick mirror. It was so much easier to be fuelled by bile: now I was felled by disgust at how we'd treated her.

'*You're* sorry, Rachel?' she said, cocking her head. 'It wasn't you,' she added softly. 'It was all your parents. You've done nothing but try to make things right. The fact is, it's an impossible task; they're beyond redemption. This is the final piece. Now you can begin to make a real difference.'

My thoughts were scrambling again, trying to make sense of what I knew and what I didn't. 'What happened to the baby?' I stuttered, even though some part of me already knew. A sick kind of anticipation lurched inside me as she carried on.

'Your mother found out about the affair . . .'

'From me?'

'From you,' she confirmed, looking almost proud. Coldness slithered down my spine. It hadn't been pure spin – in some twisted way Amber did care for me. I didn't know if that was better or far, far worse. 'And then she found out Esther was pregnant.'

'But . . .' It was so hard to form a coherent sentence – no wonder the one that finally came from my lips was so naive. 'Where's the baby now?'

The look on Amber's face made her words almost irrelevant. 'There *is* no baby, Rachel. Not now. Your mother convinced her to scrape it down a drain.'

I buried my face in my hands – felt the deathly coldness of my skin against my palms. 'Does Dad even know?' I whispered.

'She paid her off, made her promise not to tell anyone, including him,' Amber said. As I let my eyes peel upwards, I met her ice-chip gaze. 'Your mother spends her Christmases unwrapping Barbies and Lego with her grandchildren, while we're left with *nothing.*' A smile briefly slashed its way across her face. 'Well, most years at least.'

The chill sunk even deeper into my bones: Christmas had been an elaborate trap, and I'd walked straight into it. My fury about the drugs spurted up again – my suspicion now was that the bitter tea she gave only me before my turn was laced with something – but I pulled back before the accusation could spill out of me. If I thought about how large and sprawling Amber's trap really was – all of us running down invisible tunnels she'd spent years crafting – I wasn't sure I'd be able to reach the end of the story I so desperately needed to dig out.

'Esther's still young,' I said. 'She's still got time to make a good life for herself. Have a family.'

It's so ridiculous the way we try to make sense of an unfair world by creating happy endings for even the bleakest of stories. By now, I of all people knew it was fantasy to suggest we can just magic our wounds away, and Amber's look of contempt reminded me of that fact.

'Your family broke her. She can't hold down a job, she can't hold down a relationship. She's still obsessed with your dad, even if she lies about it. By the time she found out I was her mum, it was too late . . .' For the first time, her voice broke. 'It was too late for me to heal her.'

Was that what she was doing? Trying to create her own happy ending by finding surrogate daughters – me, Hannah, countless others – and sticking them back together with the glue she hadn't had the chance to use on Esther? In some cases, perhaps, but in mine the story was far, far darker.

I forced myself to ask the inevitable question. 'Are they still . . . My dad and her . . . ?'

Amber shrugged. 'She says not. She says she's just back there for the money. But she's never let him go, however much I try to tell her it's a delusion. He's her lost youth – she can't face up to the fact she's never getting those years back.'

Acid lurched up my throat again. Hearing that, it was hard to know if it was more tragic if she was still his mistress or if she wasn't.

'And on top of that, your mum left herself in a nasty fix,' Amber said, that grim, mirthless smile back on her face. 'She said she'd take care of her if she did what she asked. And she can't have your dad finding out what she persuaded Esther to do – he'd know what a monster she is. So Esther reappears when she's desperate.' Her head shook with disgust. 'Your dad's too weak to say no to her and your mum can't say a word.'

I felt so exhausted, even though there was still so much further that I would have to walk. I slumped backwards against the sofa's cushions. It was no longer my refuge; it was my cage.

Amber's eyes tracked me, her gaze intense. 'But you and me, we can clean it up. We're a great team. I meant everything I said to you. The love between the two of us is real.' A soft smile warmed her face now, restored her momentarily to the woman I thought I knew. That I had loved. 'There's no greater healer than pure love, Rachel. I sincerely hope I've taught you that.'

An involuntary shudder moved through my body. I knew Amber so well by then. I could see by the set of her face that she had a plan for me.

Had *always* had one, in fact.

LILY

It's not Amber who haunts my dreams now; instead it's my lost lamb of a daughter. I'm almost grateful for those clammy night-time flights of fancy, even though they make me ache with loss. Seeing her face, believing – however fleetingly – that we truly are together, is all the joy I can find within this monochrome existence of mine.

I'm not depressed; I'm just truthful with myself. It's a very different thing.

RACHEL

'You've always had a plan, haven't you?' I said, trying to drain the rage out of my voice. I couldn't risk unleashing it just yet. 'All of this – all of this care you had for me – was just about tearing our family apart.'

Amber shook her head. 'You didn't need me to do that. Your family was in freefall without my help. Do you remember where you were at when I arrived? Scraped off the pavement, your stomach pumped.'

'Are you seriously still asking me to be grateful?'

'I dragged you back onto your feet, Rachel,' said Amber, a smile that felt real playing across her face. 'I couldn't let your mother destroy another life. Not on my watch.'

My brain was starting to focus now, working out the steps she must have taken. There was a time when Esther was buried deep in the heart of our family, in every sense. She'd been the one to care for Sophie day to day, to keep mine and Josh's schedules faithfully recorded on the calendar in the kitchen, all while Mum was cementing the business she was so proud of and ignoring Dad's bad behaviour. Esther would have walked away with a roadmap to our lives, one she could have handed over to her own mother when the time came to exact revenge.

'You need to reach for your inner wisdom,' crooned Amber, 'your inner knowing, not just your knee-jerk response.'

'What does that even mean?' I said, willing my clarity to stay in place even as she told me riddles.

'I've let you see who your parents really are. Your dad groomed my daughter, your mum finished off the job. You'd have killed yourself eventually, Rachel, I promise you that.'

I shuddered at the potential truth of that and saw her tiny nod of satisfaction at the sight. Her power over me, over all of us, meant everything to her.

'You're the sensitive one, Rachel. The one who demands honesty. Acting out your family's dirty secrets, poisoning yourself to make sure their poison was visible.'

I shook my head. 'What, so you're trying to say you did all this for *me*? My life's been destroyed by you ...'

'So you'd like to turn back the clock, would you?' said Amber scathingly. 'Your mother ...' – she spat out the word – '... gaslighted you, her own daughter, and made you think you were making up stories, destroying your perfect family. It's no wonder you've had no self-confidence, no way to believe in love. You've spent your whole life thinking you can't trust yourself because she told you that, and now you've made it true. You're barely holding on to your job; you're still one step away from a drink or a line. I'm the only one protecting you from yourself.'

Her words were like bullets: I couldn't hold her at arm's length anymore. 'I'm trying!' I sobbed. 'I've tried so hard!'

'You still need me to survive, Rachel,' she said, her voice a caress. 'The world's too much for you. *They're* too much for you.'

'All you've done is lie to me. Manipulate me,' I said, choked by my tears. 'I don't want you anywhere near me.'

'Yes, you do,' she replied softly. 'You know you do. Look how much the truth hurts you. It's not just me and Esther who deserve revenge.'

I looked over at her – at her sly, foxlike face. 'What are you trying to say?'

She paused a second, weighing her words.

'Your dad's got away with a lot, hasn't he? Thriving business, huge sums of money running through it with those property deals.'

'And?'

'He's got a massive deal going through next week. Esther's been helping with the paperwork.'

'I don't know anything about it.'

Amber stared at me, almost beseechingly. 'Think how powerful the retreat was, Rachel.'

I stared at her in disbelief, my jaw tight with rage.

'Amber, you have to answer my question about the drugs; you can't just ignore me . . .' I started, but she held up an imperious hand, her words drowning out mine. I hated myself for the way I was still letting her exert control. Shock and exhaustion made it so hard to fight her.

'Sure, you've got mixed feelings about the experience – about how you were taken to the edge – but that's because you're still processing the healing. You made an incredible breakthrough. Every single one of you did.'

She was too cunning to ever admit it to me. 'That retreat battered me,' I said, almost shouting, but she interrupted again.

'You might think that right now – when you're busy hating me – but when the dust settles, you'll see it differently. You made lifelong friends there, other people apart from me who'll support your healing. Who'll treasure you. We really are a family, Rachel.' Her voice was honey. 'And you of all people need a family.'

I started to cry again, fat tears running down my cheeks as I felt the chasm between me and Sophie. The trauma of what had likely been done to me within my new 'family'.

Her face was alight now. 'And if I had the resources, I could do much, much more of that work. I could help so many people. I could have Esther beside me: it might finally give her the chance to heal from what your family did to her.'

I curled in on myself, letting her words wash over me.

'You worked for him, all the way through university,' she said. 'He probably doesn't even realize, but you're still a signatory on the client account.' She was like a cancer that had run rampant through the body of our family, no part of our lives left unscathed. 'When that money lands, you have the authority to divert it before anyone notices. The deal closes on a Friday. I told Esther what to do, and she made sure of it. The weekend is the perfect cover. I can set up an account and we just send the money to it.'

'I could never do that ...'

She cut across me. 'All of your suffering could be over, Rachel. You could leave the country, start a new life. No more debts and formal warnings, no more pointless battles with your selfish, narcissistic parents. You could finally be your own person.'

It was strange and unexpected, the tremor of freedom that I felt as I listened to those words.

'Why are you even telling me this?' I demanded. 'Why are you risking it? I could just go to the police.'

Amber looked unconcerned. 'I don't think they'd believe you. Of course, I'd never do this, but I could just tell them you've been weaving these fantasies for weeks. I'm very convincing when I need to be. With the complaint on your records, they might even charge you with wasting police time.'

'How can you threaten me like that?'

'I told you, I'd never do it,' she insisted. 'I love you, Rachel. You're so much more than a client; you're like my own flesh and blood. You've suffered the same way my own beautiful girl has. This way I can scoop you both up, rescue you together.'

I studied her face, its planes and contours, so familiar to me now. I really could see love – or at least her version of love – shining out of her blue eyes.

I stood up abruptly. 'I need to think,' I told her. 'I have to think about all of this.' I stopped. Despite everything she'd done, I had to try to atone this one last time. 'I'm sorry – I'm so, so sorry – for what happened to Esther. For what my family did to yours.'

Amber's eyes blazed. 'They're just words though, Rachel. You've got a chance to actually *do* something. To put some healing out into the universe, to make amends.'

'But—'

She cut across me yet again, her words like a speech she was giving on the world stage. She was addressing the UN, delivering her TED Talk.

'Think of all the other Esthers – young girls abused by powerful men while the world turns a blind eye.' Her eyes bored into me. 'Do it for all of them. Do it for you, because you're one of them too. This money could do *so much good*.'

As my gaze locked with hers, it felt as if time had frozen. As if every second of my life was contained within this one.

And then I turned and walked away.

LILY

I was staring into the mirror on my dressing table, wrestling with my sense of impending dread. It was like an invisible twin these days, impossible to banish.

'Come on, sexy,' said Nick, cupping my bum in his hand through the weave of my skinny jeans. He'd been like this – appreciative, tactile – ever since that horrific police interview. 'St Pancras is going to take us at least an hour.'

I turned to face him. 'I'm not sure we should be doing this.'

'Lily, don't be like that,' he said, irritable. 'We have to keep living our lives, celebrating the wins. I upgraded us to a suite – it's meant to be a surprise, but maybe it'll cheer you up.'

'But . . . it's Sophie's hen night tomorrow. And I'm behind on my contracts.'

He wasn't falling for it.

'Lily, you're not invited,' he said, his tone deliberately gentle. That was almost the worst part of it – being treated like an Alzheimer's patient who thought doodlebugs were still dropping on London.

'Sophie and I haven't really talked about it,' I snapped. 'I think if I turned up and bought some Laurent Perrier to replace that vile Prosecco they all knock back like it's water, she'd be delighted.'

Nick seemed to select his words carefully. 'I'm choosing this, okay? We both need to choose this now. Let's make Paris a new start.'

Esther had sent me some feeble text message saying that she was leaving town this weekend, which I'd 'liked' instead of replying to. Modern life was so ridiculous: it had started making me weary in some profound, existential way that I'd never experienced before.

'Fine,' I said, applying a thick coat of red lipstick that made me look more like a sad, crumpled clown than a femme fatale. 'Full steam ahead to the city of love.'

I knew in my bones that we shouldn't go.

I've never really forgiven him for the fact that we did.

RACHEL

I stood on the cold Soho street, looking down the metal stairs into the cramped cocktail bar that Kitty had chosen for my sister's hen night. It was so ridiculous, fantasizing about what I would have chosen if I'd been given the task – how well it would have demonstrated my love for her, my forensic knowledge of who she really was. It was all a futile attempt to paper over my bottomless grief.

I took a couple of steps down the curved, wrought-iron stairs, and then froze. A couple of pissed girls squeezed past me, squashing me against the cold metal railings. At least I hadn't gone to the bottle these past few days – my pride in that fact somehow propelled me down the rest of the steps.

I stepped into the bar, looking around. Kitty had reserved a nest of couches at the back, helium balloons weighted down on the tables, ice buckets filled with bottles stretching across. My sister sat in the middle of a gaggle of her best friends, a plastic tiara perched on her head at a jaunty angle, a flute of Prosecco held in her left hand. I remembered when we found out she was left-handed, how her spidery infant scrawl would run the wrong way down the lines of her school books, to Mum's eternal frustration. All of these little, precious pieces of her that added up to a whole person, that I now had to commit to a memory box held deep inside.

I approached the table, taking in the gang before Sophie saw me. No sign of Mum: thank God I'd called that right. Then Sophie looked up, her face freezing in shock. The rest of the group followed her gaze, and the ones who obviously weren't up to speed started drunkenly shrieking at me to sit down and grab a glass. I'd never felt more sober.

'I'm sorry to turn up like this,' I said.

Her best friend Kitty, a bit of a prefect from Owl Class onwards, glared at me. The intimidation was offset by the lurid, flammable 'Bride's Best Mate' sash that was slung across her black dress.

'Rachel,' Sophie said, the syllables slurred, a hand held over her mouth in shock. 'Rachel!' she repeated, stumbling to her feet and coming over to envelop me in a tipsy hug. 'Come and have – I dunno, a glass of water. Girls, budge up for my sister.'

It was almost impossible not to break down. I hugged her back fiercely. 'Sophie, I need to talk to you,' I said into her hair, wrapped tight enough to smell the serum from her party-ready blow dry. 'I really don't want to ruin your night, but can we go outside? It won't take long.'

Sophie's smaller than me: she looked up at me, her eyes round with confusion. She'd pushed the boat out, worn contact lenses instead of her familiar wire-framed glasses. 'But – can't we just have a nice time?' she pleaded. 'Is it illegal for me to say I'm so happy you're here?' She giggled, hugging me tighter. 'I'm sorry, I'm not taking the piss. It's just so nice to be normal.'

'Course we can, but only once we've had five minutes on our own.'

I preferred my old lies – the selfish, addict variety which were only about pleasing myself. This lie was so painful that it nearly broke me.

*

We stood at the bottom of the spiral staircase, dodging the few smokers who were brave enough to puff their way through the freezing February night.

'Rachel . . .' she said, swaying on the stilts of her high heels, a goofy grin on her face.

I couldn't lose focus. I'd rehearsed this in the mirror, but having her with me made it so much harder.

'Sophie, I love you . . .'

'I know that, silly!' she said, grabbing my hand, her words still slurry. 'Can we get a drink now? Sorry . . . that was in . . . insensitive.'

'Don't worry about that now,' I said, holding her arms and looking into her soft, pretty face. 'I'm going away for a little bit. There's a big project in Scotland that they're putting me on to, and I'm leaving this weekend.'

'That's great!' she said, face lighting up. 'So it's going better again? You seem better, Rachel.'

Lying to her was like a knife in my own ribs: I hated and treasured how much my successes were her successes. Her face in that second was another treasure for my memory box.

'Yeah, yeah it is,' I said. 'And I am. But I need to tell you a couple of things before I go.'

I watched her bubbliness drain away. 'What are the couple of things?' she asked uncertainly.

This was agony.

'Firstly, how lucky Toby is and how much I hope you'll be really happy.'

'But – you can come to the wedding?'

I kept going.

'Secondly, that you being born was the most fantastic thing that ever happened to me. It might sound weird, but you're the love of my life – not in a creepy way. But I never felt, like, sibling rivalry, or that you'd taken anything away from me. You were just this gift I'd been given. When you used to sing to yourself in the mornings, or, there was this time when you'd want to sleep with an apple, instead of a teddy. It had to be red.' She looked so confused, so emotional – I squeezed the goose-bumped skin on her bare arms and hurried on. 'What I'm trying to say is, there are a million tiny details that make up you, that I will always remember until the day I die. Every single one is precious to me.'

'Rachel, *you're* precious to *me*! That's why it's been so awful having to shut you out like you're some kind of frigging devil . . .'

'But I understand why you had to,' I said, heartfelt. 'I put you through so much, and I'm truly sorry. This is the last thing I need to tell you, and I'm sorry that it's tonight, on your hen night. If I wasn't leaving, I wouldn't do it, but you have to know.'

'What?' she said, voice rising.

The cold and the intensity were sobering her up: I felt a flash of regret that I had to do this, tonight of all nights.

'Sophie, I found out for absolute definite that Dad and Esther had an affair. Mum did know it was true, but then she found out that Esther was pregnant, and she needed to keep her under our roof to make sure she had an abortion.'

I could see the battle raging in Sophie's eyes. She wanted to dismiss me, but she knew me so well. Something in the calm authority I was projecting, which was costing me so much to maintain, was working on her now.

'Rachel, don't – how can you know that?'

Was I really going to risk this?

'I heard it directly. From her.' Lies come in many different hues. The half lies, grey ones like this one was, are almost the most betraying. I had heard it from 'her', just not the 'her' she thought.

Sophie had turned pale by now, a red-tipped hand clamped over her mouth as if she was stopping herself from retching. 'Oh, Jesus. Are you sure? Are you really sure it's true?'

I nodded, hugged her properly.

'Dad doesn't know, so Esther's been able to walk in and out, knowing that she can tap Mum up for money. That's why she's been working for him the past few months.'

'How could they – how could they do that?' she wailed.

'I'm sorry. I needed you to know, and I won't be around for a while.' A sob wracked Sophie's body, and I wrapped her tighter in my arms. 'Just try to leave it alone for this weekend, okay? Try to enjoy your hen, and just let them have their stupid mini break. If you talk to Mum on the phone, she's going to try to deny it. You're better off waiting until you see her.'

Tears were rolling down her cheeks, wreaking havoc with her make-up. I got a tissue from my bag and dabbed at her eyes. I went to put my coat around her naked shoulders, but I knew if I stayed any longer, everything would start to unravel.

'Sophie, I have to go. I love you so much.'

She grabbed hold of me. 'No, Rachel! Please don't leave me with all of this shit.' She looked up at me, eyes full. 'You're the only one I can trust.' She paused. 'I'm sorry I didn't believe you.'

It took all the strength I had to untangle myself from her.

'I'm sorry, too,' I said. 'For all of it.' I put my hand on my heart. 'You're always here. You always will be.'

I broke away, half running up the dizzying loops of the metal stairs, icy tears freezing on my cheeks like stalactites. Then I cut through the crowds on Charlotte Street, pulling out my phone in the crush. Amber answered on the first ring.

'It's done,' I said. 'Now we just have to wait for Monday.'

LILY

I woke up on Monday morning and finally let myself exhale. It was a relief to be back in my own bed, even though I'd never have admitted it to Nick: I pretended that I adored the hushed luxury of our Parisian suite, that I'd loved sipping champagne out of elegant coupe glasses and sucking oysters from their shells. The truth was, it felt like we were performers in a dodgy am-dram production of a Noël Coward play, the set wobbling, our lines hard to recall. All I could do was silently seethe about Amber, about the way she'd stolen my most important role from me. I barely cared about my business now, and celebrating Nick's financial triumph felt tasteless. I was Rachel's mother. I had no idea it was a job I could be fired from, a job where a new recruit could slip into my seat.

Nick had bounded out of bed as soon as the alarm went off, and was now singing Bruce Springsteen tunelessly in the shower: his relentless positivity, as sincere as an American game show host, was really starting to grate. His phone started up, and I let it ring out, but as soon as the message beep had sounded, it began to ring again. On the third cycle, I swung myself out of bed and went to find it. Maybe he really did mean it about this new start: it wasn't like him to leave it in such easy reach. The number was regional and didn't come with a name.

'Nick Appleby's phone,' I said tersely.

'I need to speak to him,' said an equally abrupt Northern man.

'He's not available right now,' I said, clipped. 'Who shall I tell him was calling?'

'You need to go and find him,' demanded the man. 'This is urgent.'

'He's not available,' I repeated. 'I'm his wife. I can give him a message.'

'He needs to take this call,' he said. 'I'm calling from Carter & Lyle solicitors.'

Before I had time to tell him about his lack of manners, Nick emerged from the en-suite, a white towel wrapped around his middle-aged spread.

'There's a very rude man on the phone for you,' I said, holding it out to him, ensuring my voice would carry.

Nick rolled his eyes, part amusement, part irritation. 'Hello,' he said.

Then his face turned to stone, and our life turned upside down all over again.

*

The entire transaction for the Hutton sale, all three million, had disappeared from the client account before it had reached the vendor's solicitor. Of course we assumed at first it was a mistake, Nick making phone call after phone call, telling people his professional reputation had been stained and angrily demanding answers. All the while, Sophie was calling me. At first I let the calls drop, but then I thought how comforting it would be to hear her voice. My sweet, biddable youngest girl.

'Darling, we're having a nightmare,' I said when I picked it up. 'That big property sale of Dad's we've been celebrating has had some weird glitch. The money's gone missing and—'

Sophie cut across me. 'I need to talk to you, Mum,' she said. 'I saw Rachel at the weekend.'

My heart plummeted. She'd invited Rachel – in all her vicious, drunken glory – to her hen night, and left me out in the cold.

'Oh, did you?' I said, icy.

'Yes, and I need to talk to you face to face about what she told me. You're home, right? I'm driving over now.'

Before I had a chance to remind her who the parent was in this scenario, she'd hung up on me. I stood there, holding the phone dumbly, watching Nick go beetroot red as yet another person refused to let him off the hook.

So much for letting myself exhale.

*

Sophie marched past me when she arrived, heading straight through to the kitchen. Nick was still barking into the phone, and she cast him a look of such uncharacteristic contempt that my blood ran cold. She was barely looking at me at all. She turned the lock on the French windows and stepped out into the garden. All I could do was scuttle after her.

'A "hello" might be nice,' I said. 'An enquiry after what your father's dealing with.'

Sophie's face was so screwed up with rage that she was almost unrecognizable. An angry Gollum in a navy winter coat.

'I don't owe you anything,' she hissed. 'None of us do.'

I tried to quell the dread that was welling up inside me. Sophie was as malleable as plasticine. I'd made her that way.

'Darling, what are you talking about?' I said, keeping my voice deliberately warm. I breached contact, touching her arm through her sleeve. 'We all know that Rachel's unwell right now. It's destabilizing for every single one of us in this family. That's why we need to take such good care of each other.'

Sophie slowly backed away from me, like a rescue dog trapped in a cage.

'I don't think Rachel's the mad one anymore,' she said, her face devoid of love, and my heart plummeted. 'I know what you did, Mum, and I know you're going to go through the whole rigmarole of denying it – flattering me and then trying to scare me – but it's too late. She found out the truth. Esther told her.'

I crumpled backwards, my body hitting a bare pine lounger that we hadn't bothered to pack away at the end of summer.

'What did she say to you?' I whispered.

'That Dad and Esther did have an affair ...' Her hands angrily sliced the air. 'If you can even call it that, considering she was virtually a fucking child! That you found out from Rachel, like she's always said, and you did know it was true. And then that Esther was ...' she choked on the words. 'You know what happened – we both do.'

It sounds like a cliché, but as my life ended, time stopped. My gaze was dragged to Nick, my husband, bent over his phone, still disbelieving that the world wouldn't cleave to his will, the way it had always promised him that it would. The way I had, too, cleaning away his mess like an indulgent owner with a poop bag. I looked back at my daughter, flooded with so much love that it almost tranquillized me. Surely it couldn't be too late for her to be soothed by that? I couldn't lose her too.

'Everything I did, I did for this family,' I said. 'I know how it looks to you, but imagine how it would have been. It would have destroyed you, knowing that about your dad. You adored Esther so much too. You're this bright star – this kind, optimistic being who loves her life. Not like me or Rachel. I promise you, you wouldn't be that way if I'd let everything break down. I protected you!'

Sophie's finger was stabbing at me now, and I glanced through the French windows, hoping that Nick wasn't witnessing her display. There was no need to worry – he was still obliviously cocooned in his self-righteous rage. 'Don't you dare try to push the blame onto me!' she shouted.

'I'm not—'

'No! It's over now, your control over us. You've made Rachel carry the can for this for years – making her feel like she was making up lies, telling her she was selfish. No wonder she went off a fucking cliff! And I believed you, not her.' Her face collapsed with an agony that I couldn't risk feeling too deeply. 'You made me into a terrible sister!'

'Sophie, you need to calm down ...' I said, risking a step towards her.

She shook her head, eyes wild. 'No, I don't. You need to take responsibility for what you've done. What you've enabled. How many lives you've ruined.'

Rage welled up in me at that. My fists balled up into stones. 'You were a child, Sophie. It was a very different time. It wasn't

all #MeToo and victimhood. That girl came into our house –
a cuckoo in our beautiful nest – and systematically tried to
destroy it.'

Sophie looked utterly disgusted, turning towards the windows that framed her father.

'For God's sake, Mum, listen to yourself. He abused a
teenager! She *was* a victim! And you covered it up. Paying her
off – Jesus, you virtually turned her into a sex worker. She's been
left relying on you.' Her features shrivelled with contempt, her
face suddenly more Rachel's than hers. 'And, God knows, no
one needs that.'

My body arched backwards, tears erupting. I buried my face
in the crook of my elbow, trying to stifle my sobs.

'How can you say that to me? I love you all so, so much.
You've got no idea, because you're not a mother yet. I've sacrificed myself to keep this family intact!'

I risked a look upwards, convinced that Sophie's face would
have softened at my distress, but she was like a statue.

'Just stop lying to yourself, Mum, okay? We don't believe your
bullshit anymore. You shouldn't either.'

'Why did Rachel even decide to talk to Esther?' I said. 'She's
always been so hostile to her.'

It should've been my first question, but I'd been fatally weak-
ened. If I'd been stronger I would have found a way to trash them
both before we got anywhere near to this catastrophe.

'I don't know,' said Sophie wearily. 'It's not really the point,
is it, Mum?'

Before I could dissect how this disaster had happened, Nick
noisily threw open the doors into the garden. I quickly tried to
rearrange my face.

'We need to talk about this properly, Sophie,' I hissed. 'Don't say a word to him until we've talked.'

Sophie scowled at me. 'Don't even bother trying to tell me what to do.'

'You won't fucking believe this,' yelled Nick over the top of both of us, still oblivious to our distress. 'It's not a mistake. It's Rachel. Rachel's taken all that money!'

RACHEL

The sun was low in the sky when I climbed off the plane, the glare shining right into my eyes. I'd brought barely anything with me, but at least I had sunglasses – mashed-up brown ones with a wobbly arm. I'd coveted the rack of chicer options at the airport, but I knew there was no way I could risk the transaction.

I slipped them on. It was a relief in more ways than one: I had to hope they would make me invisible.

LILY

My life swiftly became unrecognizable, both practically and emotionally. Our own daughter had taken everything from us. She had exploited our trust in her – the fact she'd been trained and nurtured by the family business – to destroy everything that we'd built for all of us.

She'd called the bank as soon as the money for the sale had hit Nick's client account, smoothly lying about where it was headed. The fact that it was a Friday, that we were off celebrating that very same deal, provided the perfect cover. She had it all worked out: there was a digit wrong; could they in fact transfer it to the following account for her? In the dark of the night, I often imagine the call. How charming and witty she can be, how beguiling that is. No wonder they didn't ask any awkward questions.

We traced her complicated flight path. She'd gone from London to Ireland, from Ireland to Switzerland, and there she had met her money. Part of me marvelled at her ingenuity, at the reminder it provided that she was always the brightest of my children. She would read whole novels to herself at ten, while the other two were so bovine at the same age that they virtually mooed. It was why I had to be so hard on her: it was always difficult to steer her path when she was ten steps ahead. Sophie would agree with my assessment. 'She was the one who always saw through your bullshit,' she shouts when I see her, red-faced and ugly in her grief.

That Swiss bank account provided an important clue: her co-signatory was one Amber Greville. Amber had been looking forward to her share of the cash, but my clever girl was one step ahead. The money briefly landed in the bank, one of the few that opened on a Saturday, before she swiftly withdrew it and turned it into Bitcoin. Then she boarded a plane to San Diego, upgrading to business class at the airport. I study these little clues like a spurned lover, trying to imagine her state of mind at each pivotal juncture: was she thinking of me? Did she know how much I yearned for her to come back to me?

After that, the trail goes cold. It's close to Mexico, easy perhaps to smuggle yourself over the border without too much fuss. Or did she fly further into South America, Costa Rica perhaps, hiring a discreet private plane with her fistfuls of money?

What about me, I hope you're asking. What about the mother, who tried to do everything right for her children and faced some impossible choices along the way? Perhaps what I tell you next will win me some redemption in your eyes.

Nick's situation was extremely precarious: as a lawyer who was now in breach of contract, having failed to protect his client's funds, his entire livelihood was left in jeopardy. Our daughter, and the cash, were nowhere to be seen. Amber Greville claimed total ignorance as to her whereabouts, and I felt, with a grim sense of satisfaction, that she was telling the truth. Rachel had summarily rejected her, leaving her to face the music without a penny to show for it.

Nick, meanwhile, needed all the money he could get to buy his way out of jail. Unluckily for him, I'd finally had enough – had made enough sacrifices, had cleaned up enough shit. He'd always been a whizz with taxes, determined to ensure we paid the least possible amount. One of those ruses was keeping our home solely in my name. The revelation about Amber Greville's real identity was the last straw and I point-blank refused to make myself homeless to save his skin. He had the nerve to blame me for 'hiding' Esther's pregnancy, like he really would have been wise or noble enough to turn that awful mess into something we could have all survived. There are no winners here, only different levels of loss. I'm not a total monster – I include Esther in that sad equation.

The truth – her version of the truth – was her mother's legal defence. Her daughter's life had been ruined by our family, and she'd had no choice but to seek revenge. As it was Rachel who'd pulled it off, and ultimately left her with nothing, Amber got away with little more than a slap on the wrist. My daughter, meanwhile, is an international fugitive – I wonder if she finds something rather exciting in that? After all, convention never handcuffed her the way it did me.

I'd been right all along about Amber: she'd been trying to steal my child away from me from day one. And lest we forget, her clock started ticking on our family many years before we even knew she existed. When I finally knew the whole truth, it infuriated me that I hadn't worked it all out for myself, but they were emotional tinkers, the pair of them – masters of deception. Despite the years they spent estranged, Amber moulded her daughter just as much as I did mine. At least my clever girl ultimately outwitted her.

Nick had no choice but to declare bankruptcy, holing up in Josh's basement once I'd kicked him out, like he'd fast-forwarded twenty years into geriatric neediness. He's still obsessively trying to trace the money, but I know in my bones that it's fruitless. Rachel defeated us all. I can't help but be proud of what she pulled off, even as my heart breaks in half at the loss of her.

She was always the one. She was my shining star.

EIGHT MONTHS LATER

AMBER

This is no mellow autumn day, all golden light and tumbling leaves. No, the weather is biblical: the universe has provided the perfect backdrop for their sins. Rain and sleet slice the sky, the odd flash of lightning sending the satisfyingly large gaggle of journalists scuttling for cover. Patience, I think, the voluminous hood of my olive mac giving me all the cover I need. I wipe droplets from the glasses that I don't strictly need, and as my vision clears, they're pushing their way through the courtroom doors and starting down the steps. My heart starts to thump in my chest. What is it? Fear or excitement? I think, most of all, it's pride.

The size of the crowd momentarily shocks them: Nick grabs desperately for Lily's hand, his own shaking. Only someone with my gifts would discern these tiny tells. Now Lily begins to speak over the shouting, jostling crowd.

'We're not doing this for us,' she says self-righteously, the rain soaking her pale pink skirt suit into soggy darkness. 'We're doing this for every other vulnerable family who might be preyed on by an, an ...'

It takes all my strength not to fight through the throng

and set her straight. But then I remember, fastening my hood a little more tightly, that this is the most powerful place for me to be.

'. . . unscrupulous therapist,' she continues, swallowing something far more vicious. *Sticks and stones*, I think. 'These people ruin lives! We need stronger regulations to stop them tearing other families apart the way . . .' She falters now, her gaze briefly turned upwards towards the slate grey sky. She doesn't even pretend to look to her useless husband for comfort. '. . . the way that ours has been,' she says, her final words quietly stuttered out, the energy visibly draining away. They're neutered, diminished. I did that.

Journalists are shouting questions at them now, calling from left and right. A groomed blonde woman holding a microphone steps in front of the fray.

'But you were involved with Amber Greville's daughter? Can you speak to that? She was your children's nanny?'

Now Nick wakes up, lurching forward furiously like a sad, old drunk. Again, I have to consciously root myself to the spot, so strong is my desire to hurt him. Esther will come back to me, I can feel it. She just needs more time to appreciate that my whole battle was devoted to her healing. Love can be fierce – a mother's most of all. In time she'll understand that I still won, even if the spoils weren't quite what we'd looked forward to.

'That's not relevant to this case,' Nick shouts, a finger jabbing towards the blonde. 'Amber Greville tried to embezzle money from us. She gave our daughter the plan that bankrupted us. This is a civil case, related to that. Check your facts.'

'You're separated now, is that right?' asks the blonde, undeterred. No surprise really, he doesn't cut the powerful figure he once did. As I've always known, life is nothing but a confidence trick. Lily's head swivels towards her, her eyes like slits.

'I stand by my husband. Our family stands united.' She inclines her head, and now their awful son and his wife are fighting through the scrum to complete the line-up, rictus grins plastered on their faces. No sign of Sophie, I note with satisfaction. Rachel would be so happy at the cast-iron evidence that her sister took her side. Took *our* side. Still, it's a little unnerving how they emerged from the crowd: I take a step backwards, keep my gaze trained on the ground. I'm taking a huge risk today, but I know in my heart that it's worth it.

'But isn't it true that your husband's been declared bankrupt because you refused to sell the family home?' shouts the blonde terrier, but now they're refusing to reply to her.

'And the judge just threw your case against Amber Greville out,' adds another journalist, thrusting a mic towards them, his cameraman at his shoulder. 'He said any claim you'd be entitled to is against your daughter.'

Lily rounds on him, furious.

'I would never betray my daughter in that way. And those who have betrayed her will pay the price.' She looks into the camera, almost beseeching. She's speaking directly to the child I know she's lost forever, even if I don't know where she's gone. 'I won't stop fighting.'

Now they're elbowing their way through the crowd – it's safest to let myself be sucked into it, obscured by the crush of bodies. The whole family cram themselves into a taxi, but I know, ultimately, she'll be home alone.

The light will click on in the master bedroom – the window is top right from my vantage place across the street – shortly after 9pm. It's not like the old days when the lights in the living room would often blaze till 11pm – the two of them watching their favourite crime shows in a bad parody of marital bliss, or, alternatively, Lily numbing herself with Sauvignon Blanc solo, waiting for him to deign to make a reappearance. It was uncanny to finally go inside, that first day I met Rachel – like walking into a book you've read a hundred times, the pages thumbed, the spine broken.

I won't put the book down, won't stop fighting. My girls – both of them – can trust in that. I know in time they'll be ready for me to tell them.

I know – have always known – how exquisite it can be to wait.

Acknowledgements

Infinite thanks are due to my incredible agent, Eugenie Furniss, who signed me long before there was any sign of a new manuscript, and yet was unfailingly generous, enthusiastic and supportive. Massive thanks also due to the rest of the 42 Books Department – Marilia Savvides, for sterling work at the point when it got exciting, and the amazing Emily MacDonald who keeps everyone in order. To the 42 Production Department, for being so supportive of my side hustle. And to the endlessly patient and loyal Lucinda Prain at Casarotto, my TV agent, who is luckily also very good fun.

Huge thanks to the whole team at Simon & Schuster. I couldn't ask for a smarter, more engaged editor than Bethan Jones. Thanks, too, to Victoria Godden for a thoughtful copy-edit.

Thanks to Caroline Haughey, QC, for her amazing knack for making a crime plot stack up in a (hopefully) entertaining way.

Thanks to my incredible early readers for putting up with the spelling mistakes and the excessive exclamation marks. Ray, Rhonda, Miriam, Carol B and Matthew – I so appreciated your compliments and deftly delivered criticisms in the depths of lockdown.

Talking of which – thank you to Miriam and Kingsley for turning the N5 office into an octopus appreciation society. To Anne, for going with the whole concept of white wine in keep cups. To Sophia, for all-round sanity and a lot of soft rock. To Kay, for deeming me worthy of a Jump bike ride up a steep hill. To Stef, for making the LA/London time difference work so many different ways.

And to all the not Ambers who have helped me along the way – Cabby, Bee, Foxy, Gill, Kitty, Ross. Your wisdom and kindness is never something I take for granted.

Did you love *TELL ME YOUR LIES?*

Then don't miss

PAYBACK

The next edge-of-your-seat thriller
by Richard & Judy Book Club pick
Kate Ruby.

She wants what's yours.
And she'll do anything to get it ...

Turn the page to enjoy an early extract now.

**SIMON &
SCHUSTER**

SASHA

The howl that comes from somewhere deep in the undergrowth sounds like someone's being brutally murdered. I startle as my gloved hand jiggles the lock, the key on the other side rattling against the doorframe, the sound loud in my ears. An amorous fox, I've identified the cry now, but the shock is enough to momentarily break me out of my trance. To make me realize how foolhardy it is for me to be here, in the dark of the night, trying to inveigle my way into the house. But the problem is, I've come too far. I've burnt my life to ashes, and the only way to salvage anything from the wreckage is by proving that someone else lit the match.

A minute later, I've finally succeeded. I've forced the key from the lock with the paper clip I keep in my handbag – it tinkles as it hits the tiled floor, every sound magnified to my straining ears. I take a gulp of air, try my best to squat on the ground next to the cat flap, the tight dome of my pregnant belly agonisingly squashed between my knees and chin. I roll backwards, land on the cold ground, my hand cradling my precious bump. If I Facetime Steve now, showed him the depths I've sunk to, could we laugh together? Would it prove to him how sincerely I want to make up for what I've done?

No, I think, pushing myself awkwardly back up onto my heels. It would simply confirm to him that his wife is a delusional sociopath, and his decision to walk away from me – from us – was the only one he could make. The sole way to convince him I'm not who he thinks I am is with cold hard facts. With the evidence I'm convinced I'll find in her bedroom if I can manage to get inside.

I use my own keys for the next part, sliding them along the rim of the cat flap, working my way past the magnet that's meant to keep it firmly shut from feline invaders. The manufacturers clearly didn't give enough thought to forty-something women with a taste for vengeance. Before long I've made it through, the twin rings on my left hand, which I stubbornly refuse to take off, scraping against the plastic door as my fingers scrabble on the cold floor, grasping desperately for that key.

Finally my palm is wrapped around it, the metal spikes cutting into my flesh. I struggle upwards, lean against the wall to try to catch my breath, panting like a panicked animal as I look at the time on the glowing face of my phone. When we were in the office, she told me that she'd be out clubbing with all five of her flat mates tonight, an air of smug satisfaction radiating out of her at the shiny new London life she'd built for herself. *It was me*, I wanted to scream. It was me who gave you the keys to the city, when I chose to look past your average degree and stammered answers and give you a job no one else would've hired you for. How is it that one year later it feels like she's the one deciding who passes Go?

I push the key into the lock, keep it still for a final second. This is my last chance to turn back, to stay in the realm of a professional woman with a questionable personal life, instead of a crazy person in danger of being sent to prison.

I swivel the key to the left. I left the first persona behind too many weeks ago to snatch it back now. The door creaks open and I step inside. This is who I am right now, for better or worse. This person, the one I barely recognize, is the only one who can deliver the real me from the trap she's ensnared in.

It's time to see if I can win.

ONE YEAR EARLIER

JENNA

Cheese. A sweaty, shiny lump poking out from under the fridge like a chunk of skin that has fallen off a sunburnt arse. Jenna forced herself to look away before the girl – Penelope, a name she knew would've made her mum crease up laughing – could follow her eye line. The last thing she needed was her potential new flat mate judging her hygiene standards.

'It's gorgeous!' Jenna sang, looking around the dingy kitchen, wincing at the sound of Cardiff pushing out of her vowels. She wanted to sound like she belonged here, like she'd be able to blend into North London as well as any wild animal released into a new habitat.

'Thanks!' said Penelope, as proud as if she were the queen of a castle. 'We really love it.'

She said 'thanks' like it started with an F, like she'd wandered here from Albert Square, but Jenna was savvy enough to know that she was posh – properly posh – from the weird flowery dress that was more like a kimono that hung from her lean body, from the way her skinny limbs dangled out of it and swung confidently through the air when she made a point.

'It feels really cosy,' said Jenna, keeping her enthusiasm as high as she could pitch it. 'A proper home.'

This time it was as if Penelope heard another note, suddenly seeing the chaotic kitchen through a stranger's eyes. There were a few wine glasses abandoned on the table, red wine still puddled in a couple, an ashtray with some butts that didn't look entirely legal. 'We were at school together so sometimes it gets a bit like a sixth form common room,' Penelope said, whipping up the ashtray and emptying the contents into an overflowing swing bin.

Jenna couldn't think too hard about how mucky it all was. Archway was only a twenty minute tube ride from Bright, whereas the other two places she'd seen that day would mean journeys nearly as long as the coach ride from Wales, and they were both total shit holes. She shifted her weight in her new pinching black pumps that she'd splashed out on in favour of a train ticket. She had to get this job, had to get this room. The list of reasons why was too long, too scary, for her to count, even in her head. She doubled down.

'But that's so great!' she said. 'Living with your best mates!' She pushed away a stab of dread about trying to join a tight-knit gang with a kimono for a uniform – the Brownies had been bad enough. Penelope was wiping a mangy sponge over the table now, her left boob poking out from the soft cotton, no bra in sight. 'What's the landlord like?'

Penelope at least had the humility to look a bit embarrassed. 'It's actually my aunt's. She's moved to Normandy, let me take it on for her. She's a bit crazy.' She made a gurning face, red lipsticked mouth twisting upwards, eyes rolling, like the two of them were in on the joke. 'That's why the rent's a bit mates rates.'

Jenna swallowed. Did she honestly think that £650 a month was some kind of favour? The room was like a short landing strip, a single bed squashed against a damp wall. If she got the job at Bright she could just about make it work if she lived on boiled rice and never went out drinking, but it was hardly a bargain. Still, she thought, as she had no friends in London anyway, that wouldn't necessarily be a problem.

'Got a few crazy relatives of my own hidden in the attic,' Jenna replied, grinning back at her, feeling a little aftershock at her own words. 'It's really generous of you, passing on the love.'

'Thanks,' said Penelope, glowing with pleasure. She paused. 'We've got a couple of people coming round later. Well, four actually. Just . . . so you know. Full disclosure and all that.'

Jenna felt a hot starburst of anger. Why did everything in her life have to be such a battle?

'They won't be me, though, will they?' she said, holding Penelope's gaze, letting the silence pool between them.

Penelope giggled nervously. 'What's the job you're interviewing for, anyway?' she asked.

'Creative assistant at a branding agency. The boss is . . .' Jenna felt like she knew Sasha Fulton's Ocado order by now, the amount of research she'd done. She struggled to keep the awe out of her voice. 'She's a legend in that world.'

Although, maybe Ocado was too down-market for her. Maybe there were other, more glamorous food sources in Hampstead, where she lived. It wasn't far from here, but it was also a million miles away – grand homes built from grey stone, dumped as wide as Monopoly houses on tree-lined streets. It had been a risky detour, but she'd felt she had to make it.

'Right,' said Penelope, blank faced. 'Isn't branding just the same thing as advertising?'

'Definitely not,' Jenna said, her self-control finally deserting her, the words sharper than she intended. 'It's *way* more subtle. Everything you buy, every club or bar you think you're choosing to go to – it's been branded. It's been made to seem a certain way so you connect to it. Like you're a better person because you chose it.'

She was starting to worry that she was losing her grip on this situation, accidentally sounding like the kind of flat mate that'd hypnotize you and then feed your remains down the waste disposal.

'Sounds really interesting,' said Penelope in a bored drawl that suggested the absolute opposite. 'I'm an actress.'

Jenna didn't reply immediately.

'And I work in the Whole Cup on Junction Road between jobs. It's full of creatives,' Penelope added, voice on fast forward now. 'It's a real . . . hub.'

'That's amazing!' said Jenna, after a tiny pause, enjoying the way her affirmation visibly flooded Penelope with relief.

She took another look around the kitchen, enjoying feeling desirable again. The oven was crusted with a thin brown film, a lone baked bean taking centre stage between the four rings. Jenna felt an unexpected prickle behind her eyes, sideswiped by the knowledge that her Mum would have taken a Dettol wipe to it the very first time she'd visited, unable to help herself. It was a visit that would never happen now, even if everything else about this day went her way. She picked up the stiff black handbag she'd borrowed from her cousin Claire, readied herself to leave.

'I should've mentioned, it's actually my second interview. I think it's more of a . . .' – she made air quotes, something she'd never done before '– formality. So I'm pretty much all set if you'll have me. It's . . .' She paused, as if searching for words of sufficient depth. 'Whoever gets to live here is really lucky.'

'Thanks!' said Penelope. 'And good luck for today,' she added, earnestly. 'I really want you to get it.'

Jenna felt like she already knew she had, even though there was no evidence to suggest it. After everything she'd done to get this far, including a few things she couldn't risk thinking too hard about, she couldn't afford to fail. She took a final look around the kitchen, imagined her Diet Cokes already nestled in the fridge, her mug on the draining board.

'I really appreciate it,' she said.

SASHA

I look back now and wonder whether, if that Tuesday morning had started better, my whole life would be entirely different now. I lever myself backwards on the hard scratchy sofa and wrap my palms around my round belly. Of course I wouldn't wish away this pulsing life inside me, but trapped in this short term rental, my due date rapidly approaching and my only emotional connection to Steve found via our weekly cringingly awful therapy sessions, it's hard not to blame that idiotic earlier version of myself for the bin fire of my perfect life.

Of course it wasn't actually perfect, but the fact it looked that way in a certain light almost made it so. But maybe my even thinking that suggests that everything that's been said about my character is justified.

Jack was the first person I saw that day. His shoulders were humped high around his ears, his head hanging low over his phone, more tortoise than teenager – hard shell, didn't speak human. I didn't have time to try: I was rushing, as normal, traversing that large, beautiful kitchen to stick a pellet in the Nespresso machine and trying to work out if a butter smeared frozen pitta bread, fresh from the toaster, counted as healthy. The nutritionist, who the fertility doctor had sent me to as a last resort, went on endlessly about how food was 'Mother Nature's Medicine' and her toneless drone had become a radio frequency all of its own inside my anxiety-ridden brain.

As the pitta noisily popped up, and Jack didn't even flinch, I started to feel guilty. I was some version of a parent to him, after all. He needed rehabilitation.

'Shouldn't you think about . . .' His brown eyes turned upwards toward me, a slow, deliberate roll. 'You've got German, haven't you?'

'No. I mean, yeah. But Mr Griffiths is off.'

'Right.'

His eyes returned to his phone and I stood there, my coffee cup suddenly too hot in my hand. I was halfway to the table, but now I backed away, let the coffee splash down the deep white sink, rendering it a crime scene. A little bit spat up at me, soaking into the cuff of my green silk shirt. I grabbed a J-cloth, made it worse.

'I thought I'd just work here this morning,' added Jack, innocently.

Work looked suspiciously like TikTok from where I was hovering.

'Right. Well your Dad's already left.'

'Obvs.'

Four whole syllables was clearly way too much effort to expend on your stepmother.

'So don't forget to double lock.'

'You've got it, Sasha,' he said, a lazy smile playing across his face now that he'd got his way.

I grabbed my bag and slammed out of the house, a wintry gust of air immediately reminding me that I'd forgotten my scarf in my hurry to leave. Should I call Steve, ask him if he thought his pride and joy was heading for a life of aimless drifting? No – I didn't have fifteen minutes to stand outside the tube in the cold, listening to his frustration spitting down the line. And besides, Jack would be fine, his easy charm and paid for social confidence would ensure it. Even worse than that, I didn't particularly care either way.

That realization made it unexpectedly hard to breathe, my heart suddenly shrink-wrapped inside my chest. Because what if this was it? By then, I'd cursed enough periods and peed pointlessly on enough sticks to know that there were no guarantees that this wasn't my only shot at parenthood – the two surly, shaggy-haired teenagers who made me feel like a lodger whose rent was so low she couldn't risk asking for an extra slice of toast at breakfast. And of course Steve cared, but it felt like a semi-detached kind of sympathy, a card sent in lieu of attending the funeral. He was a parent twice over, the job almost done. I couldn't help suspecting that if his forty-year-old wife decided to give up her demented quest to hold her own baby in her arms there'd be an element of relief, even if he'd never be cruel enough to admit it to me.

I'd involuntarily stopped on the pavement, frustrated commuters reduced to weaving around me. I forced myself to rejoin the death march to the tube, pulling the collar of my grey wool coat around my exposed neck to try to stay warm. I couldn't risk this much self-examination – in order to keep going, I had to stay intact. I reminded myself I had interviews that day, a process I enjoyed. I liked the way people offered themselves up, the chance to hold their stories about themselves up to the light and look for their truth.

I liked to think it was because I was caring, interested in my fellow human travelers. Now even I wonder if the desire was born out of something far darker than that.

JENNA

Bright's offices were near Old Street, although none of the lunchtime crowd clogging up the streets looked remotely old. For the over fifties, age was nothing but a number, hair dyed and cropped close to their heads, all big glasses, equally big trainers and 'statement jewellery'. Jenna's nerves started to ripple through her again, her interview get-up suddenly seeming like an unexploded bomb – she could've saved the money on her stupid black pumps and worn trainers instead, and the black Zara shift dress had started to look more suitable for a funeral. The funeral of her career – what if Sasha Fulton thought she was so off brand for the branding world that she sent her packing the second she set eyes on her?

Soon Jenna was sitting in Bright's reception, taking tiny sips of the sparkling water the receptionist – her black rimmed eyes surfing her unfortunate outfit – had handed over when she arrived, telling her casually that Sasha was 'running a few behind'. Jenna weighed the green glass bottle in her hand, not allowing herself to swig – she couldn't afford to need a toilet break at a critical moment. She examined her surroundings instead – bare lightbulbs illuminated the stripped pine floor, the sofa shaped like a lower case 'b', a pink neon 'Bright' sign shining above the reception desk. It was more like how she'd imagined a Michelin-starred restaurant would look like than an office, a million miles away from the grey Cardiff cages where she'd temped in the university holidays.

As the minutes ticked by, anxiety tightened around her throat like a noose. What if the candidate before her was so extra-ordinary – Double First from Oxford, boarding school polish and the biggest, whitest trainers on the block – that she'd already lost her chance? What if the fact she'd asked to be scheduled after lunch, so she didn't have to pay for a night's stay in London with money she blatantly didn't possess, meant that she'd never have that money? Just as her paranoia was reaching fever pitch, she realized that the receptionist was trying to get her attention.

'They're ready for you!' she hissed, from behind the desk.

'Sorry . . .' said Jenna, flustered, jumping to her feet. As she did, she realized that Sasha Fulton had already glided into view from behind the frosted glass partition that kept mere mortals at bay. She was taller than Jenna had imagined from her photos, a green silk shirt with a complicated knot that tied around the waist of her skirt emphasizing her waspish figure. The kind of boy that Jenna had been dreading to see was trotting behind her, a wiry character with dark hair that stuck up in clumps as if he was too posh to brush it. Sasha fixed him with a warm gaze that made Jenna's stomach turn over.

'Thanks so much for coming in, Jeffrey. Can we get hold of you if you're halfway up the Himalayas?'

'Hey, that's the magic of 5G!' he laughed, sticking out his hand, the sleeve of his white shirt webbed with creases. She laughed as she took it, simultaneously turning to survey the sofa. By now, Jenna's smile was more of a nervous line that cut her face in two.

'It's Gemma, isn't it?' said Sasha.

Jenna didn't bother to correct her, just nodded mutely.

'Follow me,' she said, turning on her heels.

The handbag was the only part of her outfit she could ditch. She subtly kicked it backwards under the sofa – it was hardly like anyone here would want to steal it.

Then she did what Sasha asked, followed in her wake. It was something that would, in time, become a dangerous habit.